The Knowers

by Nina Martineck

To Max,
who has taught me that
hair doesn't need hairspray
to be bouncy and that
the world spins how
we want it to.

Chapter One

If we can find a reason,
a reason to change,
looking for the answers.

"Cigarette Daydreams"
Cage the Elephant

We live in a world in which there are two types of people: the raindrops and the meteorites.

The majority of the population comprises the benign raindrops, who fall to the earth at a gentile twenty miles an hour and barely make an impact in its soil. Then they evaporate back into the sky in the blink of an eye, leaving no trace of their existence in the first place.

A select accursed few, the meteorites may be drastically outnumbered, but they don't rely on quantity to leave a resilient dent in the planet's crust. Like a fiery paintbrush streaking across the sky, they vaporize raindrops, incinerate entire cities, and cause explosive chaos just by existing. They are the ones who are remembered, the illustrious, exalted for destruction. The days are named for them, the memorials constructed—there they are, in every third grader's social studies book, the namesake of elementary schools, their bronze statues erected in parks, their distinguishable faces adorning posters and oil paintings.

One would think that a meteorite's life would be a miraculous saga of adventure after adventure, and one would think they should like to be one, as a planet in upheaval at a breath from your mouth sounds like a wondrous way to be living. But the world needs the raindrops more than the meteorites. If the world were completely made of meteorites, we would live in unadulterated pandemonium, and the fires would never be put out. Earth would turn into yet another circle of Hell reserved for the living.

If you indeed are a raindrop, relish each moment of your typical, commonplace life. An existence full of minutia and pointless worries like your cereal preference or color of your socks is one that is calm, orderly, and fulfilling. You never need to be concerned about saving the world, or saving someone's life, or even saving yourself. To you, the world isn't a blank canvas, but a Monet painting you'll just sit back and enjoy without daring to take a brush to it and risking the contamination of such a masterpiece. You'll never concern yourself with someone who lives in a country you've never heard of, or even a neighbor who lives a few doors down. Your life is solely yours, until the day the sun finally reaches you as you lie about a scorching chunk of pavement in a languid yet anguished puddle.

You will never amount to much because you are a single drop in an ocean.

And it is for this reason that I, an unobliging meteorite, envy you.

"You're skipping."

Hallie and I can finally walk to school again. The very last snowman-cores have melted, and the air smells like freshwater with twinges of fish from the river instead of stale snow and misery. I soak up the feeling like a sponge, the cool air warming up my chest and my arms through my sweater. The whispers of leaves on the trees against a milky blue sky and the squish of mud beneath my feet—I walk on the grass for that very reason—ignite a smile on my face.

"Oh. Sorry." I try to make my walking more methodical, but the day is just so beautiful that I can't contain myself. We're no longer at the mercy of the bus. "Everything is just so springy today, which accounts for the increase of energy, and I swear I saw a robin this morning. Surely it's about time. It's April. This time last year, they'd already built their nests."

"I guess it's nice not having snow," Hallie agrees. A very tiny smile dances on her face, but she doesn't let it show. "And having a day with something to be excited about. Doesn't happen a lot."

"Every day is exciting," I say. "Yesterday was a full moon. That was slightly unusual."

"That happens every twenty-eight days or whatever. Doesn't count."

"Still. It's somewhat interesting. And tomorrow, there may be even fewer muddy snowdrifts in the grass. And soon there are going to be dandelions—"

"Oh, fun, weeds my mom'll make me pull."

"No, they're flowers, and they're pretty flowers at that."

"They're weeds, Skylar."

"Well, then they're beautiful weeds." I sigh a sigh made half of awe in the weather and half of boredom with everything but the weather.

Hallie pulls her jacket closer to her and brushes a strand of hair out of her face, one that the the breeze blows right back. Somehow the Great Hallie Giovia can make a drab school uniform of an evergreen polo and a khaki skirt look effortless.

"Five bucks says we'll have a pop quiz in global," Hallie decides.

"I hope not. I didn't do the reading. What was it on?"

"You think I can remember? That was, like, nine hours ago."

"Well, could you please try?"

She looks at me out of the corner of her eye and sighs. "One of the Henrys, I think. The one with all the wives."

"Oh, then it must be Henry the Eighth," I tell her. "Divorced, beheaded, died, divorced, beheaded, survived. If we can remember that, we'll be fine. That's practically all of French history."

"Henry the Eighth was English."

"This is why global readings are essential."

My phone rings. There's only one person in the world who calls me, and it's because her mom won't let her have a cellphone and is therefore confined to the landline. "Hold on, it's Harlow," I tell Hallie, answering my phone and putting it on speaker. "You're supposed to be at school."

I hear my cousin sigh from the other end of the line. "No one's school starts as early as your island school," Harlow reminds me. "Just calling to see if you're freaking out about this weather. I'm taking a wild guess and saying you are."

"She's actually *skipping*," Hallie says into my phone. "Like she's five."

"I woke up and saw that the boys' snowman was gone and knew you'd have an aneurism as soon as you saw," Harlow says. "The three of them—man, you would've thought someone *died*. They're planning a funeral, I swear." She makes a sound of disgust. I can barely deal with one brother, so I have no idea how Harlow deals with three. Being the only girls in our family, we have a special bond that straddles the two-year age gap and the river between us.

"I almost wish it would snow again so she wouldn't be so annoying," Hallie says.

"I feel you. 'Kay, I have to get ready. Don't lick a tree or eat a butterfly or anything." She hangs up.

"You can belittle my excitement all you want, but it doesn't make the first day post-snow any less enthralling," I say.

"Almost as *enthralling* as the last day pre-snow."

"Even more so if you hate the cold."

"And you hate the cold."

I smile at the springtime—the sunshine, the birds, the squishy grass—and resolve never to change it. Summer can come with its heat and its plethora of beach balls, and I'll still long for spring, the seasonal hanging fire.

Chapter Two

Yours is the first face that I saw,
I think I was blind before I met you.
Now I don't know where I am,
I don't know where I've been,
but I know where I want to go.

"First Day of My Life"
Bright Eyes

The only thing worse than being a freshman in high school must be being a freshman in high school who has to take algebra. I am strict on my belief that there is no way there should be that many letters in any form of math. I should not have to use the entire alphabet to graph a line. (Not only that, but I don't think I should ever have to graph lines.)

Miss Felding smiles at us as we walk into her class. Wearing a black and white polka-dot dress and a red cardigan, she looks like a china doll: her pale face is accentuated by rosy cheeks, her brown hair would be plain if it weren't for the fact that it falls in perfect ringlets, and her hazelnut eyes could pass for handblown glass. Dainty and delicate, she teaches our class in a calm, even voice with a gentle smile on her face. I wish that I, like her, could float instead of walk and constantly glisten like ripples in a pond. Though she certainly can't be over twenty-five, she's as timeless as a clock without arms.

I take my seat between Jacob Connelly and Blake Kingston as Miss Felding glides from the back of the room to her place in front of the whiteboard. Then she twirls to face us and says, "Good morning, everyone! I have some very exciting news for you all."

"About math?" Lexie Petterson says without raising her hand, though I don't think I've ever seen her wait for permission to speak. "Sorry, Miss Felding, but the words 'exciting' and 'math' just don't go together."

"I certainly hope to change your opinion on that." Miss Felding's grin only grows as she glances at each of her students. As always, her gaze stays on me a little longer than it does on Blake. I self-consciously smooth out my hair and adjust my glasses.

"Today, we will be starting an in-class project to finish up our unit on systems of equations!"

"Sounds riveting," Hallie mutters.

"I promise, it'll be quite fun."

"Give it a chance, Hallie," Lexie responds with a smirk.

"How big of a chance?" she replies.

"It could change your entire perception of math. You could walk out of class today a different person."

"Yeah, right."

Miss Felding beams again before explaining. "You're going to all become teachers!"

We blink back at her.

"Isn't that exciting?"

Blink, blink.

"That doesn't sound exciting to anyone? Not even to you, Skylar?"

"I guess I just need more information on the matter," I answer carefully.

Miss Felding doesn't falter. "Jacob? Please, tell me *you're* interested."

Jacob Connelly raises an eyebrow. "Of course, Miss Felding. I'm always up for standing up in front of my entire class and talking about math. Sounds like a great way to spend a period."

She paces up and down the rows of desks as she explains. "We've learned four different lessons this unit. In groups of four, you'll be planning your own lesson to reteach the concept. You may come up with any way to teach that, be it a Powerpoint or a worksheet or whatever else you can come up with . . ."

I zone out around here. It's a shame that I find math so excruciatingly boring, since the wondrous Lea Felding excels in her job of attempting to keep us engaged—the operative word being *attempting*. I'm guessing this project is another one of her plans to get us interested in algebra, but unfortunately for her, that probably won't—

"Oh, and I almost forgot the most exciting part!" Miss Felding's hands flap around like tiny bat wings. "The group that creates the best presentation will get to join me at a conference for teachers coming up with new ways to teach their students! I am hosting a panel on student-to-student teaching, and I would love to have you join me."

There it is again, the funny, too-long look she often gives me but no one else.

"I have picked your groups for you," Miss Felding says next. "Sofia, Meredith, Alex, and Brielle, you'll be solving systems of equations by elimination. Jacob, Skylar, Lexie, and Hallie, you have solving by substitution. Blake—"

I conceal a sigh as I push four desks together and patiently wait for Hallie. Yes, I could have gotten stuck with a much worse group. I know Lexie from yearbook staff because she's the only one there to whom I'll voluntarily-yet-reluctantly talk, but I've only talked to Jacob twice, and one of those barely counts because he was soaked in orange juice (long story). But both of them terrify me, since I can see all their potential energy bouncing around them like sparks just waiting to set flame to whatever they can reach.

First off, Lexie Petterson is a literal bundle of energy in every way you can think of, like a capriciously blinding highlighter. Every single class she's in is often steered off into tangents with her at the helm. She's got this permanent smirk on her face that makes you wonder what she's up to this time, and whenever I'm in her vicinity, I do end up wondering. She leaves her dazzling yellow ink all over your hands and makes you feel this natural high just from breathing her in. Her audacity is contagious, so I try to stay away from her—she's got the capacity to change people just by drawing on them, turning them from whatever they were to her felicitous shade—because I don't think yellow is my color.

And then there's Jacob. He's a freaking hurricane. With strange eyes that aren't quite brown and messy hair that's not quite black, Jacob Connelly is perhaps the most impetuous person I've ever met. Yet every little mark he makes is tiny, like arguing with Ms. Redding on why articles should be considered a part of speech or his constant sarcasm (and I mean *constant*—he'd have a gold medal by now if sarcasm were an Olympic event). I can't quite wrap my head around the fact that the boy who just came to this school this year, the new kid, the commodity normally torn apart limb-by-limb by the kids who've been here since birth, has the nerve to be so *there*. He's not a meteorite so much as a storm of thousands of raindrops falling at once. I avoid him at all costs. His smile alone is dangerous; it can shoot a bullet right through you.

Jacob comes over to join me. "Hey, Skylar," he says.

"Hi, Jacob," I reply. Dear God, I hate using people's names. I always worry they'll find it strange that I know their name, which is by far one of the stupidest things I've ever thought, yet here I am, cringing as the word *Jacob* passes my lips.

Hallie pulls another desk to our circle and sets her books on it. "Okay. Solving by substitution. That shouldn't be that hard.

You just rearrange the first thing and stick it in the second thing and solve it like a long, normal thing."

"That's quite the minimalistic explanation, Hallie," I say.

"It's more than you have, isn't it?"

"A lot more."

Lexie comes over next and drops her books onto the floor. "Hey, guys. Who agrees that we should do the crappiest project ever so we don't have to go to that convention thing? Okay, so what if we did a board game? Like Monopoly, but with math. That has to be so boring and so awful that she couldn't possibly *bear* to watch us play it twice." I'm amazed how many words she can get out in a single breath.

"Mathopoly," I say. No one heard me, I hope.

"Mathopoly," Jacob repeats to my horror. (So much for hope.) "That's actually kind of hysterical."

"Why don't we just make a worksheet?" Hallie groans. "It's so much easier, and then she really won't want us there."

"But that's not any *fun*," Lexie protests. "And everyone else is doing a worksheet."

"Which is precisely the reason we should do a worksheet," I counter.

"No, we should do a board game," Jacob says. "Miss Felding might give us extra points for creativity, and I love being told I'm creative."

Hallie blinks very slowly, like a sloth. "Are you told that a lot, Jacob?"

"Nope. That's why I love it. It's a rare occurrence."

"Except those extra points for creativity could contribute to our chances of being chosen," I remind him.

"Except they maybe could *not*," he replies.

Hallie capitulates: "Fine, I really don't care. Can any of you draw? Skylar and I are out."

"Hey, I can draw pretty great whales."

"We don't need any whales, Skylar. No one *ever* needs any whales."

"I draw pretty epic rectangles," Jacob says. "We'll need some paper."

"And a ruler," I add.

"No, I don't need one," Jacob replies.

"Your lines will be all wobbly."

In his math book, he draws a nearly completely straight line without the aid of a ruler. The steadiness of his hands is astounding. Mine would shake and my lines would go all over the place.

"I stand corrected."

"I'll go ask Miss Felding for supplies," Lexie says. "If she's got nothing good, I'll just grab something from the art wing tomorrow."

Jacob takes out a smaller piece of paper. "I'll come up with sample problems. Hard or easy?"

"How much do you hate the people in our class?" Hallie responds with.

"Hard, then."

"No decimals, though," I remark. "That's cruel and unusual."

Something indistinguishable crosses his face, bordering between annoyance and amusement. "But cruel and unusual is the best way to go in math."

"Okay, when people start to grumble about the amount of effort needed to solve those things, you're completely welcome to take all of the blame."

"You're so sweet, Skylar."

And then maybe it's the light, or maybe I'm just being irrational, but I swear his eyes actually change color. His eyes are usually chocolate brown, but they slowly shift into a weird sepia with very tiny twinges of gold and maybe a fleck or two of green. They're very perplexing, as if someone edited a photo of a forest but the vintage filter they used didn't erase all the color. Those tiny flecks in the iris, they're like trees surrounding a lake.

"What's wrong? You're staring at me."

"Nothing." I turn away as fast as humanly possible. "No, I wasn't."

"Yes, you were."

"I wasn't."

"You literally were just staring into my eyes."

"Oh my gosh, I was not."

Hallie shoots us both glares. "You know what would be fun? Finishing this before my funeral."

Lexie comes back with a piece of poster board, a ruler, and some markers. "Here, this stuff is good. I'll do the sample problems, Jacob, and you design the board."

"Can we put sparkles on it?" I say without thinking. *Skylar, don't talk about glitter, these people are dangerous.*

"Ooo, I love sparkles," Lexie says. "Sparkles are great. They're so sparkly. Do you have any at home?"

"I've got some," I say, picturing the drawer in my desk housing eight different shades.

"'Kay, then bring them," Lexie says, "and we'll add some *shine*." She accentuates this with jazz hands.

Hallie sighs. "Sparkles? Really? I'd rather glue actual bones to the board."

"Yes, sparkles," I repeat. "They won't hurt you. I can't say the same for the bone idea."

I look up from the pages of my textbook to see Miss Felding is watching us from a couple feet away. I smile at her. She smiles back quickly before shifting her eyes to another group, not before I notice the color of her eyes switch. There's some awfully weird lighting in this classroom.

"You know Sasha Capernault cheated on that global pop quiz?" Hallie asks me as we walk home from school. I rely on her for all the gossip because I'm very, in her words, "out of it". "Guess she didn't know about all of Henry VIII's wives."

"She must not be a fan of the Anglican Church," I reply. "What did Mr. Hallawin do to her?"

"Well, he put her name in the Box of Doom for the rest of the semester," Hallie says. "And she obviously got a zero on the quiz. I don't know what else. Knowing him, that could be it."

"Knowing the rest of the faculty and the dogmatics of the education system, though," I counter, "she could be burned at the stake."

Hallie shrugs. "If she's kicked off the track team, I'll actually cry happy tears. She's always dragging down our relays, since she's always first. I'm always the anchor leg."

I smile to myself.

"What?"

"You're an anchor."

"... okay?"

"If it weren't for you, I'd be suffocating from a loss of oxygen I'd be so high up. You ground me."

"You're such a freak," she says, but she actually smiles a real, haphazard smile. They always start slow, like she can't exactly remember how to form one, but then it comes back to her, like the lyrics of a Christmas song she hasn't heard since last year. I absorb it, as genuine smiles from Hallie are like diamonds: rare, crystalline, and shimmering. "You do that for everyone? Come up with an object?"

"A couple people," I admit.

"So what are you?" We climb the steps to her porch.

"I—" I pause. "I've never thought about that."

"Come on. You must have, at least once."

"Not in my conscious memory," I say, "and I think that would be something I remember."

"You, Skylar, are weird. I'll see you tomorrow." I walk the rest of the way home with my brother Evan, who walked with Hallie's little brother, and he talks about something that I can't focus on under any circumstances—I think it has something to do with squids.

"Good, you're home," Mom says right when we walk in. "I need taste testers for these muffins. I tried a new recipe." A pencil holds her dark bun to her head, and her forehead is beaded with sweat. Judging by the muddy boots in the corner and the pile of garden tools in the garage, Mom couldn't wait till the day after the snow melts to get started on her garden.

I take a bite of the muffin she's handed me. "Carrot?"

"And apple."

"I like it," Evan says.

"Good. They've got a ton of vitamin A." She starts rinsing the muffin tins. "How was your day?"

"Fairly boring." I grab a towel and dry the tins. "We started a project in math."

"I've never heard of a math project." She puts some dishes into the dishwasher. My mother never stops moving, especially when there's work to be done. "Is it a group project or just you?"

"A group."

"Who's in yours?"

"Hallie, Lexie, and Jacob."

"Jacob . . ."

"Connelly," I finish.

"Oh, I know his mom. She's a chatterbox, that one. And which one's Lexie?"

"Petterson," I say. "I'm on yearbook staff with her."

"Oh, right. Petterson." Lexie's family is known around the island through whispers. She's got two dads, and conservative islanders either think that it's an outrage or that her house is like a petting zoo. I see absolutely no big deal in the fact that she's got two fathers and that her sister is adopted from Korea while she's adopted from Morocco. People think of them as objects of either ridicule or intrigue. I think they're people and it's not much more than that. "Well, it sounds like a good group."

"I hope so," I say. "They're . . . influential, to say the least."

"I'm sure you'll have fun," Mom reassures.

"Yeah, I guess," I say. I fiddle with a pen on the table. "I don't know. Lately, I haven't been feeling . . . I don't know . . . *challenged* enough, yet all my classes are too difficult. It's a pretty contradictory mentality, really—I'm always bored, yet I can't seem to get anything done."

"You don't feel *challenged* enough?" Mom repeats. "You're taking all honors courses."

"Expect for math. I'm very bad at math."

She ignores this. "What more could you need?"

I sigh, unconvinced. "Yes, you're probably right. Maybe my classes are just so hard my brain is numb and thinks that they're easy." I smile at her and go upstairs.

I start my global outlines, but when Evan decides to start practicing the drums and my dad decides to blast Journey because why the hell not, *I* decide that this noisy house simply won't work for the hiking of Mount Homework, so I put it all in my backpack and ask my parents if I can take a walk.

I'm bending the truth a bit, though. Strictly speaking, I *do* take a walk, but only down to the banks of our river. There, between the trees in an area no one knows about but me, is my favorite place in the world.

The little rock-covered beach that Harlow and I christened Starlight Cove can't be more than eight feet long and five feet deep. Sometimes, after rainfall or snowmelt, it's not even there because of the water levels. A rock sits in the very center, one that is just barely big enough to seat two people side-by-side. An old willow tree drapes over the hideout, creating a leafy umbrella that shades the area. This is my happy place, found when I was playing Truth or Dare with Hallie and some other girls as kids and I was dared to see what was on the other side of these trees. My hideaway belongs only to me; it's my place to read or do homework or think or work on yearbook layout. No one can ever bother me here because *here* doesn't exist in anyone else's world.

I shed my coat so I can feel the cool fishy air on my arms, and I put in my earbuds and start my entire music library before donning my hiking boots in light of the conquest of Mount Homework. It manages to take me to a different time and a different place—probably because it's a global outline—as does my entire secret: my escape from a place that most people would escape *to*, certainly not *from*.

Chapter Three

I smile
because I want to.

"Pools"
Glass Animals

"Guys, hit the triplet!" I'm in orchestra the next afternoon. When we had the option to sign up for music electives at the beginning of the year, I signed up for orchestra with no hesitation. My wishful thinking had gotten the better of me that day. Getting to play the violin three days a week for forty minutes? A sizable amount of stringed-instrument experience and a drastic expansion of my musical intellect? Where could I possibly go wrong?

Well, I overlooked the detail that to be in orchestra, one must be able to read music.

I'm hopeless. I know the basic symbols, but I can't register them in my head fast enough to sight read. They seem like foreign symbols to me. I guess I just need more practice/dedication to wanting to be fluent in music, but it's seriously difficult, like learning an entirely new language. Sure, I can play things right because I can pretty much play something after hearing it a few times, but what's the point if I can't read it when it's written? It's like being able to speak French fluently without reading a word of it. Pointless.

My stand partner must absolutely hate me. She's a sophomore and actually can play, and though she's very sweet and patient, I'm sure she gets sick of me not actually reading our sheet music and just piggybacking on whatever she's playing. The truth is, though, that I'm actually not that bad—when I learn a song aurally, that is. I mean, my vibrato sounds like a sheep and I can't shift at all, but my notes are in tune, and I can do slurs and stuff. Reading everything at the speed of light is where everything becomes difficult. Then you throw in the time signatures—I believe Hell is composed of time signatures. The fact that some people are able to hold a note for a certain amount of time is beyond me. A sixteenth note and a whole note clearly look different, but it's impossible for me to tell exactly how long they each are. Time eludes me.

The first time I heard the orchestra play together, I had to suppress a smile because I'd never heard anything like it before. The notes blend together perfectly, like a big, puffy cloud of a G-minor chord. I'm still in bit of awe every time we play a song, because every section is playing something different yet blending with the others so perfectly. Sometimes I wish that I could rip the walls of the room down and make the whole world listen to us. Other times I want to bottle up this sound and keep it only to us because it's more special that way.

"Piano!" our conductor, Mrs. Darner, cries over us. We quiet down until our playing is barely audible. "Violas, play measure forty-eight with more vigor please! Remember the forte at fifty-six! Dynamics are always nice! Firsts, accidentals, please! I have pencils if you need to mark them!" She looks at the clock without stopping her conduction. "Okay, stop, guys. The bell's going to ring . . ." she trails off and points to the clock as the bell rings. I call it the Darner Instinct; for some reason, she has the strange skill of knowing the bell schedules by heart and can tell us right as they ring. I can never figure out how she does it; sometimes this class feels like it lasts five minutes, other times five hours. I find it so impressive that she knows it's the same length every day. "Instruments in their lockers if you're leaving them overnight! Sign your concert permission slips! If you borrowed rosin or a pencil, on my desk please! Have a great day everyone!"

None of my friends are in orchestra, so I don't really talk to anyone besides my stand partner, and our conversations are strictly music-related. *Can I borrow your rosin? Do you want to play top notes or bottom notes? Is my A string in tune?* I kind of like that none of my friends are in it, though. It's my thing; I don't have to share it. Just me and my violin and my inexplicably horrible note-reading skills.

Unlike just about everyone else, I never put my violin back into its tiny cage because there isn't any room. Since my locker is on the third floor and most of my classes are on the first and second, I keep my books for those periods in my music locker rather than my regular locker. This way, I don't have to carry six periods' worth of books, and I don't need to walk an approximate mile a day within the Main Classes Building—I get my fill of walking between the library and Main each study hall, as that's (as Hallie and I have figured out) a full fourteenth of a mile. I grab my global books and slip out of the music wing.

My least favorite thing about orchestra is having to walk to global alone—I hate doing anything by myself, especially if I'm with a lot of other people. It makes me feel like everyone is looking at me and wondering why I have no friends. I shouldn't think this; most of them are walking alone, too.

Someone is suddenly in front of me. How they just materialized there, I have no idea, but there they are, as if they teleported, or as if I missed them walk right in front of me. Panicked, I try to move over to one side to avoid them, but I end up tripping over my own feet and spewing my books all over the floor. Embarrassed, I struggle to pick them up. The only thing worse than dropping your books in the middle of the hall with everyone watching is if you do so, but then your butterfingers inhibit you from picking them up without dropping them yet again.

"Let me help you."

I look up and see Ms. Parkins standing over me, though she makes no move to actually help me. I gulp. "No, thank you, Ms. Parkins, I've got it." *Please tell me that didn't come off as rude.*

She frowns. "Why, you'll be late to class. And you certainly don't want a demerit."

According to her sophomore geometry students, taking help from Ms. Parkins is like buying jewelry off a guy in the street —is it real gold, or is it dyed plastic that's going to turn your wrist green? My guess is that she's accepted that no one really likes her so she's selective with her aid.

I grab everything at the speed of light and thankfully stand up without another wipe-out. "Thank you anyway, Ms. Parkins. Have a great day." I give her a smile and walk away as fast as I can. I'm inevitably going to be late for class now, but Mr. Hallawin would have to be in a terrible, puppy-squishing mood to resort to demerits. I hurry in right after the bell rings, but no one turns to look at me.

"Okay, take out your chapter questions from last night," Mr. Hallawin says. "Surprise! I'm coming around to check it. If you don't have it, you know what that means."

"The Box of Doom," the class choruses. If someone doesn't have their homework during a surprise homework check, their name gets written in a box on the whiteboard labeled "DOOM" in heavy black letters for the rest of the day, and they have to face the humiliation of being irresponsible. I've been in it four times; the first time, I cried for a few minutes.

I dig through my pile of books for my blue global notebook, where my homework is done. It's not there. *Really? I didn't think you could find a way to mess this up, Skylar. They were just chapter questions, for God's sake.* It's probably still on the floor of the hallway. I sift through my books again, slightly panicked. *Seriously?* Hallawin is extremely nice, but if he sees that I don't have these chapter questions with me, he'll be ruthless as he writes my name in that objectifying Expo-Marker gulag. Nevertheless, his class is one of my favorites. It's very freeform because he's pretty young, like mid-twenties. He often brings in people to talk to us; once, our congressman was in town and came to school to talk about the legislative branch, and another time, Ms. Redding's brother came to talk about his job in the Department of Interior and to babble about his son Thomas's position in Homeland Security (did you know that there are botanists that work for Homeland Security? Me either.).

I get up and quickly grab the hall pass, hoping to be back in time for Mr. Hallawin's arrival to my desk.

It's not on the hall floor. The bright turquoise should stand out against the speckled gray of the tiles, but it doesn't. Someone must've picked it up by accident or turned it into lost and found in the office. I don't have the time to get to the office, though, because Mr. Hallawin will be at my desk any second and I'll be put in the Box of Doom and forced to drop out of school and raise guinea pigs for a living.

I retrace all my steps, from the door of the orchestra room to the door of Mr. Hallawin's. There isn't even a hint of blue on the floor.

"Skylar." I hear a harsh whisper. I turn around and see Hunter Athan slip out of Parkins' geometry room. Hunter is one of the most serious people I know, which is why he reminds me of a plain, smooth piece of shale. His thin face, olive-tinted skin, and dark hair only solidify this. Fairly smart—and kind of a know-it-all, in all honesty—he takes the geometry course usually taken by sophomores, but his laconism makes his intelligence a little hard to believe until he corrects you on something. I haven't talked to him since seventh grade when I had to build a model cell with him, so I can't help wondering why he's talking to me now, and breaking the rules by doing so.

"Um, hi, Hunter," I whisper back awkwardly.

"You're looking for this, right?" He hands me my notebook. "I was gonna give it to you next period, but," his eyes glaze over me, "you need it now."

"Oh. How'd you know it was mine?" I ask. "Oh, sorry, thank you. For finding it, I mean. Thank you. I just said that. Sorry."

"It's completely covered in whales, and so is your pencil case and folder. Also, it's got some American Girl doll stickers stuck to it, and you're the only one in high school who still likes those things. It's an A-schedule day, which means you go to global from orchestra, which is over in the east wing across from sciences, and you probably wouldn't come through here unless you were coming from the east wing."

I blink at him.

"That, and your name's on the cover in big purple letters."

I hope I'm not blushing as hard as I think I am. "Right. Well . . . thank you." I quickly smile at him before hurrying back to class, arriving just in time for Mr. Hallawin to draw a smiley face on my homework, marking it as done.

Lexie and I sit next to each other in our after-school yearbook club meeting. She talks so much, she's barely breathing between her words. I watch her for signs of suffocation rather than listen to a word she's saying. Something about her kittens, I've gathered, and maybe a box of cornstarch.

"We need the spring sport teams pics taken soon," Mr. Hallawin announces. "Emma, I've got you penciled in to take those over the course of next week in homeroom. And we'll need to finish the—"

It's like a puzzle piece falls out of the world, because suddenly everyone is standing and surrounding the computers. I frantically glance around the room, confused as to why I completely missed what seems like a few minutes of information. I can't even recall what I was thinking about or what the last thing Mr. Hallawin said was.

Seriously freaky, I think, but I brush it off and join Lexie at one of the computers. "I'm sorry, I missed it, what are we doing?"

She shrugs. "I have no idea. I'm just following them." She gestures to everyone else at our computer. "They seem to know."

"Someone grab the class list," Emma McCarter says. She's the editor in chief and is totally annoying about it. *I'm better than you 'cause I've got fine print under my name on the yearbook staff page. Whoop.*

"Oh, I gave it to Miss Felding," Mr. Hallawin says. "She needed it for something. Skylar, why don't you go get it? She's probably still in her room."

It's just Miss Felding, I tell myself as I walk down the hall towards her classroom. *Here, rehearse what you're going to say, that always works, right? "Hi, Miss Felding, Mr. Hallawin needs the class list back. If that's alright. If you're finished with it. We're doing the sport pages, I think. I haven't been paying much attention today but—" Okay, you know what? Just stop there.*

I'm about to enter her classroom when I hear her talking to someone. As the conversation seems to be very one-sided, she must be on the phone. I wait in the hall for her to finish, so I don't count this as eavesdropping because I'm not *trying* to listen, but there's her voice, the only sound in the hall. It's just begging to be heard.

"Yes, I think I have all of them," she says.

I lean against the wall so I can hear better. (Okay, maybe *now* it counts as eavesdropping.)

"They display all the signs. I . . . No, I haven't mentioned it . . . I don't think it's time, Margaret, it's such a lot to take in."

I can hear her pacing around her classroom.

"I'm just waiting until I'm absolutely sure . . . I'll be sure to do a pause when I pinpoint them to let everyone know . . . I'll let Eula know as well."

She stops moving.

"They are truly wonderful. I cannot wait for you to meet them." A pause. "No . . . Please don't worry. Just because they're exceptional doesn't mean they could ever take your place."

She's back at her desk now.

"Yes . . . I did. Thomas Redding is expecting your phone call within the hour. He says he can help you in any way and at any time, especially with the Serbian biohazard containment. He's got a few contacts. I've forwarded all of your contact information as well." Another pause. "I will see you at the Meeting, then. Best of luck with the containment units."

She hangs up. I wait a full twenty seconds, counted out in Mississippi's, before going in and asking for the class list. Miss Felding hands it to me with no fanfare or even a trace of her phone call.

Except, of course, her irises fluctuate between hazel and jade, and I really don't know if the light is just playing tricks this time.

Chapter Four

Well, don't stop now—
you won't forgive yourself.
Tiptoe around what you don't want to tell;
no need to speak,
oh, your face says it all.

"Tiptoe"
Coin

Beads of sweat form on my forehead. My foot taps frenetically on the floor but my fingers can't seem to work fast enough. Every detail of my room is far too garish and threatens to steal my focus from what really needs it: an English essay due in less than twelve hours I haven't started, on a book I haven't read. SparkNotes becomes my savior; my abnormally extensive vocabulary pleads for some extra points for finding a way to use "nosocomial" in a sentence.

"Skylar?" I can barely hear Evan calling from downstairs—his speaking voice is a loud whisper, so his yelling voice is a normal person's talking voice.

"I'm a little busy," I call back.

He runs up the staircase, his light footsteps barely making a sound. I sigh to myself; I love my brother, but I'm not in the mood to be a good older sister at the moment.

"I would love to go to the thrift store, and Mom says that you should take me." Evan jumps onto my bed.

"Stop! You'll mess up my animals!" I jump up from my desk and fix the alignment of my stuffed whales sitting atop my pillow. "I'm sorry, but I have an absurd amount of work to finish."

"I think you said those exact words yesterday."

"It was, in fact, three days ago," I say, "and high school does not diminish the workload just because we have workloads from other classes. Please, Evan, let me work for a bit."

"Skylar, take your brother to the thrift store," Mom shouts from downstairs.

I close my computer and put a bookmark in my book. "Fine. Get your shoes on, then. We're not going to go for very long."

Evan loves walking down to Twice Loved Thrift to find new action figures and books about space. I personally love their moderate selection of old vinyl records that were most likely found in an old lady's basement posthumously. They smell like mothballs and are probably carrying previously-thought eradicated diseases, but I love the crinkling paper jackets and the smooth ridged vinyl laden with scratches that look like battle scars.

The tiny bell jingles as we enter the store. "Hi, Mr. James," I greet the man behind the counter, and Evan repeats me.

"Hello, Skylar, Evan," he says with a tiny nod and gruff smile. "We just got some new records. I haven't looked at them yet. You'll be the first."

"Thank you," I say, going to the back of the store. Evan stays in the front and begins to sift through the bin of action figures.

I absentmindedly leaf through the brittle vinyl records, but I don't find anything that interesting. Most of these are either ancient folk singers or cheesy blonde women with horrible, incurable cases of Eighties Hair™. Although they all smell musty and some leave a sticky residue on my fingertips, the piles of records in Twice Loved Thrift are among my favorite things on the entire island.

"Skylar, hurry up." Evan comes over, six action figures in his fists. "You've been looking for at those things for eons, and *you're* the one who said you didn't want to stay long."

"It's only been five minutes," I brush off.

"No, it hasn't," Evan says. "It's been much longer. Like I said, it's been eons."

"Evan, don't be so vexatious."

"It *has* been over twenty minutes, in his defense," Mr. James calls from the front of the store. "He looked through the entire bin twice."

"No, it couldn't have been twenty minutes." I look around the store to all the ticking clocks. Yes, they do say that my time here is edging on twenty-five, but it certainly didn't feel that way. And not like a *time flies when you're having fun!* issue. It honestly feels as if I've been here for a quarter of that. "I have to be writing my essay right now! How could I have lost track of time so carelessly?"

"You must've been enjoying the albums," Mr. James says with a shrug.

"No, no, with all due respect, you don't understand," I try to explain. "The time— We've only been here five minutes."

"You get some sleep tonight," Mr. James suggests. "Maybe herbal tea beforehand. Peppermint is my personal favorite."

I sigh; it's fruitless to attempt an explanation at whatever just happened. "Thank you, Mr. James. Tea *is* a panacea. Well, come on, Evan. Do you have enough quarters for all those?"

He holds out a dollar and fifty cents in quarters.

We leave the store as quickly as I previously believed we'd been in there. The clocks have certainly not been working in my favor as of late.

Naussie shuffles through her rocks. I go over to her, needing to get up from my desk anyway because it's got to be around feeding time and my legs shake from sitting for so long. I have an alarm set on my phone that won't shut up until my hermit crab's got her snack, but I stop it before it starts and fill her tiny dish with tiny food pellets and some apple for dessert.

When I was little (well, really, I was fourteen) and in the midst of my Jurassic Park phase (that I haven't quite left yet), I asked my parents for a velociraptor for Christmas. Naturally, they couldn't find one that had survived the mass extinction and were skeptical about housing a carnivore, so I got a hermit crab instead. I named her Naussie because I thought it was a velociraptor-ish name at the time.

Hallie has a giant golden retriever that's bigger than me. Harlow just got a tiny cockapoo named Gerard after Gerard Way from My Chemical Romance (I helped pick the name; Aunt Clara still doesn't know her beloved pooch's namesake would literally make her faint). Lexie, I've learned, has a bunch of kittens roaming around her property all named after *Friends* characters. I have a hermit crab with a spotted shell named Naussie. It's just how the world happens to work.

She playfully snips at my finger—at least, I *think* it's playful, but as she gets crabby in the evening sometimes, it's hard to tell. I pick up her tiny terrarium and move it closer to the windows so she can see outside—it's not nearly hot enough for the sun to hurt her. She crawls to the other end where she has her tiny log that she likes to climb on. Sure enough, she makes her way to the top.

My phone rings. "Hey, Harlow," I say into it.

"You speak French. What's pig?"

"*Le cochon.*" I spell it for her. "Why not just look it up online?"

"Mom said no, obviously, since it's homework," Harlow groans. "That woman will be the death of me, I swear."

"She just wants the best for you," I assure her.

"Yeah, sure. So, what's up? Anything interesting?"

"I was writing an essay," I say, "and now I'm talking to you."

"I'm so much more interesting anyway." I can almost hear her flip her hair.

"I'm not graded on talking to you," I remind her.

Harlow pauses for a second, and I hear rustling paper. "Okay, what's cow?"

"*La vache.*"

"How do you know all this?"

"I take French."

"I do, too, but I don't know uselessness like farm animals. Only kindergarteners care if the cow says moo."

Naussie's eaten all her apple already. I contemplate giving her more but decide against it; I really don't need her getting a stomachache. Last month, she was pretty sick, but all she needed was an eyedropper of Pepto Bismol. In hindsight, you probably aren't supposed to give a crab human medicine like that, but it didn't kill her, and within the hour, she was back to moving around her rocks and scurrying up her log.

"—so then Freddie steps on Liam's Star Wars guy and he totally freaks out, right, 'cause he's obsessed with those things—"

"What are you talking about?" I interject. Somehow I missed whatever she started discussing, though I can't even remember what I was thinking about before. (Logs, maybe? I don't even take calc.)

"What, did you fall asleep or something?" Harlow prods.

"Something like that," I say. "I don't know. It seems to have been happening somewhat frequently lately."

"Eh, my story wasn't funny, anyway. Maybe you should just get some sleep."

"I have to finish this essay," I tell her. "I'm only on the second developing paragraph."

"Don't beat yourself up over it," Harlow says. "Sleep is more important than homework."

"I don't know what kind of school you attend, but I'm not graded on sleep."

"Still. Try your best. 'Night."

She hangs up without another word.

Dwindling sunlight hangs low in the sky, but it hasn't quite hidden behind the trees yet. I open one of my windows to let the cool air into my room. I sit back at my desk and attempt to work on my essay again but can't seem to refocus due to the new spring verve that engulfs the island, the terrifying yet invigorating feeling that makes you want to jump up and *do* something.

It's days like this one that make me wonder if changing the world isn't such an impossible feat, what with this air full of springtime. I almost close the window in efforts to stop myself, but I end up leaving it open.

Chapter Five

But you know
that I could crush you
with my voice.

"The Pros and Cons of Breathing"
Fall Out Boy

If moods were colors, this one would be a maroon-ish red—dark and powerful. It's an explosion of energy and a longing to run as fast as I can, out of my life and into an empty field, where every blade of grass screams at me and the sky is made of blood and there is no one to hear every thought I've ever composed erupt out of me like some vivacious volcano about to engulf the Earth to the point where the magma of the core fuses with incandescent words coming out of every pore of my body; it's a place where the voice in my head is louder than anyone's ever was, and it forces everyone on the planet to listen to me vociferate everything I need to before they slowly burn to death as the world melts around them like a cherry popsicle in July—

Good God, what the hell is wrong with you?

I get up and put on my glasses before I end up surrendering to the extrinsic urge to set the island aflame. This must be how the other half lives, how meteorites feels every day—but if this is how those meteorites feel every day, then I'm surprised they haven't all spontaneously combusted yet.

"Hi, Skylar," Evan says, drumming on the kitchen table with the end of his spoon. For someone generally so quiet, he sure drums a lot. Most people think quiet kids play the piano. Evan does not.

"Stop that. Please. It's really irritating." I sit at the table.

"Good morning to you, too."

"Everything okay there, Skylar?" Mom says, eyeing me with her mother's eye.

"Yes, I'm fine." I *am* fine. Completely fine. Everything is just annoying me more than usual, that's all. I'm as raindroppy as ever.

"You seem . . . edgy," my dad adds.

"I'm about as edgeless as a sphere, but thank you for the concern." I manage a smile that's about as convincing as special effects in monster movies in the fifties, but it's the most I can give them right now.

I go to get some cereal, but nothing in the pantry seems appetizing, not even the Rice Krispies I eat every single day (with bananas and blueberries). I stick a granola bar in my bag instead before slipping on my shoes. "Can you hurry up please, Evan?"

"I just made this waffle," Evan groans. Nevertheless, he shoves the rest in his cheek like a squirrel and gets his sneakers on. We start our walk towards Hallie's house, but I realize halfway down the street that I left all my homework sitting on my desk, so I have to run back and get it. Evan giggles to himself, and I sigh angrily as I shove it all in my backpack.

Hallie waits on the porch like always. "Hey," she says to us, and we begin to walk, leaving Evan lingering on the porch to wait for Hallie's youngest brother so they can walk together. "How are you?"

"Okay," I say. "I'm in a bad mood."

"Your bad moods are my good moods," she responds, kicking a stone on the sidewalk.

"True," I say, "but I'm in an *actual* bad mood. Tired, I guess—I didn't go to bed until about one-thirty last night because of that insipid English essay, which I didn't even finish, by the way, so I'll have to do it in study hall. Or I'm stressed. Probably stressed. It's always just stress in high school. Stomachache? Stress. Headache? Stress. Feel like dying in a hole? Just more stress, you melodramatic, hormonal teenagers."

My hands fumble around the combination lock on my locker once we get to school. I sigh, frustrated, when the third try is to no avail. I don't understand locker locks; do you really think someone's interested in stealing some old biology notes or half-chewed pencils?

"Lock got your locker?" Lexie asks me. She leans against her locker which is right next to mine, on the left.

"That's not clever," I mutter. "What was it supposed to be, a play on cat's got your tongue or something of the sort?"

"Not sure. It wasn't one of my better jokes." Lexie plays with one of the curls in her bouncy hair. "Did you bring the glitter for the math thing?"

"Oh, no, I'm sorry. I totally forgot. I'll bring it tomorrow."

"It's fine. We can add it whenever."

Details fire at me like bullets. Too much is going on in this hallway—is it this exhausting to walk down this hall every morning? Someone's dropped their papers all over, and two juniors pick them up. Mrs. Darner hangs a poster asking people to come to the music electives' spring concerts. Jacob and Hunter lean against the lockers and talk—those two are best friends, and they talk there every morning before homeroom. How haven't I noticed? It's been almost eight months of the same routine, so how haven't I picked up on it? Jacob's laughing and even Hunter, whom I've never seen laugh when he's not around Jacob, smiles with his whole face.

We walk into homeroom and sit down right before the bell rings, and then the morning announcements begin, which I hate because they always seem so irrelevant. Our principal talks about swim matches and chess meets—no, that can't be what she says—but everything is just so *much* today, all dramatic and flagrant. It all sounds like noise that mixes with the noises in my head and it creates this horrifying symphony that sounds like a thousand of me trying to sightread four different pieces in five-eight time all at once.

"Do your English essay instead of reading," Hallie says, turning to face me and gesturing to my book. She sits in the desk in front of me every day; she says it's so she can easily turn around to scold me.

"We're *in* Redding's homeroom," I say. "If she caught me .. . I couldn't handle her shouting all those words at me of which I don't know the meaning. It makes me feel like my vocabulary is menial at best."

"Well, it's your fault you didn't finish it," she says.

"I literally fell asleep at my desk, Hallie," I say, "and I'm not very good at writing in my sleep."

"Okay, cool." Her voice teems with apathy. "Good for you."

Lexie spits, "Hallie, stop being mean to Skylar."

I glance at her out of the corner of my eye. Lexie Petterson, defending me? Seems strange, but is welcomed nonetheless.

"Stop siding with her," Hallie says to her. "She didn't finish her essay, and that's her fault. Not mine."

"Hallie," I warn, "we're not going to fight, and no sides will be taken."

I mill through my morning classes, my mind fuzzy. It's thinking very un-Skylar thoughts, telling itself that it's . . . capable of things? I yell at it to be quiet for once because I really hate it right now, but, then again, I always have, really: I can't remember things people asked me to do three minutes ago; I can't get through a class and retain all the information they shove at us; I can't sit still, and I say weird things out loud without realizing it, and my stupid, *stupid* brain can't think about anything without playing leapfrog with other thoughts running around. It's absolutely useless, and it's absolutely *in*capable of anything.

"Jacob, why haven't you finished the board yet?" Hallie groans while we work on our math project during third period. He isn't listening to her. "Jacob!"

"What? I'm sorry," he replies.

"Why haven't you finished the board yet?" Hallie repeats.

"Oh. Sorry. I'll finish it."

"Skylar, your card piles are uneven." Lexie paces the scene, inspecting everything.

"I'm trying," I say. "I'll make more for the other stack."

"Hallie, you can't complain about me not finishing the board if you're not helping," Jacob retorts.

"I *am* helping!" Hallie spits back. "I'm doing all the sample problems."

"You're making them too easy," Jacob says. "Anyone can solve number six in their heads."

"Really, Jacob? You can combine two equations and solve for x right in your head?" Hallie sounds dubious.

"Yes, I can." Jacob crosses his arms and stares Hallie down.

"Skylar, can you stop tapping your pencil please?" Lexie asks.

"Then can you stop tapping yours?"

"I'm not."

"Yes, you are."

"Both of you are," Jacob says.

"Finish the board." Lexie throws a pencil at him.

"I told you, I'm *trying*," he says, putting his pencil back to the board. "At least I'm *attempting* to get something done." He throws the pencil back.

"I *am* trying!" Lexie shouts back. "I'm just . . . not interested in any of this crap."

"We've gotten next to nothing finished," I lament. "Only a bunch of half-started components. Can't we make an effort to get some of these things off the ground?"

"Skylar, stop biting your nails," Hallie reprimands without looking up from her computer.

"Hallie, I appreciate your concern, but could you maybe shut up?"

I catch Miss Felding looking our way. She doesn't say a word to us, even though we're being uncooperative with our group members, which should result in a point deduction. She only looks at us with the same funny face she always has when we're in her line of sight and drums her fingers on her desk, one finger after the other: tap, tap, tap.

I'm not hungry during lunch, so I mindlessly pick at my food instead. Hallie and I sit with Lexie and some of her friends like Meredith Pandey and Brielle Aberson and some other girls to whom I don't pay attention, the ones who are all on the tennis team in the spring and political debate club in the winter. "I'm just saying, *Shrek Two* is a cinematic masterpiece," Meredith declares.

"The first is the best," someone replies. I don't know who because today everyone's voices sound the same. "*Definitely* the best."

"No, the third!" another says.

Something's got to be up, or else Lexie would have shot her down and said the first movie was the best; she's got very strong opinions on Shrek. Her color is off today: more of a mustard than a highlighter yellow.

I get up to throw my garbage out. This, here, the getting up by myself to go to the front of the cafeteria, is the reason Hallie and I only started eating in the cafeteria around a month ago. First off, the cafeteria is a separate building across the quad (Hallie and I think that they put the cafeteria, library, advancements building, and the like in separate buildings to keep us active and make up for only having two gym classes a week), and if you're going to cross the quad for any reason, it really should be for the library. And if it's raining, it's not worth it to leave the Main Classes Building at all.

So we'd either stay in Main or go to the library, or to the quad, if we were really lucky to not find any upperclassmen already there. It was only when Lexie, Brielle, Sofia, and Meredith asked why we were never at lunch that we decided to give the cafeteria, the epitome of high school Hell, a try.

I put everything in the garbage and turn around so I can quickly skirt back to the table. With my flat-out amazing luck and unfortunate talent of benign awkwardness, after throwing out my things, I quickly turn around and run smack into Alex Summer-held. His mouth opens in a little *O* and begins to drop his plate.

But I *see* it. The plate falls as if it were in slow-motion, taking far more time to hit the ground than one would expect. Moving straight down, there's no argument that it will shatter on impact, and that'll cause the entire cafeteria's attention to latch right on to me. Smashing plates is always the highlight of any lunch period—seriously, once there was bake sale with our principal dressed as a penguin selling cupcakes, and all everyone talked about how some freshman dropped a soup cup and shattered it. That can *not* be me today. The very last thing I need is attention at the moment. All those eyes on me and I try to clean up ceramic shards without crying would be an absolute nightmare.

I make a split-second decision to reach out and catch it like a Frisbee, closing my hand around the edge of the plate, the force of it landing on my fingers. It stays in my hand. Then I cast a glance at the rest of the cafeteria to see if anyone noticed, but those who were looking at me have already turned their attention back to their friends. Then I look in awe at whatever I just managed to do.

Alex's eyes flit between me and the plate in my hand. "How'd you do that?" His voice seems too generous for his face; it's somewhat full of life whereas his face seems to be permanently blank. He's one of the "popular" boys, the ones that keep telling themselves that popularity is an issue in a school so small. Before the Great Plate Catch, I hadn't talked to him since third grade, even though he's in yearbook club with Lexie and me (though he doesn't really show up at the meetings) and I hadn't been planning to start talking to him again, as his thick following of girls would destroy my next to nonexistent social life if I were to even breathe in his direction. Not that I would care, anyway. I hate to say it, but Alex is about as flat as a piece of paper. Even his appearance—while fairly attractive, I won't discredit him—is a bit bland, with plain round face adorned with plain brown eyes topped with plain brown hair. I can see nothing in him, as if he were made of cellophane and clear Scotch tape.

"I— Honestly, I have no idea," I reply.

"Seriously, are you trying to be a Jedi?" He takes the plate out of my hands.

"'Do or do not, there is no try'," I say awkwardly. Now that I'm not clutching a dirty plate for dear life, I don't know what to do with my hands. I clasp them in front of me, but that's uncomfortable, and hanging them at my sides makes me feel like

Sasquatch for some reason. I decide on crossing my arms. It's how I naturally stand anyway.

"That's funny," he says. "Well, I thought it was cool."

"It was nothing," I assure him. "I was merely trying to minimize humiliation."

I practically run back to the table. Then I stare at my hands and wonder how they managed to do that.

Maybe eating in an empty English classroom wasn't such a bad idea.

Chapter Six

"It was so weird," I explain to Hallie as we walk home from school. "Everything slowed down so I could see what exactly was happening in extreme detail. And then without thinking, I just . . . I *caught* it."

"Maybe you can actually get an A in gym this quarter," she responds. She seems very on edge today, constantly glancing at the watch on her wrist and throwing looks over her shoulder.

"I'm serious," I say. "I have no idea how I did that."

"Just plain luck."

"Hallie, it feels like I'm . . . I don't know. Time doesn't seem like it's working right, and people are becoming, like, high-definition versions of themselves, like there're suddenly *so many* more details about them that must be memorized."

"You're so annoying," Hallie says. She always forgets that I usually can see right through her as if she were a clear sheet of ice over a pond—underneath, I see all the fish waiting for spring and avoiding ice fishermen. This isn't because Hallie can't lie—she's the best liar I know—but I know her incredibly well. "Stop being so overdramatic."

"You think so, too," I continue. "You're not as ignorant to this as you're pretending to be. You're just as nervous as I am, but you're a lot better at not showing it."

"Nervous about what? That you caught a plate midair? Newsflash: you may be terrible at sports, but you're bound to catch *something* in your lifetime."

"In study hall, I did the math," I say.

"You don't finish your essays? No shit. You waste your time on extra math."

I ignore her. "Assuming the plate weighs about eight ounces, it was dropped from four feet off the ground, and knowing that a free-falling object accelerates at nine-point-eight meters per second squared, it would have only taken roughly four seconds to hit the ground. Human reflexes usually move at about point-twenty-five seconds for a visual stimulus, but for me to get the timing just right to grab it with little effort—the numbers are next to impossible."

"*Next to.* Not *completely.*"

"No formula I could possibly use could tell me why I was watching it fall much slower than thirty-nine-point-two meters per second."

"Can you stop with the creepy math?"

"Hallie, I watched it fall in slow motion."

"Really? I'm a Russian queen."

"Tsarina, I watched it fall in slow motion."

"I stopped a Bolshevik revolution yesterday."

"Something is happening to me."

Hallie and I stop walking right in front of her driveway. "Nothing is *happening* to you, Skylar. You just want something to be excited about. Because maybe if you worry enough about something, it'll turn into something you actually *should* worry about."

"That's not true!" I cross my arms.

"It's totally true. You just don't want it to be."

"I actually want to *do* things, not just wait for other people to do them first. When have you ever seen me like that?"

"Never, but people change." With that, she marches right up her driveway and goes inside her house, leaving me standing outside, watching her.

She doesn't believe the words she's saying—I can tell—which means the Great Hallie Giovia is scared of something.

Harlow slept over at my house for the first time when I was thirteen and she was eleven. Mom told us to be asleep by midnight, but at one-thirty, we were still high on chocolate and popcorn and giving each other outrageous dares and wondering what we'd do when we grew up. I was half-afraid the neighbors would call to complain about our giggle fest and half-too happy to care.

"You know, Harlow, you're a star," I said to her.

"Why, thank you," she said in a horrible movie-star imitation with a flip of her hair. Harlow's hair is a single shade lighter than mine but falls in perfect curls. She looks like me but prettier; her legs are long and her freckles are orderly and her sapphire eyes are confident rather than an indecisive gray.

"No, I mean, like an actual star," I said, pointing out the open window. I'd been playing with the idea for awhile, and our sleepover merely solidified it. "Like in the sky."

Harlow was glued to the window at this point. Unblinking, she stared at the sky. Her eyes were blinding me because of the white light that was coming out of them.

"What's wrong?" I asked her. She hadn't spoken in a minute, which may have been the longest she'd gone without speaking since she'd learned to talk.

"I've never seen real stars before," she murmured, "so I never thought I'd be one."

"What do you mean, you've never seen stars before?" I asked. "You went camping last year."

"It was too cloudy to see anything."

"That night at Grandma's? The super clear one?"

"I didn't have the heart to tell you that was a helicopter search party for some loose criminals."

"You mean to tell me that in all of your eleven years, you've never seen a single star?"

"Does the sun count?"

"No. Well, yes. But— How could have you never seen a star? How is that even possible?"

"I live in the city, and it's smog central. And even if you *could* see them through the gunk, my bedtime is, like, seven thirty."

I was almost as in awe at this than she was with the stars. Then I got the most ludicrous idea ever and blamed my cousin; I still only ever get this ambitious and reckless when she hangs around me. "Let's go."

"Where?"

"I'll show you where."

We tiptoed down the stairs, each creak threatening to give us away. After putting on some shoes and grabbing some sweatshirts, we exited through the back door because it didn't squeak as much as the front door.

"Now, you have to promise not to look up at the sky until we're there," I told her.

"Why?"

"Trust me."

"Okay."

Walking down island streets at night is a precarious feat. If one nosy neighbor sees you, you can be sure the police will be on your tails and take you home to receive a talking-to courtesy of your parents. In this town, people can recognize each others' silhouettes.

And though I knew the island like I knew my house, traversing the curving and interlocking streets at night was basically traversing Daedalus's labyrinth. Harlow and I had to stop a few times to get our bearings and so I could find the way. Any time we saw a light on—which wasn't really that often—I'd make her get down and crawl.

"You know what?" I finally said. "Let's just go."

"Go where?"

"Back home," I answered. "We'd get in so much trouble if anyone were to catch us."

"And you know what? I don't care." She took off running.

"Harlow!" I chased her.

And there we were, running through the municipal streets of the island with absolute impunity and unabridged joy. The absurdity hit me at once and I starting laughing really hard, trying to do so quietly but having no idea how successful I was being. I was guessing not very, but Harlow and I were having too much fun to care one bit.

"You're terrible," I told her when we had to stop for a second. "You're absolutely terrible and I can't stand you." My laughter made it completely unconvincing.

"Can I look at the sky yet?" she pleaded.

"No, not until we get where we're going."

"Come on, please?"

"Harlow, I promise you, you will see each star that hangs up there in the sky, and then I will give you a mirror so you can see all the starlight inside of you, too, and then you truly can say you've seen each and every star."

She was quiet for a second before she said, "Which Shakespeare play is that from?"

"Hey!"

"Cut the melodrama, 'kay? It's too late at night for this." But I could tell that what I said actually meant the world to her. Thank God—I've always wanted to give her the world.

And when we got to the tiny beach I'd found when I was dared to see what was on the other side of the trees, Harlow exploded into a shower of golden flecks that coated everything in a layer of sparkles. She extracted light directly from outer space and swallowed it.

That light, it shines through every pore of her body. When she opens her mouth, you need sunglasses before listening to her speak or you'll go blind. It travels to the ends of her fingers and illuminates everything she touches.

And today, as I attempt to get my homework done without throwing my textbooks into the wall, I feel that spark of reckless-ness that Harlow gave me—it makes my body staticky and my heart pound. I'm afraid that the spark might have started a fire, and I really don't want that; how many raindrops are needed to put out a wildfire?

Stars burn out completely, caving in on themselves and tearing the universe apart. Raindrops, they're merely reabsorbed into the air and fall again. I certainly know the safer option.

Harlow does, too. She just won't take it.

Chapter Seven

So it seems
I'm someone I've never met.

"That Green Gentleman (Things Have Changed)"
Panic! At the Disco

A straight jacket holds me me as its hostage. It whispers to me: *You're nothing, but since nothing is truly nothing, aren't you everything?* You're a complete mess, what with that muddled mind of yours. You, my friend, are something that you don't know exists yet, because you *don't.*

The clock is ticking; every second brings me closer to the moment I unleash all those flames coursing through my veins. I kind of wish it would stop ticking all together so I never would have to worry about that happening.

Math class is more dismal than it usually is, being a math class and all. The four of us have to present today, and the four of us have stopped caring about this project completely. Besides, if we put any effort in it, Miss Felding might take us to that teacher convention thing, and I can't afford to miss any classes—and also, playing Mathopoly in front of a group of math teachers sounds like a medieval torture technique used on alleged witches.

"Just make this presentation as crappy as possible," Lexie says to us. "Like, just make it suck *so bad*, she won't want us."

"I'm cool with that," Hallie agrees.

"As am I," I say. "I'm not up for any medieval torture. The allegations of witchcraft against me are false."

Jacob looks at me. "That makes some sort of sense. A weird sort, but still a sort."

It seems like Blake Kingston's group had the same idea as us: their presentation of a worksheet is about as enthusiastic as a funeral home. Then we all cheer extra loudly for Meredith's group because they launch into this intricate rap about how to solve systems of equations by elimination into which they clearly put a ton of time, making them the only group who really cared.

Then we set up Mathopoly and go through a round as lackadaisically as we possibly can. Miss Felding's face lights up when she sees what we've made.

"No one has ever made a board game before," she comments.

"Oh" is all Hallie says.

Then she gives us the rest of the class as a study hall, but right before the bell rings, she announces, "I have picked the group to come with me to the alternative teaching convention on April sixteenth!"

Everyone inaudibly groans.

"Skylar, Jacob, Hallie, and Lexie!"

We exchange looks and force smiles that don't fool anyone.

"I didn't even know they *had* conventions for teachers," Jacob says as we walk out of class.

"Sure they do," Lexie replies. "But having students there, now *that* seems a bit weird. I thought teachers went to those things to get away from kids for a bit. Also, Miss Felding didn't mention anything about permission slips. Sketch central right there."

"My mom's taught for ages, and I've never heard of students ever going to those things," Hallie says. "I can ask her."

"No need," Lexie says. "Meet me in the library sixth period."

"You're going to make us walk all the way across the quad?" Hallie groans. "It's cold out."

"Bring a coat. You all have study hall with Parkins, right?"

"I was moved into Darner's study hall at the last minute," I say. "So was Hallie."

"Me too," Jacob says.

"Well, either way, you all have study hall," Lexie says, "so meet me in the library. You know that table in the corner, right? Go to that one. If there're other people at that one, then go to that other table—you know, the one near the bookshelf?"

"Every table is near a bookshelf. It's a library."

"You're smart. You can figure it out." She turns on her heel and walks towards the stairs, and I've never seen so much yellow in my life. It spirals up from each of her footsteps and with each bounce of her curls, and it permeates the hallway until it's the only color I see.

At the beginning of sixth period, Hallie gets the three of us a pass to the library and we make the trek across the quad and towards the library, which is the furthest building away from Main, because why not add copious amounts of physical exertion to a high schooler's day that certainly isn't crappy enough at this point? We spend the entire time grumbling and hugging our green cotton uniform polos to our bodies for a bit of warmth.

Sure enough, Lexie is there, sitting at the table in the corner, her books scattered about so no one else tries to sit with her. She sees us and stacks them up.

Hallie plops her books down. "Okay, so why are we here?"

"To do some research on this convention."

We all sigh. "I have an outline on ATP structure due tomorrow," I say.

"Yeah, and I have French next period, and I haven't even started the homework assignment," Hallie says.

"And Hunter and I were going to do global notes, but now I'm here instead." Jacob adds. "So do we have to do this now?"

"And you couldn't have done this in a classroom in Main? We had to walk all the way here? It's freaking cold out."

Lexie is adamant. "I don't know about you, but I don't believe Miss Felding. It's something about the way she's talking about the convention. Have you noticed how she always twists that one section of her hair—front, on the left—as she talks about it, and *only* as she talks about it? And she only looks at us. Yesterday she glanced at Danny for only a second, and then she looked right back to you, Jacob."

We look at her in stunned silence.

"And," Lexie starts slowly, "you're gonna think I'm losing my marbles, but Miss Felding's eyes change color."

My chest surges. "I've noticed."

"All of your eyes change, too."

"That's impossible," Jacob says. "Like, your eye color usually changes with age or as warning sign of certain diseases, not all the time or with your moods. That would mean the iris's content of melanin would have to change every couple of minutes. Like I said: impossible." Hallie raises her eyebrows at him. "What? My mom's an ophthalmologist."

"But, she's right," Hallie says. "All of your eyes . . . I noticed it while working on the project. They *do* change. It's freaky. Can't believe I didn't notice it before. Guess I just wasn't paying enough attention."

"Seriously, eyes can't just *change* color."

"I'll prove it to you," Lexie says. "Skylar. Happy whales."

I smile. "I love whales, especially when they're happy."

"Oh my God," Jacob says, "her eyes *did* change. They got a bit more blue."

"Whales make me happy."

"So, what do you *think* Miss Felding is gonna do with us?" Hallie asks. "Kidnap us? Test our retinas?"

"I don't know," Lexie says. "Gonna get deep here, guys, but have you ever felt, I don't know, *different*? Like, I can't explain it, but— you just feel like everyone is taking too long to catch up to you?"

"Not you, too," Hallie groans. "Skylar was saying that, what, yesterday? It's stupid. There's nothing wrong with any of us. Nothing even a little bit wrong. Come on, you've all lived long enough on this floating pile of dirt to know that no one from here will ever be anything special."

"Well, I don't agree," Lexie says. "Does anyone else feel like time's not working right?" I nod, as does Jacob. "Like you're missing stuff, or like stuff takes too long to happen? It can't just be me. So I'm going to find out what it is and who else it's happening to. Even if I have to ask Miss Felding myself."

"Good luck," Hallie scoffs. "She's gonna have no idea what you're talking about and think you're losing it."

"Then why'd we all get put in the same group for a project? All in the same homeroom? Global class? Something's up, and Miss Felding totally knows it."

"Miss Felding just started teaching this year, and she's already got seven classes a day, plus a study hall and Math Team coordinator. I think she's a little too busy to worry about messing up our lives."

"Yeah? I don't." And with that, Lexie stands up with all of her books and walks away.

"Lexie, wait," I say, picking up my books and following her. Jacob follows me, and Hallie follows Jacob. Lexie leads us back across the quad, into Main, and right over to Miss Felding's classroom, which is filled with her study hall students.

"Miss Felding," Lexie says, "if you have time, I'd like to talk." A few people look up from their homework to see what she's talking about, but most of them don't seem to care. Everyone is pretty much numb to Lexie's Lexieness by now.

"About what, Lexie?" Miss Felding appears calm, but people can appear a lot of things without actually being them.

"This convention. And your eyes. They weren't that color in class."

Her hesitation is borderline imperceptible. "I'm sorry, I don't know what you're talking about."

"Why did you put us all in the same project group, then? If not for us to realize that there's something weird about us? That I'm not the only one that watches five minutes turn into twenty in a couple seconds or that loses bits of conversation because I fall asleep or something? And you do this, too. When you're teaching, sometimes you suddenly stop in the middle of your sentence and you start a new one. Or you write super quickly on the board but your handwriting still looks like you spent a minute per letter. There's something about you, and that something's about all of us, too."

A brief look of panic crosses her face, and, as if on cue, her eyes morph into a more of a moss color. She rises from her desk, touches something on her cell phone, and says in a voice almost too soft to hear but could still shatter glass, "I would brace myself if I were you."

An earsplitting *BANG!* causes a shudder to move through the building like a child caught in the rain without a coat. It shakes everything from the inside out, a quake that makes Pompeii's seem like a hiccup. My brain tries to turn itself inside out, causing a jiffy of searing pain that's completely gone within the second. I automatically cover my head with one hand and grab the desk with the other one. Then I slowly open my eyes, expecting to see the immaculate classroom in ruins and hear screams of anguish.

But that's not the case. In fact, it's quite the opposite.

Alex sits with his pencil touching his paper but not writing a single word. Kyle's book which he'd dropped is suspended in midair. Brielle's mouth is open in mid-whisper, and Meredith's and Sofia's are in mid-giggle. The second hand on the clock has ceased ticking. Everything in the room is frozen, like if someone hit the pause button and everything just stopped where it was.

I slowly bend each of my fingers, making sure I can still move them. I open and close my eyes. Everything and everyone remains in their standstill.

"I was right." Miss Felding is standing behind her desk, animated and completely alive, a placid grin spreading across her china-doll lips. "Thank goodness, I was right. I'd hoped it was you. I'd *always* hoped it was you."

"Right about what?" Lexie grips her pile of books tighter with one arm and runs her other hand through her curls as she surveys the room with her wide brown eyes. "What's going on?"

"What . . . There's something wrong with us." Hallie's voice trembles, and that alone causes my hands to shake harder. Hallie doesn't get scared, yet she now sits as frozen as everyone else in the room because of fear.

"How'd you . . . " Jacob is unfrozen as well. "How did you even . . ."

Miss Felding plays with the phone in her hands, tossing it from one to the other methodically. "You are the Knowers I'm looking for." She says this simply, as if we couldn't possibly be unaware of her meaning. "And I'm very happy that you are."

"How . . . what . . . Miss Felding . . . What did you do?" I look around at the unmoving classroom. I see a bird through the window that's stopped in the middle of the sky. Not only is everything in the room frozen, but it appears the whole world is. The island landscape is captured by whatever force is causing everything to stop. Tree branches are stuck in a non-moving breeze and cars are parked in the middle of the street.

"I knew it was you," she says, more to herself than anyone else. "The eye color, the inattentiveness in class, the fidgeting, the fighting, looking at the clock disbelievingly—it *had* to be you."

"I'm sorry, but what the hell is going on?" Hallie says. Her worry has half-melted into confusion. She carefully paces the room, weaving in and out of the frozen bodies. She stops to stare at Alex, who's stuck staring at math homework. His finger touches a button on his calculator, the cursor unblinking. "I swear to God, if you're going to harvest our eyeballs—"

"I really have no idea where to start," Miss Felding admits, "but I promise that your eyes are safe."

Hallie sets her books on a desk and crosses her arms. We set our books on the floor.

"Well, let's start with the basics," she says. "You all are extremely smart. You surely already know that. I certainly do."

Lexie actually laughs. "Smart? Not me, then. Just ask Redding. My grades suck."

"I'm not even sure what month it is," Jacob adds, "and I'm just about failing global."

"Yeah, there's no way you could mean me," Hallie says. "I completely bullshit my way through school."

"Me either," I say. "I study for about twenty-four hours a day and still barely make grades high enough to keep me in honors classes."

Miss Felding looks at all of us. "This is why I hate the education system."

"You're a teacher," Lexie says. "You can't hate school. That's, like, paradoxical."

"You have a lot of trouble focusing and sitting still, too. And you're terribly impulsive. So school is naturally hard for you. It wasn't *designed* for you."

"What does that have anything to do with you being able to freeze time like this but not freeze us?" Hallie asks.

Miss Felding brushes her question aside. "You're so incredibly smart. You're the world's greatest thinkers. You're Knowers, for crying out loud, yet being in the classroom still makes you feel worthless because of your ADHD."

"Wait, how'd you know about that?" Jacob says, and he's suddenly very tense. "Do they, like, tell your teachers or something?"

"They made me tell all of mine," Lexie shrugs. "No big deal."

"No, seriously," Jacob says. "Can you just tell? Is it that obvious? I— I didn't think it was, but . . . "

Miss Felding takes a deep breath. "You are four of the world's greatest thinkers."

We stare at her blankly. Clearly, if we think well, we would have thought we're great by now.

She looks at each of us calculatingly, her eyes making these tiny movements and slowly changing color, as if she's trying to gauge how we could possibly grasp this concept. "The Knowers make up a top-secret organization that solves most of the world's problems without the world even knowing that we're here. We work one-hundred percent underground and use our extensive connections to get solutions to worldwide problems out there into mainstream life."

"What—"

"Just listen, please, it'll make it easier, hopefully. You've heard of natural selection, right? We're basically continuing that. We're growing slowly, but we're growing. You know about dominant and recessive genes, too, right?"

"Yeah, it's what we're doing in biology right now," Lexie says. "Your parents can pass genes to you, and some are more common than others. Like, if your parents have blue eyes and brown eyes, you're more likely to get brown eyes because it's the dominant trait. It's easier to get because it's less specific."

"Exactly. The gene combination for a Knower is extremely, *extremely* rare—about one in just under three million, since you need an exact sequence of fourteen genes for it to work. But it does happen, and when it does, it makes you a bit more than human. You are an evolved form."

"Wait, we're not human?"

Miss Felding smiles at that. "No, you're completely human. You're just a *better* human. You're quicker at math. You have semi-photographic memories. Your minds are so strong that they can't keep on one topic for long without jumping to another. You're impatient and restless. You possess the best and fastest problem solving skills ever. You have eyes that change color with your mood.

"Yet the most amazing thing you can do: time doesn't affect you. You see right through it, as it really is just an illusion. It's why you don't keep track of it very well, because you are constantly conscious of the fact that it doesn't exist. And why your perception of it allows you to be unfrozen right now, while we freeze everyone else. And you miss things sometimes, because it will speed up and slow down without your knowledge. A minute can feel like an hour and vice versa. You take in more details a second, making things seem slower and giving you what feels like more reaction time to you but is nothing to anyone else.

"In a couple million years, everyone will possess these traits and abilities and the Knowers will have nothing to work for because we can all work for ourselves. Right now, though, there are only a few Knowers worldwide, including you. We may not expand, even by a single person, for another thirty or forty years."

"Wait, can we only have kids with other Knowers then?" Hallie wonders. "Because members of different species can't interbreed. Are we going to have to marry other Knowers, then?"

"No. You aren't a different species. Only a further along member."

"So, wait, all Knowers have these . . . these traits that make us Knowers?" Lexie asks. "Like the eye color?"

"Of course you've noticed that," Miss Felding says. "Your eyes will change color approximately fourteen times on a normal day, and a more taxing day where you go through more emotions, up to about forty-two."

"That's so weird," Jacob says. "But pretty cool."

"And the ADHD?" I ask. A thousand things click together at once—the Rubik's Cube solves itself . "We all have it?"

"Yeah," Miss Felding says. "School is probably hard for you, which seems weird because you have the best minds in the world, right?

"It's all in your head, literally. In your brain are these chemicals called neurotransmitters that are running your entire body. ADHD is characterized by low natural levels of two of these neurotransmitters."

"Dopamine and norepinephrine," I say. "Right?"

"Exactly," Miss Felding continues. "The label is a mere side effect of your ability to disregard the rules of time."

"A side effect." Jacob seems unsatisfied with this definition.

"Perhaps that's the wrong term, but yes, it's essentially a side effect."

"Good to know."

Miss Felding takes a deep breath. "Okay, this is the hard part."

"Harder than learning we're new age humans," Hallie reckons.

"What's the date eight days from today?" Miss Felding asks.

"April sixteenth," Lexie replies after thinking for a second.

"The first or the second?"

"The only," I say skeptically.

"Nope," Miss Felding says. "April sixteenth is the Knowers' Day, with a capital D. It's the day all of us, from around the world, meet at one of the Knowers bases—which is the base in Washington, D.C. this year. This is the Day on which we meet, for various reasons, which differ from year to year. You are all coming this year—we could use some fresh brains."

"Oh, so *that's* the conference you were talking about," Jacob figures out. "It wasn't a conference at all."

Miss Felding smiles guiltily. "Yes, I needed a way to get you all out of school that day, even if no one else remembers. If I just took you from the building, the police would be here before we were halfway to Washington, D.C."

"Wait, so what does the first and second day thing mean?" Lexie asks. "And what do you mean no one else will remember?"

"The first April sixteenth is nonexistent."

"No way."

"We've engineered an entire day that is completely not there for everyone besides us. If you aren't a Knower, on the second April sixteenth, you will have no recollection of the first. This is to ensure the secrecy of our organization and all the innerworkings."

"So, wait, no one except us will remember April sixteenth?" Lexie says. "Like, the calendar goes from the fifteenth to the seventeenth?"

"No. All Knowers will remember the *first* April sixteenth, and no one else will. The second will be the one to actually exist and happen, the one everyone remembers, on everyone's calendar.

Unlike the first, which only can be remembered by us—only we will remember because of our withstanding to changes in time."

"And the other seven billion?"

"It will be like waking up from a dream and forgetting everything about it immediately after."

"But we don't?"

"You remember everything."

"And how does that work exactly?" Hallie, always the skeptic, asks.

"We've engineered something called the Mechanism which allows us to have minimal control of time. That's how I'm freezing time right now. Using an app on my phone," she holds up her iPhone to demonstrate, "I can practically freeze time. All the Knowers have it in case something dire happens and we need to make sure there are no mundane ears listening. Not only am I explaining to you away from prying ears, but we've sent up a signal to the other Knowers around the world that you've been found."

"So you can make days not exist from your smart phone?" Hallie crosses her arms. "Apps have come too far."

"You can't make days nonexistent from your phone. That's more complex and takes a Knower manipulating the physical Mechanism. The app only allows one to freeze time for less than twenty-six minutes."

"Okay, but why are the Knowers so secretive in the first place?" I say cautiously. "I mean, you've taken it to the extremes of a day that doesn't exist. Why is that?"

"We control practically everything from underground," she says. "Anything anyone could possibly want us to do, we can do. If people knew we existed, we'd be tested on, expanded possibly, and maybe taken over by the government. We're protecting ourselves and our work."

"Still, a nonexistent day?" Jacob says. "Don't you think that's a *little* much?"

Miss Felding brushes over this, and the room is quiet for a minute, completely silent—I haven't heard true silence till this moment. There's always an air conditioning unit running or someone else whispering or the scratch of pencil on paper, but now, when there's no movement, there's no sound. Everything is stiller than a frozen pond. Even the water rushes under the ice in a frozen pond. Here, now, there is nothing. Is my heart even beating? I feel my chest to make sure. Still, it makes no sound.

Then Jacob shatters it and says, "Okay, but why us?"

"What do you mean?" Miss Felding wonders.

"Like, if there's only a few of us in the whole world," he clarifies, "then why are five of us right here? Like, that seems . . . "

"Highly improbable," I supply.

"Yeah. 'Highly improbable.'"

"Well, Knowers often became close friends," Miss Felding says, "and there is safety in numbers." Safety from *what*, I don't ask. "Sometimes a small group of Knowers will move to one place to live. In the early nineteen hundreds, five Knowers moved to this island, and those five families have stayed here over the years, and here you are, the second generation of Knowers of this island."

"So why did this all happen when we're fifteen?" Lexie asks. "Like, we all mature differently, right? So, then, why now? And if you've frozen time before and we've never noticed, then—"

"Have you ever felt as if your brain has fallen asleep and you've missed a large chunk of information?" We nod. I hate those. It's like when I have something in my hand, and I set it down, but I have absolutely no recollection of when and where I put it. "That was a time freeze. Your mind could sense it but had no idea how to interpret it, so it stalled. But, once you've reached around the age of fifteen, give or take a few years, the small part of your brain that handles this time freezing is mature enough to display full effects.

"You all can withstand the time freeze, luckily. That is absolutely vital for an active Knower, so that is why we wait until you are fifteen before allowing you to attend the Meeting."

She looks at us all individually. "I was sent by our Eminence Margaret White to teach at this school because we believed there would be four of you this year. We were right, and I'm glad we were. In the few months I've known you, I've realized you've all got something special about you. Each of you is powerful and important. But you cannot say a word about any of this. You can't tell people that you're this special. People don't like people that are special. I need you to promise not to tell."

We all nod.

"Good. Now get back into your exact positions you were in before I froze time. I will give you more information as it comes up."

Then Miss Felding taps something on her phone, and at once, everything starts moving again. People become animate again, Kyle's book continues to fall, Alex continues to write without a hitch, Brielle continues her story and Megan begins to whisper to Meredith, the clock begins to tick again.

It's like the world never froze, like it all happened in our heads.

Chapter Eight

And the sound,
it's so loud
in my head.
Another kind of red
is written in the snow;
today I am a bird.

"Another Kind of Red"
Tula

Every part of me asks questions. My hands inquire about their dexterity, and how quickly they could catch any other falling plates. My lungs wonder if this means they breathe differently; my eyes are indecisive when it comes to their their color. Each cell in my body shouts at me, each one asking me why I have to be different and demanding that I fix this. I try to tell them I would if I could, but you can't change genetic makeups; not one of them listens to me.

An evolved form of a human? Impossible; it's far too sci-fi to be realistic. But it's not like I can un-hear the things that I heard or scientifically prove that everything didn't just freeze and start up again. Like someone pressed the pause button on the whole world but I was exempt.

My mind is as turbulent as a storm. The Knowers never leave my thoughts.

The word is taboo; it doesn't pass any of our lips. Not one of us will vocalize any thoughts to each other. We are quiet, communicating through discreet looks to verify that we weren't just dreaming. Brief expressions are all it takes to assure each other that we aren't losing our minds, but rather finding them.

The first one to get asked about her sudden change in demeanor is Lexie. Meredith Pandey asks her why she's suddenly so quiet. She says nothing but, "I'm fine. My throat hurts and I need some sleep." Meredith believes it because it would take a Knower to see through Lexie's lies.

I can see things about people that I've never noticed: tiny, little things that are seemingly insignificant factoids but that actually tell so much about people. Everyone is just a mixture of tics and habits like nail bites and eye twitches and secret looks with their friends. And I can tell things about them because of it, like how Rocca Barns plays basketball because of the patterns of dirt on his shoes or that Savanna Reid wears the same perfume that Gemma Fischer does. It's like more details come into my brain per second, and I can see everything about people.

Miss Felding freezes time during study hall again, two days after the first time. We're less startled this time. "You've discovered the ability to presume," she says, "I presume."

"Presume?" Hallie repeats. "Like, make assumptions?"

"Exactly. You have the beautiful ability to look at people and notice little things and tell things about them."

"Oh, like Sherlock Holmes's deductions?" I ask.

"Yes, exactly like Sherlock Holmes and his deductions. In fact, Sir Arthur Conan Doyle was a Knower. He was the best presumer in his day. A complete genius. He wrote about it in his Sherlock novels, changing *presume* to *deduce,* of course. He ran into a bit of hot water at the time with the Knowers, as they were afraid people would try to falsely presume about people. They thought it may cause issues between communities."

"Or it was a power play," Jacob adds. "Like they didn't want people to know how to know stuff about other people."

Miss Felding doesn't acknowledge him.

"Oh my gosh, are you serious?" I gush, feeling my face light up. "We're technically related to Sherlock!"

Miss Felding chuckles. "More along the lines of *spiritually,* but I suppose so."

"So, basically, we can deduce stuff like Sherlock does?" Lexie says. She's beaming, too, so she must also be a Sherlock fan (basic presuming). "I've always wanted to do that. Like, I'll be walking down the street and I'll try to deduce stuff about strangers. I see why the Knowers didn't want to people to know about their skill. I'm not very good at it."

"Well, now you can do it for real," Miss Felding says. She walks over to Brielle's frozen body. She's got her earbuds in and her fingers resting on the keyboard of her computer. "Tell me everything you can about Miss Aberson, please, Lexie."

"Okay," Lexie says, walking closer. "Um, she's not over One Direction breaking up yet, because the tab for Spotify on her computer is playing *Made in the A.M.*"

"More," Miss Felding implores. "Look deeper. Always look closer than you think you have to."

"Okay?" Lexie says uneasily, getting closer to Brielle. "She's writing an essay on *To Kill a Mockingbird,* so she must be in Redding's non-honors class because that's what they're doing now. Her favorite character was Jem because she can relate to him because," she pauses to read, "they're both older siblings with semi -present dads and no moms. Wow. I never realized." She looks at her face. "She's wearing lip gloss. Strawberry, I think, be-cause she was saying earlier how she just bought new strawberry lip gloss. But it's starting to fade, so I think she must've—"

"Don't think, Lexie, only know."

"—she must've put it on a long time ago, probably between third and fourth period because she's got a study hall fourth so she's got time to stop in the bathroom to reapply before going to room 108 for study hall. Besides, 108 fourth period study is proc-tored by Parkins, who's super slow and has to come all the way from 121, so there isn't a ton of fear of being late."

"I'm very impressed," Miss Felding says. "You're very good at this." She looks at my hands, and in that quick glance, I watch her eyes gather facts about them like berries off bushes. "Hallie, please tell me everything you can about Skylar, by only looking at her hands."

"I already know everything there is to know about Skylar," Hallie replies. "I don't need to look at her hands."

"How much can you tell about me by just looking at my hands?" I say, looking at them. "They're fairly nondescript."

"Let's see. Jacob, can you do it?"

"Um, I can try," he says uneasily. He takes my right hand. "Okay. She bites her nails a lot, that's pretty obvious. Um . . . She must write with her right hand because there's a tiny callus on her her middle finger which must be from holding a pencil too tightly, so she writes really small because you have to hold the pencil tightly to write small. There's also a tiny scar at the base of her thumb that looks like a knife cut."

"I tried taking up wood carving for a bit. It didn't work."

He takes my left hand. "I can't see anything on this one."

"Always look closer than you think you have to," Miss Felding repeats.

"Um, sure?" He runs his fingers over my fingertips. "You have really hard fingertips. Oh! From violin, probably. You— you play violin, right?" I nod. "And there's a callus on the base of your palm. That must also be from your hand rubbing against the base of the violin while playing. It also means that you play really quickly because I remember when my sister took violin for a bit she said 'no pancake hand' but she'd always flop it playing fast . . . either that, or you don't listen to your violin teacher because you think your way is better."

"Wow," I say. "I didn't know my hands held so much. Pun totally intended."

April tenth: the hundredth day in a year (hundred and first day if it's a leap year). Birthday of Daisy Ridley (famous in her role as Rey in the third Star Wars trilogy, born in 1992) and death day of Jimmy Dawkins (American electric blues musician, died 2013). It floats like a leaf falling off a tree, moving slowly yet too quickly, its gliding trip to the earth delicate but at an alarming speed for something so light.

The eleventh: the anniversary of the day Kellogg's stopped giving public tours of its cereal factories in the fear that other cereal-spies would infiltrate the facility (1986; this is the stupidest reason to discontinue tours because who gives a flying fudge about espionage of the Mini-Wheat variety). Birthday of Morgan Lily (young actress who played little Raven in *X-Men: First Class,* born 2000) and death day of Ahmed Ben Bella (Algeria's first president, died 2012). Today is a Big Test Day in global. I study for two hours and still barely finish the test. I think I do okay, though, because I know about Ancient Greece (mostly from Rick Riordan books, if I'm being honest).

April twelfth: voters in Lockport, NY, become the first voters to use a voting machine (1892). Birthday of Brendon Urie (lead singer and frontman of Panic! At the Disco and one of my favorite people in existence, born 1987) and death day of President Franklin Delano Roosevelt (died of a cerebral hemorrhage in Warm Spring, GA during his fourth presidential term, in 1945). Today is a very important day in American history, so I wear my Panic! shirt, bake brownies with frosted exclamation points, and listen to *Vices & Virtues* on repeat.

The thirteenth: Dolly the Sheep Clone gives birth to a healthy baby lamb (1998). Birthday of Thomas Jefferson (third President of the U.S. and author of the Declaration of Independence, born in 1743) and death day of Muriel Sparks (author of *The Prime of Miss Jean Brodie,* died 2006). The day moves like dried up glue in a glue bottle. I find myself staring at the clock so much you'd think he'd start to get self-conscious.

The fourteenth of April is the slowest day so far (President Lincoln is shot in Ford's Theater in 1865; birth of Peter Capaldi, the twelfth Doctor in *Doctor Who*, in 1958; and death of Burl Ives, famous folk singer, in 1995), mostly due to the fact that it's Monthly Obligatory Family Dinner Night.

Once a month, all the Rawlings and the Rainers congregate in the tiny city-bungalow belonging to my grandparents. Grandma cooks something inexplicably delicious and we sit wordlessly at the table while the grown-ups talk. I don't necessarily *dread* the dinners—Grandma, Aunt Jessamine, and especially Harlow are three of my favorite people—but I have been looking for ways out since I was four.

The family piles into the car for the trek into the city. We drive over the bridge, and after a half-hour in pure country-bump-kin town, we enter the urban nightmare of crumbling concrete forests, postage-stamp-sized yards, and demonic pigeons. Evan likes going into the city, but I couldn't hate a place more. Even the sparse green seems manufactured. I would never tell my grand-father this; he thinks living on the island is the equivalent to a diagnosis of Small-Town Mentality.

I'm welcomed by a warm hug from Grandma as soon as I push through the rickety screen door. "I found this darling craft we'll have to try," she says to me immediately. "Save your toilet paper tubes."

Aunt Jessamine is an eccentric bundle of energy, but she hardly speaks louder than a mouse's squeak. She's my dad's sister, not that you can't tell by the identical glisten in their icy blue eyes —Aunt Clara has eyes that are a much darker blue and shine in a completely different way. It's funny, because Dad had Grandma's ingenuity and Aunt Clara has Grandpa's iron fist, but Jessamine is neither, both, completely different, and completely the same. Sometimes I look at the three of them together and I see a flower-pot you'd find sitting on a windowsill in any elementary science classroom: my dad is the terra-cotta pot, the oldest one, the one who holds everyone else, sturdy and reliable; Aunt Clara is the soil because she seems plain but she hides so many nutrients and vital elements for the plants that you can't see by just looking at her; and Jessamine, beautiful Jessamine, is the sunflower.

"Hey, I tried a new recipe," Jessamine whispers in my ear when I hug her. Grandpa is not a fan of trying new foods, so Aunt Jessamine and Grandma hide all their experiments in the kitchen, the one place Grandpa won't dare traipse. "Hint: asparagus."

"I'm intrigued," I say. I usually hate asparagus, but I'll try any Jessamine-made dish. I'd eat worms if she sautéed them with garlic and olive oil. I actually tried her artichoke-chocolate cake though was unamused when I unearthed a stem from my frosting.

"Sky Sky Sky!" At this moment, Harlow comes in through the door and squeezes the air out of me.

"Hey, Harlow," I greet her once I've got enough oxygen to speak.

"Oh my God, I have the *best* news in the *whole* world. You're never gonna believe it."

The rest of the Rainers file in: Aunt Clara and Uncle Henry, and Spencer, Freddie, and Liam. There are six kids in the entirety of the extended family, four of them being boys; Harlow and I are the only girls, which may be why we're so gravitated to each other.

The adults send us outside into the tiny backyard while they have their grown-up talk about NPR or coffee or whatever they talk about. Liam and Freddie are eight and eleven, so Evan has no problems playing with them; in fact, the three are able to cause more trouble together in one day than I have in my whole life. Spencer, who's seventeen but has the mentality of a twelve-year-old, runs around with the younger boys as they shoot Nerf darts at him, occasionally taking refuge atop the metal playground to check his phone when he's sure Aunt Clara isn't watching.

Harlow and I are barely to the top of The Climbing Tree before she claps her hands and says, "Guess what!"

"What?"

"Okay, so—oh my God, I'm so freaking excited—the guidance counselors came to talk to all the seventh grade classrooms about high school and crap like that, you know, stuff I don't really care about. But then they said that if we want to transfer out of the public school system for high school, we can shadow a day either at the end of seventh or the beginning of eighth. I signed up already to shadow at—guess where—your school! And I wrote your name down to be my guide! I'm gonna shadow you for a whole day!"

It takes me a second to process what she just managed to get out in a total of three seconds. "They let you sign up to shadow at a public school in a district of which you're not a part?"

"You don't go to public school."

"Yes, I do!"

"Then why do you wear a uniform?"

"Some public schools wear uniforms," I say. "That's not a factor in the publicness of a school."

"Either way, I'm gonna shadow you in two days! It'll be so awesome—"

"Wait, you're shadowing in *two days?*"

"Yeah! This Thursday. I mean, I should've told you sooner, but I wanted to surprise you. Why?"

I can't tell her that I'm not going to be there because I will be there for the second day she shadows, so I only say, "No reason." But of course the always cunning Harlow Rainer could subconsciously and unwittingly find a way to make my Day so much harder.

"Kids, come in, it's dinner time!" Grandma stands at the sliding glass doors, her faded blue apron tied around her willowy waist. Harlow makes a noise that's simultaneously a squeal of delight and a groan of dread.

We wash our hands and take our places at the foot of the dining room table. Grandpa is at the head of the table, and the adults fill in.

We're the last to get served, as always. Our mouthwatering mashed potatoes, roast beef, green beans, and honey-roasted carrots sit untouched in front of us as Grandpa says blessing, which, no hyperbole, lasts about seven minutes. He rambles about various things as our food lay getting cold. At last he says "Amen" and the eating may commence.

Children are to be seen and not heard. These words have followed me since before I could remember. At home, I can talk all I want. Hearing Evan's and my voices twenty-four-seven is commonplace, if not encouraged. At Obligatory Family Dinners, however, we are silent as the grown-ups talk. If Grandpa hears one word out of us at the table, we're sent away without finishing and with absolutely no hopes of dessert unless Grandma can think of a way to slip us some without him seeing.

Spencer continuously tries to make Harlow and me laugh by making funny faces. Liam suppresses a snicker and receives a glare from Aunt Clara, but Harlow and I are well-trained against his attacks. I make some funny faces back in recoil. He isn't fazed.

Aunt Jessamine's caught us. She raises an eyebrow at me that only means one thing: Don't mess around, especially around Grandpa. *It's not worth it,* her glance pleads.

I make a cutting motion across my neck to get Spencer to stop. He's about to launch into another caricature when Grandpa says, "You'd better not be fooling around, kids."

"We're not, Grandpa, sorry," Harlow says.

The grown-ups restart their conversation and pretend to pretend that we don't exist for Grandpa's sake. I don't know why my grandfather is so conservative: he sticks to old ways like syrup sticks to pancakes, keeping half of his values absorbed inside of him and spreading the rest of them so they get over every other piece of bacon and egg on your plate.

Dinner ends, and we go back outside. It's colder and a tad darker now; the April days aren't as long as we wish them to be. The boys put their Nerf guns into the Rainers's car trunk, and the six of us sit in a circle in the damp grass, huddling close for warmth.

"Hey, sorry I got you guys in trouble," Spencer apologizes, kicking a rock. "I was just joking around."

Harlow blinks and says, "Next month, you're dead meat."

Spencer turns to me. "So, island kids, anything interesting going on on the other side of the river? Did you see a squirrel last week?" The circle snickers.

The Knowers are immediately called to the front of my mind. Every month, Spencer jokes about how nothing happens on the island. He always tries to probe me for symptoms of Small-Town Mentality, and he almost got me last month when I told a previously-thought riveting story about a switch in our mailman and rumors that our previous mailman got promoted to package-delivery. Although you don't get too much more exciting than a secret society of geniuses, Spencer could be an evil government guy and he could slit my throat at the mention of the Knowers. *Come on, even you know that that's really unlikely; you're just a worry-ridden snail. Yes, I know that doesn't make sense, but it doesn't make it untrue.* Still, I'll have to fabricate something quickly.

"I . . . Well . . . Um, there was a fire at school. Like, the fire alarm rang and everything. Well, I mean, that's a given, but the . . . the trucks came. Like, the fire trucks. The red ones. With the big ladders—Evan, please shut up, it *did* actually happen. But the fire . . . the flames were orange and really hot."

"You're lying through your teeth."

"Yes. Yes I am. How'd you know?"

"Lucky guess."

It slowly begins to rain onto us. At first it's fun to pop up the hoods on our sweatshirts and splash around as Grandma's grass is turned to soupy mud. Then it starts to rain harder and lighting rips apart the sky, so we trek inside.

The grown-ups sit in the living room, reclined in various overstuffed floral armchairs. Grandpa converses to Dad and Aunt Clara. Mom loves talking to Uncle Henry because both are in the medical field and find conversations about spleens or kidneys interesting, so the two of them talk with Grandma.

Jessamine sits in the corner fiddling with the tassel of a fading throw pillow. I feel the same as she does, like I don't belong in this dated and dusty room because I'm different than everyone else in it.

It's weird, though, because it's evident that *everyone* in the room feels the same exact way. Harlow's far too bright for this room to hold her in, Spencer and Freddie and Liam don't like the stillness, Evan doesn't like talking to people, and my mom and Uncle Henry are additions into the family so they naturally feel as such, and my dad is too progressive, and Clara and Grandpa both like to be in control, and Grandma is too restless. Everyone looks just *slightly* uncomfortable, like if you mix Mega Bloks and Legos and the pieces don't sit exactly right with each other. I guess the ubiquitous feeling of having no place to be ironically gives us somewhere to be.

"Kids," Grandpa says to us as we linger in the doorway. "What brings you inside?"

"The rain," I say, trying to erase all the Captain Obvious tone from my voice, which admittedly is very hard to do. "It started thundering, so we came inside. It . . . it didn't seem safe, what with a metal playground and the looming threat of lightning." Harlow elbows me in the side to get me to stop babbling.

"Fair enough," Grandpa says. "You can go play upstairs then."

"Thanks, Grandpa," Spencer says.

"Be careful," he says in reply.

The boys head right to my dad's old room, which houses all his old Matchbox cars and G.I. Joe's. They ransack his splintering toy box. I remind them to put everything back exactly where they found it, as the upstairs of Grandma's house remains a time capsule and shouldn't be overly disturbed.

Harlow and I decide to explore Aunt Clara's room, a placid place where almost everything is pink, from a fading flowered comforter draped on her bed to just-about peeling wallpaper glued to the walls. Porcelain dolls are lined up on a shelf. Her dresser is covered in tarnished picture frames of faded smiling faces and bottles of acrid perfume.

"We should find my mom's diary," Harlow says. "Knowing her, she probably did some daily journaling."

"I don't know if I want to read about your mother's deepest secrets," I reply. "Especially her thirty-year-old secrets."

"Then let's go to Jessamine's room. It's more fun, anyway."

Aunt Jessamine's old room is my favorite of the three, though it looks exactly like Aunt Clara's except in purple, with porcelain dolls that look like Miss Felding and sticky makeup and fraying books. But Jessamine's space is so much more loved. I can see her floating around in here, humming to herself—she always has loved music. Even today, though she's finishing up studies in law, she's always singing and tapping on tables as if they were her piano—

"Jessamine wanted to go to music school," I say suddenly.

"What? Where'd that come from?"

I move over to her old desk and gingerly open one of the drawers. Only normal desk things sit in there, so I open the next one, then the next one, then the very last one at the bottom. Squirreled away in there is a stack of yellowing paper. They're mostly old report cards and drawings, but towards the bottom I find a pile of staff paper, each one written on front and back.

And at the very bottom: a college letter. No, a college *acceptance* letter—from Juilliard.

I hand it to Harlow. She gives me a confused look but reads it over and concludes with, "No way."

"Juilliard," I say. "And she didn't go."

Harlow lets out a breath. "You think that was her decision?"

"Nope."

She neatly stacks everything and puts it back into the bottom drawer. "Jessamine, my God. She could've gone to— I can't even think about it." She falls back onto Jessamine's bed, and I fall right next to her.

The ceiling is cracking, the white of it now more of a cream color. The tiny window is dressed in three layers of dust. Her comforter is still soft, but it carries the strange old-fabric scent most old fabrics have. We've lay in this position innumerable times, so we certainly know how to start the conversation that often starts here.

"When I grow up, I'm going to go to the Galapagos Islands," I say.

"When I grow up, I'm going to be the CEO of my own company," Harlow says.

"When I grow up, I'm going to live in an old house that I've renovated myself."

"When I grow up, I'm going to travel a lot and see the entire world."

"When I grow up, I'm going to be stronger and not scared of everything."

"When I grow up, I'm not going to need karate because everyone will already be scared of me."

I chuckle. "When I grow up, I won't really be growing up because I doubt I'll ever be able to sleep without stuffed animals."

She chortles. "When I grow up, I'm going to get Jessamine to re-audition for Juilliard so she can be a musician. Give her a second chance. 'Cause if anyone deserves a chance to redo everything, it's her."

"When I grow up . . ." I'm starting to run out. As we've been playing this game since I was seven and she was five, it's hard to come up with new things. We've touched on my dreams of being a marine biologist and Harlow's of revolutionizing the karate *gi* industry. We've gone much more lighthearted ("When I grow up, I'm going to be able to drive to the store for midnight ice cream fixes") and deeper ("When I grow up, I'm going to have to be responsible for everything and I'm going to fail miserably"). I don't know if I have anymore goals for myself.

"Did you give up?" she says.

I surrender. "Yeah. You win."

"When I grow up, I'm going to continue to beat you at this game every time we play."

"When we grow up, we'll have no need to keep playing this game because everything we've ever said will have happened and the two of us will be ruling the world."

"Well, we *never* stop growing up, I guess," Harlow says.

"Oh, wait! When I grow up, I'm not going to be clumsy anymore. I don't think I've ever used that one."

"You're too late," Harlow points out. "I won."

"Fine. But next time, you're going down."

"Yep. Keep telling yourself that, loser."

"Harlow Amelia Rainer, that is very rude." I put on my best Aunt Clara voice.

"No! No middle names, Skylar June."

I chuck a tasseled throw pillow at her. "No! No middle names! I won't call you Harlow Amelia anymore if you stop with the June talk."

She whacks me in the face with another pillow. "Come on, June isn't as bad as *Amelia*."

"It's a freaking month! One I wasn't even born in! I mean, if I had to be named for a month, Skylar December would make the most sense, but then that's cheesy. Maybe people should refrain from all month names."

"Yeah, but at least it's not some old lady name."

"I'd rather be Skylar Amelia than Skylar June."

"I'd rather be Harlow June," she says. "If this were some elementary lunch table, we could trade or something. Like, 'I'll have those pretzels for this cookie'."

"Terrible trade. I'd much rather have a cookie than pretzels."

"You get my point, though," she says. "We should trade."

"And what? Just erase our names on our birth certificates?"

"Maybe white-out. They're probably done in pen. We just sneak into the office or wherever we keep our birth certificates and just change the middle names. Simple. And I'm pretty sure not-law breaking."

"Harlow, you're unbelievable," I say. "In the absolute best way possible."

"You're unbelievable, too," she says. "Don't go throwing stones in a glass house."

"When we grow up, we'll still be unbelievable," I say.

"Doesn't count, Skylar Amelia." Harlow looks at me as she says this, and she smirks. "I still won."

Chapter Nine

You and I, we're both living in the strangest time.
Our hearts breaking, and the sky's falling down.
Every night, dark or light, I see a fire burning in your eyes;
they're wide open.
Yeah the sky's falling down, we better hide
downtown, don't be afraid.
She said,
"This could be heaven, or it could be a curse,
The world is shaken—for all I know this could be our
last night, our last night, our last night on Earth."

"Last Night on Earth"
Dreamers

I anxiously navigate the morning of April fifteenth, hoping that no one will notice my nerves. Hallie and I walk to school and barely speak because any conversation would somehow remind us that tomorrow we are facing a room of geniuses.

"You know that today in 1899, Thomas Edison organized the Edison Portland Cement Company? And it's Leonardo DaVinci's birthday and Abraham Lincoln's death day."

Hallie rolls her eyes at me.

As soon as we get to school, Lexie comes up to us. "Miss Felding wants to see us."

I brace myself for the news that I can talk to elephants or something of that nature.

We're barely through her classroom door when the extrinsic *BANG!* sounds through the hall. Everything freezes on cue. "Hello," Miss Felding says as we carefully walk through the forest of frozen students milling about the homeroom. "It's very nice to see you again." She paces around the room, unfazed by its stillness. Her rhythmic footsteps keep the silence from returning, and I'm grateful for that. The pure silence makes me uneasy; I much prefer when it's tainted.

"Hi, Miss Felding," Lexie says. "What is it you needed?"

"We should discuss the plan of action for tomorrow," Miss Felding says.

"What's there to discuss?" Jacob asks. "Haven't we pretty much covered everything? Or can we breathe underwater, too? Maybe read people's thoughts?"

Miss Felding gives him a little smile and begins to explain. "At the end of homeroom, you are to tell your teacher that you're coming on the algebra field trip and are asked to come to my classroom. I've already sent emails to them, so it shouldn't be an issue. And then we will leave for Washington, D.C. It's very simple, but I wanted you to know what's happening."

"Alright, that sounds simple enough," Hallie says.

"I'm sorry, but I'm about to add a hurdle," I say. "Harlow's going to be here. She's shadowing."

"Who's Harlow?" Lexie asks.

"My cousin," I say. "She signed up as a seventh-grade shadow, and she just happens to be coming tomorrow."

"That shouldn't be an issue," Miss Felding says. "I don't like to say this, but you only need to lie. You need to lie a lot. It's imperative that you don't give any unnecessary information to anyone who doesn't need it, and though I'm sure Harlow is a very sweet girl, she doesn't need it."

"I'm just forewarning you that when I lie to Harlow, she can see right through it," I say.

"Just hand her off to someone else," Hallie suggests. "And then when she actually shadows, she'll be with you."

"I guess that would work," I say. "At least I hope."

"I have a question," Lexie announces.

We wait for her to ask it. Then Hallie says, "You waiting for an invitation?"

"Oh. Sorry. Why do we even need to stage a conference? Why can't we just get out of school and drive to D.C.? It's not like anyone's gonna remember, and it seems pretty complicated for something that no one's gonna remember."

"You think we could just get out of here?" Hallie crosses her arms. "No way. Security in schools is tighter than security in prisons. There're cameras everywhere, active-duty security guards, alarms on all the doors—before we made it to the parking lot, somebody would stop us and make us go back inside and probably fire Miss Felding. Then we'd never get there."

"That's exactly it, Hallie," Miss Felding says. "It goes back to my request for you to bend the truth until it's unrecognizable. Though no one will have any recollection of the ordeal, we must be cautious so it doesn't interfere with the situation at the moment."

Lexie shrugs. "Makes sense."

Jacob then says, "You say that like any part of this *actually* makes sense."

I pace my bedroom later that night, once the sun is gone. I'm restless; nothing I try, from counting sheep to camomile tea, gets me to settle down. My mind is racing so fast I can barely keep up with it, and each of my limbs is an earthquake.

I call Harlow, just because hearing her voice makes me feel better. Even when she's talking, she sounds like she's singing: she's a music box that you can't stop winding up because its glass-like tinkles make your chest feel like it's filled with warm maple syrup.

"Hey, Skylar Amelia," she says when she picks up.

"Hi, Harlow June," I respond.

"Oh, thank God it's actually you," she says. "I answer every phone call with that. Mom's hairdresser lady wasn't happy with me last night." I force a laugh, but even through the phone she knows it's fake. "Okay, what's up?"

I sigh through my bit lip. "I have this . . . this thing tomorrow," I start with. "During your shadow time."

"What kind of thing?"

"It's very hard to explain." Each of my words is tentative. "But I'm not looking forward to it at all. I mean, I certainly should, as it's an experience in which most people don't get to partake, but it seems so daunting, and I don't think I'm the right person. Oh God, Harlow, I'm petrified."

"Like a million-year-old tree, it sounds like," Harlow says. "Now can you stop being all twisty-turny and tell me what you're doing?"

"I'll just explain tomorrow," I cover. "It'll be easier. I shouldn't have even brought it up tonight."

"Okay, then. I'll just take your word for it."

"Thank you. Sorry. I'm probably being horribly annoying, aren't I?"

"Not *horribly*. Look, Sky, whatever it is you have to do, you're gonna do it well. I have full faith in you. You'll be fine."

I wish, with all of my being, that I could believe her.

Once we've hung up, my mom pops into my bedroom. I quickly hop onto my bed and grab a book off my nightstand to pretend that I'm reading. "You going to sleep soon?" she asks me.

"Yeah," I reply. "This book is so good though." I turn back to it for good measure.

"I thought you finished that yesterday," she says.

"I'm reading it again," I cover. "You know how it's my absolute favorite." It's not, but she doesn't need to know that.

"I thought Harry Potter or Percy Jackson was your favorite. Or maybe Lord of the Rings? Or anything by Agatha Christie. Or Hemingway. Maybe Laura Ingalls Wilder? She's pretty cool. Or—"

"See? You just proved that I could have multiple favorites."

Mom sighs and smiles. "Okay, well, don't stay up too late, You have school in the morning." *Do I, though? You don't know that.* "Goodnight."

"Goodnight."

I actually do read for awhile, but when the clock hits ten-thirty, I decide that I really do have to get to bed, whether I am going to school tomorrow or not. I turn on my nightlight and bury my head beneath the covers so it's just me and the blankets and a couple hundred stuffed whales. When the rest of the world is falling asleep, however, is when my mind decides to wake up.

How my best friend happened to also be a Knower is the first question I ask the darkness. It's intriguing, nevertheless. It seems strange that we're friends that also bear the same label. Maybe that's why we were drawn to each other in the first place, because we had underlying similarities our subconsciouses recognized. Maybe I could see parts of myself in Hallie's darting eyes or her argumentative flair. Whether it was science or magic or just pure luck, though, I'm glad that she's with me. I could never have gotten through this without her by my side, nor could I have ever hidden it from her. Now the two of us can hide it from the world.

This thing may be the thing that brings me and Lexie inevitably together. I mean, part of me *wants* to be her friend, but the other part is terrified. She'll get her blinding yellow ink all over me, and though I don't really know what my color is, I know it's not anything in the yellow family. Still, I may need Lexie to complete my rainbow, as yellow is vital in a rainbow.

And then there's Jacob, the hurricane. I never would've guessed that he's a Knower, too. I mean, in hindsight, I can see it. He's extremely good at math, too impetuous for his own good, and seems pretty intelligent. I may just not know him well enough. He's only been at this school for a year, and it's far too perilous for me to get close to without getting shot with a bullet from his smile. It's always too dangerous to get close to people whose smiles have the ability to kill you.

Not to mention Miss Felding, too. She's my favorite teacher I have this year, and possibly ever, which may go back to my theorized Knower draw. I could always tell that there was something special about her, but I always told myself that I was biased. Which isn't untrue, but looking back, I was right. There is something very special about her, and there's something special about me, too.

Part of me still doesn't believe any of this. First of all, I didn't think *Homo sapiens* were around long enough to start evolving, but I guess I was wrong, because here I am. The thing is, though, I feel no different after hearing this information. Maybe normal people are just different than I am, but I've never noticed because I thought I was normal and everyone just thinks and functions like I do?

Normal: a term so casually tossed around that it's, well, normal. A word everyone knows but no one wants to conform to. Except me, though, since I want so badly to hide in the shadows and keep to the outskirts of humanity. If no one ever knows my name, I'd be okay with that. Standing out is precarious. The brightest stars burn out the quickest.

Sleep finds me eventually, and all my worries are absorbed into to the dark.

Chapter Ten

But,
in the end,
I learned it rains in hell
and angels could be bad.

"Angels"
Vicetone ft. Kat Nestel

At first, as I walk to school silently with Hallie, I'm surprised by how ordinary this day is. No fires are in the streets, and no gunshots are fired through the air. I yell at myself and the ideas disappear. No one else knows that everything that they do today will be inconsequential. For everyone else, today is just another forgettable day of island life.

"You know, today, back in 1851, a big gust of wind in Minot, Massachusetts took down an entire lighthouse," I tell Hallie. "A whole lighthouse. Is wind really powerful enough to collapse a whole lighthouse? I think that's amazing. Nature tried to take itself back because it never gave us the right to use it to our advantage. There are just some things in this world that aren't up for human alteration."

She looks at me out of the corner of her eye but doesn't say anything.

"And it's Charlie Chaplin's birthday," I continue. "That old movie star from before movies had talking in them, the one who made everyone laugh, even though he hardly spoke? It's fascinating how we can make people speak without ever saying a word to them."

She lets out a breath.

"Oh, and it's Rosalind Franklin's death day. She was truly amazing yet next to no one knows about her achievements—you know Watson and Crick, the DNA guys? She was written into history as their lab technician, but, oh my gosh, she was so much more than that. She practically discovered the structure of DNA by X-rays, with this photo called Photograph 51. It's how they learned about the double helix."

She kicks a rock on the sidewalk.

"She died of ovarian cancer in 1958, today, on April sixteenth. So she died twice. How terrible it must be to die, just to be brought back, just to die again. Sounds like sleeping: a half-commitment to death."

"Are you nervous?" Hallie says suddenly.

"No," I say, hoping that if I vocalize it, it'll be true. "We'll be with Miss Felding. How bad could it be?"

"There's no way *I'm* nervous and you aren't." She looks paler than normal, and the tiny spark in her eyes is dimmer. I was too wrapped up in my nervous babbling to notice.

"Okay, I'm extremely nervous and I really don't want to go and I wish I weren't whatever I am and I want everything to stay the way it is because I hate change and I'm especially nervous about what I'm going to do about Harlow."

"That's more like it."

"What if being Knowers ends up changing us? You know how little I like change."

"It won't. I'll still be Hallie, and you'll still be Skylar. The same people when we get out of D.C. You might be even more annoying post-super genius meeting. Who knows."

"Except . . . I have a feeling we won't leave this unscathed. I mean, every day changes us in one way or another. Yesterday I found out I like mini chocolate chips better than big chocolate chips, and now I can spend the rest of my life knowing that about myself."

"Walking to school with you is tiring," Hallie sighs. "You always make me think harder than I want to at this time of the morning."

We go to homeroom first, where people congregate and chat like normal. I scream at all of them: *Today is different than other days. Do different things. Be different people. Just do* something, *because you'll wake up in the morning with no recollection of any of it.* No one hears me, though, and the usual homeroom affairs continue.

It's just a day, lowercase D. That's all it is. A Day is no different than any other day apart from the capital. It's nothing worth getting worked up about because no one else has any clue that it's written differently because they don't have to write it.

Then, once I'm all unpacked, I walk to the Advancements Building, which isn't too far from Main, but it's far enough to make me irritable. I find the admissions center, where a batch of eighth graders from the middle school are sitting in wooden chairs that look almost as stiff as they do. Then, in the chair farthest to the left, wearing a baggy lime green polo and a wrinkled khaki skirt, is Harlow.

She jumps up at the sight of me. "What do you think? Do I look like an islander?"

"Hardly," I say. "Are you all signed in? They gave you the free lunch pass and the information packet? Did you bring a book to read in case I have a quiz? And did you bring your own pencil, or will I need to lend you one? I say *lend* because I'm going to want it back."

"Geez, Sky, calm down." She crosses her arms. "Are you always this uptight here? No wonder Hallie's the only one who'll hang out with you."

"I have plenty of friends."

She sighs. "I signed in, I got all the stuff, I forgot a book, and I'll find a pencil on the floor if you care so much."

"No. Floor pencils are always chewed. I'd rather you lose one of mine." We walk across the quad, and I point out all the buildings. "There's the cafeteria, the library, the auditorium, the gym, and health and infirmary. We're going to Main."

"Did whoever built your school ever see a school that's only a building before?"

"Hallie and I are convinced that this is their solution to keeping us active."

As we're walking through the halls of Main, I point out everything: the science wing, the music wing, the art wing. She's absolutely enthralled. "It's so much more exciting to go to someone else's school than it is to go to your own," she comments. "It's like going to someone's house and seeing how they live when they're not around you. Like you're in a part of their lives you've never seen before."

"You're very happy not doing any actual work today," I respond.

She's quiet for a split second before saying, to my dismay, "What's that thing you have to do today?"

It takes me a second to form a good answer. "Oh, Harlow, I'm so sorry. I have to go to a math convention today. I'm presenting a project with a few friends. You'll have to shadow someone else for the rest of the day."

I can watch her heart break as if her face were a window. "You're kidding."

"I'm so sorry," I repeat. "You'll have so much fun shadowing that you'll completely forget I wasn't here. Literally."

"And you *forgot* to tell me this?"

"I . . . I didn't want to tell you last night and burst your bubble."

"It would've been a lot nicer. Maybe I wouldn't have bothered coming to spend a day with my cousin if I'd known she wouldn't even *be here.*"

"I wish with every ounce of my heart that I could stay here with you," I say. "I don't want to go to this convention, and I don't want to miss out on you shadowing, and there are a million things that could go wrong, and I have no power to stop them because that power lies in someone else's hands."

"In that case, I'm coming with you."

I turn to face her. "What?"

"You heard me. I'm coming with you."

"You can't do that." I turn back around and continue walking.

She runs up next to me. "Why not? The whole point of shadowing is to follow a normal day of a typical student."

"But this Day is a complete one-hundred-eighty degree turn from *normal,* and it would appear that I'm anything but a *typical student.*"

"So? I want to be there. I want to be with *you.* So I'm coming. I'll convince anyone I need to, I'll hide in the back of the bus—hell, I'll call my mom and ask for permission if they make me, and you know I must love you to do *that.*"

"Harlow. You don't *want* to come to this thing, as you have no idea what you're getting yourself into," I tell her. "You have a choice if you want your life thrown off its course, so I would advise taking advantage of that and choosing to go back to your own school and have these parts of our lives run parallel to each other."

"If a math convention has the power to throw your life off-course, then hell yeah I'm coming. My life could use some throwing-around, and yours does, too, and there's no way I'm not gonna be there for that."

"Why are you so difficult?" I exasperate. "Normal cousins see each other, like, a few times a year. You, well, you quite literally crossed a river today. I can't complain about you because not many cousins would do that, but, oh my gosh, Harlow, you're simultaneously the best and worst person I've ever met, and I don't know which of those is a better thing to be."

"Is that a yes?"

"No!"

"Yes!"

We've made it all the way to Ms. Redding's homeroom on the third floor by this point. I stop in front of the door and turn to face her again. "If there were ever a time for you to finally decide to listen to me, then please, let it be this one."

"Skylar Amelia, I think we both know that I am *never* going to listen to you."

I try to stare her down, but I've always been bad at glaring, and Harlow's always been very good at it. In duels like these, with our eyes as our only weapons, she tends to beat me within seconds. "Talk to Miss Felding," I say. "She'll tell you exactly how much I'm lying right now."

"Lying? What do you mean?"

"I mean that you've singlehandedly made my Day so much harder. And not because we have to descend three stories now to go talk to my math teacher, which doesn't fall into the *easy* category."

Miss Felding's homeroom is occupied by sophomores who look at Harlow like she's a polar bear in the jungle. Even Hunter Athan, who's making up a test in the corner, looks up at her for a second before turning back to his paper. "Miss Felding, we have an issue," I say, and I shove Harlow in front of her.

"Why, hello," Miss Felding says. She looks to me. "Is this your hurdle?"

"No, I'm her cousin," Harlow says. "Nice to meet you. What a beautiful school. You teach math, right? Well, I want to go to the convention."

Miss Felding looks to me. "Well, I'm afraid that's impossible," she says, "for more reasons than you think."

Harlow crosses her arms and says, "With all due respect, Miss Felding, I want to come. Skylar said she was nervous, so here I am, fixing that."

"Or making it far, far worse," I comment.

"You'll have a wonderful guide here to be with you while Skylar's on the field trip," Miss Felding assures her.

"No thanks," Harlow says. "I would like to come. Like, a lot. A day in Skylar's life, right? I need to be there for that."

"You don't," I say. "Today won't be an accurate portrayal of my prosaic island life."

She stares me right in the eye. "Skylar, you will physically have to murder me if you don't want me to come with you."

"I'm sorry," Miss Felding begins, "but—"

"Oh, let her come." Lexie comes up behind us—Hallie and Jacob following—and holds a hand out to Harlow. "I'm Lexie. Nice to meet you."

"Nice to meet you, too," Harlow says, a little stunned. She turns to Hallie. "I already know you, Hallie."

"A little too well, Harlow," Hallie responds.

"And I'm Jacob," Jacob says. "You probably haven't met me."

"No, definitely not. I didn't know Skylar ever talked to a living, breathing boy."

"You're welcome to shut up at any time now, Harlow," I tell her.

Lexie looks at Miss Felding. "Can she please come? It's not like she'll remember it anyway. Everyone should get to live a day they know no one will remember. And I mean *live*. And from what I've heard, this girl's pretty good at living."

I cross my arms. "Lexie, she—"

"Please?" Harlow throws me the puppy-dog eyes. "I *am* very good at living."

"It's against so many rules, I'm afraid," Miss Felding begins to explain.

"I don't care about *rules*," Harlow says. "Like, I don't care at *all*. I don't care if I get in trouble with your school or my school, or what my mom would do to me if she ever found out, or if I get so bored at this thing that I literally *die*. Skylar obviously needs me, and if she needs me, I need her. So please, Miss Felding, let me come."

Miss Felding sighs a long sigh and eventually says, "Alright, Harlow. I suppose you could come. We'll have to tell you everything, though, and it may not be easy to her."

So we do, and it's clearly not. Harlow's jaw drops a little further with each word we say. The other people in the room are either apathetical or hang on every word we say. It doesn't matter what they hear, though, because not one of them will have any recollection of what they've heard.

By the time we finish, Harlow's eyes are made of handblown glass. "Why didn't you tell me?"

"I couldn't. I'm so sorry."

"What about that one day when you were seven and I was five in The Climbing Tree when we swore to tell each other everything?"

"When I made that promise, I never thought I'd get mixed up in something of this magnitude."

"The worst part is that tomorrow morning, I'm going to wake up and believe again that you have full faith in me."

"I'd tell you if I—"

"Oh, I know *why* you can't tell me, and I perfectly understand that, but that doesn't make it any less . . . *boom*." She plops down in my desk and flips open one of my textbooks. "Help me blend in till we get out of here, Island Girl."

Can people tell that I'm different? My eyes dart around the room. Everyone appears to see straight through my cellophane facade and tell me that I'm not normal. They all watch me with saucer-sized eyes. They pick apart every movement I make. They know that I am something that they're not and hate me for that. They can all see the spark in my eyes I'm so desperately trying to keep hidden, yet they know nothing of the flame it can create if ignited. They should be terrified of me, but I'm terrified of them. I blow each of them up with my eyes until nothing of their glaring glares are left but ashes.

Woah, slow down there. No obliteration, you weirdo.

Hallie hopes we don't have to do anything: "I swear to God, if I have to take that bio test today and then retake it tomorrow—"

"It would give you a glimpse at the material you need to study," I suggest.

"Yeah, but when would we have time to study?" Jacob wonders. He's doodling something on the side of his global notes. "We'll be in DC until midnight, probably."

"I'm just going to study in the morning tomorrow," Lexie says.

I cast another glance at Jacob's notes. "What's that?" I ask.

He seems surprised I noticed. "Nothing, really. Just a house."

"They look like blueprints."

"More like 'global-notes-prints', but yeah, kinda."

Harlow leans over to me. "So, this is what you do in Island School homeroom?"

"Isn't this what you do in City School homeroom?"

"Yeah, pretty much." She sighs. "But unless you do all this again tomorrow, I'm never gonna know that, am I?"

"Probably not, but I guarantee that it'll be something similar."

"But I won't remember *this*. I'll never remember that look Ms. Redding gave you when you dropped all your books or laughing at your horrible locker-lock skills or watching you flirt in the nerdiest way possible—"

"Excuse me?"

"—or ever going to Washington, D.C., and then a ton of stuff's gonna happen there that I won't remember, too."

"I'm sorry," I tell her. "I really am so sorry."

She shrugs. "Eh, I can't be in *every* part of your life, right? You would've jumped off your bridge by now if I were."

The principal comes on the announcements and begins her daily ramble. At the end of her message, she says, "Miss Felding's Rewonk math club will meet in her classroom immediately following homeroom. Have a great day."

"Rewonk? Is that us?" Lexie asks.

"It's Knower backwards," Jacob says.

"Jacob! Don't say it!" I exclaim. "You never know who could be listening."

"Skylar, it's not like it's 'Voldemort'," he replies.

"You shouldn't say that, either. *You-Know-Who* works just fine."

"I'm just glad we don't have to do any school stuff today," Lexie says. "If anything sucks more than school, it's school *repeating itself.*"

"If we actually did have classes," Hallie says, "I'd say we just hide in the woods till we leave."

"The *woods*?" Lexie repeats. "Absolutely *not*. I hate the woods. There're so many sticks."

"What do you have against sticks?"

"They're just so pointy," Lexie says, mock-shuddering.

"I will never understand your conversations," Jacob says, peering up from his global notes.

"You should start trying to," Hallie says. "Looks like you're stuck with us for life."

And *how* exactly do you protect yourself from a hurricane for your entire life?

Chapter Eleven

I can design an engine,
sixty four miles to a gallon of gasoline.
I can make new antibiotics,
I can make computers survive aquatic conditions.
I know how to run a business
and I can make you wanna buy a product;
Movers, shakers, and producers.
Me and my friends understand the future.
I see the strings that control the system.
I can do anything with no assistance 'cause
I can lead a nation with a microphone.

"Handlebars"
The Flobots

At the beginning of first period, we stuff our books in our lockers and head to Miss Felding's room. I check my pockets to make sure I have everything I need in case of emergencies: my phone, three bobby pins, a hair tie, a small rubber elephant, an eraser.

"Are you sure you want to do this?" I ask Harlow. "Are you absolutely, one-hundred percent sure you want to get yourself mixed up in this?"

"Relax, Sky," she says. "It's not like I'm permanently in this thing. I've got twenty-four hours, that's it. I'm not gonna do anything that's gonna end up actually mattering. I could set your entire little island on fire and then watch it burn and guess what? No one would care."

Then we're in the car with Miss Felding. She has a small sedan that can only fit five people, but since there are six of us, we're riding in extremely tight quarters, and Hallie doesn't have a seat belt. I'm squished between Jacob and Harlow.

Lexie won the straw draw and got the front seat next to Miss Felding. Not only does she have her own chair, but she gets DJ privileges. Some electro-pop song is on right now and makes me want to rip my ears off my head. I almost ask her to change it until I realize her fingers dance across her leg to the beat. She seems pretty content.

"So, this should be fun," she says after a few minutes of driving in silence with the staticky radio in the background.

"Yep." Hallie stares out the window.

"Possibly," I add.

"Probably," Jacob says.

"For being so smart, you'd think you'd have come up with a better lie," Harlow comments. "Like, a math convention? I didn't think anyone, even math teachers, cared enough to do numbers out of school."

"Yep," Hallie repeats.

"Sorry, just speculating. Isn't that what you guys do?"

"Harlow," I warn.

She sighs. "I'll shut up."

"Thank God," says Hallie. Harlow elbows her.

"Let's play a game," I suggest.

"Skylar. No."

"Hallie. Yes. Let's play I Spy."

"No."

"Come on, Hallie," Lexie prods.

"We'll die of boredom otherwise," I add.

Hallie blinks. "I welcome death with open arms."

"I spy something yellow," Harlow announces.

Hallie groans.

"It's that blinking light on the radio," Jacob replies. "So I spy something green."

"You wouldn't go with our shirts since that's too easy, so it's the superfluous cardboard tree handing from the rear-view mirror," I say.

"I spy something blue," Lexie interrupts.

"It's the sky," Hallie sighs.

"I always thought she was more of a peach color," Jacob says.

"I've always preferred 'cooked salmon'," I tell him.

"Okay," Lexie says, "that one was easy. So I spy something red."

"The label on the windshield," Jacob answers.

"They're *all* too easy," Hallie says. "I mean, judging from his angle, he wouldn't be able to see the red tag on the side of this seat, and unless there is some red I can't see because of my angle, the only thing he could be looking at is the sticker on the windshield. He could, of course, be talking about the tiny red flower on Skylar's necklace, but first of all, he most likely can't see it well enough, and second of all, it's almost always tucked in the collar of Skylar's shirt because she has no idea how to put on a necklace."

"Dude, slow down," Harlow says. "I can't keep up with rapid-fire I Spy." She crosses her arms and looks to Hallie. "How do you do that, anyway?"

"I don't know," Hallie admits. "I just kinda did it."

"You have a different perception of time," Miss Felding reminds us quietly. "You can solve things at what seems to be 'faster' than everyone else, but it's the same amount of time to you. You see time differently because you subconsciously know that it isn't relevant."

"That's so weird," Jacob says. "So, like, a minute to us could be like two minutes to someone else?"

"Exactly."

"Hey, Miss Felding?" Lexie asks after a minute of silence.

"Yes?"

"Are the Knowers threatening?"

Miss Felding thinks for a second. "No, not really. Just be good and nothing bad will happen. Follow their rules and you should be fine." Luckily, I'm great at following the rules, I like to think.

Trees conceal the landscape, their April green leaves lightly blowing in the bright spring breeze. The scene looks like a painting that a big hand painted. It paints me as well. I'm a flurry of messy brown waves and evergreen cotton and pools of muddy grayish eyes set on my pale face dotted with freckles and shrouded by thick black glasses—I am entirely color.

This entire car is color, really. The royal blue anchor that keeps me from floating off into space, the striking yellow highlighter that brightens anywhere she walks, a cerulean storm who only transferred this year and has already wreaked havoc, a china doll math teacher, and the blinding white-light of my starry cousin who is every color at once: we're an unorthodox rainbow junk-drawer.

"Welcome to Vienna, everyone," Miss Felding announces as we drive into a city.

"We drove all the way to Austria?"

"No, Lexie, the city right outside Washington, D.C. is called Vienna as well," Miss Felding clarifies.

"Oh, that makes so much more sense," Lexie sighs in relief.

Then after driving through the city, Miss Felding announces, "Alright, we're in Washington, D.C. now. As stated by Charles Dickens, welcome to the City of Magnificent Intentions." I can sense the excited relief in her voice. "We've made it."

"Intentions," Hallie repeats. "So stuff doesn't get done. They just want people to think it does."

"It depends on how you look at it," Miss Felding replies.

The Capitol rises before us. The old marble buildings assimilate with the new office towers, the mounted policemen trot alongside the latest cars, and the historic architecture is constantly being renovated; perfect contradictions for a next-to-perfect capitol.

"That bush looks like a narwhal," I say, pointing to a bush shrub of the window.

"That one looks like a teapot," Harlow says.

"That one is shaped like me," Lexie comments. "See the hair?"

"That's an oddly Ms. Parkins shaped bush," Hallie says.

"Doesn't that one look kinda like Samuel L. Jackson?" Jacob asks.

Miss Felding looks out Hallie's window and immediately whitens so that her pale skin is almost translucent. She looks petrified by what seems like an empty garden to me and accelerates the car a bit. There is a fear called botanophobia, which is the fear of plants, so I assume she's an undercover botanophobe. Or perhaps she's a pteridophobe, meaning she has a severe fear of ferns. There are some ferns over there, and their feigned spikiness is a bit unnerving.

Miss Felding parks on a street just outside the National Mall. There's so much wonder in this stretch of land: the Smithsonian Institution with its immense collection of everything you could think of, the abstract sculpture gardens ridden with picnickers, the monuments in all their glory, and all the different people and cultures exploring our Capitol together. Something about just screams that *this place is as close to utopia as we can get.*

"We're going to the Smithsonian Institution Building, better known as the Smithsonian Castle," Miss Felding says as we enter the Mall—she seems rushed, talking a bit too quickly and walking just a few steps ahead of us. We approach the sprawling building made of red sandstone and stacks of windows. It lives up to its name with its turrets and general regality.

"Why the Castle?" Hallie asks

"Headquarters is right there," Miss Felding says. She gestures to the circular rotunda of frosted glass atop the building. It's the tallest tower, standing guard for the rest of the Castle like a soldier. It salutes to us while we wonder what's inside of it.

"That's seriously awesome," Jacob says. "I love this place. The sandstone is awesome.

"I've always wondered what was up there." I stare at it.

"Well, you're about to find out," Miss Felding tells us.

As we're walking towards the entrance, a tall, fluid boy walks towards Air and Space, and I watch his eyes change color, morphing from moss into almost chlorophyll, marking him as a Knower. What things has he done in the world, and am I familiar with any of them? Or has he eradicated some disease with which I'll never have to be familiar because of him? Has this boy inadvertently saved my life?

We walk into the Castle. A fair amount of people mill about, gazing at early pieces of the Smithsonian collection and pictures and drawings of the Institution Building in its early days. They don't notice as we slip through a door in the library into a thin hallway dressed in peeling wallpaper and scratched-up hardwood. Miss Felding leads us with her head held high through twisting wings and corridors. We follow as if we're in a trance, gazing at these rooms we aren't supposed to be seeing.

"And now we climb!" Miss Felding announces as we round a corner and approach a thin, steep, winding staircase that appears to go up till it reaches the heavens.

"*Climb*?" Lexie groans. "I don't *climb*."

"Well, you'd best start," Miss Felding says, bracing the steps headfirst. She skips steps as she guides us up them.

We reach the top a lot sooner than I expect, though everyone but Miss Felding and Hallie, the track star, is breathing a bit heavier than normal. The stairs open up into a large octagonal ballroom-like space. The tremendous ceiling must be thirty feet above us, and long, intricate windows connect the ceiling to the shiny hardwood floors. The room is outlined in twenty-five desks made of frosted glass and muted chrome. They are all clear except for very organized but average desk paraphernalia. Five of the walls between the windows support sleek whiteboards with no marks. One has a table leaning against it, covered in bits of metal, hand tools, various screws and fasteners, and microscopes and lab equipment. The remaining two are laden in thousands of sticky notes, stuck in no apparent order. In the very center of the room, a large and complex hunk of metal whirs dimly; it's a fantastical machine with countless levers and dials adorning the curved surface of the cylinder that must stand over six feet tall. It gently hums a monotone song as the room moves around it.

There are eight people in the room: a thin young woman with hair like red autumn leaves and a splatter painting of freckles on her face; two siblings—twins, I'm fairly sure—with dirty blond curls and gleaming opals for eyes; a petite woman wearing a gray business suit with pale blonde hair swept back in a tight bun click-clacking on high heels around the room; a severe looking man with dark brown hair and eyes to match; two women talking rapidly in a language I don't recognize; a tall man with dark skin and a playful laugh. The diverse collection of people mills about the room, unfazed by its strangeness. They talk and laugh in a way of old friends and past memories that I could become part of if this whole super-genius thing works out.

The boy whose eyes I watched change color is not in the room.

The woman with the blonde hair clicks over to us in her high heels holding an iPad. Her face is lightly creased with well-earned wrinkles, and her strong brown eyes smile with the rest of her face as she speaks, though there's a fire of authority behind them. Whatever this woman's place is, she is very secure in it. "Hello, newbies. My name is Margaret White, Eminence of the Knowers. It's nice to finally meet you in person."

"Nice to meet you, too," Hallie ventures. She's the only one of us who does.

She looks us up and down. "You're Hallie, surely. And you must be Alexandria, but you prefer Alex? No, you like Lexie, don't you? I should've known by your hair. Then you have to be Jacob, being the only boy, that one's easy, and if you weren't, I could tell by those big brown eyes of yours. Your brother's eyes don't look like yours, am I correct? And you—" She stops and looks at me for a while, her eyes flitting around, their colors fluctuating. "You're Skylar. There isn't any argument there."

She offers no explanation as to how she knew.

But I already know some critical things about Margaret White, though I've only just met her. There's no way that Miss Felding didn't supply her with entire dossiers on each of us. As soon as we walked into the room and her somewhat bleary cedar eyes flitted in our direction, she knew our names. The only reason for her to go through that monologue was to show off to us, as if rattling off a few facts about predetermined strangers could make us wary of her, but I'm going to need a bit more than that. Pomposity doesn't scare me.

Margaret types vigorously on an iPad as I marvel at the speed of her fingers. There is unequivocal power in all parts of her body. "Excellent. All our scheduled newbies this year." Then she sees Harlow. "Then who are you?"

"You don't already know?" Harlow asks with a smirk.

"I asked you a question and I expect you to answer it."

"Oh. Sorry, then. I'm Harlow. Harlow Rainer. Just here for moral support."

"There's no *moral support* when the Day doesn't exist, Miss Rainer."

"Just because the hours aren't real doesn't mean the enthusiasm doesn't have to be," Harlow says with a smile on her face. "Besides, I won't remember seeing this freaking awesome room, or ever meeting you, so what's the difference?"

Margaret looks annoyed but brushes her off. "You all are from Lea Felding's island." She says this, not asks it.

"Right," Hallie says. "We're all freshmen."

"Yeah," Lexie says. "Miss Felding said that she got assigned to us or something."

"Yes," Margaret says. "We were expecting four new Knowers this year descended from Ruthie, Akram, Larkin, and Elizabeta. Any of those names sounding familiar?"

I nod. Larkin was my great-grandma. She's the reason my name is Skylar, like a skylark. We don't even have any skylarks in North America, but my great-grandma was obsessed with them according to my mom. I never knew her—my mom's side of the family is composed of gremlins—but I still can't imagine her shaking as she looked around this place.

"Good," she says. "They moved to that little island back in the early nineteen hundreds. Safety in numbers." She tucks her faded hair behind her ear, but it immediately falls back out again. "The Meeting will begin shortly, but we are waiting on some people that are flying in."

"So can you, like, show us around?" Lexie asks. "Since you've got time."

"Honey, she *is* time." A woman walks up to us, her steps far more gentile than Margaret's, probably because she wears purple sneakers (with memory foam inserts, by the looks of it). She looks like an amber honey jar and her voice sounds as such: warm and sweet and gooey like hot fudge on a sundae.

"Are you actually?" Lexie's eyes look like saucers. "Like, are you a goddess or something? I wouldn't be surprised, really, if you said you are—"

"No, darling, I just meant that Margaret here can milk a minute out of a second."

"This is Eula Bevrot," Margaret says. "She's the other Eminence. There are two—she and I—and we are the leaders of the Knowers."

"I do the Mechanism stuff," Eula says.

"Is that thing the Mechanism?" Jacob asks, pointing to the whirring thing in the center of the room.

"It sure is," Eula says. "You . . . you're Jacob, right?"

"Yeah. Was it my eyes?"

"Only boy."

"Right."

"Anyway, dearies, the Mechanism is the thing that allows us to mess with people's perception of time. It's super complicated but super cool."

"How does it do that?" Jacob asks. "Mess with our perceptions?"

"It doesn't mess with *our* perceptions," Margaret says, as if the idea were preposterous. "It alters the way everyone else experiences whatever's happening in order to give us complete discretion in our studies and execution."

"Still. That didn't answer my question. How does it work?"

Margaret is about to say something to Jacob, but Eula thankfully cuts her off. "You know, pumpkin, *I'm* not even sure, and I was elected to run it, can you believe that? But it makes people believe that everything that happened today never happened at all. They all wake up in the morning and forget it immediately like a dream they can't hang on to."

"And the freezing thing?" Lexie wonders. "How does it do that?"

"Well, time isn't stopping. Your perception of it speeds up, and everyone else's perception of it slows down. Then boom. Their brains are working too slow to see you guys moving, and to you guys, they don't appear to be moving at all. The way we've got it, a minute for you is sixty-thousand nanoseconds for them."

"That's amazing." Harlow is in awe, as are we all. But she's the one who shows it the most.

Hallie, on the other hand, crosses her arms. "You know how much power that thing must take? What does it run on?"

"Carbon dioxide." Eula wears it like laurels.

"That's impossible," I can't help pointing out. "You have no catalyst. How is the power generated from a simple gas?"

"A series of chemical reactions with the carbon dioxide. Energy is released and then harnessed."

"I—"

Margaret gives me a warning glance. I don't ask another question. Then she walks swiftly away from the Mechanism. Eula winks at us as we follow Margaret over towards the circle of desks. "This is the Meeting circle," she says, gesturing to the neat arrangement of desks around the Mechanism. "Needless to say, this is where we have our discussions during the Meeting. These are your desks. Since a lot of the Meeting time is spent developing and researching, each Knower has her own station at which to work." She walks from desk to desk, tapping on each one she passes. "Hallie, this one is yours, and Skylar, Jacob, and Lexie."

I run my hand over the smooth frosted glass of my desk. The chair is a schoolhouse chair made of dark wood that doesn't have a single scratch. A metal cup is in the right corner, stocked with pens, pencils, a small ruler, and an ExactO knife. There's a drawer filled with crisp sheets of paper and a sleek black iPad.

"And this is the tinkering station," she says, leading us to long tables covered in bits of metal and hand tools. A man screws something into what looks like a miniature dishwasher, and another girl attaches pieces of cardboard to each other with some sort of industrial tape. "Meet Dakarai and Coira."

"Welcome aboard!" Dakarai says with a pure smile. Coira gives us a wave.

"You're also completely welcome to add sticky notes to the Wall of Beginnings." As she says this, I can tell that she doesn't want us to go near whatever that wall is. Like even though she offered, it's not our place to take her up on it.

"The universe started with just one atom and a whole lotta bang," Eula says. She's made her way back over to us. "One small idea stuck to the wall can always lead to so much more."

I look at the wall. The sticky notes must be four or five layers thick. Some of them are dated today, and others are so faded I can hardly read them. Some aren't even sticky notes, but rather scraps of paper held by tape. Each one has a different handwriting style and idea on it. I have to resist the urge to write on one and stick it to the wall—though the notion quickly fades when I see Margaret's disapproving visage. She seems as if she can't decide if she wants nothing or everything to do with us.

"Well, then, I think that's it," Margaret says, surveying the room. She's not looking at the room itself, she's watching the people, her Knowers. How much intelligence and power is in here right now? I suspect enough to take over the world if that's what they wanted to do. "I'm going to take attendance, and if we have most of us, we'll commence the Meeting."

Miss Felding walks over to us gently, like she's walking on cracking ice. She doesn't look like she's seen a ghost, but rather she became one—she's translucent. The rest of the room seems to notice her demeanor, and their chatter's volume fades just a little bit. "I apologize for the interruption, but Margaret, may I talk to you?" she asks. "In private?"

Margaret says, "Just let me take attendance, Lea—"

"I'd like to talk immediately, if you will." She doesn't apologize for interrupting this time.

Margaret stares at Miss Felding for a second before leaving us standing in the center of the room.

The other Knowers in the room take notice of Margaret and Miss Felding's conversation. The air gains weight by the second. Everything suddenly has a vignette like an old fuzzy photograph that's been sitting in an old steamer trunk for too long. Miss Felding looks faint and Margaret looks lethal.

"What are they talking about?" I whisper to Hallie.

"You think I know?" she replies. "These people run the world. They could be talking about anything."

"Probably nuclear weapons," Jacob speculates.

I cast another glance at their urgent murmuring. "Nuclear weapons don't sound as detrimental as this does."

"I don't want to know your definition of *detrimental* if 'nuclear weapons' doesn't fit in it."

Margaret comes back to us. She tries to hide the ashes smearing her face, but it doesn't work; she wears a pantsuit of omnipotence but the face of a last-minute improv troupe addition.

"Everything okay there, Margaret?" Lexie asks tentatively.

"Yes. Everything is fine." She sighs and plasters on a smile. This woman has trained herself to discern frauds from angels just by looking at the way they've done their hair. She picks up tips for her own lies along the way like mementos from each time she's reduced a person to the cells that comprise them—but if I didn't know this, I wouldn't know that her grin is fake.

Chapter Twelve

No need to feel offended;
born to a time
when the quiet ended.

"Loud(y)"
Lewis Del Mar

"Wait, I thought we were here for the Meeting." Hallie crosses her arms.

"Yes, you are," Margaret says, "but there is important business that must be addressed without young ears listening."

"But we just got here," Lexie says. "You gave us the tour and everything! Now you want us to leave?"

"I thought you'd want our help with whatever it is you have to deal with," Jacob says. "Isn't that why we drove all the way here?"

It takes Margaret a second to concoct an answer. "Something has come up. Now, you are going to go downstairs with Miss Felding and do as she says. No arguments, no questioning her or me. Is that clear?"

"Not really," Jacob says.

"Don't lie to me, Mr. Connelly. You have twenty/twenty-five vision, so seeing things clearly should be no issue for you. And I know you struggle with directions a lot, unless they're illustrated, but I don't think I need to draw this out for you. You're too smart for that. Follow Miss Felding. Do as she tells you. She's your teacher, after all, and I expect you to listen to her as you would listen to me."

She turns away from us and moves towards Eula and the blond twins, and I decide that messing with this woman has got to be suicidal.

Miss Felding wordlessly leads us back down the twisting staircase and into a room on the first floor of the Castle. This wallpaper is green with swirly, floral shapes. The windows all have those metal X's dancing across the glass, and though they look a little misty, they coat the room in glorious untempered light. It's mostly empty except for a line of empty glass cases and a stack of cardboard boxes covered by sticky canvas tarps. "Stay here, please," she tells us. "I will be back for you in about two hours."

"Why are we just sitting here while all this goes on?" Hallie demands. "Whatever it is, we can help."

Miss Felding chews her lip then answers, "You will attend the next portion. For now, please stay put."

"If I may say so," I start, "I think we could offer you some assistance. We could potentially have some good ideas."

"I'm terribly sorry." By the way Miss Felding says it, I can almost believe her. "We will try to sort this out as soon as we can. I'm sorry your first Meeting has to be so abnormal."

She gives us a china-doll smile and turns towards the staircase.

"Well," Hallie says once she's sure she's gone, "guess we're not changing the world today."

"So what are we supposed to do?" Jacob says. "Just sit here?"

"It does seem a little counterintuitive," I admit.

"So much for a smart person meeting," Harlow huffs. "I thought I was gonna see things explode or something. Maybe an engineered earthquake."

"The whole Day isn't actually happening and you want an earthquake?"

"The Day thing is unnoticeable," she sighs. "I would never have even guessed there was such a thing if you didn't tell me."

"Yeah, well if you hadn't just shown up at my school— You'd best be glad that today doesn't exist, or your mother would never let you see sunlight again."

"Hey, she knew I was coming. She just didn't know I'd be doing whatever the hell it is we're doing."

"Sitting in a forbidden room in the Smithsonian Castle has got to be a substantial reason for grounding."

Lexie's eyes dart all around the place, and then she sighs. "Well, I'm done with this room. So, let's go."

"Where?" I ask warily.

"Not here, that's for sure. Let's go to all the museums and the monuments! This is such an epic place, and I really don't want to waste time just sitting here. We only have a few hours to do stuff that we'd never do, since no one's ever gonna know we did it. Now, I don't know about you, but I've got a pretty long bucket list, and I bet I can cross half off today."

"Wait, what? Lexie, you know we can't do that. Miss Felding—and Margaret, more importantly—told us to stay here."

Hallie's fingers play with the edge of her skirt. "You know, I've always wanted to lick a Monet painting."

"If you don't mind me asking, why in the world have you always wanted to lick a Monet painting?"

"That's besides the point. Today could be my one and only chance to do that."

"Miss Felding told us to stay here," I repeat.

"Yep, and I don't care." She throws me a devilish grin before she runs at the speed of light out of the room.

"Hallie!" I yell after her, but the track star can't hear me because she runs like a gazelle.

"I'm totally in," Lexie says, following her at almost the same speed, which amazes me because her legs are shorter and she's not on the track team. She is incessantly full of surprises.

"Finally, a Day where I can't get in trouble," Harlow sighs before following her.

"You guys are going to get in so much trouble anyway!" I call after them.

"Skylar. Live a little," Jacob says. A dangerous smile plays on his face.

"Once I tried to live a little and I fell out of a tree and broke a metal watering can with my left leg."

"Oh. Well. That usually doesn't happen when you live a little, just so you know."

"Hey! I know that! I'd lived a little before, you know," I say.

"Really." He raises a single eyebrow—something I've always wanted to be able to do—incredulously.

"Yes, I have! Once, while I was at the grocery store with my mom—in the *city,* mind you—I purchased an entire gallon of almond milk without any adult assistance. *And* it was the sweetened kind."

"What were you, five?"

"I was fourteen!" I cross my arms.

"You just proved my point even more."

I narrow my eyes at him before breaking into a sprint.

I make my own wind that fights with the already-present spring breeze over the right to play with my hair. My legs cheer, not screaming like I thought they'd be; the air is cool and crisp like a freshly picked apple. Air whizzes by my ears, thumping against them like drumbeats.

The sky is a pure cerulean, and melodramatic cotton-candy clouds drift through it. I can outrun every piece of it, gliding across green grass that tickles my ankles. I don't see a single person staring at me.

Hallie, Lexie, and Harlow lay in the grass in front of me. I collapse next to them in a flurry of wild giggles—I've never heard myself laugh like this before. Jacob falls right next to me—he laughs like this all the time, so it's nothing new for him. The five of us are so elated that we shake the ground. Pure and unabridged happiness jolts through me like electricity. There is not a single thing that can destroy anything. The spinning rock on which I lay is perfect in every single way.

"Can we please go lick some Monet now?" Hallie breathes, barely audible through her laughter. Her smile is a diamond.

The weight of exerting myself like that catches up with me once I'm standing. My head swims around a bit and my limbs burn. I inhale gulps of air so cold it burns my lungs; I hug my thin uniform cardigan closer around me. Yet I can't wipe the blinding smile off my face. It's stuck there as if it were superglued.

If such unadulterated ecstasy only exists when time doesn't, I hope the clock never starts ticking again.

Jacob distracts the guard in the National Gallery with stupid questions on various art pieces while we watch as Hallie marches right up to "The Japanese Footbridge" and licks the corner. We burst into a fit of laughter when she makes a face and proclaims, "It tastes like old, stale, dirty French fries."

We dart out of the Gallery as fast as we can when the guards all start screaming, "Who in their right mind would lick such a masterpiece?" Honestly, I can't help but wonder the same thing, but the whole ordeal is just so hilarious and so incredibly Hallie that I ignore them without thought.

The birds stalking the reflecting pools are thrilled when we start tossing them pieces of a donut we found abandoned on a bench—after having to telling Lexie she shouldn't eat it. She then throws the rest of the chunk into the center of a flock patrolling the artificial coastline, and they attack it like a pack of hungry velociraptors.

"Hey Lexie," Hallie says, "you should jump in the reflecting pool."

"That's such a terrible idea," I protest. "You know how many types of bacteria are growing in that cesspool? There isn't a current, so microorganisms can live and reproduce freely with little fear of a ripple taking out their colony. It's also a breeding ground for mosquitos, seeing as though it's an unmoving body of water. You could get pecked to death by angry ducks, too—"

Lexie's in the water before I finish my tirade. "Ooo, it's cold," she says. She can stand up in it, and it only goes to her thighs. "And slimy."

"Exactly. That would be the algae."

"Eww. It's worse than river water."

"Okay, guard coming, climb out," Hallie says.

"Who thinks we should piss off as many guards as we can today?" Harlow cheers.

"I'm in," Lexie replies, wringing out her khaki skirt. She pulls her soaked phone out of the pocket. "Oh, man. I forgot about that."

"Rice," I say. "It works as a natural absorber."

"Or time," Jacob says. "That'll dry it out even more."

Lexie throws it back into the reflecting pool. I open my mouth in objection but she simply shrugs and says, "It's not going to work, so I'm not going to carry it. Too much extra weight, and today's a light Day."

The Lincoln Memorial is one of the most magnificent things I've seen. The marble all looks like frozen waterfalls carved into a larger-than-life Honest Abe, his lap open like a mall Santa waiting for kids to tell him their Christmas wishes. "I've always wanted to sit in his lap," I say out loud.

"Then do it," Hallie says.

"Yeah, you'll never get another chance," Lexie says. "Better do it now."

"I couldn't possibly do that," I say. "First of all, he's super tall, and I'm, like, five-three."

"Hmm, that's pushing it a little."

"And I could be brutally yelled at, and I'm in a skirt, so—"

"Yeah, you're right, you probably couldn't make it," Jacob shrugs.

I raise my eyebrows. "Well, I never said I *couldn't.*"

"You literally just said that, but okay."

"Hey, I could climb that thing if I really wanted to!"

"Sure you could."

"Are you saying I can't climb it? Because I can prove you wrong. I'm very good at proving people wrong."

"Really."

I narrow my eyes at him before marching over to the statue and attempting to hoist myself onto it.

The base of the statue is mostly flat, so there aren't a lot of footholds. People definitely stare at me now, but surprisingly, I don't care in the slightest. *Let them gape, and for a few hours at least they'll think I'm capable of something.*

I make it to his lap in a couple of minutes, awaited by a smattering of applause by the spectators and the freezing marble underneath me. I sit there and wave to Hallie, Harlow, Lexie, and Jacob. They all wave back, except Jacob, who only smiles at me. Maybe he's impressed, or maybe he's surprised. Maybe he knew I could climb it all along.

The man in the red shirt to my left is a painter, evident by the oil (or maybe acrylic) paints on his otherwise nice sweater. The woman to my right holding a baby in one arm and the hand of a toddling girl in the other is a single mom; she looks a bit worn out but fully content with her Vera Bradley diaper bag and Fisher-Price stroller. I can tell that that guy is a doctor because of his hands and that the little girl over there has a twin that isn't with the family at the moment because of her sundress, but I can't for the life of me discern anything about Jacob Connelly.

"Okay, how do I get down?" I call.

"Jump!" Hallie shouts back.

"That's a terrible idea!"

"You have to!"

"And what if I break my arm?"

"No big deal," Hallie yells. "Just jump already!"

I'm about eight feet in the air, so it seems unfeasible to make it without injury, but then I'm slowly slipping down Lincoln's knees, I notice. If I don't jump soon, I'll fall, and that's much, much worse. If you're going to end up hundreds of feet below where you've started, you might as well choose to do so.

I leap and land on my side on the cold marble floor with a tiny thud.

Jacob holds out his hand to help me up. I get up and smooth out my skirt without him. "That wasn't as bad as I thought it was going to be," I remark, fixing my crooked glasses.

"Well, I'd hope so," he says, "seeing as though you thought climbing that was the end of the world."

"What now?" Harlow says.

"We could go to the National Aquarium and see all the fish!" Lexie claps her hands.

"No, we should try to get into American History's vaults," Hallie says. "See if they have Thomas Jefferson's spleen!"

"Eww, no," I say. "We have to go to the Library of Congress and go in the underground connections. The actual library is in three buildings that are connected underground. Doesn't that sound fascinating?"

"No, we should go to the International Spy Museum," Jacob says. "It's so cool there. All spy-ish."

It's my idea to walk around the Tidal Basin, and everyone agrees to it. I've never done it before, and I've always wanted to. We cross the street and the blue-gray man-made lake sinks into the grassy ground.

"Headquarters is really cool," Lexie says.

"I know," I reply. "It's so open. I wish our classrooms were like that. Wouldn't that just be amazing? It would be so much easier to learn in an environment like that. And just imagine sticky notes all over the building. Think of the ideas you'd find scattered about."

"Think of all the dirty jokes you'd find," Lexie says.

"Lexie. Don't make my idea all Lexie-fied. It could do without your ink."

"My what?"

"Nothing. I didn't mean to say that aloud."

"Well, she's right, though," Harlow says. "You can't give people too much freedom or they take advantage of it."

"It *could* work. Hypothetically, at least," I say. "People are generally good."

"No, people are generally bad," Hallie says. "The human race is made up of awful creatures."

"You're so dark."

"You're so bright, I need sunglasses."

I turn to Jacob, who hasn't said a word since we started walking. "You're quiet. Seems unlike you."

"Just. . . I'm just thinking," he says.

"About what?"

"Nothing. Everything. I don't really know."

"Well, when you figure it out, I'd love to know."

"How are you so positive all the time?"

"I don't know."

"Talent?"

"'Talent', 'curse'. Either one."

"I bet I could get around the basin in three minutes," Lexie comments, surveying the diameter of the basin.

"Yeah? I bet I could get there a full minute before you," Hallie challenges.

"I bet I'd get there a full minute after you," Harlow adds.

"Really?" You're on."

"No," I say. "Splitting up sounds like a terrible idea."

"You two stay here and time us on your phones," Hallie says.

"Hallie, you're getting too into this," Lexie groans.

"I said it as a joke," Harlow sighs.

"No, really, I want to see if you guys are right," Hallie says, drawing a line in the dirt with her finger. "This is the start and finish line."

"That's an extremely not-good idea," I say. "We really shouldn't separate."

"No, Skylar. Stop. We're going to do this," Hallie says, "and I'm winning."

Harlow sighs again but says, "What the heck? I'll do it."

"Fine, I'm in," Lexie says. "Let's go. Skylar, say go."

"No," I say at the same time as Jacob says, "Go."

They take off. I glare at him. "What? You weren't going to say it."

"Yes, because I don't want anyone to get hurt!"

"They'll be fine."

"And how can you be sure?"

"Because even if someone did get hurt, they'd be fine in the morning."

"Yeah, but they wouldn't be fine *today.*"

"There isn't really a *today.*"

"Tomorrow *is* today!"

"You know that makes no sense, right?"

I groan. "We're supposed to be timing them."

"Oh. Right."

"Agree to tell them that they're right and avoid future arguments?"

"Agree."

The silence is somewhat excruciating. I try to think of something to say, but everything I conceive sounds redundant or like I'm trying too hard for conversation. Then he mercifully says, "Do you trust them?"

"The Knowers?" I clarify. "I trust *some* of them. Miss Felding, for instance. And maybe Eula—she seems like she's sure of herself. And they could very well be it. I definitely don't trust Margaret. Powerful people like her are difficult in which to place all your trust."

He thinks for a second before he says, "Do you get the feeling they're hiding stuff from us?"

"Oh, they're obviously hiding things; there's no debate there. They can't go spewing out the world's top secrets to a few teenagers. It goes back to the trust thing, you know? They have to test our waters and see if we're raindrops or meteorites."

"I know—kind of—but still, I'm getting the feeling that they're not telling us everything. Like they know something that they know we want to know but won't tell us because we want to know it and we're not supposed to know it since it's something only they can know."

"... I'm sorry, what?"

"They know something that they know we—"

"That's not what I meant."

"Oh. Sorry."

"Anyway, though, I suppose you're right. But I'm not going to turn against them until they give me reason."

"Yeah, maybe they—"

He's cut off by the sound of a needle piercing the sky, followed by a thousand breaking windows and the coarse crackle of fire. I see it and almost collapse: the outline of the Museum of Natural History, filled with dancing orange flames.

Chapter Thirteen

Let me go,
I don't wanna be your hero.
I don't wanna be a big man,
just wanna fight with everyone else.
Your masquerade,
I don't wanna be a part of your parade;
everyone deserves a chance to
walk with everyone else.

"Hero"
Family of the Year

"What the actual hell . . . " Jacob trails off. "Did . . . did that building . . . Oh my God—"

Smoke begins to waft over here; although there's barely any, it suffocates me and I can't breathe. *Not in front of Jacob, he'll inadvertently destroy you, you know he will. He'll be nice to you or get you to Hallie—if she's not dead—and then you'll be dead, so stop. What are you even talking about, a Smithsonian just* erupted, *stop worrying about people that have menial effects on your life. Where's Harlow? She's dead, you know it. Hallie and Lexie, too. All of them. Everyone you know is dead now. You know they were all in there.*

"What just happened?" I turn to him frantically. "God, what happened? See, this is why I like to know where everyone is! They could've been in there for all I know! Why did we let them go? Why did we split up?"

"Skylar, calm down," he says with force yet reassurance. He puts his hands on my shoulders, which are shaking like the rest of me. "They weren't in there. They're running around the basin, re-member? They wouldn't be in there."

"But what about Miss Felding? And Eula and Margaret and everyone else? Where are they? What if they were in there?"

He takes a breath. "They probably weren't either. They're at the Meeting, remember? I'm sure everything is absolutely fine."

"You say that as one of the Smithsonian museums is up in flames! How can everything be *absolutely fine* when a building just exploded?"

"It'll be okay," he says, though he's biting his lip, so I can tell he's lying—he's not a very good liar. "It'll all be erased. This isn't happening, right? None of this will ever have happened."

"But it's happening right *now*, and that counts for something."

It's like every firefighter in the world is here in an instant. There are policemen, ambulances, news crews; everyone is bustling and screaming so loudly that I can't tell if it's millions of shrieks resonating together or one giant's cry that could cause an earthquake if we were closer to a fault line.

We move closer to the site of the explosion, where the large flames bully the innocent periwinkle sky. What has it done to you, flames? You can't leave it alone? I keep reminding myself that nothing exists and that the sky, like everything else, will be fine, but I can't get enough oxygen into my mind for it to think clearly and my vision is blurred like a watercolor painting left in the rain overnight. I only get worse as we get closer to the fire.

A paramedic rushes up to us. "Come on, kids, let's check you out," he says.

"No, we're good," Jacob says, and we hurry away from him and dodge everyone else. A woman in a bright magenta blouse tries to grab my arm, but I kick her in the shin and keep following Jacob because he seems to have at least a partial idea of what to do.

"There are speculations of a terrorist attack," a man says to the lens of a camera. "The entirety of the National Mall and its surrounding areas are currently being evacuated."

"Children, over here!" another paramedic calls to us. "We'll help you!"

"We're fine, thanks," Jacob says. He keeps moving, and I struggle to keep up with him. It's in times like these where I really wish my legs were longer.

Another news anchor materializes next to me. I swear, these people can teleport. "Miss, will you give us a comment on what just happened here?"

"She's in shock," Jacob says to her. "Good luck finding someone who isn't." He takes my hand and we continue weaving through the human labyrinth. This is the largest amount of people I have ever seen congregated in one place. They're all rushing around, some crying, some screaming in hysteria, others acting completely calm as if it were just a fire drill at school. They move as a single mass away from the Mall.

"I'm not in shock!" I tell him.

"Yes, you are," he says, "but I kind of am, too."

Then I trip over something on the grass. Jacob catches me, but I see I've tripped over a man lying on the ground, and I scream.

"He only fainted," Jacob says. "Look, he's breathing."

"That doesn't make it much better!"

The sky doesn't even look blue anymore. It's a stark and splenetic gray.

"There you are!" I turn to see Miss Felding coming towards us. "I thought I told you to stay in the Castle! Where are the others?"

"We're so sorry, and I don't know," I say. I grip my shirt to keep my hands from shaking. There's so much of everything going on. Colors flashing, sirens blaring, smoke sitting low in the sky— and the smell, oh it's awful, like burning rubber and steel and everything in between. "I don't know where they are."

"I'm pretty sure they weren't in the building," Jacob adds. He turns to me. "They're okay, Skylar, I swear."

"You can't be sure," I say, trying to get my voice to stop quaking. "You can't be sure that they're fine, and I think you know that."

"I'm sure they're fine," Miss Felding says, though she's obviously still worried.

"Where are the rest of the Knowers?" Jacob asks.

"We're all fine," she says with no other comment. "Don't worry. No one got hurt."

"You mean none of the Knowers got hurt," I correct, gesturing to the fleet of ambulances and army of paramedics. "I can't imagine how many people were in there."

"But they'll all be fine in the morning," Miss Felding reminds me.

"Still," I say. "That doesn't change the fact that they all got hurt today. Just because they can't remember doesn't mean it didn't happen."

People flood out of all the other buildings. Helicopters fly overhead like a flock of mechanical birds. Millions of guards escort people off the grass and towards the city. The underground subway station overflows as if someone put too much water in a pot then boiled it.

The entirety of the National Mall falls under lockdown, and we stand in the dead center of it.

"Skylar! Jacob!" I hear Lexie yell. Unscathed, the three of them run towards us. She looks like she's about to slap me or hug me—most likely both. "Oh my God, where have you *been*?"

Harlow engulfs me in a rib-crushing hug and whispers in my ear, "Does stuff like this always happen when I can't remember it?"

"We're fine," Jacob says. "So is everyone else. Don't worry."

I look at them and breathe a shaky sigh if relief, and then I say, "I told you we should have stayed together. But *no*, you saw that running around the basin was the optimal choice. Well, now you can see exactly how suboptimal it was."

Never having gotten an answer from me, Harlow asks, "Does this stuff happen to you guys all the time?" She surveys the Mall with wide, glassy eyes. "How much do you not tell me, Skylar?"

I barely hear her because I catch a glimpse of a boy, whose mossy eyes soon shift into a lime green.

And then I decide that he is not a Knower.

"Miss Felding?" I ask.

"Yes?" she responds.

"Are we really the only ones who are affected by this Day?"

The shift in her demeanor is perceptible to everyone standing around her. "Why do you ask?"

"Because I'm beginning to think that maybe we aren't."

Miss Felding looks extremely agitated, like when you mix baking soda and vinegar. So bubbly and disconcerted that she's overflowing her plaster volcano. "They are nothing of your concern."

"But they are *something*," I press, "and if they've had anything to do with this, then I'd argue that they *are* our concern."

"You can't leave us hanging." Leave it to Hallie to back me up. "We drove all the way here, so we're in this now. We have to be."

Miss Felding pauses before she says, "The Eradicators are a group, much like the Knowers, except far more sinister. They believe in extreme equality, to the point where they justify violence when trying to reach their goal. But they are of no concern to you." She adds that last part quickly.

"Did they do this?"

She doesn't reply.

"Do they know about us?" Hallie asks.

"Yes," Miss Felding responds. "Like us, they have the ability to remember the Days and can't survive them—"

"What do you mean, can't survive them?" Lexie interrupts.

Miss Felding looks like she's mentally kicking herself for ever opening her mouth. "Well, if a normal person were to die today, she would wake up in her bed in the morning with no recollection of dying. But if a Knower, or an Eradicator, were to die today, she would fall brain dead. She wouldn't wake up tomorrow. Her brain would be unable to revive itself like a mundane person's but also unable to let go of itself."

"So, the Eradicators are against us then?" Jacob is walking in slow circles. Even though we just ran around for ten solid minutes, he's still got energy left. "They . . . So they're out to get us. This totally could have been them."

"We don't know that for certain," Miss Felding says. "You can't—"

"How could you not know for certain?" he says. "If you even had the smallest idea that they could be out to hurt you, wouldn't you try to learn everything about them?"

"They are not our main focus," Miss Felding says.

"Okay, but why not? They—"

"They are not our main focus," Miss Felding repeats sharply, and Jacob stops arguing with her.

But I know that there is nothing accidental about these waltzing, roaring flames. They were quite obviously placed here and told to dance. Choreographed, even, and controlled by an anonymous force, something—or someone—that told them to incinerate us. I would simultaneously love and hate to know why.

Within thirty minutes, the Mall is empty of all tourists. All who remain are police or firefighters or people in business attire who scurry around like mice. I can just about see their whiskers and affinity for cheese.

"You can't stay here," Miss Felding is muttering, more to herself than to anyone else. "This isn't safe."

"So? Who cares about 'safe'?" Hallie crosses her arms. "Don't you need us? We're Knowers, too."

"It's only your first Meeting," Miss Felding says.

"And next time will only be our second, and time after that will only be our third. So when do you want us to actually start helping you? If you didn't want us here, why'd you bring us here in the first place?"

"You could stay on the first floor of the—"

"No. Why did you bring us here in the first place? Answer my question."

Miss Felding only sighs, like she's not surprised by Hallie's disrespect. "You were supposed to have a normal first Meeting, but something's come up, and Margaret doesn't think you should be a part of it. It's out of my hands. But I am in charge of you today. It's best to go back to the Castle."

"They'll look for us in the Castle," Hallie points out. "It's close to Natural History. They'll think the bomber is hiding in one of the nearby buildings."

She sighs again. "I suppose you're right. Air and Space—oh, no, definitely not. American History—"

"With all due respect, Miss Felding," I interject, "they're going to look in all those places, too. If you'd like to send us somewhere where we would be out of the way, either your way or their way," she stiffens at this, "then I would suggest leaving the Mall entirely."

"Yeah, I agree," Lexie adds. "If you're not gonna let us stay, for whatever reason, we should go somewhere that no one will find us."

"What about Tyson's Corner?" Harlow suggests. All eyes turn to her. I'd half-forgotten she's here, she's been so quiet, for the first time in her life. "There's stuff to do and no one could think to look there for us."

"Great idea," Miss Felding says. "Please, go now. Take the metro. Someone will fetch you if we need you."

"*If,*" Hallie scoffs.

Our railcar on the metro is completely full yet almost completely free of noise. No one is talking. A muffled sob escapes someone once in awhile, and sometimes a phone rings and someone will answer. But there's no chatter, there's no excitement, and there are certainly no smiles. I'm not used to seeing a world without smiles.

Once we're at our stop, we get above ground as fast as possible. Though no one feels like talking, Lexie makes an effort by saying, "Did you hear that Becky Clarin is going out with Garrett Walaski?"

"Seriously?" Hallie replies. She's still angry with Miss Felding, I can tell. "They won't last a week, I bet."

"Becky Clarin is an absolute nightmare," I say.

Maybe petty gossip can make you feel normal, and maybe that's why people gossip in the first place: because talking about how weird other people are make you feel like maybe you're less weird. Sure, I've just seen a building explode, but Becky Clarin is going out with Garrett Walaski, can you believe it?

"I thought she was dating Alex Summerheld," Jacob says.

"He broke up with her," Hallie says. "She'd stop at his locker every day when she got to school and give him a kiss on the cheek or something stupid like that then leave without ever saying a word to him. Then one day, she didn't do it, and she hasn't done it since. He doesn't ever look at her, but she still glances at him from time to time. In math, she sits next to him and tries overly hard not to look his way. He didn't like her. Definitely not in a dating way, probably not in any way. She's super insecure about him breaking it off because he never gave her a good reason as to why. She's been meaner to everyone lately, and it doesn't take a Knower to point *that* out."

"Wow," Lexie says. "Did you notice a few things or what?"

Hallie shrugs. "I just pick stuff up, I guess."

"That girl hates literally everyone," I say. "Except anyone of the male gender."

"She hates me," Jacob mutters.

"Why?" Lexie asks.

He shrugs. "She told me I'm a flighty mess." This bothers him a lot more than he's willing to share, I can tell. "Very original."

"She hates me, too," I say.

"How could she possibly hate you? I didn't think anyone was soulless enough to hate you."

"There was an incident with some chicken blood in bio."

"Still, she must be soulless." he asks, crossing his arms. "You're, like, a bubble of sunshine."

I'm not the whole sky, just part of it. A tiny bit of something so powerful encapsulated in a thin, iridescent blanket. Easily popped but strong if you give her the chance to be. A shiny, iridescent bubble that floats off into space often and lives more inside herself than out.

A necessary anchor, a raging hurricane, a blinding highlighter, a star of pure white light, and—finally—a bubble: the most unconventional collection of stuff ever.

"Thank you," I say to Jacob. I dodge his smile, knowing perfectly well the likely outcome of a bubble falling into a friendship with a hurricane. (Hint: *pop!*) "That's . . . probably the best thing anyone's ever said to me."

"It's true," he says.

We find a map of the mall as soon as we walk into the building. It's so complicated that not one of us can read it, except Jacob. He takes a single glance at the thing and says, "We came in here, at the entrance near Pottery Barn. Where do you want to go?"

"I don't care," Hallie says. "Anywhere you want, I guess."

"Then let's go to the Lego Store," Jacob says.

Hallie groans. "Not there."

"You literally just said, quote-unquote, 'Anywhere you want, I guess'."

"Yeah, but not the Lego Store."

"Fine. Any other suggestions, then?"

"Oh my gosh, the Disney Store's right there," I exclaim when I catch a glimpse of it. "Can we please go, just for a second?"

"Yeah, can we?" Lexie asks. "It's so cute in there."

"They have this giant plastic castle inside. It makes you feel like a tiny princess."

"A museum just exploded and killed hundreds of people and you want to go in a plastic castle?" Harlow crosses her arms.

"It'll serve as a well-needed distraction."

"If it shuts you up, we'll go," Hallie says. "It's not like we have anything else to do."

Lexie and I go into the store and are hit with a wave of *Frozen* songs and itchy tulle dress-up gowns. I dance down the sparkly blue tile path on the floor to the castle. I stand inside, and I feel like a tiny princess.

I pace around the castle for a bit, but then I sit on the floor next to everyone else. We're all completely silent; the only noise in the store comes from inside our own heads. We talk to each other without words, holding conversations with nothing more than glances at each other, though everyone's eyes, no matter what color they happen to be, look somewhat defeated.

Then Jacob stands up. "I need some Lego."

"Why would you need Lego?" Lexie wonders.

"Some people chew on their pencils or pace or whatever. I Lego."

"Lego's not a verb," I tell him.

"Yes, it is. Does anyone know how to get a set out of the store without setting off those stupid sensors?"

"Aluminum foil," Harlow says. "I know how to do that."

"And *how* exactly do you know how to do that?" I inquire.

Harlow shrugs. "That kid at Bible camp taught me. The one with the lisp? Those Venezuelans have interesting hobbies."

I sigh. "I told you not to talk to him anymore. That kid was at Bible camp for a reason."

"Anyway, just line a bag with tin foil. Should get you a medium-sized thing out of there."

"Okay, then," Jacob says. "And where do we get aluminum foil?"

"One of the restaurants," Lexie says. "Just ask for some. They're bound to have a roll."

Harlow and Jacob leave for the Lego Store, so I sit once again wordlessly with Hallie and Lexie. Each of us sit with our backs to the smooth plastic of the castle's faux stone, our thoughts separate but undoubtedly connected.

Then Lexie says, "So, that global quiz was hard, wasn't it?"

"Lexie, I swear to God, there are way more important things to be talking about," Hallie sighs. "Hallawin's tests are really the last thing I care about right now."

"If not ever," I add.

"Sorry," Lexie says. "Seemed like a distraction."

"We don't need distractions," Hallie responds, "only answers."

"And maybe those answers can come from somewhere we don't expect it to."

By the time Jacob and Harlow come back in about fifteen minutes, Hallie's resorted to going through Instagram on her phone and Lexie's repeatedly clicking a Nemo pen. Harlow throws a bag of tin foil into a trash can and sits next to me. Jacob opens his Lego set—I think it's some sort of Star Wars thing—and opens all of the bags, the ones that are appropriately numbered as not to have them all opened before the previous bag's contents have been completed.

"You're not supposed to open all of the bags at once," I tell him.

"I know."

I gesture to him opening all of the bags at once.

"I know."

I open my mouth to object but Hallie says, "Skylar, stop talking."

Jacob starts building something with the pieces. I try to hand him the directions that he's cast to the side, but he says, "No thanks, Bubble of Sunshine, I don't use those."

"You don't use the directions," I repeat.

"Yeah," he replies. "I don't need them. The pictures on the box are enough."

"Alright, then."

The store goes back to being silent; the only noises courtesy of us are the occasional snaps from Jacob sticking pieces together and Lexie's incessant pen-clicking. The air seems too heavy—standard pressure is a single atmosphere, but it feels as if there were five.

Lexie's stomach audibly growls. We all look at her. "I'm starving," she announces.

"I couldn't tell," Jacob responds.

"Same," Harlow says.

"Yeah, I could totally eat," Hallie says.

"You could *always* eat," I remind her.

"True. Still, can we go get something?"

I smile at them. "I have an idea on where to go, and I believe it's a good one."

"Where?" Jacob asks.

"It's a surprise," I respond, attempting to sound mischievous. It comes across as more creepy than sneaky.

I lead them out of the Disney Store and towards the opposite end of the mall. Although I'm fairly sure they'll want to kill me at first, I'm even more sure they'll thank me later. That's often what happens in these situations.

"How far away is this place?" Jacob asks. "We've been walking for, like, two minutes."

"We're almost there," I say, and when I see the magenta facade of the American Girl Place, excitement explodes in my chest like a thousand little bubbles all popping at once.

Chapter Fourteen

*Change everything you are
and everything you were.
Your number has been called,
fights and battles have begun,
revenge will surely come.
Your hard times
are ahead.*

"Butterflies and Hurricanes"
Muse

"Absolutely not."

"Come on, their food is so good!"

Hallie narrows her eyes at me. "Did you not hear me? No."

"I can't be seen in there," Jacob states.

"It's just crawling with little kids."

"If we let you in there, you're going to lose your cool and embarrass yourself." Harlow crosses her arms.

"I'll go in with you," Lexie shrugs. "I love the American Girl Place."

"Thank you, Lexie," I say. I plead to the rest of the group, "Please, guys? I promise I won't be too vexing. Well, I promise I'll *try* not to be too vexing."

"Why don't I believe you?" Harlow says.

"I pinky-promise." I hold out my pinky for good measure.

Hallie slowly and reluctantly interlocks her pinky with mine. "If you do that thing where your voice goes up six octaves, we're out."

"I won't. I'll keep my voice at approximately one-eighty-five Hertz."

Despite my promises, it takes all the self-control I have not to screech when we get into the store. All the smiling dolls and tiny accessories and raspberry pink and giggling children are the epitome of pure happiness. There's nothing more innocent and precious than a room of dolls whose sole purpose is grinning.

"You're acting like you're six," Harlow reminds me.

"You can just be quiet. I don't need your negativity." I hand her a doll wearing a pink gown shedding sparkles. "Look how cute she is!"

The corner of her mouth twitches. She takes the doll and sets it on the shelf behind her. "Fine. I would *totally* wear that dress."

"They probably have your size." I gesture to the matching girl dresses.

"All this pink hurts my eyes," Jacob says, inspecting a miniature popcorn maker. "Okay, that's cool and all, but why would a doll need a popcorn maker? It's not like they can eat any popcorn. Especially that one with braces. Why would a doll need braces?"

"You have absolutely no imagination," I chastise. "They love popcorn. And some of them need help aligning their two teeth."

"So is that why they need a Crock Pot?" Lexie asks, holding up a tiny plastic slow cooker.

"Of course. Some of them really like to cook."

"Okay, speaking of cooking, can we just go get some food now?" Hallie groans. "My stomach sounds like World War II."

"Okay," I say. "The bistro is right upstairs. Wait until you see the napkin rings. In the café is New York, they're hair ties, and here, they're little paper stars. Oh, and you all have to pick a doll to eat with. It's absolutely mandatory."

"There is no way you can get me to do that," Jacob says.

"There is, and I'll find it."

"You *have* to be joking," Hallie groans.

"Nope. Not at all."

"Don't worry, Skylar," Lexie reassures. "I wouldn't miss a chance to eat with Samantha."

The five of us—some more begrudgingly than others—select the tiny person to eat with. Our waitress clips five tiny pink chairs to the table and instructs us to put our dolls in them. I've never seen four more irritated people in my life.

"It'll be fun," I promise them. "They have pizza that looks like a little tic-tac-toe board."

"Fascinating," Hallie mutters, twisting the stem of a daisy from the centerpiece around her finger.

"You must know how much we love you," Harlow says to me.

"Of course I do." I smile at all of them, even Jacob and Lexie, and all of them, even Jacob and Lexie, smile back at me.

Once we order, I'm getting restless. "I'm going to go walk around," I announce.

"I'll come," Lexie says. "We have to go look at the historical characters."

"Definitely. We'll be right back," I tell the others.

Lexie and I wander around the store, pointing at miniatures and giggling at little girls' giggles as they anthropomorphize their dolls, asking them which outfits they'd like or placing them on a salon chair and doing their hair as if they were their little sisters. We go down the escalator to look at the contemporary Truly Me dolls enjoying a wide array of hobbies. Lexie, who's on the varsity swim team, adores the tiny bathing suit, where I squeal over the tiny ice skates that come with their own set of skate guards.

"You've got some serious guts," she tells me when I start bouncing at the sight of the canopy bed. "I don't know anyone else that would be so open about their excitement. You're awesome."

"Oh, really? Thanks," I reply, a bit stunned at the compliment but smiling all the same. That's something I'd have said to her, not expected her to say to me.

"Don't tell anyone I said this, but American Girls are freaking awesome," she says proudly. "You know what, do tell everyone I said this. American Girls are freaking awesome."

I laugh. "They're the best."

"Come on, let's go see which Truly Me's look like us."

We decide doll number fifty-five would be my twin if her eyes were gray (like Molly's) rather than green. Fifty-eight looks exactly like Lexie, down to her perfect dark complexion and corkscrew hair. There aren't any glasses that look like mine, as they're all bright pinks or blues where mine are a plain matte black. We waltz around, deciding what pieces would be in our wardrobe should we ever magically become eighteen inches tall.

"I'd totally wear that outfit," Lexie says, gesturing to a butterfly shirt and a pair of jean shorts.

"Those sandals are so cute," I reply. "I love the sparkles."

"Same. I wish they made those for girls. I'd wear them every day."

"I love that skirt, too" I say, pointing to another one. "The tulle on the bottom is just so adorable."

"You'd look cute in the top, too," she says.

"I don't know. Yellow's not exactly my color."

"Well, maybe you shouldn't make an entire wardrobe of it, but hints of it would do you good."

I finally decide that maybe it would.

"I told you so."

Hallie sighs. "Fine. You told us so. Don't let it go to your head."

Empty plates scatter the table, and not a single belly is still growling. Though no one admitted it until after appetizers, the food caused heavenly explosions in our mouths and raised the bar for all the future food we're going to eat.

"If I die, I want that mac and cheese to have been the last thing I ate," Harlow sighs, looking at her empty bowl.

"Do you think they'll give us more of those tiny cinnamon buns?" Jacob inquires. "I could eat, like, six of those."

"I know, they must make them completely from scratch," Lexie says. "My daddy makes cinnamon buns from scratch on Sunday mornings sometimes, and dear Lord, they are the *best* things in the whole world."

"Your daddy?" Hallie asks, more curious than mocking.

Lexie seems to have gotten this inquisition before—she simply says, "Yeah, one of my dads is Daddy and the other is Dad. It keeps it straight so I don't holler 'Dad' and get the wrong one." We chuckle.

"Yeah, you've only got one sister, though," Hallie says. "I've got three. *And* three brothers. I'd take two dads any day."

"I don't know, can you handle double the dad jokes?"

"You have six siblings?" Jacob asks in disbelief.

"Yep. And I'm the dead middle kid. It's something else, that's for sure, but I'm used to it."

"Still," Lexie says. "I'm impressed you're still kicking."

"Yeah, I—" Jacob freezes, looking at someone over Hallie's shoulder.

"What?" I ask him. "What's wrong?"

"What the hell is Orion Athan doing at the American Girl Store in Washington, D.C.?"

". . . who?"

I can tell who he's looking at now: a tall boy with dark brown hair and skin the color of evening. Every movement he makes through the sea of knee-high children is a calculated dance. I watch him, somewhat transfixed by the light he emanates; he radiates indigo like those black-lights they have in haunted houses that make your white clothing and teeth blue.

"Athan," Hallie says to herself. "Is he Hunter's brother?"

"I didn't know Hunter had a brother," Lexie says.

"I don't know who Hunter is," Harlow announces.

"He doesn't go to our school, does he?"

Jacob ducks a little but doesn't take his eyes off him. "He's a junior, but he goes to this elite boarding school in Rhode Island," he continues. "He's some sort of prodigy. He's only home for like Christmas and the summer and stuff. Thank God for that. He's one of my least favorite people. Like, ever. I hate him with a passion."

"Why?" I ask, watching as Orion smiles at all the little girls surrounding him. He's one of those people you'd ask to jokingly ask to babysit for you as he plays with your kids at some family event so the grown-ups can talk. "He seems so . . . personable."

"Exactly. He's so misleading."

"Like a blacklight," I say.

"I don't know exactly what you mean by that, but yeah, I get it."

"He turns all your white clothes and your teeth blue when they're supposed to be white."

"And he's coming towards us," Harlow says. "Great."

I'm surprised by how little surprise Orion shows, if he feels any at all. Without any apprehension, he leans on our table and plays with a centerpiece. "Jacob, you're far from your little island." He flashes a full-fledged grin that settles into a smirk. His eyes are a very pure green.

Like chlorophyll.

"And you're far from Rhode Island," Jacob replies, his voice even.

"I have good reason to be."

"So do I."

"I'm sure." He looks to us. "I'm sorry, I've been rude. Allow me to introduce myself. I'm—"

"You're Orion Athan," Hallie fills in. "Hunter's older brother."

His smile widens. "Yes. If I may ask, does my reputation precede me?"

"No. Jacob told us as you walked up to our table."

He winks—actually *winks*—at Hallie. "Of course Jake would think to do that."

"Don't call me Jake," Jacob says with no inflection.

"Ah, yes, I forgot. My apologies." Orion toys with one of the plastic daisies that came with our desserts. "So, if you don't mind my inquiry, what brings you to Washington, D.C.?"

"Math convention," Lexie says. "We created this game called Mathopoly and we're sharing it with some teachers."

"Sounds riveting," Orion says. I don't know if I've ever heard anyone use the word *riveting* un-sarcastically before this.

"And why are you here?" Jacob asks. "I didn't know you had a thing for dolls."

Orion's careless manner doesn't fall away or even flicker, but he brushes his belt. He's concealing something that's attached to it. "Oh, you know, just floating around, seeing the world. I enjoy moving from place to place."

"Speaking of moving," Jacob says, standing up, "we have to go. The . . . the convention is starting soon."

"In that case, it was very nice to meet you all," Orion says to us. "And Jacob, you really can't lie. Some lessons from Lexie may do you some good." He winks at us all again before turning around and walking away without looking back.

"He's not that bad," Lexie says. "A little formal, but so's Skylar, and we still hang out with her."

"I don't wink at people," I say. "But I agree."

"But he's probably trying to kill us," Jacob says quietly.

"What do you mean by that?" I try to ask him, but he's already walking out of the store. We follow him.

He stops and turns around. "We have to get out of here," he says.

"Miss Felding said to stay here," I say.

"Really, Skylar, do you care what she told us to do?"

"Honestly? No. But we can't just leave."

"Yeah, we can," Hallie says. "Look, I don't know about you guys, but I think these Eradicators, whatever they may be, are actually a threat."

"Margaret doesn't think so," I remind her.

"Margaret's kind of a bitch, not gonna lie," Hallie says. "So maybe we should take matters into our own hands."

"You mean you want to go against what all the older, more experienced people are telling us?"

"Pretty much," Jacob says.

"Do you know how much trouble we could get into?"

"What, you don't *want* to get into trouble?"

"No, I prefer avoiding that very thing, thank you."

"But if we did something, like dealt with the Eradicators on our own, then maybe the Knowers would let us help more."

"Yeah," Lexie agrees. "They'd *have* to let us actually be Knowers if we did something that serious."

"Or they could get extremely angry with us," I say.

"We barely know them," Hallie says. "So what if we make them mad?"

"They probably have access to nuclear codes, fire ants, and massive amounts of cheese. If we make them angry, they could destroy us or alter time-perceptions or something along those lines, and make us cease to exists."

"First of all, they can't do that," Jacob says. "Second of all, if we don't get caught, then we can get away with anything."

"It's worth a shot, Sky," Lexie says. "Even if it's just a small shot, it's worth one."

I turn to Harlow. "What do you think?"

She breaks into a devilish grin. "I say nothing matters so let's mess some shit up."

"Watch your language," I warn her.

And so I listen to Hallie and Harlow and Lexie and Jacob, and we and hop on the very last train that's headed back towards the National Mall, most likely in order to carry the last few detectives over. And once those automatic doors close behind us at the station of our destination, the train's motor powers down, and a shiver runs down my spine because I didn't even think these trains could turn off.

Chapter Fifteen

We won't run away,
run away in the night.
We're electrified,
energized in the light.

"Electrified"
Truslow

Luckily the room Miss Felding showed us on the first floor of the Castle is still empty, so we take it over. Hallie digs out an old chalkboard and for some reason Jacob has chalk in his pocket (and a million other weird things like an old spark plug, a pen cap, three pieces of Lego, and a little plastic hippo), so Lexie writes everything we know about the Eradicators on the board.

"Okay, so . . . so far,"she starts," all we know is that they remember Days, and that if they die on a Day, they become brain dead, like us. And that's it."

"Well," Hallie comments, "it's enough to go off of."

"Except we have no idea where they're based," Jacob says. "They could be in Bangladesh for all we know."

"Good point," Lexie sighs. "They could just be visiting for the Day."

I think about the Day up till this point. I must have seen an Eradicator at one point. Unless there's only a few of them like there's only a few of us—which I believe there must be more of them because it has to take more than what we have to blow up a Smithsonian—then at one point or another, I'm sure I've seen one. That makes me extremely apprehensive. With that logic, one could be in the building right now.

"There're here," I say without looking at anyone. "I know it. I don't know how, I just . . ." I stop suddenly. "Orion."

"What about Orion?" Jacob asks, though I think he already knows my answer.

"I saw him. When Natural History exploded, he was there, color-changing eyes and all."

"This is a fantastic time to mention that, Skylar."

"I just thought of it," I protest. "I didn't realize that it was him. I didn't know he existed until twenty minutes ago. But now that I know, I think he's an Eradicator."

"Except, do we know if Eradicator eyes change color?" Hallie demands.

"If they can remember Days, thus having an altered perception of time like we have, then it's a sure possibility," I say. "At least, it's sure enough that we can assume their position for the time being."

"And where exactly are we assuming their position is?" Jacob asks. "D.C. is huge, let alone the whole world. Seriously, they could be anywhere. Anywhere big enough to hold them all."

"Then we'll work from that," Lexie says. "We'll just rule out all the small places first. And obviously Natural History, because why would they bomb themselves? And not the Castle because we'd have noticed them by now."

"Are we really gonna just assume that they're located here because Skylar saw some dude's eyes change color? That doesn't seem like enough to me. We need more solid facts."

Harlow groans. "I thought you guys were supposed to be geniuses or something!"

Hallie shoots her a look. "And your point is?"

"Didn't Miss Felding seem really nervous when we came in?"

"What are you implying?" I ask Harlow.

"She saw one of them!" she answers. "From the moment she saw something out the window that went above *all* of your heads, she was different but didn't tell us why. She probably saw one of the Eradicators that she recognized and realized they were here. Then she told that Margaret woman."

"So they must have known we were here, too," Lexie says, "so they blew up Natural History thinking we were in there."

"So then where are they?" Jacob thinks aloud. "Again, they could be anywhere. How are we ever going to find them?"

"Trial and error," Lexie states.

"I don't know if you've noticed this," Jacob says, "but the entire city is on lockdown. There's no way we can get anywhere. No one's going in or out of any of the buildings here."

"We'll have some cover," Hallie says. "There's got to be tons of guards and police officers and stuff around. They'll be here until they find the Eradicators and realize they did this."

"And in the morning, none of it will matter," Harlow says. "No one's gonna remember it. I know I won't."

"Okay, so where could they be?" Lexie turns back to the chalkboard.

"American History?" I suggest. "It's definitely big enough."

"Yeah, maybe," she says, and she writes it under the crossed out *NH* and *Castle*.

"What about one of the art museums?" Jacob wonders. "They have so many tiny rooms and twisty hallways that anyone could hide in there. It's like the world's most expensive maze."

"And Air and Space," Harlow says. "It's got so many little corridors and stuff, but everyone's too focused on the planes on the ceilings to care."

"What about the lesser known ones?" Hallie says. "Like the American Indian Museum or one of the tinier galleries?"

Lexie adds them all.

"But are you sure they're in the Mall?" I ask. "They could be anywhere around here. In the basement of an apartment building, the American Girl Store, somewhere in Maryland, Serbia—anywhere."

"I told you, they can handle it," a hushed voice descending the stairs says. I recognize it at once as Miss Felding's.

"It's unnecessary to worry about them or have them worry about us," Margaret's voice replies. "They won't bother us if we just get them out of our hair."

Miss Felding sighs. "I don't know if I can do that to them. They're brilliant, actually."

"They'll be out of our hair completely soon enough," Margaret reminds Miss Felding. "Then we can work on our midnight plans."

"About the midnight plans," Miss Felding starts hesitantly, "I don't think they're the best thing."

"They'll wipe out an entire threat, Lea, you know that."

"But I don't—"

Lexie is almost done erasing the board when their heads pop into the room, and we have no time to hide before Margaret and Miss Felding are standing in the doorway.

"What are you doing here?" Margaret asks us, cutting Miss Felding off. "I thought I had Miss Felding tell you to go to Tyson's Corner and stay there." There is a stack of paper in her hand; they are simple eight-and-a-half by eleven, black printer ink, marked up with red pen. She must see me looking at it because she sets it on a nearby table, but she makes a huge mistake and leaves them face-up.

"It was closed," Lexie says. "Probably because that building blew up. Not good for business, I'm guessing."

"We came back here because we thought it was safer than wandering around the city," Hallie shrugs. "'Cause, you know, we're problem solvers. We solve problems."

Praying that Margaret or Miss Felding won't notice, I glance again at the papers she set on the table; the top one is a map of Air and Space, all marked up with red X's. I bite my lip to hide a smile. There it is, a substantial lead.

"So, what are you guys going to do about the exploded building?" Lexie inquires.

"It's not at all that pressing of a matter," Margaret says quickly and sharply. "It's not an issue you need worry about."

"Do you think it was Eradicators?" Harlow asks Margaret. I throw her a glance. Does she not know not to mention the enemy with the people who could thwart our investigation? An investigation of which she was never meant to be a part?

"Eradicators will not hurt us," she dismisses, unable to mask the edge in her voice. "They don't have the chance. You shouldn't even know what an Eradicator *is*," Miss Felding visibly shudders here, since she's the one who inadvertently sent us on this chase, "let alone be worrying about them hurting you. We have them under control."

Yes, but how? Can't you at least tell us how *you have them under control?* I don't ask it, though. I don't want to get caught in Margaret's crosshairs. The rest of the room seems to agree with me because no one says a word.

Margaret takes a breath and grins so placidly that you'd think it were just a normal Thursday. "Excellent. Well, I'm sorry that your first meeting is an unusual one. You just stay in here until we send for you."

"We really can't help with anything?" Hallie asks. "Why not?"

"As I've said, you're still very young," Margaret says, and she leaves it at that. "Miss Felding will be back to get you in a few hours. And, for goodness sake, *stay* in here. For your well-being." The tone of her voice adds *And for mine.*

She's not even gone a full five minutes before we're out of the room and on our way.

"Air and Space," I say. "That's where they are."

"How do you know?" Hallie wonders.

"A map. Margaret had a map for it. That's what she was holding. It was a map of the building, all marked with little X's. She knows that they're all in there."

Lexie flaps her hands around. "Okay, a solid lead. We should split up and—"

"I thought we weren't going to split up again!" I protest.

"But we don't know if that's where they are for certain," Hallie says. "I'll stay here and do research and stuff on other possible places. Harlow, why don't you stay, too?" Harlow starts to protest but Hallie cuts her off. "You three go do a sweep of Air and Space and see if there's anything that seems weird. Everyone have their phones?"

We all say that we do.

"Good. See you in an hour."

"Wait, Hallie! What are we even looking for?"

She and Harlow are already gone, and I swear to God that Margaret is watching us from the glass cylinder atop the Castle.

Our walk to Air and Space is anything but peaceful. We spend the time on the outskirts of the Mall, walking behind the buildings, attempting to avoid the thousands of guards and their overly watchful eyes. I wish I were closer to them, so I could see what color they all are. I find eyes amazing, how they come in rainbows. And mine, how they *are* a little rainbow, morphing their color like a river, reflecting whatever color the sky happens to be at that moment, be it green or blue or the color of slate—

"Skylar?" Jacob's talking to me.

"Oh, sorry, did you say something? I'm sorry."

"Yeah. It's fine, don't worry. I just have no idea what we're supposed to be looking for. Like, there's not gonna be a glowing door that say 'Eradicate the Knowers' on it. It's going to be really hard to find anything. Like, what if we end up needing a key to get in or something? Then what?"

"Well, I'd guess a secret passageway would be too forward," I ponder aloud. "Maybe not . . . honestly, I don't exactly know what to expect from these people. We may have to resort to a secret passageway hunt. I've always wanted to go on one of those."

"But how are we going to do that without being noticed?" Lexie asks. "Tapping walls isn't non-suspicious activity, really, and that's what all these police guys are on the look out for."

"I don't know," I admit. "This wasn't my plan. I wanted to ignore it all, frankly."

"Well, since we're not doing that, do you have a different plan?"

"No. I don't make plans."

Jacob gives me a sideways glance. "I wonder why I find that so hard to believe."

The front doors are not only closed, but there's a couple hundred minotaurs guarding them. Where do they even find people that large?

"So I guess the walking-in-through-the-front-door option has been eliminated," I say, "so, what now?"

"What do you think?" Lexie tilts her head and looks at me.

"Well, since going home, making a cup of tea, and binge-reading an Agatha Christie novel clearly isn't an option," I reason, "then I suggest finding an alternate entry."

"What, you *don't* want to walk right past those human action-figures right into the land of interrogation and pain?" Jacob says.

"Please, I'm trying to think," I say, and I put my hands over my ears and close my eyes to block out all the minutia interfering with my thought process. Then my eyes pop open and I take my hands off my ears. "We go through one of the emergency exits."

"Alarms," Lexie says immediately. "What if it sets off the alarms?"

"Then . . . we run?"

"I don't know— Jacob!"

Jacob's already gone over to the nearest door, which is tucked in a corner and can't be seen by the massive guards, so we follow him over. He then runs his fingers over the hinges, taps the center a few times, and puts his ear against the doorframe.

"There's no alarm on this one," he says to us.

"And how can you tell?" Lexie asks.

"I— I just can. I can't really explain it. But this door doesn't have an alarm."

"Or a handle," I point out, gesturing to the general spot in which a doorknob should be.

"That part's easy," Lexie says. "Anyone have a lever?"

"Sure, Lexie," Jacob says, "I'll just pull my handy lever out of my pocket."

"We probably have a spade, or at least a trowel," I say, pointing to an abandoned gardener's cart, left in the flowers.

Lexie goes over to it. "We have a chisel *and* a spade. Which is easier?"

"Spade," I decide.

"Perfect." She lodges it in the doorframe and looks to Jacob. "You sure this thing's not gonna go off?"

"I'm pretty sure," he replies. "A good seventy-percent sure."

"Good enough for me," Lexie says, and she pushes the door open. It doesn't make a sound. Leaving the spade in the grass outside, we enter the museum in silence.

One would think it would be quieter now than it was earlier, but I actually think there's more activity; instead of leisurely gazing at aircraft and moon rocks, people are working, moving through the museum at extreme speeds, looking for footprints or gunpowder or whatever else they think could lead them to the bomber. Then I'm suddenly overwhelmed with the worry that one of the planes swinging from the ceiling could fall at any minute, squishing everyone beneath it. I spend the rest of our journey through the main gallery apprehensively looking up with my back against the wall so no one notices me.

The three of us wander aimlessly and wordlessly. I notice nothing out of the ordinary. Everything looks exactly the same from the last time we were here. I count the floor tiles and note that there's the same amount as before. I look at display cases and see nothing that seems out of place. Each plane remains suspended on the ceiling. All things are in order.

There's a man walking past us. He is the only person I can see who isn't in uniform or wielding a badge like a shield. There's something else very curious about him: he keeps touching his belt. This is a subconscious movement. He wears a blue cashmere sweater and khaki pants with a plain leather belt that's quite worn. About mid-thirties or early forties, I'd guess; married, judging by his ring; and a father, evident by the gray dusting his black hair and his tired yet fulfilled eyes. Those eyes, they look at everyone fearfully. And, as they glaze across the room, they morph from an amber-ish brown to borderline crimson.

I find myself following him, and Jacob and Lexie follow me. He moves toward the back of the museum and approaches a door. I watch as he gently presses the fingerprint of his thumb onto a panel, opens the door with ease, and slips into it without turning the light on. I rush behind him and catch the door just before it closes.

"It's probably just a janitor's closet," Lexie says, taking the heavy door from me. "He's probably just a janitor. Or investigating the janitor's closet."

"But it might *not* be just a janitor's closet," I counter. "What janitor has eyes change that color and wears a cashmere sweater to mop, and what janitor closet has such an advanced security system to protect their brooms and their Windex? If you wanted a secret hideout, you wouldn't hide in plain sight, right? But you *would*."

"You make absolutely no sense," Jacob says.

"No, yes I do! See, it's plain enough that it's overlooked, but it's not so plain that it becomes suspicious."

He doesn't look any less confused, but he says, "Okay, we can check it out if you want, but I'm pretty sure it's just nothing."

"It's not *nothing*. Nothing's ever *nothing*. At the very least, it's a humble janitor's closet, and that man was a humble janitor."

We move into the tiny room, which is pitch black. "I can't see anything," I whisper.

"Really? I could've sworn you had night vision," Jacob whispers back.

"That didn't come in the Knower package deal," Lexie says.

"You don't have a flashlight?" he asks.

"No, why would I have a flashlight?" Lexie says.

"We're surely going walk into a wall or—" I take a step forward and begin tumbling down a set of stairs concealed by the dark. I land on my left arm, and my glasses fly off. "—or stairs."

"You okay?" Lexie calls.

I fumble around for my glasses. "I'm okay. Don't step on my glasses. I can't find them."

"Okay, well, just . . . feel around for them, I guess," Jacob says.

"Oh my gosh, I thought we were geniuses." I take my phone out of my pocket and turn on the flashlight app. The light illuminates a gray concrete floor and bland walls to match. I find my glasses and put them on.

"We're *selective* geniuses," Jacob says, and I see his light pop on at the top of the stairs.

"I'm a genius who threw my phone in the reflecting pool," Lexie sighs as she and Jacob descend the stairs in a more conventional manner. "I know, you wish you had my intellect."

"What is this place? There isn't any cleaning supplies," Jacob wonders.

"Come on, let's keep walking," I whisper, standing up. The light from our phones leads us down a concrete hallway. It's utterly featureless and seems endless.

"We're probably in the collections underneath the museum," Lexie says as we approach a bunch of other doors.

I peek behind one and see a dark room of wooden crates and the wing of a silver plane. "Woah."

"Yeah."

"This has got to be highly illegal."

"Probably."

"So, no Eradicators down here?"

"It's a pretty big basement," Jacob says. "They could be in the other half."

"Or not down here at all," Lexie counters.

"That too, I guess, but let's keep walking."

The absurdity of this mission suddenly hits me. What happens if we waltz right in and they immediately tell we're imposters and kill us right then and there? It could happen. In fact, it *probably* will happen. "We should just turn back," I say, hoping I don't sound whiney.

"If you want. But there's got to be something at the end of this, even if it's just an exit."

"Okay, fine," I capitulate. He makes a good point, even though it's not a point I would want to acknowledge as being good.

We walk for about three more minutes until a light at the end of the tunnel is visible. Our pace quickens, desperate to get out of this tunnel. I'm not even claustrophobic and I think it's closing in on me.

A ginormous room bustling with people waits for us at the very end of the hall. It's lit by flickering florescent bulbs on the low ceiling that cast strange shadows onto tables of scrap parts and weapons and people typing on clicking keyboards. Computer screens and whiteboards line the unfinished walls. Everyone's eyes are fearfully determined and sometimes change color without warning, and although I wasn't sure what to expect, this is completely what I was expecting.

"I think we found the Eradicator's headquarters," I say.

"Really? I wasn't aware," Jacob says in reply.

"You're really awful, you know."

"Okay, so what now?" Lexie wonders. "We found it. Now what? We spy on them?"

"Hey! You!" An angry voice behind us is yelling to us. I tense.

"Oh my gosh, they know we're not them and they're going to murder us," I whisper to them.

"Just act natural," Jacob says before turning to the voice. It comes from a tall, wiry man with slate colored hair and nearly black eyes. "Yes? How can we help you?"

"Neophyte initiation is in five minutes," the man shouts at us. "Why are you not in the Initiation Center?"

"Wait, what?"

"Were you not paying attention at all during the tour?"

"No, I— I was totally paying attention. It's . . . it's been a long morning."

"We'll get there right away," Lexie says.

"You'd better." The man turns away and walks in the opposite direction, not looking back at us to see if we've obeyed his orders. He must know we'd be foolish to do anything but.

"Okay, let's get out of here," I say. "We found it, so we can go—"

"No, we shouldn't," Lexie says. "We should go peek our heads in and see what this whole initiation ritual is. Dig up more information. See what their motives are and then try to stop them."

"Fine. Then let's go hide somewhere and watch—"

"Why would we hide?" Jacob says. "There's no better way to learn about the Eradicators then to become them."

Chapter Sixteen

As a child you would wait
and watch from far away,
but you always knew
that you'd be the one that work
while they all play.
In youth, you'd lay
awake at night and scheme
of all the things that you would change,
but it was just a dream.

"Warriors"
Imagine Dragons

"You can't *actually* be serious."

"I'm totally serious," Jacob replies. "If we go to this weird induction, we'll learn all about the inner workings and stuff. We'll get firsthand information that could help us later."

"And what if it's dangerous?" I cross my arms.

"Then we'll find a way to escape," Jacob says. "Come on, Skylar, it's at least worth a shot."

"There is no way in hell that I'm doing that," I say. "They'll notice that we're outsiders, especially if they can presume like we can, and we'll be incarcerated at the blink of an eye."

"But maybe they can't, and maybe we won't. We don't know about any of that."

"We don't know *anything* about them!"

"Which is exactly why we have to figure them out!"

He's right; I hate it. "Okay, fine. We've only got five minutes, so we'd best find this Initiation Center soon."

"Thank you, Skylar. You're amazing."

"Oh, be quiet."

We wander around for a little bit, to no avail, before Lexie buckles and asks someone. The woman is surprisingly kind and points us in the right direction. We thank her and she smiles a bright smile that's ostensibly genuine.

An arched opening leads into another large, shallow-ceilinged room. This one is circular and is lit only by a plethora of blood-tinted candles. I'm assuming these people have a flair for the dramatic, as I can see unlit electric lights on the ceiling. About thirty people stand around the circumference of the room, their faces concealed by the lack of light. They try not to get their clothes caught on fire, and I follow suit. They may be unnecessary and pompous at best, but I will admit that they are indeed setting a threatening mood and cause my blood to course a bit faster.

"You're almost late," a woman says to us. "Get in the circle." She points to an opening in the circle of people.

The woman strides into the center of the circle. "Welcome, Neophytes," she says. Her voice is made of old honey that's sat in the cupboard too long and is now a crunchy, crystallized mess. "My name is Andrea Jennings, and I am the Neophyte director and assistant director of the Efficacy. Some of you probably knew that already. Some of you know nothing." A few people, who most likely fit into the former category, murmur in agreement, though no one talks at her volume.

Andrea paces the circumference, looking at everyone bordering it. "You are an elite group of fighters. Some of you may have known that this day was coming for your entire lives. Others have found out maybe only today. That doesn't matter. When this day is done, washed away with time, you will have skills you couldn't even comprehend before your training. You will re-member today forever though no one else will.

"What you will be doing today is going through a series of challenges that will test your strength, mentally and physically. At the end of the day, you will be fully immersed into the Eradicator organization if we deem you ready to serve us."

The look on Andrea's pointed face is sinister. Whatever she's got planned for these inductees is surely awful, and I almost feel bad for them.

"Oral drill," she says, coming closer to us. "What is the sole purpose of the Eradicators? You." She points to a short girl with silhouetted ringlets.

"To eradicate inequalities," she states, brimming with confidence I'm somewhat surprised she has. "People must be treated equally to ensure that everyone lives a fulfilled life. Our prime targets of abolition are governments and monarchies. Also, we are researching other smaller groups that are trying to change things and trying to stop them."

"Exactly," Andrea replies. "All people that put themselves above others are considered immoral and therefore must be stopped. Our primary target is the U.S. government, but first we must take out smaller groups, like the Knowers, who we've ignored for years, believing they weren't a threat, but now, we have reason to believe they have more power than they're letting on. So to take them out, we have to extensively research them and find their weakness. Why?" She points at another member of the circle.

"Knowers have a lot of connections," his voice says. "They can do anything they want underground. They can control everything they want, even time."

"Even time," Andrea repeats. "We don't believe they know it, but we remember the day they make reverse itself, so we meet on this Day, capital D, too. Our minds are almost at their capacity. They aren't our *very* top priority as of now, but we still have to learn more about them if we want to take them out, like where they're based—"

"The Smithsonian Castle," the boy says. "They're located at the top of the Castle."

"Don't make things up," Andrea tells him sharply.

"I'm not," he says. "I overheard some Knowers talking to each other. They said they were going to the Castle today."

"And how do you know these people are Knowers?"

"I told you, I heard them talking. This morning. They were just openly talking about it. I think they were explaining the whole system to another girl—she looked scared. I heard everything about how they invented today and what they do and stuff. They're not just normal people who want to do stuff. They're evolved or something. Like, their eyes change color. And they have these heads that work differently, like they have ADHD or something like that and can solve problems super well, but it also makes them not fit in and kind of hate themselves."

Jacob tenses next to me.

Andrea gives him a long, hard stare then turns to everyone else and says hurriedly, "You all go into the Main Room and look for your desk so you know where it is. Then we'll move on. You, Athan, you stay with me. I'm guessing you already know where your desk is anyway. It's right next to your brother's." She ushers the boy out of the room without a second glance at us.

We file out of the room, and I can finally see the faces of some of the young Eradicators. They all look like perfectly normal kids, not people capable of the things they talked about in the circle. One wears a One Direction shirt and another has half of a best friends necklace. One of the boys has on a soccer jersey and another, a Nirvana tee. Perfectly normal kids, not members of a sociopathic cult.

"Okay, who knows about us, and how?" Jacob whispers once we're safely out of earshot of anyone.

"Someone from school," Lexie says. She looks more grave than I've ever seen her before. "It must be. Is there an Eradicator from our school?"

"Knowing our school," Jacob says, "probably."

"We've got to tell them," I say. "The Knowers, I mean. We have to tell them to find a new headquarters. They can't stay there now that they know. They'll blow it up immediately, just like they did with Natural History."

Jacob takes out his phone. "No cell service down here. Fantastic."

"Can we go back upstairs and call them? They have to know."

"We can't tell them," Lexie says. "We're kinda doing this behind their backs, remember? We're just gonna have to hope they don't bomb the Castle."

"I'm sorry, but when it comes to possible bomb detonation, *hoping* isn't good enough."

Lexie ponders this then says, "I'll go upstairs and call Hallie and tell her. Maybe she and Harlow can, like, keep an eye out for any suspicious activity. That's what they do on crime shows. Maybe that can help us here."

"Please be careful," I tell her.

"I'll be fine, Sky." She disappears among the rows of desks. I can't remember when she started calling me Sky.

Jacob and I pretend to find our desks and then make our way back to the circular Initiation Center. My heart is pumping so hard, I'm sure I'm about to burst a capillary. Who knows what these people could do to us, even if they believe we're their own? And if they realize that we're not . . . I can't imagine.

The PA system from the museum upstairs calls for Henry McClaim, and I wonder why. Maybe someone found the cell phone he lost, or maybe he's a little kid who can't find his mom, or maybe he's the head detective and they've just made a breakthrough. Whoever he is, he's having a better Day than I am. Most likely, he doesn't know of the capitalization. I wish I didn't, either.

"Can't we just leave?" I ask Jacob.

"No, we can't. Who else is going to get the information on them?"

"I don't know. Someone capable?"

"Are you saying we're not capable?"

"No, *I'm* not capable," I say. "You're . . . intrepid. Completely and utterly intrepid. You could probably do anything you wanted to."

"Well, I don't know about that, but thanks. And, come on, Bubble of Sunshine, you're totally capable of this."

"Jacob, I get scared whenever my parents leave the house because I'm afraid something will happen to them. I don't like being in the car because I'm afraid it's going to crash. I hate answering questions in class because I worry that I'll get it wrong and people won't like me and I'll be a social outcast. I'm, like—"

Don't get too close to people whose smiles shoot bullets.

"You're like what?"

"Nothing," I cover quickly. *I'm, like, nervous all the time. You're not helping.* "It's not important. We can stay here."

He looks at me for a second. A thousand thoughts race behind his eyes. I watch them change color in the florescent light. "You're weird. In a good way."

"Thank you. Let's go become Eradicators and possibly die."

"Or possibly *not* die."

"But it *could* happen."

"But it could *not* happen."

We get back to the cult-esque circle. One by one, the young Eradicators trickle back into the poorly-lit room and take their places around the circumference. Andrea waltzes back into the room once everyone's returned with a boy at her side. They're talking intently. She looks absolutely riveted, and the shadow of the boy's chest swells. She sends him next to me.

"I'm assuming you've all found your desks," Andrea begins. "That will be the easiest thing you do all day. We're going to take a look at the Efficacy next. You're in for a treat."

The room buzzes; "the Efficacy" must be common Eradicator lingo that we're not familiar with. The buzzing stops abruptly when Jacob asks, "What's the Efficacy?" I mentally face-palm.

"How do you not know?" the boy next to me says.

"How do all of you know?" Jacob counters with.

"You're about to find out exactly what the Efficacy is," Andrea says. I truly see her for the first time and am fairly unimpressed; she's got stringy dirt-colored hair, skin so pale it's ghost-like, and muddy blue eyes. The only thing of remote interest is her charm bracelet—it's a cheap silver chain that most nine-year-olds get for their birthdays. There are three charms on it: a purple starfish, a gold fleur-de-lis, and a silver sailboat. The starfish and fleur-de-lis are cheaply made, their gilded plating flaking off, but the sailboat looks much newer and much nicer. From where I stand, I can see tiny ropes and portholes and billowing sails frozen as if a wind were filling them at this minute, all carved into a shiny sterling silver.

The boy next to me runs right over to Andrea and helps her lead the pack. Jacob and I hang towards the back because everyone else seems way too eager to see this thing, whatever *this thing* actually is. The room we're led into is really small, and it's a tight squeeze. I'm pressed up against like three people, and I'm too short to see anything.

"Welcome to the Efficacy," Andrea says. The buzzing begins again.

Frankly, it's underwhelming. It's literally a small silver box the size of a milk carton sitting on the table. There aren't even any fun dials or buttons; it's just a hunk of silver with a thick black wire coming out the back. It's a piece of unbuttered toast compared to our Mechanism soufflé.

"This is the most powerful computer, possibly in existence," Andrea gushes. "Everything we are comes from this box. All the information we have on the government and various monarchies and small groups like the Knowers is on here. All of the stuff we have on ourselves is on here. It can store all of it and send it to our fingertips in fractions of seconds."

"Will we ever get to use it?" someone asks. The eagerness in their voice is sort of frightening.

"Not unless you're trained," Andrea says. "And you're not being trained today."

The disappointment in the room is audible.

"Okay, now get back to the circle."

Very anticlimactic, I can't help thinking, but I guess that's better than a room of medieval torture devices.

Once we've squished out of the tiny room and are in the circle, she continues with, "Next, you'll learn to shoot a gun."

"Shoot a what?" I can't help whispering out loud.

"Get used to it," the boy next to me says. "They're gun fanatics." I'm beginning to not like this boy—he's quite the know-it-all.

Andrea continues on. "Guns are an important part in overthrowing systems. Someone tell me why."

The boy's hand shoots up and he speaks without waiting to be called upon. "They promote fear. When people are scared, they're reduced to nothing but animal instincts, and that makes super powerful people nothing but freaked out little kids. Even if they're never fired, they still make people scared." Why does his voice sound so familiar?

"Very good, Mr. Athan," Andrea says.

Orion—I must be right—must be an Eradicator. That's why he's in Washington, D.C. and not in Rhode Island, why he was at the American Girl Store, why Jacob so clearly didn't trust him and clearly never has, why his eyes are so indefinite.

"We're going to go outside to the field behind the museum and there you'll be distributed your guns. We will practice shooting and learning about the guns."

Once again, we move out of the room and into the gritty light.

Jacob recognizes the Eradicator next to me before I do. "Hunter?"

Orion doesn't stand in the circle with us. No, Hunter Athan is the one who turns to face us and says, "Jacob?"

Chapter Seventeen

Now I'm freezing in winter of the heartache,
you ask me how it feels.
Well, time wounds all heals,
Ice preserves these bitter chills.

"Turning Into Water"
Maybird

"What the hell are you doing here?" Hunter's whisper is harsher than any whisper I've heard.

"You're an Eradicator?" Jacob asks. His face is hard, but his voice holds essences of betrayal. "You . . . You and Orion are Eradicators."

Hunter is silent.

"You heard *everything*. When we told Harlow . . . you were in there, weren't you? Taking a test or whatever. And you just— you just spit it back out to . . . to *them*."

"I had to."

Jacob's eyes turn from sepia brown to a dark orange in an instant. It's very cool to watch; the colors just suddenly turn into each other without warning. "No. You didn't *have to*. You didn't *have* to risk getting us all killed. Or have Natural History blown up. Do you have any idea what you just did to us?"

"I'm sorry." He teems with apathy.

"You were my best friend." His voice cracks, just barely imperceptible. "I trusted you with everything. Literally everything, and now they know *that*, too."

"I'm sorry," Hunter repeats. "I had to tell them. They needed it."

"No, you didn't," Jacob says. "You didn't have to lead them right to us, and you didn't have to tell them *that*. There's a million other things you could've done."

"I—"

Jacob turns on his heel and begins to walk away. I try to keep up with him, but he's a good four or five inches taller and his gait is twice as fast. I follow him down the pitch black hallway and up the stairs. He walks out of the museum and plops down on the front steps. Once I catch up, I sit next to him.

He's very quiet for awhile, until he says, "Why him? Of all people?"

"I'm sorry," I say quietly. "I'm really, really sorry."

"Me too," he says. "I can't believe I ever trusted him. God, why didn't I *know*? Why couldn't I *tell*?"

"How could you have possibly known?"

He sighs. "I . . . I don't know. I should've . . . I should have just *known* though. He is—*was*—my best friend. I should've realized at some point. How could I have not?"

I have no idea what to say in this situation, so I stay silent.

"Hey, guys," Lexie runs towards us. "So I told Hallie and— What's wrong?"

"It was Hunter. He's one of them," Jacob says quietly.

"Hunter Athan? Like, your best friend Hunter?"

"No, the other Hunter we know."

"And Orion? Is he one, too?"

"Yeah, probably."

"Wait, so how did he find out about us?"

"When we told Harlow, he must have been listening," I say.

"But it's really bad for him to know that."

"Yeah, Lexie, we figured that out," Jacob snaps back.

"I'm sorry, Jacob," Lexie says quietly.

"Thanks, Lexie," he says. "I'm sorry, too."

"So are we continuing with Initiation?" I ask tentatively.

"I'm not going back in there," Jacob says. "I'll just end up punching him."

"I'll do it," my mouth says without my brain's permission.

"Do what?"

"Go get initiated."

"Sky, you sure?" Lexie asks.

"No. Not at all. But if I send one of you guys in there . . . you're all made of explosives. Who knows what hell you'll unleash?"

"Um . . . well, okay." Lexie looks at me as if she can't believe me. I can't believe me either, really.

"Skylar, you can't go in there *alone*," Jacob says. "Who knows what they'll put you through?"

"Are you *trying* to make me change my mind?"

"Um, yes?"

"Well, stop. Someone's got to do it." I grin haphazardly— this isn't something to grin about. "And it's got to be me."

"At least let me come with you," Lexie protests. "No one should go in there alone, let alone you."

"Exactly. I seem so unlikely. Look at me. I'm a Munchkin."

Lexie puts her hand on my shoulder. "At the first sign of danger, run."

"I'll be running before danger even knows it's dangerous."

I mean, I knew I was eccentric, but this is absolutely insane of me.

With my back against the wall, I wait until someone else comes and unlocks the door with a touch of a thumb on the panel. It takes almost seven minutes, but someone eventually does come and unlock the door. I slip in then go down into the crypt-esque hallway. The dwindling battery on my phone serves as my light source. (In fact, this is when I realize I should probably put it on low-battery mode.) I make it back to the main room, where I'm immediately barked at to go join the other newbies outside.

"Could you help me get there?" I ask in the sweetest voice I can manage. "It's my first time here, and I don't know my way around that well."

"I would love to," a voice says. "Please forgive me, I never did learn your name."

Of course Orion Athan would be here. I shouldn't even be that shocked. "Skylar. Hi."

His little grin tells me that he knows the real reason I'm here. "Skylar. What a beautiful name. Is it Celtic?"

"Dutch, actually," I say.

"Of course. Dutch. Here, I'll show you where the Neophytes are training, and you are welcome to join them. I'm sure you're very interested in their initiation." Leading me down another hall, he asks no more questions. Not because he doesn't have them, but because he already has the answers.

There's another staircase at the far end of the hall, one that's wider and far better lit than the other one. Orion leads me up. It opens into another small janitorial closet, though this one has its light on and feels much bigger because of that. We walk through Air and Space and leave the building through one of the back doors. Orion appears to know this building as if it were his house. The little field behind the building is completely lacking any guard or fireman but is filled with the young Eradicators, each wielding a small silver handgun. I see the fire in the eyes of the Neophytes. They look as if they've been waiting ages to do this. I momentarily consider turning around and running from this precariousness. Everything about this is just so uncertain, and I hate uncertainty.

"Alright, they're just over there," Orion says to me. His smile disarms me for a second. "I hope you find what you're looking for."

"And what's that? What exactly am I looking for?"

"Oh, I don't know," he says. "I only know that you're looking for something, though I'm unclear as to what it is. Please, my dear Skylar, if you find it, I'd love to know."

Based on the spark in his eye, however, I can tell he already does.

"I will," I reply.

He gives me a little wink and saunters off.

Hunter catches my eye as soon as I join the circle. I quickly break contact and stand at a place in the circle where he can't see me. Then I realize I need to grab a gun from a foam-lined case in the center. The guns inside are a dark silver. I stop myself as I reach for one; *Skylar, this is a freaking gun, and you are the biggest idiot in the world.* I reach for one again, and I stop myself again. I've been taught since my kindergarten years that *gun* is synonymous with *bad.* I bite my lip so hard that I'm afraid I'll taste blood and snatch one at the speed of light.

I avoid the trigger at all costs as I turn it over and over in my hands. The metal feels like ice against my skin. My eyes are so wide that they're about to blow up like little balloons.

"Where are those other two?" Andrea asks me, breaking me from my daze.

My mind races for an answer. "Um, they didn't want to . . . They gave up. They suddenly decided—well, not *suddenly,* I mean, they'd thought about it for awhile, but still fairly quickly, it all happened—that they didn't want to be Eradicators. Well, at least weren't *ready* to be. Not ready for this magnitude of a commitment, you know?"

She narrows her hard eyes at me. "They aren't allowed to do that."

"Yes," I say simply. Not many people can mess up the world's simplest lie.

"Fine, I'll take care of it later. Just be quiet."

She moves back in the center of the makeshift circle. "The first thing you learn today is how to shoot. These guns were engineered by Eradicators and highlight our natural abilities. The bullets they fire are twenty-seven percent faster than those of the average pistol, and the gunshot is over fifty decibels quieter than the average. These are extraordinary little machines.

"The guns we're handing out are now your issued guns. These are yours to keep. Our facility is equipped with just about seven hundred of these things because they're cheap to make. These are yours to take with you everywhere you go. Since you'll wake up in the morning without the gun at your house, they will be mailed. Your parents will know all about it."

Then that means fifteen-year-olds—and at least one of those on our island—are keeping firearms in their bedrooms, and apparently their parents know about it, too. That doesn't seem safe to me. Imagine a teenager with raging hormones mad at his friend for kissing his girlfriend or wearing the same dress as her to a party or something else completely mundane and then bursting into a room and shooting their backstabbing friend right in the chest. The horror isn't that far-fetched, especially with these potentially unstable fresh Eradicators as the culprits.

"Isn't that dangerous?" I curse my impulsivity.

"No, it's not *dangerous,* because I'm going to teach you how to use them." Andrea is fed up with me, and it's blatant. "Be quiet."

"Of course. Sorry. I wasn't thinking. I'll just—"

"Stop apologizing."

"Sorry. Oh, wait, sorry. I mean not-sorry."

Andrea does her thing, prowling around the edge of the circle and looking everyone in the eye. I drift in and out of focus as she rambles about the pieces of violence that we're holding. I suppose it may be important for me to listen, but I've given up on her listless voice. When the circle begins to move and form a line, I try harder. From the stance our line has taken, we have a clear view of the bustling Mall about fifty feet away.

"Now, target practice is probably too basic for you, what with your natural accuracy," she says, "so we'll go right to moving targets. You'll each aim your gun at a person walking by and attempt to hit them."

Shoot a person? I almost ask Andrea to repeat herself because what she is asking of us is ludicrous. *Shoot a living, breathing, human person?*

The first person in line, a short, stocky boy with hair the color of a rotting carrot, takes his stance. He raises his gun up so he can just see over it, and he fires. A woman clutches her heart and abruptly sinks into a disheveled heap.

"They'll be fine in the morning," Hunter whispers to me, as if that somehow makes the whole ordeal better, or if it makes me like *him* better. Neither of those hold true.

"You have no right to say that." I turn to face him and hope I look as angry as I feel. "You're acting as if her life were disposable."

"For our purposes, it is."

I fire my worst insult in my repertoire: "You're a downright jerk."

"Downright." Another gunshot, and this time, followed by a scream.

"Downright."

"You don't hear many people rocking the *downright* anymore."

I turn to my gun so I can figure out how to load it. It's completely foreign; it could be made of another language. I don't want to start moving parts around because the odds of it accidentally shooting me are probably around one-hundred-twenty percent. Hunter sighs, takes my gun and hands me his, and loads it in about twenty seconds.

"Yet you hear a lot about people stabbing their so-called best friends in the backs with rusty spikes," I counter. "I'd much rather hear more *downrights*."

I swear his rock facade flickers for a second, but it's probably only because I want it to. "It doesn't matter."

"Try telling Jacob that," I say. "To him, it matters quite a bit. And to you, it matters quite a bit as well."

"Yeah?"

"Yes."

"Well, maybe I wasn't even his friend in the first place."

"I'm not grasping why you think you can fool me," I start. "I've seen you two at lunch and in homeroom and when you talk every single morning before homeroom starts by the lockers outside of Redding's room. You smile with your whole face when he says something you think is funny, with your mouth, your eyes, your ears—everything smiles, which is otherwise weird for you, because it's clear by the lack of indentations around your mouth, and by anyone who's ever looked at you. You pretty much never smile unless you're with him and he's saying something overly sarcastic or inexplicably hysterical. And he obviously told you something he either hasn't told anyone else or hates talking about; he was more hurt than ticked at you. You're actually his friend, even though you're pretending you aren't for their purposes." I gesture to the other Eradicators.

Another gunshot echoes through the air. I try to block them out, but they're deafening.

"You can't let them take that away from you."

Gunshots are like stones dropped into still ponds: they make violent ripples.

"I must say, though, you're a much better liar than your best friend."

"You're doing that stupid Knower thing," he says. "Presuming or whatever. It doesn't work on me."

I look him over. Licking lips, fidgeting hands, a very small scar under his left eye, most likely left by a blade, one on the duller side but pushed in hard enough to hurt.

"I don't know, Hunter. Maybe no one has tried hard enough yet."

He reaches the front of the line. As if it's the most natural thing in the world, his gun rises to meet his eyes, and he pulls the trigger. The bullet flies through the air and hits a girl wearing a bright pink sundress. Why is she even still here? She should be somewhere safer, in a pillow fort, surrounded by stuffed animals, squirreled away from everyone and everything that could try to hurt her. The wind picks her up and carries her away. Screams, lots of screams. I pretend that they're just angry birds and that the wind is just giving her the change to fly like a nice, non-angry bird.

I'm at the front of the line. The metal is so cold it burns my skin. The field becomes hazy, and I no longer can see the Mall without it blurring. A voice urges me to shoot. Another voice screams that I need to leave this place as fast as I can and close my eyes and wish to be home with my river and willow tree. I listen to the latter and say to Andrea, "I can't do that."

"Well, you have to," she replies flatly.

"I can't do that. I'm sorry. Is there anything else I can do?"

"No. You either don't become an Eradicator, or you shoot."

"I'd rather take the former option if you didn't mind."

"You can't just leave."

"I was just given that option."

She repeats herself, slower this time, annunciating each syllable: "You can't just leave."

"I wasn't here to begin with."

Andrea turns a shade darker and I regret saying anything in the first place. *See, Jacob? I'm so incredibly incapable.* "What does that mean?"

"Listen to me. When I say run, you run as fast as you can," Hunter whispers into my ear.

"I don't know," I finish. "I . . . I really don't have any idea. I'm sorry."

"Shoot the person!" She is livid.

"I'm not going to! I'm not going to shoot them, and you can't make me do otherwise!" I throw as much valor into my voice as I can, but it's very unconvincing.

"Okay," she says. Then she grabs a gun out of the hands of someone next to her and puts it right up to me. "Then you can go inside and talk to the head of the Eradicators, who can decide on the best way to deal with you. Most times, the conflict ends with your life."

I freeze, staring at the barrel of the gun, which is staring straight back.

Hunter breathes, "Skylar, run."

I do.

Chapter Eighteen

Heaven, if you sent us down
so we could build a playground
for the sinners
to play as saints,
you'd be so proud of what we made.

"Crossfire"
Stephen

I didn't know it was possible for me to move this quickly. I don't believe I've ever ran like this before in my life; if I have, gym class would be a lot easier. My legs feel like they're about to pop off my body, and my heart is about to explode into a horrifying, ventricle-y mess.

That may partly be the fault of the fact that I've been shot in the arm.

I couldn't have been more than six feet away when Andrea fired at me. The bullet scraped past my arm, luckily not nestling itself into my skin. Now I drip fat drops of rusty blood as I run a speed I'd previously thought impossible.

People stare at me, I can tell. A screaming girl with an arm on fire and legs about to short out and a heart made of ventricles and a silver handgun gripped by her whitening knuckles is quite the sight. My arm surges and sends a new wave of pain through my body. My head is pure static.

The Castle seems impossibly far away. The whole word pulses as if it were one big strobe light. Cherry blossoms are everywhere, blindingly pink. They stand in front of the Castle like dominos that are much less afraid of falling over and knocking all of their friends over. Even if I could get these massive doors open, I don't know if I could find our little room. I close my eyes and think but closing my eyes only makes my arm hurt more so I open them but everything is just too bright so I close them again. Then I remember where everyone is, and I run that way.

Hallie. I can see her a few feet away, talking to Harlow and Jacob and Lexie. "Hallie!" My voice is strangled and I don't get the full word out, but she sees me now. I tell myself I'm in the home stretch and push myself to go faster. My body is made of lead.

I collapse at once into Hallie and let the tears I've been holding back fall to the ground. I gape for air like a dying fish and shake like an earthquake. She catches me and sits on the floor with me. "What's wrong? What did they do to you?"

I don't say anything. Every part of my body screams too loudly for me to hear myself. Lexie says something to her and then she and Harlow run away. Jacob kneels next to me, too, his eyes a dull tree color. Like a faded forest, like the trees just injected themselves into his irises.

"Did they shoot you?"

"Yeah," I say, wiping my eyes. "It just grazed my arm. I'm sure I'm fine. Actually, I'm completely lying. Hallie, it hurts. I think I'm dying." The reality of the situation hits me. "Dear God, they *shot* me! Freaking shot me! Stuff like this only should happen in movies . . . Oh my gosh, I actually got shot with a real gun . . . Hallie—" I start crying again. "I'm dying."

"Shh. You're not dying; you're fine. Lexie's gonna find you a bandage. You'll be okay."

"There're so many police officers . . ." I mutter. "One of them is bound to notice me. I got shot. That sounds so weird when said out loud. Like, unreal. Like I'm reading aloud from a book and it didn't actually just happen. Borderline unbelievable. It hurts, oh God, it hurts so badly."

"You're going to be fine," Jacob tells me. "You've got this, Bubble of Sunshine. Okay?"

I don't believe him, but I say, "Okay."

Lexie comes back with a box with a red cross on it. "Okay, does anyone know any first aid for getting shot? I have no clue—"

"Move over," Harlow says. She pushes Lexie out of the way and tears off my bloody white cardigan. She digs through the box and pulls some things out. "This is going to sting a lot," she says, dabbing my arm with a cotton-ball that drips with antiseptic.

I bite my lip hard enough to tear it apart to keep from screaming. "Can I swear? Is that okay?"

Hallie shrugs. "You literally swear all the time."

"In that case, *flying fudge*."

"That's not even a swear word."

"What does that even mean?" Jacob asks.

"I don't really know. It's just something my dad says when he burns his pies or something along those lines."

Harlow starts wrapping the bandages around my arm. "There'll be no easy way to hide this from Margaret," she says to us. "None. No possible way."

"I'm sorry," I say. "I kind of ruined everything."

"It's not your fault," Lexie says. "No one *wants* to get grazed by a bullet."

Harlow looks up from my arm for a second. "It sucks, doesn't it?"

"Wait, you've gotten shot before?"

"No!"

"I wouldn't be surprised, honestly."

Harlow sighs. "I mean finding out the world isn't made of sparkles and sunshine." She finishes my bandage.

"Oh, wait," I say. I grab the silver gun from where I dropped it on the grass. "I brought this for you."

"This," Hallie says as she tosses the gun from hand to hand, "is weird. I mean, I know pretty much nothing about firearms, but I know that this one is weird."

I sit on my knees on the carpet of the forbidden wing of the Castle that we've taken over. We're arranged in a circle, and Hallie is the the one holding the little silver gun now.

"It is?" I ask. "It looked fairly normal to me. Then again, I've only ever previously encountered Nerf guns."

"Same here, but I still know it's not what a normal gun looks like," Hallie says.

Lexie's eyes are huge. "Are you sure it's a real gun?"

Hallie holds it up. "Do you see an orange tip?"

Lexie takes the gun into her hands. "Woah. I've never seen a real one, either."

"There's a fingerprint sensor. Maybe you need to have a registered fingerprint to shoot?"

"Maybe," Lexie thinks. "Or maybe they're tracking thumbprints to make sure the same person uses the gun every time. Didn't you say they assign these to every Eradicator?"

"That seems like it could be right," Jacob responds, taking the gun from Lexie and looking it over. "They want to remain a secret for now, right? They don't want anyone to find their stuff. And if someone does and they get a fingerprint they don't recognize . . ."

"Then they get eradicated," Hallie finishes. "Simple as that."

"Then my fingerprint is saved in their system," I say. "I put my thumb on that thing without so much as a thought. So they've technically got me registered as an Eradicator."

"Well, I guess they do," Lexie says. "I don't know if that's a good thing or not."

"They didn't seem too happy with my leaving," I comment, gesturing to my bandaged arm.

"The trigger is so oddly-shaped," Harlow says. "Look at it. It's like an S."

"You should have seen some of the shots they were making," I say. "They were plain unbelievable. Even though it was their first day of training, it seems as though they've been training all their lives."

"Maybe they have," Jacob says. "Didn't Andrea say something about how some people knew what she was talking about?"

"And she mentioned parents," I add.

"Then maybe they actually grow up as Eradicators," Hallie says. "Like they know about what they're going to grow up to be from the time they can remember."

"So the exact opposite of you guys," Harlow points out. "You can't tell your parents anything, and their parents tell them everything."

"Weird," Lexie says. "You'd think the smart people would be more open about being smart than the cult members would be about being cult members."

Harlow crosses her arms and looks straight at me, eyes wide. "So what are you going to do about them?"

"Nothing, I was hoping," I tell her. "Didn't we just want to learn about them? Prove to the rest of the Knowers that we could do something so they'd stop ignoring us? We've done that already. Now we can go back to the American Girl Store."

"No, we've got to *do* something," Hallie says. "I mean, they obviously can't blow up a building and not get in trouble."

"The authorities will deal with it," I tell her, gesturing out the scratched window to the swarms of uniformed people holding their badges in front of them as if they're magnets for leads. "It's what they've been doing all day."

"Nothing they do will end up mattering!" Hallie fires back. "They can only do stuff that the Eradicators will get out of because time is on their side."

"Time is on our side, too," Lexie says, "so why don't we use it?"

Boom. It hits me like lightning.

"In that case, I have a plan."

Jacob raises an eyebrow. "I thought you said you didn't make plans, Bubble."

"I'm trying something new."

"Well, do you have a *good* plan?"

". . . I have a plan."

Chapter Nineteen

Castle built in the sand
will only last one day.

"Feels Like Summer"
Weezer

"The Eradicators have this master computer system," I start. "It's called the Efficacy, and it's their pride and joy."

"Oh no," Jacob mutters. "Whatever you're thinking, it's not good."

"It's got all the information they have on us," I continue. "Everything they know about the rest of the world, too. It's their lifeline. Without their Efficacy, they're just a body of unstable mass murderers."

"So you think we should pour a cup of juice on it?" Lexie says.

I ponder this for a second. "No. Nothing that we do today will matter tomorrow. See, that's our issue right there. Nothing we do is permanent. We could blow the entire world up and the only thing that would matter was us."

"Well, you've got pretty good brains," Harlow says, "so just think of a way around it."

I play with a bobby pin that's in my pocket until my mind finds what it wants. "I'm right, aren't I? The only thing that matters today is us. Us! We're the key! If we do it, than *we* can do it, because we can *do* things!"

"Sky, slow down. You're doing that thing where you make no sense," Lexie says. "We can do what?"

"We can hack into the Efficacy," I say. "We'll squeeze all the things we possibly can out. If we get our hands on it and get the information in our untouchable-by-time minds, then we've got their whole organization in our heads. We'll know their next move so we can thwart it, and we'll know how the whole organization works so we can take it down. Then we've got the upper hand. No, we'll have so many upper hands. We'll be like the Hecatoncheires of upper hands!"

"The what?"

"Greek mythology. They had lots of hands."

"Do you have any idea how risky that is?" Hallie says to me, her arms crossed and her eyes darkening into a color best described as algae if it absorbed a ton of cobalt, all teal-ish and earthy. "Who knows what Margaret would do to you if she found out you were messing with Eradicators, first things first. No way does she want you around them, not now. And what could they possibly have that we don't? "

"You'd be surprised," I say. "I'm assuming they have a wealth of knowledge almost as great as ours."

"You really think so." Hallie sounds doubtful.

"I wish I could say otherwise."

"So there we go," Lexie says. "Let's start by getting to the Efficacy."

"All of us can't go," Hallie says. "We're too big a group. Two people should go. I'll go since they don't know me, and one of you guys who's been there should go to show me where it is."

"I wanted to go," Harlow whines.

"Jacob, you definitely shouldn't go back," I tell him, seeing him about to say something and knowing perfectly well that it would be an offer to go back, which he really shouldn't do. "You kind of made yourself known."

"But Lexie doesn't know where the Efficacy is," Jacob reminds me, "and we do. One of us should go with them, and it probably shouldn't be you. For obvious reasons." He gestures to my bandaged arm.

"But Hunter is there, and I'm guessing that things between you two aren't all flowers and rainbows."

"Yeah, but me going back is better than you going back. Need I remind you: they shot you."

"You can't be around Hunter. Not right now. Maybe not ever."

"I can deal with Hunter. But you . . . You were *shot*. There really should be no arguing about this."

"You were metaphorically shot in the heart."

"Skylar. You were literally shot. With a gun."

"How about neither of you go and I find the thing by myself?" Lexie interjects.

"You *could,* but I don't want you to get lost," I say. "It's practically the Labyrinth down there. I'm not even completely sure I know exactly where it is."

"Then there's really no point in you going." Lexie crosses her arms. "And there's no point in Jacob going either. So I'll do it."

The hall outside is suddenly taken over by a stampede of wild elephants. The sound of a thousand footsteps causes noises of confusion from the people outside, meaning it's not them, meaning it's someone else, meaning that it's the Eradicators.

Then Hallie ushers us into a closet and everything is too dark for me to see.

"Your elbow is in my face," Jacob hisses into my ear.

"Sorry." I try to move very slightly.

"Now your other elbow's in my stomach," Hallie says.

"I can't move that one. I got shot, remember?"

"Guys, quiet," Lexie whispers, followed up with, "Margaret is going to flip."

If it weren't for Hallie's very quick thinking and her memorization of this room we've spent too much time in, we could be incarcerated, or dead, or worse. She found a way to squish us all into this tiny cabinet that I don't think they'll look in because I'm having trouble believing that one of us can fit in here, let alone all five. I should either become a better person or stop dabbling in beliefs of reincarnation so I don't come back as a sardine.

"Search everywhere," one of them commands. Her voice holds authority and familiarity. "Find them. What did you say that girl looked like, Andrea?"

"Way too small to be a fifteen-year-old," Andrea's voice says. "Super pale face covered in freckles, dark frizzy hair, and thick black glasses. Green polo and khaki skirt. Over-sophisticated and kind of annoying."

I'm fairly sure the Eradicators outside can hear my heart pounding from where they stand.

"A new girl with glasses in a green polo," the other one says. She repeats "green polo" to herself before saying, "She's probably from my school, and she's probably one of the new Knowers. Her name?"

"She never told me," Andrea replies.

"Get Hunter Athan. Ask him what the girl's name is. If she's from the island, he'll know. All those kids know each other. We all know each other on that stupid island."

"Yep," Andrea responds, and her footsteps leave the room.

I'm hyperaware of everything: whoever's elbow is in my back, the crinkling papers beneath my feet, must in the air, breathing, shuffling, footsteps outside the room. Everything bombards me within seconds. Or has it been minutes? An hour, even? I never do know.

"Did the geneticists schedule new Knowers from that island this year, ma'am?" a new one asks.

Heavy footsteps slowly pace the room as the commander explains. "Not necessarily, but Lea Felding is a confirmed Knower who, just out of the blue, moved to my island last year and took up a ninth grade teaching position," their apparent leader conjectures. "We were predicting four new Knowers this year from anywhere, based on last year's genetic tests. But Felding wouldn't drop everything and move from Baltimore if there weren't some reason behind it, and she *especially* wouldn't teach ninth graders algebra while she's qualified to teach college-level calculus."

"Isn't Lea Felding twenty-four? How can she teach AP calculus when she's barely out of college herself?" the other Eradicator wonders.

"That's a Knower for you," the ringleader says. "Unbearably smart. Probably finished calculus before high school, if you ask me. "

Another Eradicator marches into the room. "There's no one of interest on the first floor," he says.

"Search every floor in this thing. Athan said they were in the Castle, so look around the Castle. If we don't find all of them, we'll at least find the little one, and she'll be easy to get information out of."

"Ms. Parkins, ma'am, they could be anywhere in this place."

I gasp in surprise. Hallie elbows me in the face.

"I heard something," Ms. Parkins says. "Something close. Look for it."

"What kind of something?"

"A noise of surprise. They *are* from my school, and they're in the room."

Chapter Twenty

Let them run from the violence.
The world is way too cold
and bright for their eyes.
Little boy runs beside them
as they take his hands
and jump to the sky.

"Little Boy in the Grass"
AURORA

"Do you see any good hiding places in here?"

"No. There's nothing in this room." Ms. Parkins pauses for a second, most likely surveying the area. I imagine her squinting her aged-jade eyes that peer from above her math books as she proctors study halls and pacing the room as if it were her classroom during an exam. I pray that she doesn't notice the door and decide to take a look.

"Nowhere they can be?"

Three more people walk into the room. "The upstairs of this place is a maze," one of them says. "There're so many rooms, and they don't seem to be in any of them."

He must have missed the spiral staircase leading to the glass rotunda.

He continues, "You think Athan was lying?"

"No, he doesn't lie," Ms. Parkins says, though her voice is distant, as if she's searching the entire Castle without ever moving her feet. "The girl may be in here, though, and we could use her to get to the other ones."

"There's so many places a girl her size could be hiding, Eleanor. It's not worth it. She's worthless, anyway. She's a newbie. What could she tell us? Everything we already know, I'm guessing."

"So what should we do now then? If it's not worth looking for the girl."

"Nothing is needed. They're not our main concern, and I take it we're not theirs, either. There must be other reasons for their . . . their *actions*. We won't waste much time on them, today at least, unless a seizable opportunity arises."

"Eleanor." Andrea is back, jogging and out of breath. "The younger Athan boy said her name is Skylar Rawlings."

I'm very careful not to make a noise this time.

"Skylar Rawlings?" Ms. Parkins is silent for a second. "Yes, I think she's one of the freshman. She's quiet most of the time. Not exactly Knower material, if you ask me. She always looks like she's scared of something."

"I don't know," Andrea says. "She's definitely got Knower blood in her, looking back at how she acted."

"I don't know," Ms. Parkins repeats. "She's probably absolutely worthless." She pauses for minute. "Skylar. Such a powerful name." She sighs. "What a shame it was wasted on such a weak little girl."

Jacob is the first to speak once we've gotten out of the closet and sat in our circle on the floor. "Ms. Parkins? An . . . An *Eradicator*? Like, I— I knew she was mean and stuff, but . . . but not to the point of . . . that."

The full weight of Ms. Parkins's words hasn't hit me yet. I'm still in a bit of a daze, the edges of my mind fuzzy like fraying cotton.

"That's seriously freaky, oh my God," Lexie says. "She could have been watching us this whole time. Every day in the halls, before you all got switched out of her study hall, at lunch—all that time, she was there, staring at us."

"How could we not have known?" Hallie groans. "It seems so obvious."

"For the first time ever," Jacob says, "I actually wish I were still homeschooled."

"You were homeschooled?" Lexie asks.

"Yeah. That's why I only started this year, but both my siblings have been in island school."

"You have siblings?" Hallie asks.

"This is the perfect time to tell my whole life story, isn't it?"

"They know me," I say quietly, but everyone hears me. "Hunter told them my name. Ms. Parkins knows that I'm at her school." A giant rock falls from the very top of the sky and crushes me. It forces all the air out of my lungs and strangles me and causes my heart to explode from pumping my Knower blood so fast.

"They won't be able to find you." Hallie tries to calm me down.

"No, they know where I am! Hunter told them who I was. They can put me right into their Efficacy and pull up everything on me." The entire world is shrinking, except me. I'm like Alice in Wonderland, suddenly too big for this minuscule room. The walls all squeeze my arms and legs until I'm just this tiny cube that can't move.

"Skylar, it'll be okay," Jacob says. "You're a Bubble of Sunshine. How could they possibly hurt you?" His voice is firm but still soft, like an un-toasted marshmallow. I try to think of marshmallows instead of my imminent doom. Like, when Evan was about six months old, he shoved two marshmallows into his cheeks. Dad was so worried he'd choke that he made Mom take them out. To this day, I have never seen a more disappointed baby. Evan must eat a million marshmallows a day. He's like the Stay Puft Marshmallow Man from *Ghostbusters*.

"Yeah. Listen to Jacob. We'll make sure they don't do anything to you," Harlow says. "Absolutely positive. They'd have to get through me, first, and I'm borderline unbreakable."

"I know you are," I say, praying my voice has at least stopped shaking enough for it to sound like words. Marshmallows are pretty great, to be honest. Mini-mallows are okay, but the full-sized are way better. My dad's birthday was on an Obligatory Family Dinner Night last year, and Aunt Jessamine made homemade marshmallows. From scratch. The light in Evan's eyes when he saw them was next to blinding. Ironic, seeing as though it came from his eyes. "I'm not, though, and that's the problem."

"Well, we've got to come up with a plan, and fast," Hallie says. "Even if it's just to get back at Ms. Parkins for calling Skylar worthless."

"Well, she's not wrong," I say under my breath. No one hears me; if they do, they don't acknowledge it.

Lexie sighs. "But is it worth it?"

"It's totally worth it," Hallie says. "Totally, completely worth it. No questions asked."

"They know who I am now," I say carefully so I don't spiral off into oblivion again. Aunt Jessamine's marshmallows were so good. They were all I asked for for my birthday last year, but the store only had an overstock of strawberry gelatin, and I'm allergic to strawberries. I told her I'd be fine ("There's probably no real fruit in there anyway!" I protested), but she wouldn't listen ("Not worth a potential hospital visit," she replied with a sharp look in her eye). She got me a book on whales instead, which I've read cover to cover an octillion times. I love whales. I have the intro memorized: *No creature is as majestic and mysterious as the whale. These water mammals are utterly mesmerizing and wondrous in their capabilities.*

"So we're finding the Efficacy, then," Lexie says, "and we're gonna pick it completely apart."

The blue whale not only holds the record for the largest animal currently living, but also the loudest. Though benign and docile, his heart alone weighs about the average weight of a car.

"So Lexie and I will go," Hallie says. "No arguing about it."

"I'm making a map for you," Jacob says. He's already found a piece of paper and a pencil and is sketching something. "Lexie, use it once you get down to the basement. I'm doing it from memory, so it may be a little iffy, but it should be okay."

His tongue, that weighs as much as an elephant. He can spray water from his two blowholes three stories in the air and can live for over a century. He is surrounded in mystery and folklore, forever an object of children's fantasies and sailors' accounts of the high seas.

"We'll just go through the back door we went in before," Lexie decides. "And we left the spade outside, so we really can get back in."

"Then you three stay in here and we'll call you from my phone and tell you what it's like," Hallie says. "We'll tell you everything we find, so please try pay some attention. Jacob, looking at you."

"I can't make any promises," he replies with a shrug.

And though they are the epitome of nature's perplexing brilliance—

Harlow smirks. "I've always wanted to try to get into a supercomputer."

—it's often hard to believe we are sharing the earth with creatures some may believe only exist in fairytales.

Chapter Twenty One

I know you're not a liar,
and I know you could set fire
this day. Go ahead and make me
look away. Strike me down,
I am calling your lightning.

"Implicit Demand for Proof"
twenty one pilots

"Just stay here," Hallie says as she and Lexie get ready to step out into the disaster zone. "It's too risky to go outside."

"Are you really talking about risk-taking?" I say. "With what you're about to do—which, I might add, involves going outside? They don't even want us to be a part of anything, so this risk seems foolish in my opinion."

"We're very much a part of this, so you can't be afraid of the world yet," Hallie says to me. "We're doing this, and if you're really too scared to help, then you can hang out in the Ocean Hall till midnight."

"The Ocean Hall blew up!" I say. "I'm sorry, but I have a legitimate reason to be afraid of the world right now, Hallie. A fifteen-year-old boy shot me. Someone my age, with about as much life experience as me, attempted to kill me. This time, you can't tell me that I need to get out of my little bubble. I tried that, and it almost ended my life."

"You're not allowed to be afraid of the world yet," she repeats. "Not yet."

"You know that I can't guarantee that."

"No, but I know you can try."

Without another word, she walks back out into the hall. Lexie says, "We'll be back soon. If we haven't called in ten minutes, that means we're either in prison or dead."

"That's definitely reassuring, Lexie," Jacob says.

"I know. I'm the best." She grins and runs after Hallie.

"Your friends are weird," Harlow tells me.

"I know," I respond.

"Like, I thought my friends were weird."

"They are."

"But you guys . . . it's like a whole new level."

"We've surpassed any previously established calibers of weirdness."

"If there were any way to prove her point even more," Jacob says, "I think you may have just found it."

"Point-proving is certainly one of my better talents—"

"Shh," Harlow interrupts. "For a second."

"Why—"

"Do you not understand the meaning of *shh*?"

I soon understand why she wants us to be quiet—there are footsteps coming down the hall. The Castle was practically empty just a matter of seconds ago. These footsteps aren't walking straightforward patterns, but they skip around like the beat of a ska song. I don't need to see the person to know who's walking towards us.

"There's my favorite person in the world," Jacob sighs.

Orion Athan approaches us with a smile on his face and something flickering behind his synthetic green eyes. "I must say, I certainly am lucky to encounter you not once, but *twice* today." He sees me and smiles brighter. "Oh, Skylar, this is our third meeting, isn't it? My mistake."

Jacob glances at me and mouths *Third*?

I shrug and bite my lip to tell him that I forgot to tell him.

"It doesn't count as *luck* if you came out to find us on purpose," Jacob says. He stands up and crosses his arms, and Harlow and I follow, except it hurts too much to cross my arms, which makes me uncomfortable, as I rarely stand without my arms crossed. "Which you did, I'm sure."

Orion grins even wider. "I must admit, I was curious about your whereabouts."

"How did you even get here?" I ask him. "It's impossible to get anywhere around here, what with the disaster zone and justified lockdown."

"Why, it wasn't hard at all," Orion says. He walks circles around us, as if to trap us, though he beguiles us with his conversational tone. "You walk as if you don't fear your own death."

"Okay, that's cool, but you're a teenager," Harlow says. "If you saw a— how old are you?"

"Seventeen," Orion replies, and he looks to Jacob. "The same age as your brother," and then he looks to me, "and your cousin," and then to Harlow, "so your brother as well, I presume."

Jacob raises an eyebrow. "The fact that you know that really creeps me out."

"Okay," Harlow says, "if the cops out there didn't stop a seventeen year old walking around a crime scene, then they're sucky cops."

"I believe the police are doing the best job they possibly can be," Orion replies, not ceasing his pacing. "I have an idea. What do you say we ignore all responsibilities for the time being and go wander around this beautiful Castle for a spell? You know, we could see some historic documents, investigate what explosives were used, and maybe explore some rooms that you haven't fully explored yet."

"There are so many reasons I don't want to do that," Jacob says

"Why not, Jake?" Instead of falling, his grin widens.

"First of all, don't call me Jake. Second of all, I kind of hate you."

Now Orion's grin disappears completely. His face looks blank without it. "Now, Jacob," he stresses the *ob*, "do you really think what they're doing is right?"

"Do you think what *you're* doing is right?"

"I beg your pardon, but what exactly am I doing?"

Jacob trips over words for a second. Then Harlow jumps in and says, "Come on, you blew up a building."

"No, my dear, I didn't do that. You and I both know that that little incident was not my fault."

Jacob closes his eyes for a second. "Why did you come here? Is there something you want?"

"Oh, no," Orion replies. "I merely wanted to find you. But, now that you mention it, I will also have you know that we're everywhere. Everywhere you could possibly want to go, we're already there. Keep that in mind when you decide to switch teams."

"So you're not gonna kill us?" Harlow says.

"No."

"You're not gonna probe us for information?"

"Not today."

"You just came to talk."

"Does there have to be more?"

"You're not afraid that we'll kill or probe you?"

Orion smiles again. "You wouldn't do that to me, would you?" He looks directly at me. "At least *you* wouldn't, Skylar. You couldn't fool a soul by saying you would. He stops pacing. "All in all, although I may have good reason to be, I'm not afraid of you.

Not yet. Likely not ever. I thought that would be imperative for you to know."

We don't respond.

He glances at my arm. "I offer my condolences, Skylar. Things like this always happen for a reason." He stops and exhales. "Now, let's just hope it was a good one, shall we?" With a charming wink, he walks back down the hall without looking back at us.

By the time Orion has left and Jacob's done muttering about how annoying he is, Harlow decides that they're going to call any minute now.

"Air and Space is about the same distance away from the Castle as American History," she says. "Even with all the police and detectives and stuff, they should be getting there soon."

"I'm just hoping they get to the Efficacy okay," I say. "There are so many people scurrying around. They're like a swarm of flies."

"They'll get there fine," Jacob says. "As long as no one's in the room, they probably won't even have to talk to anyone."

"Oh my gosh, I forgot about that," I say, and my brain starts fabricating scenarios of them running into Eradicators in the closet-sized room and one of them recognizes Lexie and they both end up with bullets in their heads.

"They'll find a way in," Jacob says. "This is Hallie and Lexie we're talking about. They'll get into that room if it kills them."

"And it very well may," I remind him.

"Yeah, but it very well may *not*," Jacob counters.

"But it *may*."

"But it may *not*."

My phone rings. I answer it at lightning speed. "Hi, it's Skylar."

"Kind of assumed that," Lexie replies. "You're on speaker."

I put her on speaker as well. "So are you. How are you guys? Did you get there okay?"

"Yeah, we're good," Hallie's voice says. She's a bit out of breath, and that makes me wary.

So I ask her. "Why are you so out of breath? What did you do?"

"Well, we couldn't get the Eradicator in this room out, so I knocked him unconscious."

"Hallie! How do you even know how to do that?"

"Since there was already a guy in the room," Lexie interrupts, "we don't need to worry about passwords. It's protected by three, maybe even four. But they were already all typed in, thanks to him, so we can just browse now. Thank God for that, right?"

"Yeah, I wouldn't have a clue where to start looking for a password," I admit. "So what does it look like?"

"I was expecting something like the computer from Jurassic Park," I hear Hallie say, "but it's just a Mac desktop and that silver box thing, which must be the external hard drive. At least I know how to work it, then."

"There're a ton of folders on the desktop," Lexie adds. "They're all labeled super obvious things. This one just says 'death', no joke. Hallie, go into that one."

"'Kay," Hallie responds.

"This thing is connected to the Internet, but, like, it's *not* the internet," Lexie explains. "Isn't that weird?"

"They made their own internet?" Harlow says. "That's genius. If a computer is connected to the internet, it can be tracked by the NSA, but then this one's untraceable if the internet it's connected to isn't actually an internet."

"That hurts my brain, Harlow," Lexie says.

"This folder only has a document of the different things that happen when different people die," Hallie says.

"Sounds morbid," I say.

"It says a Knower's eye color changes one last time, turning silver right as they die," Lexie reads. "That's pretty horrifying."

"Creepy," Jacob says.

I can almost hear Lexie shudder. "Yep, that's an image I can't get out of my head."

"Woah, it has descriptions of different blood types," Hallie says next, after a second of scrolling.

"Complete with photos," Lexie chimes in.

"They can tell different blood types apart by *looking,* can you believe that? I didn't know scientists who study blood could do that, let alone these guys."

"As interesting as that is, you need actual stuff you can use," Harlow says. "Like are they planning anything? Anything that can be stopped?"

"Hold on," Lexie says. A minute later, she comes back, saying, "Okay, we just found a folder called 'Knowers'."

"Oh my God," Hallie says. "They've got family trees. Really extensive and branchy family trees. Lexie, look at these things."

"Really?" Jacob says. "Any you recognize?"

"Miss Felding's," Hallie says slowly. "They know she's a Knower. They've got her name underlined, bolded, *and* highlighted. Oh, and there's her great-grandpa, Harold Reynolds. They directly traced her back. Holy—they have Punnett squares. Like, a lot of them. They must be trying to figure out the exact genes leading to Knowerism or whatever."

"There's no way they'll ever figure that out," I say. "The odds of getting the exact gene combinations needed for the title are about one in twenty-eight million. The genetic code must be incredibly specific and mostly recessive. It would take a team of professional geneticists to figure us out, and even then, it'd take years for them to learn what actually makes us Knowers."

"They do, actually," Lexie says. "Have a team of geneticists, I mean. They've got nineteen. Thirteen dedicated to Knowers alone."

"Oh. I stand corrected."

"Here's your family tree, Jacob," Hallie says.

"Seriously?" Jacob says, coming closer to the phone. He taps the screen to close the alert telling me I've only got ten percent battery left. "Am I on it?"

"Yeah, at the bottom," Lexie says; then she adds slowly, "They've got you marked."

"Hunter told them," he mutters. "Fantastic."

"Hey, on the bright side, it won't be there tomorrow," I try to console him, but he doesn't seem to be listening.

"They've got Punchy Squares or whatever they're called for all of us except me," Lexie says. "They just have my name and underneath that, 'Undetermined parents, living with parents Aaron and Hudson Petterson and adopted sister Nari'."

"Here's mine, but I'm not labeled as a Knower," Hallie says. "There are question marks next to my older siblings and me, but none next to the little ones."

"Skylar, here's yours," Lexie says. I grip my phone a bit tighter at the thought of the Eradicators having my family down. "You're labeled."

"Of course I am," I say.

"Oh, here's a folder called 'Plans'," Hallie says.

"They're all tiny little security breaches," Lexie says, perplexed. "This one's hacking into the postal service of Belgium to try to take it apart, completely done from the Efficacy."

"None of these plans are important," Hallie says. "This one is literally just for a punch party. 'Nancy Sawloski is bringing her famous lime punch again this year!' Big whoop."

"I think cherry punch would go better with world domination," Jacob decides.

"Nothing about blowing up Natural History?" Harlow asks. "No, like, other building explosions, either? Anything like that?"

"No," Lexie says. "None at all. They seem to do everything from underground, literally. They don't have anything on any explosions."

"That's so weird," Jacob says. "You'd think they would've had *something* on here about them doing that. Bomb plans or whatever. Or blueprints highlighting weakest points in the structure of the exterior."

"Hallie, what's that one?" we hear Lexie ask.

"'Code'? I don't know, it could be anything." A long pause. "Oh my God. Lexie, look at this."

"What is it?" Harlow asks.

"It's a firewall," Hallie says. "Except it's not—"

My phone screen goes black.

"It died!" I exclaim. I immediately try to turn it back on, but it only flashes the hungry-for-battery-power picture before conking out again. "My phone never dies! I always charge it!"

"Well, you obviously didn't last night," Jacob says.

I replay last night's scenes in my head. I normally plug in my phone right as I get into bed. Last night, though, I was absolutely terrified for what today would bring and in all the confusion, I must have deemed it unnecessary or something. I was very, *very* wrong.

"The one time I don't charge it is the one time it's a potentially life or death matter," I groan.

"I have my phone," Jacob says. "We can call them back."

"Okay, do you know Hallie's number?"

"No. Do you?"

"No, I was hoping you did!"

"Why don't you know?"

"Why don't *you* know?"

"Why would I know her phone number?"

"Well, why would I? No one memorizes phone numbers, Jacob!"

"Exactly! Why would I know?"

"You don't have it saved in your contacts?"

"I have, like, six contacts."

"Then we've got no way to get ahold of them!"

Jacob sighs. "I could text Hunter—wait, that wouldn't work." He toys with a piece of paper that was on the floor—he's been ripping it into tiny pieces, and now it looks like snow.

"Andrew or Blake wouldn't know their numbers, either. And Daniel . . . Great. You're sure you don't know her number?"

"No!"

"You're one of the smartest people in existence! You know more about whales then whales do! And you can't remember one phone number?"

"Um, I think Hallie's has a four in it."

"You're so helpful, Skylar."

"At least I have more than six contacts!"

"At least I charge my phone!"

"Shut up, both of you!" Harlow says suddenly. "I have a plan."

"And exactly how good is this plan?" I ask her, crossing my arms.

"My best since that plan to get those giant stuffed bears at the fair last summer," she says, turning to me. "You've had that fedora for eight months now, you know, and Spencer wants it back."

"Well, you've had my will to live for thirteen years, so."

"We don't want to go the compound right? Well, what if we just went into the museum part of the museum? They probably have a PA system, like the one at school. We just have to get to that and pray that it reaches the basement."

"It does," Jacob says. "We heard it while we were down there, right, Skylar?"

"Yes! Henry McClaim. We heard it clear as day in that basement."

"Easy, then. We just get to that PA system," Harlow says, standing up. "Aren't I a genius?"

"You're a genius, and it's snowing in Hell right now."

"Then the Devil better buy a parka."

Chapter Twenty Two

Thought you'd be quite happy there,
in that warm New York air,
but your heart's not right.
But if you sing along with me,
do you think you could
ever smile again?
If you sing this melody,
do you think you could
laugh again, my friend?
Just try,
for me.

"England Skies"
Shake Shake Go

We have to brace ourselves before we go back outside, for obvious reasons.

Outside is even worse than I remember. More people swish around, completely ignoring sidewalks. They talk into phones, into cameras, to each other, but mostly to themselves. The acrid, burnt smell doesn't just linger in the air—it's more of a main act than oxygen. But nothing in the world could have prepared me for the sight of Natural History—or lack thereof. A black shell haphazardly lay where the gold dome once stood, still smoldering.

It looks like a meteorite struck.

"How the actual hell are we going to get over there?" Harlow groans as we stand in the doorway.

"You walk as if you don't fear your own death," Jacob says.

"I'm not sure how effective that will be," I say. "Orion at least could pass as a twenty-something year old to a distracted eye. But we're in school uniforms, and whatever atrocity Harlow's wearing—"

"I happen to love my outfit, thank you very much."

"—and we look like teenagers. Also, my arm is wrapped in fraying bandages. We're going to be stopped as soon as we set foot out of this doorway."

"Okay, so if that happens," Jacob says, "we run."

Harlow shrugs. "Sounds good."

And so we leave the inside of the building, only to hug the outside. Then we dash from the outer wall of the Castle to the Arts and Industries building, which I hadn't even heard of prior to holding onto its rough red walls as if it were an inner tube and we were drowning.

I think my arm's stopped bleeding—the splotch of blood on the white bandage hasn't grown in about fifteen minutes—but it still burns and makes me wince with each step I take. All the sudden movement is so dizzying, I have to close my eyes for a bit to stop the world from swaying as if it were a boat on the ocean during a storm.

"We can take a break if you want," Harlow tells me.

"It's a five minute walk," I dismiss. "I walk more than that to school every morning."

"But not with a bullet scrape on your arm," Jacob reminds me.

"I'm fine," I say, but the fact that the boat-world just hit some whitecaps and I fear we're about to capsize doesn't help my case. "We can keep going."

Jacob's eyes bounce between me, Harlow, and the wall on which we lean. "Well, I don't know what's on the other side of this museum, so I'll go check it out and come back and figure out which way we have to go from here. You guys stay here."

Before I can protest, he's disappeared. Harlow plops down on the concrete, and, much more slowly, I follow suit.

"He's quite infuriating," I say.

"He's cute, though."

God, wouldn't the ability to control blush be amazing? To normal people, it would seem stupid, but coming from someone who's constantly embarrassing herself, I would love that. "You're quite infuriating, too, just not as much. You're not a hurricane."

"Hurricane?" Harlow asks me.

"Oh. Nothing. Sorry." Yes, controlling the color of my face would be a freaking godsend.

"Is he a hurricane like I'm a star?" Harlow wonders.

"I guess so," I say, "but you're very different people. But, then again, you're very similar, too. You're both far too intractable and horribly annoying."

"Stars are so much better," Harlow says. "They can't kill you."

"You're certainly right about that."

"And they make the night brighter," she continues. "Like, you know those lanterns you can make by punching holes into tin cans? If the world were just a giant tin can, stars would be the holes that let in the light, even when the lid is over the top and it technically should be pitch-black in there."

"Your brain is a mystery, Harlow."

"Okay," Jacob begins as he emerges from behind the wall again. "The next building is this big circular thing with these super cool supports that look unsound but there's no way this thing was built before the seventies so if it works, then that's cool. There's this path that leads to this super tiny garden area, which goes out to the street, which goes into the bottom of the concrete donut, and that's all surrounded in walls. Then we stay in there for as long as possible, and then go in the back entrance of Air and Space. Are you guys ready?"

"We've been ready since you left," Harlow responds.

We move around Arts and Industries until I see the path connecting it with the concrete donut resting on crescent moons. It's a little garden with all these tiny plants growing next to tiny labels. "There's an outer wall surrounding it," I say, "but not on the building itself, unless you could the few feet of supports holding this thing up."

"We just have to cut through," Jacob says, leading us straight through the center of the entryway. Through the middle opening, I look up and see the sky. Thick black smoke floats through it in wisps.

"Anyone have any idea where they keep the PA system?" Jacob asks as we move through the courtyard. Cerebral statues are everywhere you look. I almost stop to stare at a big yellow pumpkin before I realize our lives are at stake.

"Or how to work it?" Harlow adds.

Both look to me.

"I don't know!" I exclaim. "I'm guessing they keep it in one of the main offices. I would have no idea how to work the system were one in front of me. The one in the office at school looks so complicated. So many buttons."

"It can't be *that* complicated," Jacob says. "There's a microphone to talk into and a button that's bigger than the others to send your voice through the museum. Seems easy—" He's cut off by the sound of someone getting a text—he and I both look at our phones while Harlow comments that she knows it's not her. "Who is it?" I ask.

"My brother." He doesn't sound very happy about that; in fact, his eyes darken. "I guess I forgot to tell them I was—quote-unquote—staying at Hunter's house, and now everyone's mad at me."

"On the bright side, they're not going to be mad at you tomorrow," I supply.

"That's not the problem." He puts his phone back in his pocket and walks towards Air and Space twice as quickly. I throw a glance to Harlow and have to jog a bit to catch up with him.

"It's not your fault," I tell him. "You've kind of had a lot on your mind for the past few days. Also, they don't understand how unnecessary it is for you to explain."

"I know, but—" He stops mid-sentence.

Without him saying another word, I understand. I know that people see our minds as defective, think our thinking processes are inadequate, and claim that we're nowhere near as intelligent because we have twice as many thoughts.

What they don't understand is that they're very, very wrong.

Luckily, the gardeners were interrupted by the explosion, so I see exactly what I'm looking for dotting the grass right outside the donut. I run over to the patch of dandelions, pick one, run back, and throw it at Jacob. He picks it up off the ground and looks at it—and then me—all confused. "You know, people think dandelions are mistakes," I say. "I think they're the best part of a lawn."

He doesn't look any less perplexed.

"I mean, the only reason dandelions are considered weeds is because people decided that they were," I continue. "If people started seeing them as flowers instead of flaws, then there'd be so many fewer pesticides."

He throws the dandelion back to me. "You're literally the weirdest person I've ever met."

I throw it back to him. "Thank you."

"Excuse me!" Harlow calls from behind us. "You guys done yet? We kinda have a job to do! Lives to save!" She breaks into a sprint and moves right in between us. She grabs my shoulder to steady herself as she takes a gasping breath. "Sound good to you? Or are you not really feeling the *lives to save* thing?"

We take her word, get out of the middle of the donut, and hurry over to Air and Space.

"You know, we could just give a message to security people to say," Harlow suggests as Jacob finds the un-alarmed emergency exit and the spade still lying in the grass from our last break-in. "'Hallie and Lexie, please report to American History immediately.' So much easier."

"First off, this is a crime scene, so they'd never do it. We'll have to do it ourselves. Also, the Eradicators are too smart for that, and will know something's up," I comment. We move down the hall. Maybe if we pretend we're invisible long enough, we'll simply melt into the walls. "We need some sort of code."

"Allie-hay and Exie-lay ease-play go to American Istory-Hay?"

"Pig Latin? I'm going to pretend you never suggested that."

"Morse code?" Jacob ponders.

"They've probably got people that can do Morse code. It's not exactly uncommon."

"Dash dash dash space dash dot dash," he says.

"What?"

"Okay."

"You can say 'okay' in Morse code but can't remember to do a global reading?"

"Skylar, tell me the last time you actually did a global reading."

"Dash dash dot or whatever you said."

"Binary?" Harlow suggests.

"Do you even know binary?"

"That would be a no."

I sigh. "I don't know. We need an inside joke or something that Hallie would get. Something that would go right over everyone but their heads."

"You sure we can't just call their names?" Jacob says.

"No. Trust me. If no one else figures that out, Hunter will."

"We can write a riddle," Harlow says. "Um, phone say bye, as it die . . . um . . . come to History, or . . . we'll die a mystery!"

"Well," Jacob starts slowly, "you may not want to bank on a future in the freestyle rap industry."

Harlow throws him a look and says, "Okay . . . Skylar, does Hallie know her object?"

"Her what?" Jacob asks.

I ignore him and rack my memory. *And you're an anchor,* I think I said to Hallie once. *If it weren't for you, I'd be suffocating from a loss of oxygen I'd be so high up.* "I think she does," I say. "I told her once. It's just a matter of her remembering."

"What about Lexie?"

"No way she'd know. I'll use Hallie's."

"Finally," Jacob says, gesturing to a map of the museum on the wall. Using that map which he can somehow read effortlessly, Jacob leads us to the main office. Fortunately, it's empty.

"Ready?" Harlow asks. She hits a glowing red button on the machine, and our voices are live.

I decide on, "Would the anchor and her friend please return to the other building where they are supposed to be? Thank you."

"So, if Hallie's an anchor, what am I?" Jacob asks.

"You're a hinderance," I tell him. Telling a storm it's a storm is just reminding it of all the power it is able to unleash. And honestly, that's the last thing I need today.

They certainly did get the message; Lexie and Hallie are back in our room in the Castle before we are. They sit on the floor next to piles and piles of sticky notes. "They were the only paper in the room, and we needed to write stuff down," Hallie says. "We must have gone through three pads because *someone,*" she looks to Lexie, "has handwriting the size of a small truck."

"At least mine is legible," Lexie says before turning to Harlow, Jacob and me. "Pretty genius, I have to say. Using the announcement system and everything."

"Thanks," Harlow says. "I came up with that."

"Do either of you have a phone charger?" I ask.

"Yeah, 'cause I just carry one around," Hallie huffs. "Why didn't you charge your phone last night?"

"I was a little preoccupied," I tell her. "The whole nonexistent Day thing took up most of my mental space last night."

"Why don't we just give Jacob our numbers so we've got some contact?" Lexie suggests. "It's a lot easier."

After they've punched in their numbers, Jacob remarks, "I'm up to eight contacts now."

"Nine. Here's mine in case you need to call my dead phone," I say, and I add mine, too.

"Thanks," he says. "I'm going to randomly send you whale memes now."

"Where are you going to find whale memes?" I inquire.

"I don't know. I'll make some."

"So what were you saying about the firewall not against viruses?" Harlow asks them. "You know, before Skylar's phone kicked the bucket."

Lexie's fingers drum on the tile. Not one after the other, like most people's. Hers tap out a sequence: pinky, thumb, middle, ring, index. She repeats this over and over again, giving no though to it. "It's against time."

"Time," Jacob repeats. "And that means . . ."

"The whole thing is encrypted with, like, a million lines of code," Hallie elaborates. "It makes it so the Efficacy isn't affected by the Mechanism's time-reversing. I have no clue how it works, but you should have seen this thing. I've never seen so many letters and numbers. It was kind of awesome, but in a weird way."

"So nothing on that computer is affected by the Mechanism," Lexie says. "Everything they put on that computer will stay there, even when it's the real April sixteenth."

"Seriously?" I gawk. "That's . . . amazing."

"So, we didn't delete anything without consulting you first, but—"

"We can delete everything except the code, then," Jacob says. He's pacing the room, occasionally bumping into dusty furniture or molding crates. "Then all that stuff they have on us is gone. Anything doesn't exist like the rest of everything. They'll have nothing left."

"Well, it would be a bad idea to go back," Hallie says. "We got a lot of weird looks. As if they could, like, *sense* that we aren't them."

"Yeah, it's weird there," Lexie adds. "It's almost not worth it."

"Then maybe we can find a way to get it without going back to the compound," Harlow says. "It could be possible."

I toss my dead phone between my hands. "The Knowers have an app, don't they?"

"Yeah," Jacob says. "Eula said she'd install it for us when time is real or something like that. It sounds pretty cool, but I don't know, nothing can come close to Splashy Shark—"

"No. I mean that if we have an app, they could have one, too."

Chapter Twenty Three

We could be a story in the morning,
but we'll be a legend tonight.
I'm just a moment,
so don't let me pass you by,
and they can speak our names in a dead language
'cause you and I, we're alive.

"Outlines"
All Time Low

The AppStore has never heard of anything Eradicator. Simply searching the word yields no results. We get more creative, typing in things like "Efficacy" and "extreme-pyromaniacs", but nothing comes up.

"You really think that you could get such a strong database like that through the AppStore? Without Internet, too?" Hallie asks. "Seriously. I have no idea how they would be able to get all that information out to other phones without Internet."

"Unless the app has the information encrypted right into it," Harlow suggests. "I mean, it would have been hard to do, but if they really wanted to—"

"We could always just steal one of their phones," Jacob suggests for the third time. "Trust me, it would be a lot easier."

Hallie crosses her arms. "Explain to me how that would be easier."

He holds up his phone. "It's a long story, but basically I have Find My Phone on here hooked up with Hunter's phone. He lost it at the zoo once and we had to find it, I had to crawl into a rhino habitat, it was a mess. Don't take Hunter to the zoo, ever."

"But you know where his phone is?" Harlow asks.

"Wherever he is. He never goes anywhere without it."

"Then there's the matter of the password," I remind him.

"Four-nine-four-two. It's his house number. He uses it for everything."

"I'm going to pretend it's not weird that you know that," I say.

"What? I've seen him type it in a lot."

"Anyway," Hallie says, "if it's always on him, then how do you expect to get it away from him?"

"That's true, Jacob," I admit. "No bond is as sacred and unbreakable as the one between a teenager and his phone."

He sighs. "I guess it's kind of pointless."

"It's not pointless," someone says. "You found a way to take us down, now do it."

Hunter Athan, of all people, is standing in the entrance with his phone in his hand and a face made of stone.

"I forgot you could find my phone, too," Jacob says, "and that I trusted you once. Can you believe that?"

Hunter fidgets with his phone. "I had to. I'm sorry."

"You're a bastard," Hallie says flatly. "You didn't have to lead them to us."

He sits on the floor across from us. "You know how hard it is to grow up with the Neophyte prodigy as your brother? I thought I might have had a chance to do something he never could —give firsthand information on one of our targets—and I took it. I'm sorry. I shouldn't have."

We stare at him in silence. My bandaged arm pulses more.

Hunter slides his phone across the floor to Jacob. "We have an app. You can get the Efficacy on here and access all our information."

"I'm not falling for it again," Jacob says, sliding it back. "It's not that I don't believe you, but I don't believe you."

He pushes the phone back towards Jacob. "You have to. I'm gonna help you. Really. I promise. I won't lie to you again."

Jacob pushes it back to Hunter again. "Hunter . . ." he trails off, searching for something in his head. "You told them our whereabouts. You explained all our special traits, including you-know-what, and that *especially* ticked me off. You brought them all to the Castle, and, not that this one's a big deal or anything, almost got Skylar *killed*."

"So you're not gonna forgive me?"

"No, of course I'm going to forgive you. You're my best friend. Even though you're unbelievably stupid."

Hunter relaxes, just a little. "Thank you."

"Try anything else, though, and I actually *will* kill you."

"I don't doubt that."

I cast a wary glance at Hunter, and I make sure he can see it. Jacob may be quick to grant his forgiveness, but it'll take more than that for mine. I saw him fire at the girl. I saw his stoicism when Jacob found out his best friend had backstabbed him and left a possibility of a literal backstabbing hanging in the air. So what if he'd choose Jacob over the Eradicators? Any idiot would choose Jacob over the Eradicators.

"So you can get to the Efficacy off your phone?" Lexie asks.

"Yep," Hunter says, sliding his phone to her. "Password's four-nine-four-two."

Lexie unlocks it and scrolls through apps. "What's it called? The app, I mean."

"Fluffy Friends Pet Spa," Hunter mutters.

Jacob looks at him. "I've always wondered why you had that thing," he says. "I just thought you were an undercover puppy enthusiast."

"'Kay, found it," Lexie says. "It's protected by three passwords?"

"Yeah, and I know what two are," Hunter says. "I overhead these guys talking about today's passwords. They change day-to-day. Keeps it more secure. The first one is 'starfish'."

Hallie looks at him skeptically. "'Starfish'? Why 'starfish'?"

"Hell if I know."

"Okay, got it," Lexie says. She takes a second to type it in. "It accepted it."

"You sound surprised," Hunter states.

"Well, you kinda betrayed us once, so . . ." She shrugs.

He rolls his eyes then brushes her off. "The second is 'Fleur-de-lis'."

"I don't even know what that is," Lexie says.

"It's because you don't take French," Hallie says. She takes the phone from Lexie and types it in. "Damn Latin students. It's a dead language, you know. You've got to move on sooner or later, to —I don't know, French."

Lexie snatches the phone back. "*Numquam.*"

"Any ideas on the third?" Harlow asks.

"None. I don't know how the system works or how you know the passwords for the day."

"Does Orion have any idea?" Jacob wonders.

"Probably." Hunter shrugs. "He's training in it right now. He's gonna be an Efficacy coder by the time he graduates high school. My parents are so happy or whatever. It's not that great."

"Can you call him and ask for the password?" Hallie suggests.

"No," Hunter says. "I'm a Neophyte. I'm not supposed to go in until my third year."

"So, what next?" Harlow says. "We just guess the password?"

"I guess," Hallie says.

"Great," Jacob says. "There's only, what? A couple hundred thousand words in the English language?"

"There's over one million, actually," I correct.

"Even better."

"And that's assuming it's not a multi-lingual password system."

"Perfect. Thanks, Skylar, for making this even harder."

I shrug and smile. "I'm always such a bubble of sunshine."

He gives me a look and turns back towards Hunter. "Try 'jellyfish'."

Hunter blinks at him. "Why?"

"I don't know. Jellyfish are cool."

"No," I say. "There has to be a logical way to figure this out."

"Logical," Harlow repeats. "Guess Hallie's doing it then."

"My best guess is only as good as 'jellyfish'," Hallie admits with a rueful glance at Jacob.

"If you don't like that one," Jacob says, "'pufferfish' is always an option."

I close my eyes for a second and imagine the Eradicator compound. There has to be a hint somewhere around here, tucked where we can barely see it—there always is. A sticky note on a desk perhaps, or a picture on the wall. It must be there, hidden in plain sight: standing on someone's shelf, marked on someone's whiteboard, suspended from the ceiling, dangling from someone's wrist—

"Does Andrea Jennings do anything with the Efficacy?" I ask Hunter.

He scoffs, "She practically coded the thing."

"In that case, try 'sailboat'."

Lexie gives me a funny look. "Why 'sailboat—"

"And not 'jellyfish'?" Jacob interrupts.

"Andrea wears this bracelet," I say. "It has three charms: a starfish, a fleur-de-lis, and—"

"A sailboat," Hunter finishes. "I never thought of that. She's worn that thing for years, and the charms change every time I see her. Of course, that's how people know the daily passwords. She wears them. You're—"

"Incredibly intelligent?" Jacob fills in. "Absolutely ingenious? So freaking smart you could be a cryptographer?"

"Actually, it would be cryptanalysis," I say. "Cryptography is the study of coding things, cryptanalysis is decoding them."

"I mean, you're really annoying, but you're super smart."

I shoot him a look that I try to make menacing, but I can never pull those off, so I'm assuming it's more mildly confused.

Lexie types in "sailboat" with her lightning-fast texting thumbs. "It works," she announces with a stunned smile on her face. "It actually works."

"Meaning we just hacked what could be the highest level computer in the whole world," Harlow says. "Dear God, I wish I could remember this."

Lexie is about to dive in when Hallie says, "Don't you think we should have some sort of plan before we go in all willy-nilly?"

"Please," Lexie says, "never say 'willy-nilly' again."

"Willy-nilly. Don't you think we should have some sort of plan before we go in?"

"We can delete everything," Harlow shrugs. "There's protection against time, duh. If we just get rid of their information, then boom, they have nothing, we win, hurrah, wahoo."

"Too easy," I say. "They'd notice that right away."

"So? They still wouldn't have it."

"Still," I say. "A computer of that strength would most likely have some sort of . . . I don't know, an 'undo' function."

"My crappy PC can undo things," she says.

"Exactly my point, Harlow," I sigh. "They would almost certainly have a way to get it back, just by hitting 'command' and 'Z'."

"So what do *you* suggest we do, Miss Cryptanalysis?"

With unwarranted defense, I say, "I don't know, but not that."

She sticks out her tongue at me.

I turn to the only person who somewhat has an idea of what he's doing. "Hunter, any suggestions?"

He shrugs. He looks like Orion when he acts careless, though his hair is lighter and his eyes are darker. "You're the smart ones."

"Thank you for your help. Hallie?"

"We just delete the stuff on us and leave everything else. It was all stupid, anyway."

"A possibility. Lexie?"

"Jump in and stop planning."

"No. That never works. Jacob?"

"We replace all their information with memes."

I sigh. "I don't know why I hang out with these people."

Jacob's about to reply when someone materializes in the doorway. Each cell in my body stops respirating when her eyes lock onto mine.

"Upstairs," Margaret White says. "Now."

Chapter Twenty Four

Some saw the sun,
some saw the smoke.
Some heard the gun,
some bent the bow.
Sometimes the wire must tense
for the note.
Caught in the fire, say oh,
we're about to explode.
Carry your world,
I'll carry your world.

"Atlas"
Coldplay

Margaret's angry face is far, far worse than her reprimanding face.

As it turns out, a Knower—Coira, was her name? what a cool name—saw us poking around Air and Space. She then, as any good little Knower would do, told Margaret. Margaret subsequently flipped.

So now, though it's quite needless to say, I pray for a fire extinguisher because Margaret is fuming.

"Do you know the type of trouble you've gotten all of us into?" she shrieks. Her voice seems to go up the octave when she's upset. "I told you, those people are of absolutely *no* concern to you! If you had *listened,* perhaps, you would have noted that I precisely said that they are an unnecessary burden. Now they are aware of our headquarters location. They have some confirmed faces and can any information on you. If they find a bit of Skylar's blood—" I hate the way she says my name, like I'm a specimen she's studying "—they can begin DNA testing. Before you all came along, we had safety and security, and you've jeopardized it all."

"We're sorry," Lexie squeaks. "We thought we were helping."

Margaret paces around us. "You're newbies. Your version of helping should be sitting quietly and learning how we work."

"We're sorry," Jacob repeats. "We won't do something like this again."

"You can't promise that."

"They really were trying to help," Harlow defends.

"Why are you even here? You don't belong in here. Neither do you." She points at Hunter. "Out, into the hall. Both of you."

"Okay, sorry," Harlow says, standing up and descending the stairs. I give her an apologetic frown before she leaves, and she just shrugs back before throwing a glare to Margaret's back. Hunter follows her silently, his face a blank slate. It's always so difficult to tell what he's thinking.

Margaret runs her fingers through her faded blonde hair and whips back to face us. "Right now, I hold the entire world in my hands. I can do just about anything I want to do, with the help of the people in this room and in rooms like these around the world. So help me God, if this organization falls apart because of a few teenagers, I will pick you apart bit by bit until you're nothing anymore. I don't care about the fact that you're children. We all know that you're far more than that."

"Yeah?" Hallie says back, her eyebrows raised and her fingers twitching in her lap; she's completely unfazed by this somewhat threatening proposition. I shudder, in part because I've been on the receiving end of one of Hallie's wrathful moods. "Then treat us like we're more than children. You know the Eradicators have this computer system, called the Efficacy. I bet you didn't know that."

Margaret takes a second to answer as uncomfortable shuffles suffuse through the room. "I was slightly aware. But—"

"I'd bet even more that you didn't know it's got a firewall against time," Jacob continues. "And if we find a way to take that down, they lose a ton of their data, mostly on us."

"It's got all of our family trees on it," I say, my sudden confidence stemming off of theirs. "And a lot of genetic information. They know quite specific things about us, like how Lexie is adopted or how many siblings we all have." Margaret tenses at this. "I think that they know more than you think they know. If I remember correctly, you told us that their resources were nowhere near the immensity of ours, but quite honestly, I think theirs *surpasses* ours."

"Impossible," Margaret says. "We're the smartest—"

"Well, then the Eradicators are a very close second," Hallie says.

"We know how to take them down," Lexie says. "We just need some assistance."

"We're way more than children," Jacob says. "You said it yourself."

"So treat us like it," Hallie repeats.

"Absolutely not," Margaret scoffs. "We've been handling them all Day; we've been doing just fine without your attempted assistance. If you had bothered to listen, you'd know that they can't hurt you."

"I beg to differ, as they shot me," I remind her. "While at Eradicator training, the fifteen-year-olds were given actual firearms to keep with them and were instructed to fire at passersby to practice. Clearly, they have violent intentions."

"And they blew up Natural History," Lexie adds.

Silence, true silence, the second time I've ever encountered it. This time, it seems far more sinister. It hasn't glided into the room because motion has left and the two can never coexist. No, it was summoned by fear. Now fear grips the imperium of the Castle and those who stand in it; it slowly strangles everything. Silence cheers without making a sound.

Then Margaret becomes an erupting volcano, lava spewing out of her every pore. "*That's* the reason you went after the Eradicators? Because of Natural History?"

Hallie's the only one brave enough to speak, and even her voice trembles. "Yeah."

"You absolute imbeciles! If you'd had a clue! *We* blew up Natural History!"

My chest sets itself on fire and my mind stops working properly.

Jacob raises an eyebrow. "I'm sorry, you *what*?"

"We caused the explosion," Miss Felding borderline mouths. She shrinks into her desk and almost disappears.

"And you just *forgot* to tell us?"

"We thought you'd find our motives violent, when really, they weren't."

"Oh, right, blowing up a Smithsonian is a total pacifist move."

"You don't understand anything yet," Margaret says. "The world works in ways that are very difficult to understand, and your minds are too weak to take it—"

I solidify. A cloud drops me, but instead of gliding down to Earth like normal, I pick up speed. Colors dance around me like a running sunset: burning scarlets and ambers, singing tangelos, screaming saffrons, shrieking ecrus, and chartreuse and emerald and azure and cobalt and fuchsia and indigo and suddenly I'm like

Harlow, not one color but every shade of every hue at once, a glowing ball of white light the size of the moon.

And I run through the field again, where the sky is cherry and every blade of grass screams at me—no, they scream *because* of me—and the entire world melts at a flick of my hand. Margaret isn't in control, *I* am, *I* move mountains with a blink of an eye and I grip lightning in my hands and I hold the sky on my shoulders.

I say goodbye to the rainclouds and welcome inferno instead. It's much warmer, after all.

"Although I apparently can't understand anything of value," I say, "I certainly can understand that you're no better than they are, and that you have no right to say that you are."

"Excuse me?"

"You blew up a building," I state, "and for whatever reason you decided to do that, you believed those people in there were disposable. This Day may prevent them from dying in the eyes of everyone else, but that doesn't change the fact that they *died*, at least to us. Hell, you engineered an entire nonexistent Day, not to stay away from everyone, like I thought, but to have everyone stay away from *you*. You just want to be able to get away with anything you want with absolute impunity. You couldn't care *less* about running the world *well*. You just want to run it. I find there to be a stark difference between the two."

Margaret's eyes lunge at me. They pick me apart, atom by atom, until I'm just a pile of protons and neutrons and electrons scattering the scuffed hardwood.

But, for once in my life, I don't want to crawl under a table. I don't want my river or my willow tree. I don't break eye contact with her, and my hands are not shaking. I stand by every word I say, and I throw them at her like stones. Should she pick up each of my individual atoms and throw each one into her volcano, I'll just jump in before she can drop me. She seems to have trouble realizing that matter can't be created or destroyed, so she can't turn me into nothing.

"You have no idea what you're messing with," Margaret says. "I can destroy you."

"I can destroy you, too, Margaret. I think you often forget that."

We stand, eyes locked, for a few smoldering seconds.

"Out," Margaret says. "Get out of this room."

And we do, without a single word.

"What did I just do?"

"You excommunicated us," Hallie replies to me. "And I don't even care."

"You got pretty intense," Lexie says. "From zero to one-hundred in, like, three seconds."

"I didn't know you could be so assertive, Bubble," Jacob says.

"I—" All the adrenaline wears off and I start to shake, and not all jittery like before. These trembles rack my entire body like mini earthquakes only I can feel. "They . . . they can't do that, and they *especially* can't create a whole nonexistent day to justify doing that. I had to tell her that, since no was else was going to."

"Why would they even blow up Natural History?" Lexie wonders. She looks abjectly defeated. "We're the *good* guys, aren't we?"

Children were in that museum. Little kids.

"Good and bad are just so superficial," Harlow says. She and Hunter walk up to us, their faces telling us that they were eavesdropping. "It's all human-made stuff. One person's good is another person's bad, and vice versa. That's what makes life so hard. All those stupid blurred lines."

All anybody wanted was to visit Henry the giant elephant and see the gemstones and maybe watch a tarantula feeding. Nobody walks into the rainforest expecting a blizzard.

"Maybe they blew it up for a statement?" Hallie wonders. "Did they want to show the Eradicators that they're stronger?"

"I just got us kicked out of the Knowers." I pace around the room.

The thing about powerful people is that their power is the cause for their veneration. What they do with it is secondary.

"Seems unlike them," Jacob says, "but then again, so does blowing it up in the first place."

"And the worst part is, I almost don't care. I almost *always* care. Shit flying fudge for the love of God I'm a meteorite, how did that even happen? What did you guys do to me?"

"There has to be a reason," Hallie says.

Raindrops don't question the people who make decisions for them. All of their trust is invested blindly into whatever force is just barely out of their control. A moment of disquietude isn't questioned because the galactic bodies beyond their reach weren't built to be challenged.

The galactic bodies just wait for enough raindrops to pile up so they can create the maximum splash when they land. Forget the fact that the entire puddle will evaporate at that very moment. It's not important. They're not important.

"It's obvious," Lexie says. "They thought the Eradicators were in there."

"She's right, she can completely destroy me! She can just pick me apart and throw me into a volcano and then just erase me from ever existing." I try to think happy thoughts. None come to mind.

"I mean, I guess," Jacob says, "but why would they blow it up then? Wouldn't you guys just be alive again tomorrow?"

"No," Hunter says. "If Eradicators die on the Day, they fall brain-dead, like you guys."

"Half-alive, half-dead." Jacob lets out a breath. "Like their brains can't decide to live or die, so they kind of do both."

"Which is worse than either option, I think."

They killed people.

"So not only did I send the Eradicators after me, but the Knowers, too! Oh my gosh, why the *hell* am I all the sudden such a fireball? I should've never even come to this stupid Meeting! Everything would be fine if I didn't." Evan and his marshmallow obsession can't save me now. I try thinking about manatees instead.

But there were children in that museum.

"So there. Maybe they just wanted to kill them all and get rid of them," Lexie says.

"No, it doesn't match up, though," Jacob sighs. "Too high-profile. Don't you think they would have done something quieter if killing them all was what they wanted to do? If they made this whole Day to stay away from the government, then why would they bring the entire government to them?"

"You think they care?" Hallie challenges. "Honestly. You think they care anything about police roaming around? They're tucked up in their tower, watching down on chaos and laughing, probably, since they caused it."

Jacob plays with a twist-tie, bending and unbending it without giving it any thought. "Except they must've figured out they weren't in there, so they're not done yet, and something tells me they're not gonna try another explosion."

Not even manatees are working. "I didn't ever want to be a meteorite, never ever *ever*, and here I am, about to kill everyone who stands with me, and what do I even stand *for*? Them or us, or just *us,* not us? Why does anything matter, anyway? Why don't I just go turn myself in now and save you all? But I don't want to! What if I'm on *their* side, not ours? What if I'm not on ours either?"

"So what *are* they gonna try?" Lexie asks.

"Something worse," Hallie says. "Something much, much worse."

"No one would care, anyway, if I just turned myself in. It's not like I'm needed for anything. I'm worthless."

"When you grow up, you're going to start to realize how awesome you are," Harlow says. Everyone falls silent when she says this; she's been so quiet that I've almost forgotten she's here. "You'll finally understand why I think you're like Atlas, that Titan guy from Greece. You hold the entire sky on your shoulders, but unlike him, you don't realize that you do, and you never see how needed you are, how everyone depends on you to keep the sky from crushing them."

I'm rendered thoughtless.

"And when Hallie grows up, she'll realize it's okay to laugh when you find something funny. And Lexie won't have to deal with people making fun of her family because it doesn't fit their definition of what a family should be. And Jacob, you'll realize your mind is really cool and that you aren't defined by that stupid label. And Hunter, you won't have to be forced into beliefs you never wanted to believe in the first place."

"And you, Harlow? What will happen when you grow up?"

"When I grow up, I hope I can remember at least one second of this Day. It's the best one I've had by far."

My star competes with the sun for who can outshine the other. In all honesty, I think Harlow's winning.

Chapter Twenty Five

Once I made a man all out of snow.
He had the darkest eyes
and a button nose.
I told him all my sadness and my fear,
and he just listened
with a snowy ear.
But when I came around the next day,
my friend had gone and melted all away.
I saw his eyes lying on the ground
and I made a sound
that was something
like crying.

"Men of Snow"
Ingrid Michaelson

"Do you agree with me now?" Jacob says. "That too much smart in one room isn't that good of a thing?"

"No comment," I respond.

"'No comment' is a comment."

"Will you just stop talking?"

"Probably not, if I'm being honest."

We've left the Castle and have gone to American History. The proposition of staying in that building makes me nauseous, so we cut across the Mall in groups of two and go through the back entrance. There aren't as many police in here, but they still travel in swarms.

I feel like if someone ever asked me what history smells like, I'd tell them to walk through the doors of the National Museum of American History and inhale the ocean breeze air freshener attempting to mask the mustiness and the mothballs hiding between folds of elegant and fading fabric. Oh, and Windex. Lots of Windex because of tiny children pressing their impressionable faces against the glass keeping them out of history's way. Museum janitors have to wipe their marks away so we can see the marks that matter to a wider range of people.

"Where's a good quiet place?" Harlow wonders aloud. "With no detectives or news guys?"

"What about in there?" Jacob recommends, and we follow him to a tiny room filled to the brim with ship paraphernalia. It's mostly empty except for an older man who isn't dressed like a police man and seems far more interested in the anchors than us. He might be a detective who's either on break or bored with this investigation—I can't see either because I can't believe they'd allow breaks during this and that this isn't the coolest and most intense investigation of his career. He doesn't even cast a glance in our direction when we walk in, so we slip to the opposite corner of the room and move behind a giant coil of fraying rope. Hallie fits in perfectly here in the ship room, even if only I can see her anchorness.

Miss Felding told us not to mess anything up, that we would just watch today and not touch a thing. I didn't touch anything, but I did obliterate everything in sight. A minor infraction.

"Who thinks we should just wait here until the Day reverses itself?" Lexie questions. "There's nothing left for us to do, really, so . . ."

"That's not true," Jacob says. "They're planning their next move. Maybe even putting it into action. We have to plan ours."

"Our move to what? Stop them?" Hallie asks. "We want to get rid of them, too, don't we?"

"Not . . . not like that. They want to literally *end* them. We just want to stop them from bugging us."

The man wears a bulky, eggplant-colored sweater. I didn't know sweaters came in a color so distasteful.

"We don't even know what they're planning, so we can't stop it," Hallie says.

"Then we figure out what it is and *then* stop it."

The man who's in the room with us ambles closer to us. Hunter's watching him closely; I can see it in his dark eyes. The clunk of heavy-booted footsteps are the only noise in the room other then our occasional shuffle. The walking eggplant gazes at each display with an odd sense of hunger, like he wants to become a boat himself.

The weirdest thing about this room is that the glass is reflective. Usually, the Smithsonian museums use museum-grade glass that doesn't have any glare. This room must not have made the cut when they switched over the other glass, a far more expensive but professional option.

He's not looking at the bottled ships and types of knots. He's looking at us; he watches us like he wants to mount us on his wall.

He then brushes his belt, conveniently covered by his bulky eggplant sweater, and just barely reveals the S-shaped trigger of a dull silver gun.

They could be in every single room in every single building in D.C. There could be one on my street, on Harlow's street, even. I know for a fact that one is my teacher, and now I know for a fact that Orion wasn't playing when he said they are everywhere.

I look at Jacob and then glance towards Eggplant Man. He seems to get the message and says, "We should get back, guys."

"They don't want us back," Hallie says. "I thought it was obvious."

"No, I mean we should get back," Jacob repeats. "Soon, probably."

"You're kidding, right?" Harlow scoffs. "You—"

I put my hand on top of hers and stare her in the eye. She gets the message and glances at Eggplant Man behind her.

The man paces to a display case closer to us.

Jacob types something on his phone and hands it to Hallie. After reading, she says to Lexie, "No, Jacob's right, we've been looking at the ships long enough." She stares at her.

"Yeah," Hunter agrees, not taking his eyes off the other man. "Like, they'll be mad or something."

Lexie's eyes shift color, darting between each of us and Eggplant Man. She pretends to look at a watch on her wrist, though she only wears a woven bracelet. "Oh, wow, you're right, it's almost three-thirty. We should head back."

"Back where?" The man's voice is made of broken glass shards being rubbed against a blackboard; it makes me cringe with just two words. How can a voice be crunchy?

"Back home," Jacob replies. I close my eyes and pray Eggplant believes him. He really can't lie to save his life, and the sad-but-true thing is that in this business, you *do* lie to save your life. Lies to your family, friends, teachers, and even to yourself are the difference between having your brain dissected by madmen and going to high school and memorizing the different numbered Louises.

Lexie takes over. "We're supposed to be back to our apartment by four," she says sweetly. I wonder if she's ever taken improv classes. If she hasn't, she totally should; she'd be a natural. Then she stands up without using her hands and pushes her corkscrew curls out of her face. "Come on, guys."

In one motion, Eggplant Man draws his silver handgun tricked out with an S-shaped trigger and a fingerprint sensor. "If I were you, I wouldn't move a muscle."

"Well, you're not them, and you never will be," Harlow says. "So don't bother. I guarantee that they're better. In lots of ways. You can stop trying."

We have no weapons to draw, but between the six of us, we've got a hurricane, an anchor, a highlighter, a star, a shard of shale, a bubble, three working cell phones, and four minds that make us an unpredictable and audacious force because we lack neurotransmitters. This guy couldn't possibly stand a chance against us.

Except he's already shot Harlow, who now has a bullet straight through her chest.

Some things speed up, like how long it takes me to get to her, and other things are in slow motion, like the action in the rest of the room. I can't hear anything but Harlow's short, rasping breaths. A trickle of blood is a tiny red waterfall from the corner of her mouth. Her entire body convulses as she tries to scream but she is only given small, throaty noises in place of words. I hold her hand and say her name over and over again; she doesn't hear a thing or say anything back to me.

Her death isn't silent. It's not beautiful. There are no earth-shattering last words or violin music playing in the background. But her light does intensify, until everyone within a million miles is blinded, before it fades into a black light that turns your teeth and white clothes a bright purple, a million times brighter than Orion's, before she collapses on herself and disappears completely into the black hole she's created. The universe has been torn apart; nothing can sew up the scar she's left, not even time itself.

It's Jacob who takes me out of the shrieking room and outside the museum. I fight him on it—I think I may punch him a couple times—but he's stronger than he looks. He sits on the ground with me, holding me, and he lets me sob without a single word.

"I have to go back to her," I whisper. Everything feels hazy, like I'm watching the snowfall from a frosted-over window. The edges of all the buildings and people walking past are blurred; I can't tell when one thing ends and the next begins. "You have to let me." I try to stand up, but he keeps me where I am.

"Skylar, you need to stay here." His voice is static. My head is on his shoulder; my entire body is shaking. "You can't go back in there."

"I need her. I can't go through anything without her. Let me go back to her."

"You have to stay here," he says. "Please."

"She's gone, and I don't have her anymore."

"Remember, today doesn't exist. She'll wake up absolutely fine in the morning. Everything will be fine, Bubble, I promise."

"She won't be *fine,* Jacob, she's *dead.*"

"And she won't be tomorrow, remember?"

"She will have *been* dead, at least to me. Time can't fix the stuff that happens to us."

"I know."

"It's horrible."

"I know."

"I want her back."

"I know."

"It's been five minutes and I want her back already."

"She knew he was going to shoot," he says quietly. "And she knew there was only one person in that room who wouldn't be affected by the bullet."

Footsteps walk towards us. Someone sits next to me. "How is she?" Hallie's voice asks.

"How do you think I am?" I don't move to look up at her.

"Skylar, listen to me," Hallie says. "When you wake up, you can dial Harlow's number, and she will pick up the phone. She's completely fine. You know that."

"Is your definition of *fine* synonymous with dead on the floor of a Smithsonian?"

Hallie takes a couple of breaths before responding. "I don't lie to you. Ever. You know that, too. And right now, I'm telling you everything is going to be fine."

"It's *going* to be fine. It isn't fine *now,* is it?"

"Not really, but at least you know it *will* be okay tomorrow," Lexie says. She and Hunter sit next to Hallie. Hunter's face looks more like slate than it usually does. He looks as if he shot her himself.

"I don't want them to find her there," I say. "All black and torn apart, surrounded by bits of stardust."

Naturally, no one knows what I mean, and they don't ask.

"I don't know what will happen to her," Lexie admits. "But we tied up that Eradicator with the ropes in there and shot him with his own gun."

"Is he dead?"

"No, just bleeding slowly," Hunter says with no trace of remorse.

"That's very descriptive. What did you do to him?"

"Knees," Hunter says. "It won't kill him, but he won't be able to move for the rest of the Day."

This is no longer a matter of a one-click delete of their information and hoping they don't notice. No, I want to pick them apart, bit by bit, destroy them slowly, make them suffer, like Tantalus and his retracting fruit tree, inducing eternal torment, haunting them with knowledge that someone out there watches their every move, plucking each eyelash out one by one.

They moved their piece on this chessboard. My next move is going to checkmate.

Except I don't know if I'm playing as black or white, which makes it a difficult game to play.

Chapter Twenty Six

We walked up to the tower,
they looked down from above.
I never dreamed trouble could be coming from
so few people.
Wherever you are,
let's get loud like thunder.
Know in your heart they won't drag us under.
They can blow, every brick we lay will make us stronger.
All we heard was a whisper,
when they paid for a beating drum.
They never dreamed together we could make a sound
that would drive them out.

"Thunder"
SHAED

    I silently conspire, my head still resting on Jacob's shoulder because I don't care enough to move it. (Also, he smells like lavender. I didn't know boys could smell like lavender. I mean, I have extremely limited experience, but still.) The thing is, though, I have no idea where to start my conspiring.

    You're a Knower, now think like one, my brain tells me. I try to tell it that it can't do much of anything because it's much too jumpy and utterly useless. It screams back, You *have the advantage,* you *have a dandelion brain. Now use it.*

    Okay, I reply. So I start with water, because that's where I always start.

    I took swim lessons when I was five, as it's mandatory for all kindergarten classes, due to the fact we live surrounded by water. I remember I'd finish a lap full of triumph, then I'd dangle at the side of the pool, waiting for the instructor to give her corrections, to which I'd never listen. I'd stick my tiny fingers in the jets, attempting to thwart the water pressure, my tiny toes trying to brush the bottom of the pool. They never did.

    Our instructor was a willowy senior named Delaney Mallonski desperate for volunteer hours. She wasn't a bad teacher, but she did give you that feeling that you were always her second thought. I mean, we probably were—she was a social butterfly with a hot boyfriend and a convertible that looked like a roofless lemon. I don't think she would've cared one bit if we drowned, only if it cost her service hours and thwarted her graduation.

I read somewhere that if drowning doesn't kill you first, you can slip into an anoxia-induced coma, meaning that your brain doesn't have enough oxygen to function and kind of shuts down. That's what happens to Knowers, I've heard, when they die on the Day. Though horribly morbid, I've always secretly wondered what that feels like, flitting somewhere between falling asleep and dying.

I don't have any idea why it's called *falling* asleep, really. You don't *fall* at all. Maybe it's called that because you can't control falling. If you decided to fall asleep, it would be call jumping asleep rather than falling. Falling is the loss of control, which must be why I hate is so much. If I wanted to lose my control over things, I'd simply jump.

I was obsessed with jump rope when I was six. Hallie and I would make up our own rhymes to jump in time to. Hallie's mostly had to do with horses, as she was (and still is) one of those girls obsessed with horses with the gold horse charm bracelet and the running horses music box that plays "Home on the Range" and five million Breyers. Mine mostly revolved around whales or other marine mammals. I was (and still am) a whale girl with the silver whale necklace and the jewelry box with the watercolors of the ocean and five million stuffed sea critters.

People never believe me when I tell them I've never seen the ocean. They always remark on how it's impossible for me to love something that I've never seen. I mean, people love celebrities without ever having seen them, so it's the same thing, really. You can love something despite having never laid eyes on it without the aid of a screen or photograph.

I've always wanted to get into photography, but I've never gotten around to it. Jessamine's best friend from college, a wiry hipster who carried a red Moleskin notebook and wore fraying sweaters named Cyleigh (pronounced like Kylie—it took me a while to figure that out), is a master of the art and sends Jessamine black and white prints that she develops in the closet she's converted to a dark room. Jessamine has them pinned all over her tiny studio apartment that's got exposed brick walls and these windows that are so big and so crystal clear that you can see the whole city through them. Jessamine says she bought the apartment for the view. I don't blame her; sunsets turn the whole white-walled space into a work of art you can dance in. One sunset, she invited only Harlow and me over and we made cookies and danced in her art studio whose only paint is light.

Harlow. No, keep going.

Spencer's best friend stole a traffic light once. His name was Roger, but everyone called him Rouge. Harlow said that she told him once that "Rouge" is just "red" in French and that he probably wanted to spell his name "Rogue" if he meant what she thought he meant, but he wouldn't hear it. Anyway, he stole a traffic light, and Aunt Clara *flipped* on Spencer, even though he was at an Obligatory Family Dinner Night while Rouge stole the stoplight and had literally nothing to do with the ordeal. She said that he had to "make better life choices" and "surround yourself with friends that leave good impressions on you". Harlow had me on the phone the whole time so we could tune in, and I think we both burst capillaries from suppressing our manic laughter.

There she is again, ever present in my mind. I force her out for the moment.

Hallie came over after the Snow Ball in eighth grade. For some reason, just about everyone in my class wanted to go to this dance, and I couldn't just not go and be the only one not there. My dad picked us up and drove us home, and I walked Hallie to her front door. She'd kissed Kyle Connors and I'd eaten three brownies and some chocolate covered bananas, so we were both in these weird, giggly moods. It was cold, the coldest I've ever felt on the island. I hugged my ski jacket closer to my frail body in an attempt to warm myself up, to no avail. I trudged up Hallie's front path with her, coming to the realization that no one had shoveled. On my trek back, I fell face first into the snow. Instead of getting worked up like I usually do, I starting laughing uncontrollably. Here I was, in this freshly fallen snow, laughing like a hyena, my boots freezing onto my feet, my dress soiled. I was borderline hysterical, playing in the snow, tripping on ice and laughing as I went. It was a moment that didn't seem to exist at all.

I didn't know half of the departments of government existed at all until Mr. Hallawin taught a whole week's worth course on them in the middle of September. We thought it was stupid because what does this have to do with Mesopotamia, but it ended up being a bit interesting. Ms. Redding's brother even came in to talk about his job in the Department of Interior and his son's position in the Department of Homeland Security—

Half a face in a photograph behind Ms. Redding's desk flashes in front of me. Another glimpse of yellow hair and ice eyes, walking down the hall of school towards Ms. Redding's room at the beginning of the school year. A jawline so sharp it could cut you and nervous freckles and a quicksilver smile front and center in the basketball portrait in the gym's foyer. A name so simple that he could be anyone, anywhere, but those four syllables were dropped in both Miss Felding's phone conversations and Margaret's passing asides, thus proving their worth.

I don't know exactly what he's done, but he's done something.

And then there he is—tall and lanky, moving towards Delaney Mallonski and kissing her right on the lips in the middle of our swim lesson, pleading with the kindergarteners not to tell on him.

"I'll give you guys anything if you don't tell," Thomas Redding emptily pleaded to a pool of five-year-olds in Little Mermaid one-pieces and dollar-store water wings.

I never did tell, and I haven't taken him up on his offer yet.

The entrance to the lobby of Nebraska Avenue Complex is about as daunting as its name implies. It's just a bunch of buildings, mostly red stone and frosty glass. Hallie immediately decides the best way to get in was to be as open as possible about it. I agree with her; I mean, how difficult can getting into Homeland Security be? It's not like they're specially trained in security or anything.

My hair is pulled up in pigtails to make me seem younger. Before Hallie and I leave the other three outside and go up to the desk, she takes my glasses and puts them on to make her seem older. Her eyes cross, I think—I can't see a thing, and I take it she can't, either. She holds my hand; her height compared to my pipsqueak-ness really makes her look like my older sister. Except I must have been adopted because Hallie and I look nothing alike except for our pale skin and dusting of freckles, hers more haphazard than mine.

"Can I help you?" the secretary says. Even half-blind, I can tell that she thinks we're a waste of time; it's evident in her furrowed brow and slightly exaggerated exhales.

"Hi, we need to see Mr. Thomas Redding," Hallie says. "As soon as possible."

She sighs again. "May I ask why?"

"Well, Laura, here," she holds up my hand, "is doing a Fun Family Facts presentation in her third grade class—"

"Fourth grade," I correct her, forcing as much baby-ness into my voice as I can.

"Fine, *fourth* grade class, and she wants to surprise Thomas by doing them on his work, but I didn't want to ask and be awkward."

"I'm sorry, but that's classified information," the secretary says.

"Even for me?" I pout. "I'm Uncle Tommy's favorite!"

"Laura, quiet," Hallie scolds me. Then, thinking for a second beforehand, she says in an undertone to the secretary, "You know Margaret White?"

There's a visible change on her face. Her pupils dilate and her cheeks turn a single shade darker darker. "No, I don't know who that is."

"Really? I have a feeling you do," Hallie says. "Just about everyone who's anyone knows about Margaret White but has no idea the person next to them does."

She gapes like a fish.

"I'm with her," Hallie continues. "I'm one of her messengers. I need to see Thomas Redding. And if you won't give me his building number, or, better yet, permission to see him, I can, and I *will*, find an alternate and not entirely ethical way into his office, all on Margaret's behalf."

"I have no idea what you're talking about," the secretary protests.

"Yes you do, but you know you're not supposed to," Hallie says. Her eyes run up and down the woman. "You . . . overheard something. You were walking through the halls, were intrigued by the British accent coming from one of the rooms, and just *had* to stop and listen. Oh, but then you realized this conversation was super top secret, and you listened anyway. You could get in serious trouble for that, you know. If anyone found out."

She's completely silent for almost a full minute. At last, she pulls a sticky note off a pad and chokes out, "Building Nineteen. If there's any issue, though there shouldn't be, not at this time of day, show this to Joseph Mercer at the fifth desk from the left. Mr. Redding is on the ninth floor. Office 921. Lots of houseplants."

She signs a swooping signature that kind of looks like an eagle catching its prey and hands Hallie the note.

"I will warn you, though, that Mr. Redding is not in a very good place today."

"Thank you," Hallie says. "I'll ensure you don't lose this job because of that tiny . . ."

"Infraction," I supply, then I remember I'm supposed to be nine and follow it with, "It's my vocabulary word this week."

"And how will you do that?" The secretary stares at Hallie.

"Time will tell," Hallie says with a smirk only I can see.

And after helping me pull out my pigtails and reclaim my glasses, Hallie finds Building Nineteen, and we walk inside, no sneaking necessary, not with our glorified hall pass. Sure enough, no one asks about us, so we never even have to see Joseph Mercer. We go to the elevator and rise to the ninth floor.

Thomas Redding's office isn't that hard to find. For starters, the amount of houseplants he houses makes the room look like a jungle of wannabes. He sits in the center of it, sitting at a desk with a pile of paperwork. He practically looks the same as he did back in the days of kindergarten swim class, except his jawline is sharper and his boyish bangs are much shorter.

That, and he seems to be in the midst of a mental breakdown.

I can hear his shallow breathing from where I stand, and his eyes dart around the room so quickly, I'm not entirely convinced he can actually see anything. His left hand grips a pencil, but it shakes as if it were the epicenter of an earthquake.

He finally sees us, and if there were any color in his face to begin with, it drains. "Can I help you?"

"Hi, Thomas, Mr. Redding, sir," I say. *How do I start this? Don't be a Knower, be you, you* are *a Knower, so handle it like a you-Knower. Wait, what does that even mean?* "You most likely don't remember me, as not a lot of people do, but I'm Skylar Rawlings. I believe you owe me a favor, and I would like if I could cash that in now."

"What the hell?" he says. "Leave me alone. I'm gonna call security, I'm warning you—" The quaver in his voice makes the threat hollow.

"Remember Delaney Mallonski?"

"I . . . What? I haven't talked to her in years."

"Oh, I know," I say. "Not since graduation, I'm guessing, because," I take a prolonged look around the room for dramatic effect, "she didn't want to deal with a long-distance relationship in college? But you never really got over her, right? Well, anyway, that's besides the point. Remember that day at the pool, when she was teaching that class of kindergarteners?"

He shakes his head.

"I've never told."

It takes him a full minute, but his face shifts when he finally remembers. "You know I was joking, right? Just trying to get you guys out of my hair?"

"In the future, you may not want to joke around kindergarteners. They're a lot smarter than you think."

He sighs as if he were bored, but he obviously forces it—it comes out shaking, just like the rest of him. "Fine, what do you want? Money?"

"Information."

"On what? You're, like, twelve. What could you want information on?"

"I'm fifteen!"

"Do you know Margaret White?" Hallie jumps in.

I'm afraid he may actually throw up. "No. I've never heard that name in my life."

"Are you sure?"

"Yes. Please, just go away."

"We need your help," I say. "Clearly, something happened today, and you probably have something to do with it."

"The fact that you would imply that I had something to do with . . . with *that* is very insulting."

"But it's true, isn't it?" I say. "You're a botanist here."

". . . yes? So?"

"What do you do with your plants?"

"Research," he says.

"Any experimentation?" Hallie asks.

"Some."

"On dangerous plants?"

"Sometimes."

"Did you make a plant-based explosive?"

I almost ask Hallie to stop interrogating him because he looks as if a single breeze can pick him up and turn him to dust.

"That's classified information." His face divulges everything that may have been classified.

"Thomas," I say, "a Smithsonian blew up today. If you have something to do with it, you need to tell us. We aren't affiliated with the police, and we won't tell a soul—"

I add this last part after a moment of hesitation.

"—unless you refuse to give us information on the matter."

"Are . . . are you blackmailing me?" he asks.

"Do you see any envelopes around here?" Hallie says. "Tell us. Do you know who Margaret White is?"

I can barely hear him say, "Yes."

"And did you help her?"

He practically mouths, "I did."

"How?"

It must take him three minutes to begin the story. "We got connected through a few people. She needed some help with some biohazard containment in Serbia, so I helped her. It was all completely harmless—we actually helped a ton of people. But then, just this morning, she contacted me again and asked for help with something else. She needed explosives and some other plants. And I gave it to her before noon."

"Did she tell you why?"

"An experiment," he responds. "She said only for an experiment. But now I'm getting reports of traces of *Datura stramonium* found outside Natural History, and I'm not so sure they were used for experimentation."

He sways on the spot, and I'm afraid he's going to faint.

"Please, I'm begging you, if anyone finds out, I could lose my job and my entire life."

"Other plants," I repeat. "You said she needed other plants in addition to the explosives. What were those for?"

He actually starts to cry. "Poisonous. All of them. Cyanide, hemlock, *Atropa belladonna*, *Ricinus communis*, *Abrus precatorius*—everything I knew, I gave her."

Hallie and I exchange a glance.

Thomas opens a drawer in the filing cabinet next to his desk and produces a folder. "Take it. I don't want it. Burn it when you're done. Never let me see it again. You did *not* get that from me."

"Thank you," I say. "We won't tell."

Thomas looks at us as if he just can't believe us. Honestly, I can't blame him. If you loan a book to somebody and they return it with a torn cover and dog-eared pages, it's extremely difficult to give a book to anyone else ever again.

"That woman is going to do horrible things," Thomas tells us. "Amazing things, but horrible. Get away from her."

We leave a catatonic Homeland Security botanist shaking is his office, surrounded by his plants.

We find the other three outside. "How'd it go?" Lexie asks. "What did you get?"

Hallie holds up the folder. "All this. I haven't looked at it yet."

"Well, we can't stay here and do it," Jacob says. "Everyone here is kinda panicking. Probably because they're Homeland Security, and the security of the homeland was just totally compromised."

"That probably has something to do with it," Hunter says. "Come on. The Day is too short to wait around." We begin to walk down the sidewalk.

"Hey, Jacob," I say. As soon as he looks over to me, I regret everything. Literally *everything*. Like, from my birth to this moment. It's an alien invasion on my brain, but if all the aliens were cringes. I could totally just keep harboring this unyielding gratitude because that's what I normally do anyways—isn't it just so much easier to keep your thoughts bouncing around your head rather than share them with anyone? But this subsides rather quickly, and I take a breath, and I get my hands to (miraculously) stop shaking.

"What's up?" he replies. We lag a few paces behind the rest of the group.

"Thank you," I say.

". . . you're welcome?"

"Everyone else went to Eggplant Man first. Even my best friend. She didn't think to come to me because as much as she loves me, she doesn't think like that. But you . . . do."

"You had to get out of there," he tells me. "I just . . . got you out of there."

I can't help but giggle, just a little bit.

"What?"

"You took something of extreme magnitude and reduced it to fourteen words, with a pause in the middle," I say.

". . . sorry?"

"You really shouldn't be," I reply. "It's how your brain works. And it has nothing to do with Knowerism. And maybe not even your brain."

"And what, exactly, does that mean?"

"You're smart," I say, taking a few big steps to catch up with everyone else. "I'm sure you could figure it out."

Chapter Twenty Seven

Well, I was there on the day
they sold the cause for the queen,
and when the lights all went out,
we watched our lives on the screen.
I hate the ending myself, but it started with an alright scene.
It was the roar of the crowd
that gave me heartache to sing.
It was a lie when they smiled and said, "You won't feel a thing."
And as we ran from the cops, we laughed so hard it would sting,
yeah.
If I'm so wrong, how can you listen all night long?
Now will it matter after I'm gone?
Because you never learn a goddamned thing.

"Disenchanted"
My Chemical Romance

Over the course of the day, I have learned some things about my friends.

For starters, Hallie is excellent under pressure. I mean, we all have pretty good reflexes because we're so impulsive, but Hallie —it's like she jumps off a diving board into whatever problem it is we're facing and she just stays there treading water until the pool is devoid of any problem with which to be dealt. She gets in this state where her eyes are glossed over and her mouth sits in a thin line and the soldiers on the other side of the battlefield start praying for mercy; it's like she's got a switch that can turn her aggressiveness on or off. It's quite amazing to watch her flip that switch and become a throat-slashing goddess that's not only beautiful but immensely powerful and extremely fear-inducing.

And Lexie almost never stops smiling. Although we've dealt with some pretty un-smile-worthy endeavors today, one corner of her mouth or the other is just about always turned up. It's like a reflex, almost. I can't help but wonder if she lives in a constant state of happiness, for permanent smiles are impossible to fake, or if she'll ever encounter something that will erase that smile like chalk off a blackboard, so it lands on the wooden tray in microscopic white flakes. I pray to God she doesn't. Once one loses a permanent smile, they're so difficult to get back, and Lexie certainly deserves hers.

And Hunter isn't as stoic as I previously thought he was. His emotions are just displayed in very tiny ways. I can tell when he's happy because his eyes aren't a bit squinted as they are when he's not. His lips part just a bit when he's surprised. His ears turn red when he's upset about something. It's like he has his own alphabet that he uses, one that no one else can understand unless they really try.

Oh, and Jacob. I've learned a bunch of things about Jacob today. He chews on his lip when he's nervous, and it started bleeding after our encounter with Margaret. He looks up at the sky when he thinks about things. He wants to say a lot more than he actually says, so I can't imagine how many thoughts he must have per second. He's gone from a complete stranger into another person I've memorized like a poem. Each sagacious glance, each time he runs his fingers through his hair, each chuckle he tries to hide but can't—now these things are not just his, but mine, too. I've got them filed away with the rest of the things I've learned about people that used to be strangers. Everyone's been a stranger to me at one point of another.

Oh, and me. I learned something about me, too.

I certainly know how to fuck things up if I really want to.

Since we're running out of museums to hide in, we sit in one of the tiny monuments off of the Mall, where security isn't as high and isn't quarantined as of now. It's a small marble dome commemorating some war heroes whose names I've never heard of. It makes me feel terrible; these men and women died yet I don't know their names. I run my hand over the engraved letters of their names and swear to remember each one. Benjamin J. Griswold, Harry H. Hawes, Bertha Evan Hayes—I wish I knew their stories. If I did, I could run alongside them as they went through their lives, only to have them ended in hate, which is the most horrible way to die. Imagine dying solely because someone hated you, and you never knew why. They only saw you as a threat, not as a person; they dehumanized you. Click, boom, standing on the wrong side of the gun because of the different fire burning in your eyes. A fire extinguisher in the form of a rifle, putting you out.

Hunter is the one going through the file. He methodically reads each piece of paper, then sets them in a pile behind him, like he doesn't want us reading them.

"Hallie was wrong," he states simply.

He doesn't continue. "Are you gonna tell me *why*?" Hallie asks.

"They blew up Natural History to get the Mall on lock-down," Hunter says. "It would get all of the Eradicators into one spot instead of running all over the Mall."

He flips through some more papers.

"There's a tunnel running underground between the Castle and Natural History," he announces. "Thomas Redding hooked them up with some stuff, and they went through the tunnel to plant them in the basement of Natural History. Then boom. Next . . . next is the second part."

"And what is that?" Lexie asks, but she doesn't wait for an answer before taking the packet out of Hunter's hands. She flips through them and squints as she reads them, as if the words are moving and she needs to keep track of them. Then she hands them back to Hunter and says, "You know what, just tell me."

"A poison," he says, his voice completely flat. "They engineered a poison."

"Why do they need to engineer that?" Jacob says. "There're hundreds of poisons just floating around. Arsenic, paint, those little red berries on bushes—did they really need to make a new one?"

"'Prolonged effect'," Hunter reads. "They want it to last longer. Hurt for more time."

"Again, why do they need that?" Jacob repeats.

"Torture," Hallie says. "Maybe."

"They describe it as a 'biological super weapon'," Hunter says.

"And they're just going to make it and keep it until they need it?" Lexie speculates. "Like, use it as a threat?"

"Lexie, today doesn't exist, and nothing that happens today is real," I say, "so if they are engineering something, then they intend to use it today. And besides us, there's only one group of people that this would affect."

"So what's going to happen now?" Jacob asks. "Have they already deployed it? Or is it coming?"

"Quiet for a second, please," I say. Closing my eyes, I rewind the tape playing in my head—though I'm not exactly sure how to work a VCR because those things are dinosaurs—and I watch Margaret from the moment we met her until the moment she sent us out.

This entire thing must have been extremely last minute. There clearly were no prior indications that today's Meeting wouldn't go smoothly. Except when we pulled up to the Mall and Miss Felding saw something, something so terrible that it made her silent. That something was a someone and was Ms. Parkins or another Eradicator. And that's when the previous Meeting plans went up in flames.

So Margaret goes back to her friendly neighborhood botanist Thomas Redding and asks for another favor. He's not going to remember anything anyway, so why not get as much out of him as possible? She suggests the poison. The Knowers need no help concocting the thing—they have a fleet of biochemists and could find a way to make marshmallows lethal. They only need Thomas for help with the dispersion and the ingredients. The poison can't be more than a few hours old, if it's finished at all. Its release has been carefully yet hurriedly planned; the crosshairs are pointed at everyone who stands in the museum. Of course the bystanders don't matter to her—they never do—because their lives have less value than a Knower's in her eyes.

It's clever, really. The odorless, colorless murderers could take anyone they wanted, Eradicator or not. They would travel through the air vents, unleashed somewhere on the first floor, I'd guess, and then they would make a game of reaching every person in the building. Margaret, clad in a gas mask and hazmat suit, would laugh the entire time.

But wouldn't it be close to midnight? Then time would take care of the mess afterwards. They wouldn't have to deal with the police coming and testing the place, and they wouldn't worry about running from the authorities this time. They'd stand in the open, counting five, four, three, two, done.

And in the morning, no Eradicators, no worries, since they'll all be brain dead: half-dead, half-alive, not enough of either to fit into one category. The world would belong to only the Knowers, who could spin it like a globe and move the countries around at will. They could stick South America back to Africa if they wanted, or combine the Atlantic and Pacific oceans so there's only Ocean and no defining lines that make no sense because the water in one sea today will be halfway across the world tomorrow and considered new water when, in all honesty, that water was probably in a glacier and is a million years older than the Knowers moving it around and naming it.

So am I black or white on this chess board?
Depends on who's who.

Chapter Twenty Eight

Little ghost,
you are listening,
unlike most, you don't miss a thing.
You see the truth, I walk the halls invisibly,
I climb the walls, no one sees me.
No one but you.
You've always loved the strange birds.
Now I want to fly into your world.

"Strange Birds"
Birdy

"You went to architecture camp."

"It's not nerdy, I swear," Jacob defends. "It was really cool. I built an entire three-storied structure out of popsicle sticks."

"You think I'm a dork because I like American Girls, yet you went to *architecture camp.*"

"All architecture camps aside, I know how to seal up air vents, no problem."

"Okay, good. We'll try to find you some blueprints somewhere."

"I'm thinking we seal them from the inside *and* the outside, just to make sure no air gets through. So to seal them from the inside, I'll need someone small enough to crawl through the air ducts."

Everyone looks at me.

"I'm not doing it."

They blink.

"Fine, I'll do it."

But I really don't want to.

"And you'll need something to seal up the air ducts with," Hallie reminds us.

Lexie smirks and says, "Easy. Duct tape. The solver of all problems. They sell that everywhere. All you do is cover the vent with it. And since it's already sticky, you don't need to worry about other adhesives. Win-win-win."

"And the matter of the blueprints?"

"Got them," Hunter says, typing voraciously on his phone. "Jacob, I'll send you—" He groans. "My phone just died. Fantastic."

"Are you serious?" Jacob sighs.

"Yeah. Sorry."

He lets out a breath as his eyes dart around the room. "Okay, guess we're doing this the hard way." He stands up.

"And what exactly is the hard way?" I inquire.

He's looking at the ceiling and paying no attention to me, but then he says, "I'll just have to do it myself." He walks out of the room.

I look to Hunter. He only shrugs and says, "He does this all the time. I just ignore it at this point."

I look to Hallie next, who doesn't even acknowledge that I'm looking at her, and then I follow him out of the room and into the hall.

"Jacob. You can't walk around here alone," I protest. "There are far too many guards, and you-know-whats are probably lurking like moray eels in seaweed—"

"I need paper," he says to himself. I follow his gaze towards the ceiling. "And a floor plan would be helpful, so I don't have to do that from scratch."

I follow him to a circular information desk, and he takes a stack of paper maps. Then he grabs a stack of paper from the printer and four mechanical pencils from a plastic cup. He leans against the desk and starts drawing something, occasionally stopping only to close his eyes for a matter of seconds before adding new lines.

"What are you doing?" I ask.

"Bubble, I'm sorry, but please be quiet," he responds without looking up. He unfolds a map and makes little notes in the margins, then he turns back to his original drawing. Sometimes his pencil moves so quickly that I can't see the tip, and other times so slowly that I can't tell it's moving at all. His lines are straight without a ruler, and all of his angles look right without a compass.

He takes his stack of paper and moves briskly down the hall; I try my best to keep up with him. His hands move across walls, he measures door frames with his palm, and he moves around the halls in zig zags. As he sprints up and down the stairs about twenty times, I hear him counting in numbers that don't seem to match up. Once all of his papers are haphazardly scattered across the floor, he goes through fourteen more sheets and an entire mechanical pencil, just by sketching out the things he's found. In no more than a minute, his papers are all stacked again, and he's running down the upstairs halls, until he stops abruptly in the center, measures the air with his palm once again, and scribbles something onto one of his maps.

"Skylar," he calls from inside an exhibit.

"Yes?" I answer.

"I need another pencil. Could you grab me one please?"

I go back to the information desk, grab three more mechanical pencils, check to make sure they have lead, and go into the exhibit, where I find him perched on a chair and peering into a vent. I give him the pencils, and he adds a few lines to two of his drawings, then hops down and goes back into the hall. I take a breath and realize just how tiring following him around is.

As he's counting how many steps it takes for him to get from one of the hall to the other, he drops one of his maps. I pick it up and look at it. In every available space, he's made notes and little sketches in sloppy handwriting but pristine artistry. Over half of it appears to be various numbers and equations, ones that I know I've never seen before. On the layout, he's drawn in other little things like doors and windows, obvious by little arcs and rectangles, but he's also added other tiny symbols that make no sense to me, but that's because I didn't make them.

After almost forty minutes, Jacob once again spreads everything across the floor. Except now, he's ordered each of the printer sheets in a larger rectangle. On each one sits gentle lines interlocking to create a large and intricate map of the museum. Then with the calculator on his phone and another sheet of paper completely covered in numbers, he adds measurements of each little wall segment and puts slash marks on some of them. After a solid minute of looking it all over, he adds darker lines around some of the wall segments, most of them being those with slashes. In a few minutes, the pencil falls from his hand.

With only his brain and some scrap paper, Jacob has blue-printed all of Air and Space.

"This is the vent." He points to one on the right side. "This is where they're going to let the poison go. And this," he points to another one, "is where you'll climb into the system to seal it."

I can't even process what he's saying. "Did you actually just do that?"

"Do what?"

"Just drew all of Air and Space."

"Oh. Yeah." He points to another area in the middle of the museum. "So, here is where—"

"You just drew all of this museum *by memory,* with nothing but some stick-figure maps and sheer intuition, yet you're shrugging it off like everyone in the world can do this. I guarantee that ninety-nine-point-ninety-nine percent of the world can't do what you've just done."

He looks up from his map. "So? Ninety-nine-point-ninety-nine percent of the world can't call out the Eminence of the planet for being a jerk, but you did."

"I— That's not nearly as impressive."

He gives me a look and then neatly stacks all the sketches and maps. "Come on, we should get started soon. We're already almost an hour behind. Sorry."

"It's certainly not your fault. I blame the inadequate longevity of iPhone batteries."

"There you guys are!" Lexie exclaims once we get back. "Where'd you go?"

It takes Jacob only a second to lay out the sheets in their formation. "Okay, so here is the vent—"

"Dude, you drew this?" Hallie crosses her arms and looks dubious.

"Yeah. Anyway, this vent is on the exterior side—"

"You actually did all this?" Lexie's eyes are wide.

"Yes!" Jacob exclaims. "Would everyone stop acting so surprised? It's not that big a deal."

"Okay, then I'm going to whatever architecture camp you went to."

"This vent here," Jacob continues, pointing to one and paying no attention to Lexie, "will be the one where they'll set the poison off, I'm pretty sure. Look, it's on the exterior wall on the side closest to the Castle. Chances are, they won't want to walk too far with deadly stuff in their hands, especially because there're so many guards swooping around here, looking for people like them doing suspicious things, which they will be doing."

"Sounds reasonable," Hunter says.

Jacob takes a pencil and makes little stars in some of the rooms. "All of us except Skylar are going to be stationed in the rooms with the main ventilation duct openings. Skylar—I hope you're pretty good with directions—is going to move through the vents and seal them from the inside while you seal them from the outside, creating a double seal which is twice as strong. Then, once everything's all covered, we get out of here at least hour before midnight just in case."

"Perfect," Lexie says.

"It does appear to be infallible," I comment.

"Nothing's completely bulletproof." Hallie's arms are still crossed.

"Well, this is pretty freaking close," Lexie decides.

"First off, it's freezing in there," I say, crossing my arms. "Second, I'm in a skirt. I still have a bullet graze on my arm, and it still hurts—it's a miracle I'm even walking around, if I may say so. I'm wearing flats, which are *so* not the preferred type of shoe for inner-vent endeavors. And—"

Jacob cuts me off. "Are you nervous?" He asks this gently, not like he's accusing me of not wanting to go into the air ducts.

He's dangerous, I think. "I'll be okay," I say. I'm lying.

His look tells me he knows this.

"Ms. Parkins is right, you know. I *am* fairly week. I don't know where you got this big idea that I'm not."

"Remember when I told you you couldn't climb Big Lincoln?"

"That was only a few hours ago, so—"

"I was lying. I said that because I knew the only way you'd do it was if someone told you that you couldn't."

"But I'm not like that. I don't do things people tell me not to."

He takes my hand and brushes his fingers over the callus on my palm from violin playing. "You wouldn't have this if you'd listened to your violin teacher. And you wouldn't have climbed Big Lincoln if you'd listened to me."

"So are you telling me that I'm not who I think I am?"

"I don't know where *you* got this big idea that you're a perfect rule follower, but you're not. You do things. You *don't* listen to people, and that's a good thing, because sometimes you really just can't let people tell you what to do. You're actually really defiant, Bubble. You just won't let yourself look at you like that."

"So how do *you* see me?"

"Honestly? As someone who can do anything."

"I can't do anything." My voice is far too small.

"You're the only one saying you can't change anything, you know that? Hallie's not, Lexie's not, Harlow's not, I'm certainly not. So you should probably stop saying it."

I look at him for awhile. Really look at him, not at his exterior but at who he is inside, trapped under his own skin. I see him as someone who's not labeled as a ninth grader or as an architectural camper or as ADHD or as anything but a person who can't be labeled because there's too much to him and not even a hurricane can contain him.

"I'm going to tell you that I don't think you can go into the air ducts because I know you won't listen to me anyway."

And without a single word, I climb into the air duct, the roll of tape around my wrist like a bracelet. "I've only known you for a Day and you already drive me absolutely insane," I tell him eventually, once I'm a bit down the shaft and I can't see his reaction.

"Take the first turn left," he says.

I do. "Done," I call back.

"Okay, at the next intersection, go straight."

His words still buzz around my head like honeybees, so I have to ask for clarification: "Which way?"

"Straight at the first intersection."

I find it and go straight. "Okay."

"Go straight until you find a grate underneath you." His voice is fainter now. "Hallie should be underneath. Tell her to get everyone out of the room and to seal it."

I shuffle through the air vent. It's very cold in here; I wish that I had my cardigan that was torn by the bullet. Goosebumps line my arms. My knees are starting to become red from crawling along the metal, and black from the muck floating around the shaft; my eyes sting because of the circulating air. There's a metallic taste in my mouth, like blood, but not blood. I assume it's from the walls, which are sheets of trying-to-be-shiny metal.

And there it is, just like Jacob said, the grate looking down on Hallie. "Hallie," I whisper harshly, though she's the only one in the room. "Hallie!"

She sees me. "How is it up there?"

"Terrible. Jacob says you can seal this one."

"Okay," she says. "Look at the size of this duct tape." She holds up a roll of tape the size of a dinner plate. "Did you know they made them this big?"

I show her my roll, too. "It certainly is a lot of tape." I move over so I'm not right on top of the grate.

"I know, it's great. I'm gonna tape a bunch of stuff together before we leave."

"Sounds riveting."

She's already ripped pieces of tape that match the width of the grate. Methodically, she sticks them across the metal grid until no light comes from inside the room. When she says, "Your turn", her voice is muffled.

"Okay." I rip the tape and lay it across the grate, taking care to stick all the pieces into one thick blanket encompassing the metal.

"My arms are so going to hurt so bad when this is done," Hallie says. "All this ripping is tiring."

"I have no sympathy. You should see my knees. They're like that newspaper riddle: what's black and white and red all over? Skylar's knees."

"Why are you so weird?" Hallie's voice is muffled by the tape. "You're taking two lefts and then a right until you're over the next grate. Hunter should be there."

"Thanks," I say. "Good luck in all your vent-sealing endeavors. Don't accidentally tape yourself to anything."

"I hate you." It's made unconvincing by the spark of a smile I can hear flitting across her mouth. When you've known someone for most of your life, you can hear their smiles.

"I love you, too."

Left, left, right, I whisper to myself so I don't forget my directions, to the point where they don't even sound like real words any more. I wonder if those weird whistling sounds that air conditioning makes on occasion are actually just people like me who are crawling through and trying to remember their directions.

But, according to Jacob, I wouldn't listen to directions anyway. How could he see this about me but *I* couldn't see this about me? I've always assumed that I follow the rules—I'm never out of uniform and you'll never catch me cutting class—but, looking back, I'm no angel. I skip homework and I tell white lies and I have a callus on my hand because I don't play the way my violin teacher wants me to. But I'm not terrible, either, because I try to be nice to people (though that proves to be very difficult).

If you're not an angel or a demon, then do you end up in Heaven or Hell? Or are you stuck in between the shades of gray, where nothing is all good or all bad? A field of smooth, flat slate, where you fall on a spectrum, trapped in a war between vice and virtue with no idea which side to support?

I'm not black or white—I'm gray, stuck right between day and night like dusk or dawn, in a state of constant ambivalence.

Wait, how many lefts have I taken?

Better yet, how many lefts was I *supposed* to take?

I curse at myself. *Left right left? Right left left? Left left right or right left right? You mean to tell me that you couldn't remember three directions?*

I try taking a deep breath, but it's fruitless. I'm lost in a maze where each turn looks the exact same as the last, and I have no idea how long I've been out and how many turns I've taken or passed.

"Hallie?" I whisper. Her name bounces off the metallic walls.

"Jacob?" His name follows suit.

The whole "don't move if you're lost" rule is not applicable in this situation. No one will know that I'm lost, and no one will come and find me.

I think that if I'd come across a vent next to me, I would have snapped out of it and have called for Hunter. Then again, I can't be certain that I didn't miss it. I was pretty invested in my philosophy of the color gray.

And Harlow's dead.

I don't know where I see her in these halls of metal. Maybe it's the small white glint the walls have, or maybe it's the way the moving air sounds like her laugh. Then I'm choking back tears because Harlow's going to be fine tomorrow for God's sake, but then I'm sobbing because I'm lost and I don't belong here or anywhere else but my Starlight Cove with my starlight cousin and there are people out there that want me dead and I'm defiant apparently and none of this even exists which makes it all the more real. I can wake up tomorrow morning screaming for Harlow and praying for the throbbing in my arm to stop and only geniuses who somewhat understand the arcana of time will know what I'm talking about, but only three will care, and I'm completely alone because no one knows where I am and the world is going to keep spinning even if I'm lost.

Because as much as we try to believe the Earth stops for us, it doesn't, and none of us want to accept that maybe a nonexistent day actually still exists esoterically and it tears these people apart and these people matter because their lives and their brains are not disposable.

"Skylar?" Jacob's coming towards me, a worried look on his face, his entire stack of paper in his hand. "What's wrong?"

I wipe my eyes. I've let myself get too close for him for one Day. It took me years to work up that level of trust with Hallie, so why has it taken only a few hours with him? I push Harlow out of my mind; it feels like a betrayal. "I'm okay. I just got lost. Then I got scared. Really, I'm fine."

"Okay, good," he says. "You're not that far from Hunter—you only missed one turn." He points to a spot on one of his maps that means nothing to me.

"I got distracted," I say quietly.

"I've been there," he sighs. "Come on, let's go find him."

We've been crawling for a few minutes before I finally say, "You did it again."

"Did what?"

"Rescued me. I'm not a damsel. I don't necessarily need it."

"You were crying. In an air vent. Leaving someone crying in an air vent's got to get you a nomination for the Worst Person of the Year award."

"They have those?"

"Margaret runs it."

"Also, semi-unrelatedly—"

"You totally made that word up."

"—if you can fit in here, then you should be the one crawling around in here."

He holds up his stack of paper. "Carrying this? And duct tape? And making sure that everyone is in the rooms they're supposed to be in? You have the fun job, Bubble."

"I'm covered in *soot*, Jacob. It's not exactly a picnic in the park before noon on a summer day in August."

"Not only was that oddly specific, but if you haven't been to a picnic where you get covered in soot, then you haven't been to a good picnic."

We reach Hunter's grate eventually. Jacob reassures me that he'll come get me if I get lost again—half-jokingly—and weaves his way back through the twisting metal.

I don't really know what say to Hunter, as Jacob explained everything to him already, so I sit next to the grate awkwardly silent as he methodically rips the tape into long and equal strips and I rip mine into jagged, two-dimensional icicles.

"So," I say, trying to break the tension. "How are you doing?"

"Fine," he responds shortly.

"Okay, good," I reply.

It's a couple of minutes before he says, "How's your arm?"

"It's fine," I reply.

"Good."

"I know."

He finishes putting up the board. "Okay, you can go," he tells me.

Dismissed, he could've said instead with that tone.

"Wait."

I stop crawling.

"I'm sorry you got shot."

I stop myself from saying "it's okay" because it's not, not really. I could say "I forgive you", but I'm not sure I do, not yet. "Thanks," I end up with.

"Look, I shouldn't have turned you in."

"I know."

"I was caught up in trying to tell people that I'm just as good as my brother and I knew stuff that I heard you guys talking about and I thought that it was maybe my chance."

So he apologizes with excuses.

"Anyway, I'm sorry."

"Thanks for your apology," I say, "but you put Jacob through hell, not me."

"*You* got a bullet across your arm."

"Yeah? I'd rather have that." I crawl away before he can respond to me.

Let's be honest, right here, right now: I've never especially liked Hunter, but I've never hated him, either. He's always been standoffish, like no one could possibly be worth his time. I mean, he's nice enough, never said a mean word to me, at least. I've never gone out of my way to avoid him, but I've never sought after him. I have a feeling, though, that our paths are going to cross a lot more often now in one way or another.

He'd better not get me shot again if our paths are going to keep crossing.

Chapter Twenty Eight

Got so much to lose,
Got so much to prove,
God,
don't let me lose my mind.

"Trouble"
Cage the Elephant

Jacob and Lexie are waiting for me when I crawl out of my halfway stop in a small plane exhibition room. They give me high-fives and help me out of the vent so I can take a breather before starting the next half of the building. I wish there were a water fountain nearby because my throat is killing me. It must be the dry air in the vents.

At this point, my entire body feels like it's coated in a veil of grime. I don't want to imagine the things floating around up there that are now adhered to my skin and clothes. The thought of a hot shower and fuzzy socks makes me want to curl up like an armadillo with a book, surrounded by stuffed whales. Compared to this, that sounds like heaven. (Really, though, compared to this, even medieval Russia sounds like heaven.)

"What time is it?" I ask them, curious as to how long I was crawling around in there. It felt like at least four hours, but I've learned not to trust my internal clock—no amount of melatonin supplements could ever fix it.

"Four-thirty," Jacob replies.

"Do you know how worried our parents must be?" Lexie says. "If today were, like, legit, my dads would kill me. Really. I'd be grounded till I die."

"Aunt Clara's probably having a fit right now," I say, "and trying to find a way to pin it on Spencer. Or Small-Town Mentality."

"My parents are probably planning all the ways they're going to yell at me," Jacob muses.

"Mine are probably just pacing around, waiting for me to come home," I say. I pull my phone out of my pocket and attempt to turn it on, but it's so dead that it doesn't even flash the no-battery screen for half a second. "I wonder how many times they've tried contacting me."

Lexie's about to add something when a stampede of frenetic feet comes barreling into the room. Jacob takes his stack of blueprints and slips them under an exhibit case.

Each one of them holds an Eradicator-issued gun.

"Stop right where you are," the one in front says. It takes me a moment to recognize her because of the circumstances. A fraying tuft of plain brown hair sits on top of her pinched-up face as if it were a bird perched in its nest. Her lips are curled in a twisted grin and her eyes are hungry—for what, I don't want to learn. It's her outfit that gives her away: a faded floral skirt, a pale pink cardigan, and scuffed-up black loafers. She looks as much like a math teacher as a person can look without physically holding a plus-sign in their hands.

"Hi, Ms. Parkins," Jacob says, slowly putting his hands up in a half-surrender. "Look, I know that this sounds kinda weird, and you're not going to *ever* believe us, but we're actually trying to help you. Weird, I know, like I said, but you kind of have to trust us and let us finish up here with no, like, war or anything."

"Trust you?" she repeats, a little dumbfounded. "I'm sorry, Mr. Connelly, but I don't think that's possible."

"Well, do you think you can *make* it possible? Look—" She cuts him off with a shot of her gun into the air. The bullet lodges itself in the ceiling. Weird, seeing a teacher with a gun—it seems so contradictory, like a librarian on her phone in the middle of her library. "Okay, that works, too."

"Ms. Parkins," I start, attempting to reason with her, "hi, I'm Skylar, you probably already know me—I'm worthless, apparently—and it's against the little training we've had today to talk to you, let alone attempt a negotiation with you, but—" I stop myself. How angry did we get with Hunter once he sold us out to the Eradicators? Very. Now, imagine Margaret's wrath when I attempt to explain that *we* sold out the Knowers to the Eradicators. Instant death. Faster than one could make instant noodles.

The man to her left asks, "Negotiate?" and I swear that all of their weapons lower just a bit.

"Yeah, we're trying to help you," Lexie says. "Believe it or not."

"I'm sorry, but based on past actions, I have to go with *not*," the man says again. Now I recognize him; he's the man that told us to get to get to initiation once we found the Eradicator's headquarters. What was his name again? Philip, I think.

"Hear them out, Ranchald," another voice says. I assume this is his last name. It's a horrible name that makes him sound as if he's spent his life on a ranch, but judging by his wrinkled and Sharpie-defiled button-down, soft hands with long fingers and a thin palm, and hastily gelled hair, he lives in a suburb. (He could, however, live in a ranch-style house in a suburb.)

"Thanks," Lexie says. "Basically—"

"Don't tell them too much," Jacob hisses in our ears. "It'll give them more of a reason to hate us. That's, like, the last thing we need."

"Basically . . ." Ms. Parkins is waiting for a continuation.

"Basically, there's gonna be some bad stuff coming through the air vent," Lexie explains, attempting ambiguity but not exactly succeeding. "Like, really bad stuff. Stuff that can kill you guys. We're trying to stop it."

And then we're each being held by Eradicators with guns to our heads at the direction of Ms. Parkins. "Is this really necessary?" Jacob asks. "Standing there was too threatening to you?"

"Jacob, stop being so facetious," I huff. "Your sarcasm is going to be the death of us."

"Well, that *is* how I want to go out."

I groan.

"You've given us no reason to trust you," Ms. Parkins says.

"We've also given you no reason *not* to trust us," Lexie counters.

"You blew up a Smithsonian."

"Okay, that wasn't us," Lexie says. "That was Margaret and her crew."

"Who are Knowers, like you." Ms. Parkins is no-nonsense.

"Look, I'm not exactly sure we're Knowers," I say. "They care about power. We care about people. There's a very big difference between controlling people and working with them, and we support the latter."

Ms. Parkins studies me. Up and down her glances go, taking in every inch of me. "Tell me, Skylar," I shudder when she says my name—it sounds so wrong and out-of-place coming from her, like a storm cloud drifting through a blue sky, "do you have ADHD?"

"I guess so," I say. "I'm not professionally diagnosed."

"And your eyes, they just changed color."

I see what she's getting at. "The Knower label doesn't define me. I'm not power-hungry because the melanin content in my eyes fluctuates by the minute and my brain doesn't produce enough dopamine and norepinephrine."

"Well," Jacob remarks, "she told you."

"Why do you always have to be like this?" I sigh.

"Well, as much as you're trying to 'help us'," Philip Ranchald says, "we're going to have to take you into custody and ask you a few questions. You know, basic cognition tests and DNA analysis. Nothing too difficult."

"We both know you can't keep us past midnight," Lexie says.

"But we can keep your information," Philip says, thinking he's being mysterious but ignorant to our knowledge of the Efficacy's capability, and to the fact that we've dismantled the firewall—

Wait.

We were caught by Margaret and sent away from the Knowers. We sat in the boat room in American History until Harlow was shot, then went to Thomas Redding, turned Margaret into the enemy instead of the Eradicators. We came here and began to seal up the air vents to protect them all from Margaret's poison.

And in this stretch of time, we've forgotten about the Efficacy and all the information it holds on us.

Harlow was five and I was seven. Aunt Clara had taken the two of us to spend the day at the little beach on the island, where the sand is made of rocks and the water is never more than sixty degrees, and we were absolutely in love with it because it was a warm day and summer had just started and summer means freedom for a little kid. Little kids don't get a lot of freedom.

Grandma had sewed us these adorable little calico purses with ribbon handles and button closures. Harlow and I brought them to the beach with us to collect rocks that turned smooth by the tumbling waters and the occasional bottle cap.

Harlow was very particular about her rocks. She would only pick the very shiniest rocks and bottle caps that had the paint worn off. I, on the other hand, somehow gained an emotional attachment with every stone I saw. I picked each one up and placed it in my calico purse with the ribbon handle and the button closure. The purse got pretty heavy, but I still held it by the handle and carried it all the way to the car.

Except as we got into the parking lot, the handle gave out, ripping my purse clean in half, sending the button flying, and causing my smooth rocks to roll across the gravel and get scratched up and lost.

I began to cry.

"See, Skylar?" Aunt Clara chided. "This is what happens when you bite off more than you can chew. You forget what matters most."

I huffed; I never liked listening to Aunt Clara because she always seemed to have something to say to me. I wish I would have remembered her words sooner.

Now, the Eradicators know everything about me. Harlow is dead. The Knowers are planning on killing all of the Eradicators in the compound, and if we're in custody in the compound, then they'll get us, too. My rocks have fallen and are now covered in scrapes and gashes. They have us with our hands completely tied in twisting coils of fraying rope that dig into our wrists and leave raw red marks. Every movement we could possibly make causes them to scream in pain.

No, they don't actually tie our wrists with rope. They simply hold the guns to our heads as we walk with them. God, does that freak me out. If the guy behind me trips and accidentally pulls that trigger, I'll be dead in a heartbeat (or lack thereof). And Ms. Parkins informs us that they will certainly shoot if we don't cooperate. I don't attempt to find out if she's bluffing or not.

Ms. Parkins and Philip lead us down the stairs into the headquarters and down a hall I didn't notice last time I was here. At the end of it is a stark gray room with nothing in it but a single florescent light stuck to the ceiling. "We're going to prepare some tests for you," Ms. Parkins says. "Expect us back in ten minutes' time. Do make yourself comfortable."

"*Do make yourself comfortable,*" Lexie mimics once they've closed the door and we've heard the click assuring that they've locked it.

"You do understand that as soon as they let that poison through the system, it's going to get to us?" I remind them.

Panicked silence. "I didn't think about that," Jacob says quietly. He's already begun pacing the length of the room.

"And now we have no way of warning the others that we're down here and that I'm not coming. They all could be waiting in there until midnight, and then, boom. The poison's going to get us all."

"Can you text them?" Lexie asks.

"I can try Hallie," Jacob says, "but there's no service down here. You had to go upstairs to get to them last time." He types on his phone for a bit then says, "Nope. All my texts are getting those angry red exclamation points."

Lexie taps out a rhythm on the wall. "We really messed this up, didn't we?"

"We tried to take on too much," I say. I rock back and forth slightly, just out of habit. It calms me down, repetitive motion. "We jumped in too quickly. Now nothing is done because we started too much at once. We're *fifteen*, for God's sake, so why did we think we could handle world-changing?"

"We can handle world-changing," Lexie tells me. "I mean, changing the world is just changing people, really. We know how to smile at people and tell them off for being jerkfaces and we can pet puppies and tell people they look nice. We can do those things, right? And maybe it doesn't change the world for everyone, but it can for *someone*. Doesn't that count for something?"

Jacob keeps pacing, and now he fiddles with a plastic hippo that was in his pocket. "Are you claustrophobic?" I ask him. "This box of a room would certainly trigger a claustrophobe's anxiety levels to rise drastically."

"I'm not claustrophobic," he replies. "I just can't stand boring spaces where there's nothing to look at," he says. "Understimulation. Seriously, they couldn't have held us in, like, an art gallery or something? Maybe a playground?"

"Let us swing before you get to work probing our minds," Lexie adds.

We're strangely calm, given our circumstances. I think my well of worry has run dry for the day. It's like the world has thrown everything at me today so now I can pretty much catch anything. Except my arms are getting tired and one of them is torn open, so I really don't want to catch anything else. My experience with the world, though, proves that it's never done throwing.

Lexie still taps out her rhythm, except her fingers dance across the floor now. Jacob draws on the floor with his index finger. They each create something different, but I have no idea what. Then I decide that I would like to know what.

Part of me wishes that Hallie were here because I can talk so easily with her, but the other part—without the former part's permission—suddenly states, "I don't really know you very well."

Although Jacob can kill you with a grin and Lexie constantly threatens to turn you yellow, I'm going to know them my whole life, so it's worth getting to know them. Besides, as much as I don't want to admit it, I really do want to know every part of them that they're wiling to tell me about.

"Yeah, I don't really know you guys, either," Lexie agrees. "Just basic stuff, really. Skylar, we've gone to school together since we were five, yet I don't even know your favorite color. And Jacob, I don't know anything about you. You didn't go to school."

"I went to school, just not *your* school," he says.

"Does homeschooling even count as school?"

"No, not really."

"Thought so. What's your favorite color?"

"Blue," Jacob says. "Like, bright blue. The color of the sky when there's only puffy white clouds. Like it was today."

"So poetic," Lexie remarks. "I like yellow."

"I knew it." I twirl the roll of tape that's still on my wrist. "You seem like a yellow person."

"Do I seem like a blue person?" Jacob asks.

"Yes, actually, you do," I say. "My favorite color is purple." It's not, really, but that's always my answer to this question. Most people don't take gray for an answer. From experience, they usually just file you as pretentious for picking an unusual favorite color. *Oh, you'll remember me because I said gray instead of pink. I'm so special.*

"I play the drums, did you know that?" Lexie says next.

"No way," Jacob says. "That's awesome. I play piano, mostly, but I know a lot of weird instruments like the clarinet and the sousaphone because of this music thing my parents put me in when I was little."

"Seriously? The *sousaphone*?"

"I asked for the flute but they didn't have any left."

"But the sousaphone is really cool, if not a little unusual," I say. "I want to learn piano really badly. I play violin, but you guys most likely knew that. Lexie, how'd you start playing drums?"

"Well, I started playing them back in Mrs. Gallowsyki's music class in third grade, remember? When she made us each try an instrument?"

"Oh, yeah," I say. I was exempt from that because I'd already been playing violin for two years.

"Yeah, I started with bongos and other small percussion, and then I got a set, but then I started African drumming. I love it. It's so cool."

"That's awesome," Jacob says. "I've always thought African drums sounded so cool. You can actually play them?"

"Yeah! I take lessons every other week from this guy named Emeka who's, like, the coolest person I've ever met. He's Moroccan. I was born in Morocco, you know. My full name's Alexandria." She pronounces it the French way, with little em-phasis on the *x* and a long *a*. "My dads adopted me when I was two months old. They called me Lexie for short. Alexandria doesn't really fit me. You're out of energy by the time you're done saying it."

"You're so cool about having two dads," I remark. "I admire that."

"Because I'm not ashamed of it," Lexie says. "My dads met and fell in love like anyone else. It's not a big deal, really. People just make it one."

"You're so interesting," I tell her. "I can't believe we haven't talked like this sooner."

"I know," Lexie says. "I kinda forgot you were a person whose existence isn't based on the library."

"Oh, but my existence *is* based on the library," I counter. "Now you've just solidified that belief."

"You're twenty-five percent whales, twenty-five percent big words, twenty percent useless facts, and thirty percent raging spite," Jacob tells me.

"That seemed to be premeditated," I say.

"Yes, Skylar, all of my time is devoted to your chemical composition."

"Is spite a chemical?"

"An organic acid, I think."

There's a brief pause.

"Do you think we'll all still be friends when this is all over?" I ask.

"I don't see why we wouldn't be," Lexie says.

"I don't know if I can handle you when time exists," Jacob sighs.

"I don't know if I can handle you when time *doesn't* exist," I reply.

"Look, I'm glad we're all doing this together," Lexie says. "I was kinda nervous when this started because you and Hallie were so tight already, but I don't feel like a third wheel. Not like I thought I would."

"I know," Jacob agrees. "I think we've all bonded. Like, a real bond that the time-reverse can't break."

"Like the covalent bonds of spite," I add.

I though the last thing I needed was a hurricane and a highlighter—and now I cannot fathom how incredibly wrong I was. I'm glad I don't listen.

"And now," Lexie declares, "about getting out of here."

"What about it?"

"How are we gonna do it?"

I survey the room; it's constructed of bricks painted over with sloppy white paint. I love it though, how all these tiny bricks can make up this whole room—I've always loved how everything is made up of smaller pieces, and those are made up of even smaller pieces, and so on and so forth until the world is completely broken down into protons and neutrons. I could split this room in half a million times until it became the closest thing to nothing if I could only achieve nuclear fission. Except nothing doesn't actually exist, so I can't reduce this room to nothing. (Which is unfortunate, because it would be far easier to get out of this room if it weren't a room at all.)

There are no windows, not that I was expecting any in the basement of a building this size. The floor, predictably, is solid concrete. The ceiling is yellowing white and a plaster of some sort.

This means the only way out is the way we came in. Ms. Parkins has locked it from the outside, but there's a lock on the inside of the door, one that takes a standard key. And if it's a standard key, I daresay I actually have a way out.

In my pocket, there are only a dead cell phone, three bobby pins, a hair tie, my small rubber elephant, an eraser, and a square of tinfoil from Harlow and Jacob's Lego excursion. Our adventures at Tyson's Corner seem to have taken place days ago. Can it have only been a matter of hours before? It doesn't seem possible. I put everything but the three bobby pins back in my pocket.

You see, I think it's necessary to carry a bobby pin or two everywhere I go because you can use them for practically anything, if you know how. One Christmas, Harlow got me a whole book solely on different ways to use a bobby pin. I've memorized it.

"Sorry, Sky, but it's gonna take more than that to fix your hair," Lexie remarks.

"It's not for my hair," I say.

"You're going to pick the lock?" Jacob asks. "Isn't that super hard?"

"Yes, it's extremely difficult," I say as I rip off the rubber tips on the ends and use the leverage of the door to bend the first bobby pin into an L-shape, "but I've done it before."

"You have?" Jacob seems surprised, but not really. "You've picked a lock before."

"Yes," I affirm. "I get locked out of my house a lot." I bend the second pin into the shape of one of those plastic swords they put in cocktails. "Keys are a very hard thing to remember in the morning."

"That's so cool," Lexie says. "Not that you get locked out of your house all the time, but how you know how to do this."

"Thank you." I insert the first bobby pin into the lock and turn it as if it were a key, and then I use the second one to move the first around.

"Where'd you learn?"

"Harlow. Where else?"

I regret saying her name. Now I'm thinking of her. I think of locks instead.

The inside of a lock looks like one of those torture things they show in cartoons, with the giant pulverizing cylinders coming down from the ceiling and smashing people as they try to cross. Except they're are attached to springs and they're always in the air. For the lock to unlock, the little pins have to be in the right area.

I insert the L-shape into the bottom of the lock. On top of it, I put the sword-shaped one. Using the L as a base, I wiggle the sword-shaped one to get the pins in the right places.

"How long is this gonna take?" Lexie asks.

"Anywhere from five minutes to an hour," I say.

"We don't have an hour."

"I'm trying my best."

At first, I think I'm making progress. I've gotten at least one of the pins in place. But when the door starts to open, I rip the pins out of the lock and stuff them into my pocket.

Chapter Thirty

Oh, won't you let me finish?
You drive me insane.
The world will keep on turning,
even if we're not the same.

"Paracetamol"
Declan McKenna

Ms. Parkins was wrong. It takes them thirteen and a half minutes to come get us. She comes into the room, takes Jacob by the wrist, and says, "I think you would be an interesting one with whom to start. I'll be back for one of you two once I've finished with Mr. Connelly."

"This should be fun," Jacob says bitterly, and Ms. Parkins leads him out of the room. He doesn't even fight her on it.

She then locks the door behind her.

I waste no time moving back to the door and inserting the bobby pins again.

"Do you have to start over?" Lexie asks.

"I'm so sorry to be rude, but could you be quiet please?"

"Oh. Yeah. Sorry."

I close my eyes and rely on my hands to feel if the seized pins are moving at all. I hear the exuberant *click* of the first. I move on to the second, then the third, then the fourth, and finally the fifth. "Lexie, open the door please."

She turns the handle with ease, and the door swings ajar.

"That was so cool!" Lexie says. "How'd you do that?"

"Practice, luck, and sheer persistence."

I put my homemade lock-picking kit back in my pocket. We tiptoe out of the room and attempt to find the stairwell that leads to the janitors' closet. It's very much like a maze in here, however, and the pure gray room has messed with my sense of direction. But it didn't affect Lexie; she leads me right to the stairs and marches right up them. We sit at the top.

"How are we going to get Jacob out?" I ponder. "They've got him now, but when they get back to grab one of us, they'll see that we're gone. And if we don't get Jacob out by midnight, then . . ." I shudder at the unthinkable.

"We have to finish taping up the vents," Lexie says. "That's our first priority. We have to tell all the others what happened, and then maybe they can get Jacob."

I ask, "What do you think they're doing to him?" though I'd be better off not knowing.

"Mind tests, I'm guessing," Lexie says. "You know, what do they call those things with the inkblots? Rochambeau?"

"I think you mean Rorschach testing," I supply.

"Yeah, that's what I mean," Lexie says. "I think they're doing things like that with him. To see how a Knower mind works or whatever. I'm sure it's not *that* bad. I've always wanted to do a Rochambeau test. I wonder what I'd see."

"I took one online once," I say. "I either saw whales or flowers, mostly."

"That's super cool. Okay, back on track. Wait, will you send me the link tomorrow? No, back on track. We have to get you back into the vents."

"I don't have Jacob. He's pretty much what was keeping me from getting lost in there. I have absolutely no idea on the inner workings of this place. I would find myself lost in a heartbeat."

"Do you even know where the others are stationed?"

"No," I groan. "Jacob planned everything. I couldn't read those blueprints for the life of me. I have no idea how he could make them, read them, and then plan everything around them."

"So we have no idea where everyone else is, and since your phone is dead and mine is still in the bottom of the reflecting pool, we have no way to contact them."

"You're right."

She groans. "This must be what the pioneer days were like. You know, with no cell phones or ways of knowing if your uncle died of cholera or how many chickens you'd need to trade for a new hatchet."

"Remember how we used the loudspeaker last time we had to reach you guys when we had no phones?" I remind her. "We can do that again."

"It'll get labelled as suspicious activity if we do it again," Lexie reasons. "The first time, we got out of the building so quickly that they wouldn't have noticed. This time, we can't do that. We're lucky enough no one's seen us sealing the vents. Then they'd totally be on to us."

"Yeah, I agree. So, um . . . we could—"

"Let's just run around the museum and find all of them!"

"Why? That's horribly dangerous, and the guards—"

"Come on. Don't you want to have a little fun? Make it a little more interesting?"

"Not when all of our lives are possibly at stake!"

I see it again: her permanent smile that rests on the corner of her mouth. It's still there, despite everything, like a lighthouse that's been through countless raging storms but can still find a way to shine that yellow light. Ships are drawn to her.

Just when I thought I've gotten Lexie Petterson figured out, I see something like a rare permanent smile and need to rethink my entire evaluation of this girl.

"Look, Skylar. I'm just gonna say it, okay? Don't hate me. You're a freaking *stickler*."

I almost get angry until I realize it's true, and I don't get angry with people for speaking the truth. Nevertheless, I protest against it. "I am not! I have lots of fun. Buckets of it."

She raises an eyebrow. (First Jacob, now Lexie, too? Can *everyone* but me raise a single eyebrow?) "Right."

"But now just doesn't seem like the appropriate time."

"Come on! Don't you think we should do some of that whole world changing thing now?"

"All of our lives are at stake!"

"I don't know about you, but if I'm going out, I'm going out with a bang! Come on, Sky, please. Life's supposed to be fun. This whole Day, these few untouchable hours—aren't they supposed to be the highlight of our *lives*?"

"Well, I can see where you're coming from, but I'm not sure I agree."

"Well then, stickler, why not just start agreeing?"

I've lived my whole life trying not to touch anything, to pass unnoticed like a shadow. Why should anything that's happened today change that?

Because I am not who I was, even if by changing, I just uncovered whom I've been all along. I will not wake up on the real April sixteenth and be the same Skylar that I was on the fake one because on the real one, the real Skylar peeked out from behind her little black glasses.

Who knows? Maybe they'll wish she'd just put those glasses back on.

"Fine," I acquiesce. "Let's do it your way. There aren't any consequences for changing the world on a Day that doesn't exist."

Her permanent smile widens. "I knew you'd come through."

I first go back to the exhibit where Jacob hid his stack of papers. I find them all crammed under a case of old pilot uniforms. Though I know there are much more pressing matters, my curiosity gets the best of me, and I leaf through them. They make no more sense to me this time than they did earlier, but I notice more things. He's got more numbers and equations than your average math textbook, and there are more drawings than the entirety of the National Gallery. I carefully stack them in order, and I go to look for Hallie.

I find Hallie sitting alone in a room of old military paraphernalia. "Why aren't you in the vents?" she asks when she sees me, her icy blue eyes darkening into more of a moldy blue raspberry. I've noticed that they do this when she's nervous, especially when she doesn't want to admit it. It's like her eyes know her better than she does.

I fill her in on our conversation with Ms. Parkins and our trip to the Eradicator compound. Then I tell her that though I may have his blueprints, Jacob, who has the ability to read them without wanting to poke his eyes out, is still down there, that only half of the museum vents are closed, and that we never dismantled the Efficacy's firewall. Oh, and it's five-thirty now, so we only have six and a half hours until a deadly poison, killing people whose lives are not disposable and possibly us, too, sweeps through the building and all efforts against the Efficacy must be held off a year.

"Man, we're screwed."

"I know, right?"

"Well, we're just gonna have to find every vent in this place by ourselves and patch them up."

"With no Jacob, illegible blueprints, and not even a working phone between us?"

"Relax. We'll use yours."

"Mine is so dead it won't even light up to tell me it's dead."

"Lexie's?"

"At the bottom of the reflecting pool."

"Hunter's?"

"Died a couple hours ago. And yours?"

Hallie groans and takes a shattered piece of glass out of her pocket. Out of context, I wouldn't have even known it's her phone.

"What in God's name did you do to it?"

As she flips it over in her hands, little glass shards fall off like sprinkles. "Dropped it. And then as I was picking it up, I dropped it again. After all the shit we've been through, I killed my phone by *freaking dropping it*. Why couldn't I have caught it like you did with Alex Summerheld's plate?"

She hands it to me, and I take it from her. I try turning it on, but the screen is literally falling off. "Okay, then, I'm going to make the executive decision to declare that there are no working phones. Jacob has the only one."

"Hm. I would've thought he'd be the first to lose his."

"People are incessantly surprising," I say.

"Alright, then, let's take some lucky guesses and find the rest of the vent openings." She starts for the door.

I hesitate. "Hallie, we can't leave him down there with them."

She turns back to face me. "He's Jacob. He'll just talk their ears off and make them *want* to let him go. He can take it."

"He shouldn't *have* to," I tell her.

"Look, Skylar," she sighs. "We can either go get Jacob, jeopardizing finishing the vents, or we could ultimately save everyone in the building, including Jacob."

"But we could get the vents done so much faster—"

The loudspeaker beeps. "The National Museum of Air and Space is now closing. Thank you for visiting."

"Does that mean all the guards and investigators are going home?" I ask.

"I doubt it," Hallie answers. "If anything, there's even more coming now."

"So I win," I say. "We *have* to go downstairs so they don't find us. We've gotten lucky with none of them finding us, but now we're running a higher risk. So, ha. *Ha* a thousand times."

"I'm actually going to punch you."

"You know I'm right."

"I never thought you'd *want* to go into Eradicator headquarters," Hallie sighs.

"Oh, I don't *want* to. It's more of a *need* at this point."

Chapter Thirty One

There's a mad man looking at you,
and he wants to take your soul.
There's a mad man with a mad plan
and he's dancing at your door.
Oh what to do, oh
what to do,
when the walls are built to crumble.
There's a mad man
with a mad plan
and he waits for us to stumble.
Oh, but our eyes are open.

"Jump on My Shoulders"
AWOLNATION

We wait outside the door of the janitors' closet for a bit, hoping someone will unintentionally lend us their thumbprint, but no one seems to be coming in or out. After three minutes, Hallie gets aggravated.

"How're we gonna get in?" she huffs.

I think for a second, and then I realize I have the solution, right on my very own thumb. Since we haven't destroyed the Efficacy, they still have my thumbprint saved because of the gun's scanner. I put my thumb against the scanner, and the door lets out a click.

Hallie opens it. "You should've done that five minutes ago."

"I forgot the evil super geniuses have my identification saved as their own, therefore making *me* an evil super genius."

There are fewer people in Eradicator HQ now. I wonder if some of them packed up and went home because they live around here. They do have lives aboveground, I've learned.

Before I can stop her, Hallie asks a woman with blue tips in her hair and silver dangle earrings that touch her chin, "Where did everyone go?"

"Where have *you* been?" the woman responds with. "They found a bunch of Knowers and they're with one of them now."

"Who's *they*?"

"The entire genetics team," she replies, "and Parkins, of course, and Ranchald, obviously, since he's, like, the head research guy, and some data analyzers I'm guessing, and Jennings and her Efficacy-coding posse. Like, literally everyone who's not in here is in there."

Of course. They didn't go home; they're all with Jacob.

"Where are they?" I ask.

"The testing room, duh. Where else? It's down that hall over there, last room to your right. You're noobs, aren't you, can tell by your size, you pipsqueaks. Even you, tall and beautiful—you look scrappy. Personally, I don't, like, *get* the whole fuss with the Knowers, like, they'll probably leave us alone if we just let 'em go, but *no*, we have to *probe* one. God, no one listens to anyone else around here. It's unbelievable. I'm just in it for the community service hours. That desperate, you know? You gotta have hours to graduate, and I really wanna get into a good engineering program. Like, Columbia is my dream school. But my parents, *no,* be a damn Eradicator. Like, really? You want me to give up Columbia for this shit? No way, man, I'm leaving as soon as I graduate. I hate it here. Get out while you can, noobs. They're all psychopaths here."

"Okay, thank you," I tell her. "Um, good luck with all your issues."

"Don't mention it. Like, actually don't mention it to anyone."

We move quietly down the hall. I ask my ears to report back on everything they hear, but it's unnecessary as a rumble of murmurs is coming from one open door at the end of the hall. We tiptoe into the back of the room, but there's not a lot of room. If I sit on the ground, I can see Jacob and Andrea Jennings at the front of the room through the gaps in everyone's legs.

She holds up a card with a splash of red on it. "What do you see here?"

"I don't know, an inkblot? You do know how stupid these are, right? Like, seriously. They'll teach you nothing about me. Nothing."

"What about this one?" She holds up another.

"An inkblot."

She changes the card. "This one?"

"An inkblot."

"This one?"

"An inkblot."

"This one?"

"An abstract representation of the perceived verbal abuse I received as a child from my school that didn't accept non-conforming students because they were deemed as unteachable and felt they needed to remind us of that by putting us in special education programs that were more demeaning than effective."

"Really?"

"No. It looks like a freaking inkblot."

She groans and holds up another.

"Okay, that one actually looks like a fish."

"Fine! We're done with these. Did you get all that?" She looks to the audience.

Everyone mutters and scribbles things down in their notebooks.

"Okay, Eleanor, what next?" Andrea asks Ms. Parkins.

She thinks for a second. "We can hook up the TOVA and test his attention deficit."

"Is that really necessary?" Jacob groans. "Like, there's nothing else you can do? I've done those TOVAs before, and they kind of suck. You, can't, like, dissect me or something? Trust me, it would hurt less."

"We have to get him out of here," I whisper to Hallie.

"No shit. His salt is gonna dehydrate them."

"Any ideas?"

"No."

"I have three, but two an a half call for bees."

"Diversion?"

"Nothing we can possibly come up with, let alone execute, can get these guys out of here and make them let go of Jacob long enough for us to get him."

Hallie looks at me for a long time before breathing, "As you would say, 'I beg to differ'." She stands up and shouts, "Look, if he doesn't wanna TOVA, don't make him have to TOVA! For God's sake, people. It's not that hard. Yes means yes and no means no! Do we need a kindergarten teacher over here?"

"Hallie, I hate you."

"Love you, too."

The room turns to look at us. Thankfully, Jacob does, too. He sees me and his eyes go wide. I tell him with facial expressions to get over here. He throws up his hands and raises his eyebrows. I shrug and shake my head. Then I crawl, literally *crawl* on my hands an knees, through the legs of the crowd to the front of the testing room.

"You know we're never getting out of here, right?" Jacob says. "There's a huge angry wall of Eradicator meat blocking the door."

Hallie's still yelling. I think she's running out of things to be mad about because she's turned to ranting about how you don't know if a plum is sweet or tangy until you bite into it. They're starting to get bored and turn their attention back to Jacob.

"Can you run?" I ask him, handing him his stack of paper. "Can you run as if your life were dependent upon it?"

"I can try."

"Good, as your life may actually be dependent upon it." He looks a little wary, so I ask, "You trust me, right?"

"Of course."

"Okay, good."

Ms. Parkins is looking up from her clipboard, too slowly, like she's in a horror movie.

I wait for her to lock eyes with me.

"When I say run, you run as fast as you can," I whisper to him.

"Skylar? Is that you?" Ms. Parkins is staring at me. "How did you—"

"Jacob, run."

He does.

The next things happen within a couple seconds so I have trouble registering everything.

All I really see is Jacob sprout wings and fly out of the room. He pushes right through the Eradicators like a knife cutting through softened butter. Most of them are stunned and don't move a muscle, but a few, including Ms. Parkins, leap into action and begin to move after him. Hallie doesn't hesitate for a second; she takes a yardstick from a testing table and beats on whomever she can reach. I gasp at first but quickly realize that Hallie isn't the least bit scared of distracting them like this while Jacob escapes. She's intrepid.

Then a burst of colors appears in front of my eyes. Letters and numbers swim by like lazy fish. Fireworks are set off and the ocean explodes into a thousand tiny droplets of water raining back on to the surface. I run, too, right towards the thin door.

People don't pay as much attention to me. I'm guessing they don't immediately recognize me or perhaps don't care—there are way more interesting Knowers at hand than me, anyway. I'm grateful for their inattention, though, because it gives me a chance to get out of that room. My head hurts pretty badly; I'm most likely dehydrated and exhausted, but this headache feels different. Like someone has set me on fire and my head is burning.

There's a couple guns sitting on the desk of the woman in the main room. "I need one," I get out between breaths.

"Go ahead, noob," she tells me. "I've always hated those stupid things—"

I don't stick around to find out why.

Disoriented by the location of the testing room, I close my eyes to picture where the Efficacy is. I try the first door to my left, and sure enough, there's the Mac monitor and metal milk-carton, guarded by a burly orange man and none other than Orion Athan.

"Oh, hello, Skylar." Orion smirks and flashes his white teeth turned blue by his black light. "It's a pleasure to see you again."

"Get out of this room," I tell them. My voice doesn't seem like it's coming out of my body; it's too firm, too sure. I hold up my gun and my hands don't shake, not a bit. "Both of you."

"Mr. Harding, you are welcome to leave," he says to his companion. "I can certainly help Sky out."

"You have no right to call me Sky," I say. My temples throb.

"Alright then, Skylar," he emphasizes the —lar, "What brings you to our humble Efficacy?"

"I'm no longer afraid to shoot, Orion, so I would suggest getting out of here."

He leans against the wall. "What are you even doing here?" he muses. Every word he says is light. Like feathers.

"Isn't it obvious?" I reply.

"You're not with us, obviously. But you're also not with the Knowers, it seems. So for whom do you fight?"

"Honestly, I'm just trying to live for twenty-four hours." My gun lowers an inch without my permission.

"So, why are you against us?" He walks circles around me now, as fluid as a raindrop rolling across a hydrophobic surface. There's longing in his eyes—he longs for control over me. This guy is smart. He's Rhode Island boarding school smart. He knows that it would only take a few words to transfer my gun to his hands and to agree to a bullet in my head. He can read me like I can read him. He might as well be a Knower because of his intelligence and his ability to make everyone lower their shields when he talks.

Because I was told to be against you? No, that's not right. I don't listen to people. I wouldn't believe an entire community was bad because Margaret told me they were. So why *am* I against them?

"The same reason the Knowers have come to bother me," I say. I bring my gun back up the inch it lost. "You pull people's strings as if they were your puppets. You tend to believe that others have no worth, that you can take and leave people as you'd like. You think can pick them up and drop them as soon as you're finished. People are not toys, Orion. You can't decide how and when you'd like to play with them."

"Is that coming from you, or is that coming from Margaret White?"

"Margaret White, as ostensibly powerful as she is, has no power over me. I fight for myself, not for her."

"I don't know why you think you're different than all the other Knowers." He stops circling me and stands right in front of me, staring down the barrel of my pistol. "I don't know why you think you're different than *anyone* else, Skylar, my dear."

"I'm no different at all," I say. "You see, you could walk down the street and pass me four days in a row and each day you'd think you've never seen me before and you'd certainly never once question if I'm any different than you because I'm *not*. I just have a worse chance of surviving this Day than anyone else."

As he stares at me, his eyes fluctuate between moss and the color of leaves at the very end of summer, when they know they're going to die soon so they start surrendering to the dwindling sunlight. "Ms. Parkins is just going to love breaking you."

"You're going to leave this room and tell no one I'm here," I tell him, moving the gun closer to his chest. (It creeps me out too much to point it at his head.)

"I'm sorry, but I find that impossible." He smiles again and takes a gun out of his back pocket. Seems like a horrible place for a gun, your back pocket. Imagine accidentally sitting on it. "I do apologize, Skylar, that it has to be this way. But unlike you, I know what I want and from whom I'll get it." He speaks so softly and nonchalantly that the words he's saying don't seem to have any meaning. He could as easily talk about his favorite cake recipes.

I brush a strand of hair out of my face and adjust my glasses before giving him a hard stare. "I want you to know that I'm not afraid of hurting you."

"And you should know that I've been trained to hurt you since I was born."

I shoot him.

I actually do. Like, with my gun. *I actually shoot Orion Athan.* In his right shoulder, enough to cause pain but probably not to kill him, at least not quickly. "Holy shit. Did I really just do that?" I almost drop the gun.

Orion falls back against the wall, his gun flying out of his hand and clattering on the ground and making a louder noise than he does. Showing very little, he seems to absorb the pain like a sponge. Then he grimaces and limply grabs at his shoulder. "I must say, I'm certainly impressed."

"Thank you."

"But I really must ask: do you have any idea the game you are playing?"

"I'm somewhat aware of the rules and lack thereof, though I appreciate your concern," I move over the the monitor and type in the three passwords: starfish, fleur-de-lis, sailboat. "I just shot you, didn't I? I'm sorry, by the way. Violence isn't the answer to problems. But in this situation, I felt it was applicable. Surely you can see my point of view."

"Certainly." Though his voice is strained and his teeth are clenched, he sounds almost exactly the same. "I do believe I may have done the same thing in the situation."

"At least it'll only be a hinderance for a mere five hours." I study the Efficacy desktop, reading each of the folder titles. "And no, I don't think you would have shot me, despite your initial threats. You're a very good person at heart, even if you're good for all the wrong reasons. You see, I *thought* I was good until I pulled that trigger, and now I'm not so sure. Well, I have a few more hours to figure it out. "

"Perhaps one day, somebody around here could teach you to shoot properly," he says. "Your form was horribly wrong."

"I'm sorry," I say. "I wasn't exactly thinking about my body situation."

"Next time, I won't bombard you with death threats until after you've settled into correct formation."

"Well, I take it I'll need to know for some things in my life at this point."

"Oh, surely. This is a dangerous business. You never know whom you're allowed to trust. Very tiring, the distribution of trust. Seems like a waste of time until you need something."

"I almost trusted you, you should know," I tell him. "I almost do a lot of things."

"If I may ask, why did you decide to withdraw the prospect of said trust?"

"She seems to be pretty careful with that whole *trust* thing," Hunter says. He walks right into the room like he owns the place. He looks at me, then he looks at Orion with feigned pity. "She did this to you?"

"Hello, Hunter," Orion says. "I feel like I haven't seen you in eons. We really should spend more time together, don't you agree?"

"You're bleeding to death," is all Hunter says in reply.

"This? Oh, a mere discomfort, that's all. It will clear itself up in due time."

"In that 'due time', you could die."

Orion looks at me. "Did you hear that, Skylar? You have pushed me so forcefully that I'm stumbling near the cliff of death, and, if you allow me to be so honest, I was concerned that you wouldn't be able to lift the gun."

"Hey! This thing only weighs, like, a couple ounces." (Yes, I'm exaggerating.)

"I do apologize for my preconceptions. You have proved me wrong, my dear."

"I'll help you over to the infirmary," Hunter tells Orion. "Then I'll take care of her." He pretends to glare at me as he helps Orion to his feet. Orion winces, almost invisibly.

"She's certainly capable of taking care of herself," Orion says, a smile passing over his colorless lips, tight in imperceptible agony. "I am positive in that belief."

"Alright, come on," Hunter says, leading him towards the door.

Orion looks over his shoulder. "I do hope we meet again, Skylar. In any circumstances."

I don't reply to him.

"Perhaps next time, I'll be the one holding the gun."

They limp out of the room, and Hunter locks the door behind him.

Staring at the Efficacy, I immediately wish I'd thought this through more. I have absolutely no idea where to start looking for the entrance to the firewall and how to dismantle it once I've gotten to it, as I know next to nothing about computers besides the basic graphic design principles we use in yearbook, and I don't think any graphic design skills could help me in this situation. To make matters worse, it's just after seven, according to the clock on the computer, so there's less than five hours to tie up all the loose ends we've left, and we've left more loose ends than a shoelace factory.

The door's lock un-clicks and Hunter comes back in. "What were you thinking?" he demands.

"In all honesty, I wasn't," I answer.

"Now he'll tell people you're here," Hunter says.

"And if I'd just let him go, he would have done the same exact thing *without* a bullet lodged in his arm."

Hunter doesn't respond. I don't apologize for shooting his brother.

"Any idea where to start?" I ask.

"A few," he says. "Move over."

"No, I'll do it," I say, elbowing him. "I got here first."

"And you have no idea what you're doing," he reminds me. "I do."

"I've actually been here more times than you have," I say.

"No you haven't."

"This is my second time to the Efficacy today, but Hallie and Lexie snuck in and called to explain everything about it. That counts as a third time. It was pretty in-depth."

"I was born an Eradicator."

"I was born a Knower, with a pretty good brain and eyes that change color. Your point is?"

He moves over and lets me handle the Efficacy.

I think back to the conversation we had with Hallie and Lexie on the phone back in the ship room where they gave us a tour of the computer system that seems complex but is actually just a simple Mac with complicated information. It feels like that chapter of the Day took place years ago. Today stretched minutes into hours, like a film in slow-motion. Everything moved too slowly—waking up this morning feels like a lifetime ago.

They found the firewall in a folder, I know that. Was it called "Firewall"? No, I don't think so. I decide "Code" is the most likely candidate. I don't want to ask Hunter for any help, so I double-click on the little picture of the folder without consulting him first.

There's exactly one thing in the file: something labeled "The Firewall". I mean, they couldn't have come up with a more creative name? "The Firewall" doesn't sound the least bit threatening. "Time Thrasher" would have been better. I click on it and the screen immediately lights up with lines and lines of code.

I couldn't read this if someone actually gave me coding lessons. Each one of the millions of letters and numbers are a half-millimeter tall and a uniform black color. They all are in a nonsensical order that doesn't seem to say anything, let alone anything important.

"So?" Hunter asks. "What next?"

"I was hoping you'd have an inkling on the matter," I reply, scrolling through billions of symbols.

"Well, I would just highlight it all and hit the 'delete' key," Hunter says, "and that's why we shouldn't do that. Because it's the first place anyone's mind would go."

"It's not where *my* mind went first," I tell him. "I was thinking that we mess it up. Like, copy and paste that bit of code and move it there. Delete that section. Add something there. That way, nobody will be able to figure out why their information is gone because the firewall looks completely normal."

Hunter looks at me for a while. "Fine, we'll do that."

"What, was my idea better than yours?" I don't know why I want to rub it in, but God, do I want him to admit that I just came up with something pretty cool and most likely infallible and drop this whole tough-guy facade.

"No," he says curtly, "just more likely to work."

Chapter Thirty Two

What the hell am I doing here?
I don't belong here.

"Creep"
Radiohead

Playing with the code is like playing with virtual clay. I mold it into a misshapen heap of unreadable words and complicated numbers, thus taking a mismatched jumble of letters that makes sense to someone and morphing it into one that makes sense to absolutely no one. I take the last line and add it to the middle. I move the entire second quarter to the end. In the exact middle, I write in all caps "SAVE THE WHALES" and put numbers between each letter so it looks like "S7A7V3E4T8H6E6W8H7-A5L5E2S".

"Add some periods and semicolons," Hunter says. I make a smiley face with a colon and a right parenthesis. "I didn't mean like that."

"Do you think we've maimed it enough?"

"A little more can't hurt."

I play around with the virtual clay for a few more minutes and decide it's good enough. Then I exit out of the "Code" folder and power down the computer. My throat is getting extremely sore; I decide I must be dehydrated and I try to remember where the nearest water fountain is, but my brain drops that as soon as it hears Hunter speak.

"Why didn't you delete all the stuff on you guys?" he asks, his arms crossed.

"Because that won't matter tomorrow," I tell him. "It's all going to be deleted anyway because of the firewall. And anything else they add won't save. Besides, we mostly wanted to get our information off the system. The rest of it is probably engraved in someone's head anyway, and information can't be created or destroyed, much like energy. We can't remove it entirely."

"Come on, let's go find everyone else," he says. I don't think I've ever heard him say anything that didn't sound abrasive.

"Do you have any idea as to where they could be?" I wonder. I'm beginning to realize that Hunter knows both more and less than I previously thought.

"Jacob, who knows—I never know where he is. Hallie, she's your problem. Lexie, I haven't seen her in ages. Is she still alive?"

"You're so helpful," I comment. "Hallie's most likely still fending off the Eradicators. Jacob is probably still running from said Eradicators. Lexie's right there." I point at her, standing with her back against the wall.

She sees us and walk over. "Hey, here you are! Skylar, I was looking all over for you! I couldn't find Hallie." I tell her that I found her, and a look of relief washes over her face. "I've spent the last, like, century or so hiding from security guards. They're crawling all over the place up there. There're even more than before."

"It's seven-thirty-eight," Hunter says, looking at a clock right above us. "We don't have a lot of time left."

"And half the vents are still open and the Knowers are coming in four hours and twenty minutes to kill everyone in the building," Lexie groans.

"I need Jacob," I say. "Then I could get back into the vents and finish sealing them with you guys."

"We need Hallie, too, and we need to finish with these vents." Lexie sighs. She looks like she could fall asleep at any moment. "At the beginning of the Day, I couldn't wait for it to end, and now I'm praying for a few more hours. Weird how time works."

Hallie sees us and immediately runs over, completely out of breath. "Get me out of here," she whispers desperately. "They're coming after me."

We don't hesitate; we move right up the stairs hidden in the janitor closet and double-check for security guards before emerging from the dark room. Though you think Hallie would be the one to stay towards the back, but she marches upstairs head-first. I don't know if Hallie does anything not-headfirst.

The museum looks vulnerable at night, like there aren't enough people to cover it up. It stares at us like it's embarrassed to not be the center of attention. The planes sag and the tiles aren't as shiny and the floor-to-ceiling windows act as mirrors because there's even less light out there than there is in here.

And then there's Jacob. He sits on the tiles in a tiny ball next to all his strewn-about blueprints. He gets up as soon as he sees us but sways on the spot a bit, inarguably exhausted. "See, this is why I'm not in the Olympics. Or ever picked for teams in gym class."

"Are you okay?" I ask him. Legitimately concerned he'll collapse, I put my hand on his shoulder to steady him. "How did you manage to lose them?"

"I'm fine. Just tired. They didn't really come after me," he says. "Hallie kinda knocked most of them out."

"Hallie!"

She glares at me. "What do you think would have been better? A tea party where we eat crumpets and talk about our feelings? It doesn't work like that."

"It worked with Orion," I say proudly. "I only had to shoot him once."

"You *shot* him?" just about everyone says at once.

"Yes, I did. He was being atrociously annoying and certainly deserved it. No offense, Hunter."

"None taken," he replies. "He probably did."

"Anyway, it had to be done," I justify. "I didn't kill him or anything. I'm just making him suffer a bit. You know, basic stuff."

"Then you can't yell at me for knocking people unconscious anymore," Hallie decides.

"Oh, what a life we lead," Jacob says. "Hallie, don't make fun of Skylar for murdering people because you led a torture brigade on someone else. Sounds like the best way to spend a weekend, if you ask me."

"No one did," Hallie reminds him. She rubs her temples.

"So we messed up the firewall," I say. "Hunter and I did. We didn't just delete it, but we messed it up a lot."

"Thank God for your quick thinking," Lexie says. "Imagine if we forgot to do that. Like, all the trouble we caused would have been for nothing. Now *that* would have sucked."

I look at Jacob. "We really should finish sealing the vents. It's already just about eight."

"Yeah, we probably should," he sighs. He's pacing again, as he has an inability to stay still. "But what's the point? Next year, we're going to have to do the same thing again. We're going to run around, try to survive the twenty-four hours, keep Margaret from killing us, keep Ms. Parkins from killing us—it's just an endless cycle of living and dying and fighting and surrendering. And it's never going to stop, really, and even when we're gone and not Knowers anymore, the world's still going to turn in the same direction and we can't stop it with our science-y magic because it's still turning for us. And we matter, right? We're people. Isn't that enough?"

His words bounce off the walls and the floor for awhile before they become brittle, like a rubber ball dropped in liquid nitrogen, and shatter across the ground with a crash that sounds like a song sung by ghosts: chilling and stunning.

"So you want to just let all of the Eradicators die?" I say quietly.

"No, definitely not. I just wish there weren't a reason we had to save them."

I cross my arms. "That doesn't change the fact that we do. If I've learned anything today, it's that I'm not going to listen to you. So I'm telling you—not asking, *telling* you—to fight against *and* for the Knowers *and* the Eradicators because it's gotten to the point where we've become the epitome of ambivalence. This contention ends now. You'd best be on the side that ends it."

"I— Um . . ." This is the first time I've ever seen him rendered speechless.

"Did I stutter, Jacob?"

He stares at me for a while, just studying me, like I'm a code he's trying to crack but can't for the life of him. Maybe I'm not the only one that takes in the details of people and stores them. Maybe he's cataloguing everything about me: the calluses on my fingers, the scratch on the left lens of my glasses, the necklace I wear just about every day, the one with the red flower. Maybe to him, I'm not just a bubble but something more than that. Maybe I'm the whole sky in his eyes.

"Fine, we'll finish the vents," he says at last. "And, my God, you can be terrifying."

"Thank you," I say. "Now, where did we leave off?"

Chapter Thirty Three

The blood surrounding my body,
crushing every bit of bone.
The salt, it seeps in through
the pores of my open skin.
I wait on you
inside
the bottom of the
deep blue sea.

"Bottom of the Deep Blue Sea"
MISSIO

I don't know if I have ever been so tired in my life. It's not like my eyelids are heavy and I'm stretching and yawning. This is more like my legs are crying and there's a hammer inside my head pounding against the wall of my skull and my knees are almost to the point of bleeding because of all the crawling and my stomach screams at me because I haven't given it any food in several hours and every one of my joints needs oil and my cells set themselves on fire and my arms feel as if for the past million years, I've been holding up the entire universe.

It's been just about two hours of crawling in the vents and meeting the others in the rooms where the vents must be sealed. We've finished over three-quarters of the route, but this half is taking longer than the first half did because crippling fatigue hinders all of us, not just me.

Hallie has sealed the most vents out of anyone. Being a star athlete and all, Hallie's energy levels are higher than the average person's. But still, she works in complete silence, making her movements a bit more carefully than normal and taking extra time to make sure the tape is secure. Her face is pale; her shy freckles are more visible now. Her eyes look like melting glaciers.

Lexie seems to talk even more when she's tired, like she's trying to keep herself awake. She tells me stories of her cats—the ones that are all named after *Friends* characters—while she rips the tape and sticks it to the grate. As interested as I am to hear about the time Chandler got into the pantry and knocked over a box of cornstarch—which I've actually heard before—her stories actually make me want to fall asleep even more. But she talks on though her voice sounds strained, like it physically hurts her to speak.

Hunter, surprisingly, doesn't seem the least bit worn-out at first. He's got all his tape measured and ripped before I'm even over the vent, and he puts it up right as I direct him to. We both move on without saying a single word to each other. And then I see it: a moment where he flickers and looks like he's about to cry.

You see people as they are when they're tired because they don't have the energy to hold up facades. I think that's the reason most people love sleepovers: if you can survive an overnight expedition and learn a new part of a person, you'll probably be friends for a bit.

"Skylar," I hear.

"Jacob, if you're trying to freak me out," I say, "I'm really not in the mood."

"Where are you?" The panic in his voice assures me that no, he isn't messing with me.

"Over here," I say.

"That's descriptive."

"What's wrong? Where are *you*?"

He turns the corner right before I see him frantically crawling towards me. His eyes are both brighter and duller and his face is paler and his messy black hair is even more messy. Even worse, he seems to be on the verge of both mentally and physically collapsing. "Oh my God, Bubble, I'm so sorry . . . I had no idea— I can't believe I missed it— I'm so, so sorry."

"Slow down," I say. "What's wrong?"

"The poison," he manages. "We were wrong. They're not going to release it at midnight. It doesn't work that fast. The Knowers aren't that nice."

"Jacob, what—"

"I was going through my blueprints again, and I missed an exterior vent on the west of the building. It's low to the ground, right across from the Castle, part of the main circulation—and I missed it. If the gas were released there, it could permeate the entire museum in less than fifteen minutes. Every single room would be exposed. I went to go look at it in person, and—" For a moment, I'm worried he won't be able to speak. "—an empty gas containment unit. In the vent."

My heart freezes mid-beat, the blood stopping in my arteries, not having the momentum to continue coursing through my blood vessels, because I already know what he means. "No, they couldn't have already released it."

"We've been inhaling it for at least an hour."

"Which means we're on the verge of dying."

"And I've killed us all."

How do you detect an invisible, odorless killer? You can't, not really. There could be one sitting right next to you and you wouldn't know unless it decided to hold your life in its hands.

Unless, of course, it's been killing you the entire time you thought you were avoiding it.

"Jacob, we have a quarter of the museum left," I say, "and we don't even have enough time to get out of the building."

"I know," he says. "I made you go up here, and now—" He doesn't finish. He doesn't have to.

"You didn't make me," I say, but I've begun panicking, so it doesn't sound convincing, regardless of its truth. My body is too cumbersome for me to keep it up, my eyes feel like tiny balloons, and each strand of my hair is too heavy for my head.

"Your head," he says. "Does your head feel like it's exploding?"

I try to nod, but it hurts too much to move it.

"And your throat?"

It's slowly setting itself on fire.

"Mine too."

Jacob and I pry open an unsealed grate and drop through. He helps me up when I manage to land flat on my face. When I stand up, my entire body gets a head-rush. I can't breathe for a second. "Come on," he says. "How do you think we can get everyone out of here?"

"It's going to kill us. It *has* been killing us for God knows how long." My entire body burns from the inside out.

Not that Jacob looks any better. His hair is limp and falls all over his face, and he's very pale, and his brown eyes are losing their vintage-forest look. But does he let that bother him? Absolutely not. Instead, he only says, "Come on, they have to know a cure or something. They're Knowers. They know everything, right?"

The unequivocal fear in his voice is what scares me the most.

"They can help us, I promise."

"No, Jacob, they won't, meaning you're making a promise you can't keep. They don't care. Why would they have made a cure if they never intended on curing people? They wouldn't waste their time on that, having much more important things to worry about and all, like what vent they'd use, how long it would take to affect them, how long it would take to travel around the building. They're cold and calculating. They don't think about people as people, they think of them as subjects, or obstacles, or objects they can control, and— dear Lord, we're going to die, aren't we?"

I don't remember starting to cry, but here I am, crying—for the fourth time today. Jacob doesn't say a word until he asks, "Can you run?" and I nod.

He takes my hand and we run, not towards the door, but to the janitor's closet. I press my thumb against the scanner, and the door lets us pass. Then we descend the pitch black concrete stairs, move down the catacomb-like hallway, and enter the Eradicator compound, where the fluorescent lights are garish and the slightest movement sounds like a jet taking off.

"You okay?" Jacob asks me.

"Please tell me you're being ironic."

He goes over to the woman at the desk, the one with the black hair with blue tips and silver dangle earrings who wants to go to Columbia. She takes out one of her earbuds when she sees us approaching. "Look," Jacob says, "we need help. How can you get everyone out of here?"

"Only a direct order from Parkins can get everyone out of here," she replies, fiddling with a ballpoint pen, her foot tapping to the rhythm of whatever song she's listening to.

Jacob glances down each hall and then turns his attention back to the woman. "Okay, so where can I find her?"

"Jacob, no," I plead. "She'll never listen to you. Then she'll execute you."

"Her office." The woman seems unfazed by our conversation. Either she doesn't care, or she hears stuff like this all the time. "That hall, third door on the left. Can't miss it. Only room down here with a window." She doesn't babble about this window; she gives us a grudgingly encouraging smirk and sticks her right earbud in.

Third door on left, I repeat over and over in my head until they don't sound like words anymore. Jacob doesn't bother knocking; he opens the door and walks right in, closing it behind us.

The aforementioned window is only a foot-by-foot square that touches the ceiling. It's grimy, scratched, and the catch is rusted shut, but it lets in some moonlight, so I can see why Ms. Parkins, who, from what I've gathered, is a very important Eradicator, chose this as her office. But the rest of the details are muddled—is that scuff mark on the floor from a sneaker or a high-heel? Why is there a pink cardigan on the floor? Who's in that picture on her desk? I ask more questions than I answer.

"Jacob?" Ms. Parkins sits at her desk in a leather spinning-chair.

"Come on, you have to be a *little* impressed," he states.

"At what?"

"At the fact that we found a way to get me out of that room, which was wall-to-wall with you guys. I mean, that's pretty cool, right? Are you going to give us *any* admiration? Maybe just a little?"

"Oh, darling, I already knew you would find a way out." She motions to two chairs in front of her desk. "Please, sit."

"We don't have time," Jacob says. "You have to get out of here."

"What do you mean, you already knew?" I ask, mostly out of curiosity, but also for the chance to sit down and maybe for a second stop my head from spinning like a carousel. Little horses with painted saddles run by in a circle. At the carousel in the park near Harlow's house, I'd always go on the Palomino with the purple saddle. Harlow took the white one with the blue saddle. It looked like her eyes.

"You think I'm unaware of your intelligence?" Ms. Parkins asks us. "My dears, I know you're geniuses, and I know how geniuses think. I can only imagine the speed at which the thoughts run through your heads. I've seen your reflexes, your calculating glances, the way your brains can't stay on one thing for very long because it can't wait to think about the next. I've gotten to watch Lea Felding firsthand for the past few months, a Knower in action. Please, don't think I am not in awe of your brains."

I wonder if putting my cold hands on my forehead will make it feel better. I try it. It doesn't work.

"Ms. Parkins," Jacob continues, "you need to evacuate the compound. Get everyone upstairs and outside, all while holding your breath. Look, it sounds unbelievable, I know, but you need to trust us."

"Oh, you're trying this again," Ms. Parkins muses. "An interesting tactic, repetition. I must say, you especially are unpredictable. Most would move on to another way to remove us from the compound."

"He's not kidding," I say. "Poison. There's poison coming, and it may already be here. We've already inhaled a ton of it, and honestly, we could die at any second—I have no idea what is going happen to us. You need to get outside and then as far as you can from this building." It's gotten to the point where each of my individual teeth scream. Isn't that my vocal chords' job? I hate when parts of my body feel the need to switch roles.

Ms. Parkins presses her fingertips to her lips as she contemplates. "Prove it, then. Explain to me why you feel we should believe you."

Tick, tick, tick. Like a clock or a bomb. Maybe both. Do bombs have tiny clocks in them? Maybe that's why they tick.

Or maybe clocks have tiny bombs in them.

Jacob, who's still standing, crosses his arms. "We literally could die any minute and we chose to come down here and warn you. That should be proof enough."

"I—"

"Look, Ms. Parkins, we've done more that enough to save you. You think all the Knowers are trying to get rid of you? We've just spent the last couple hours turning our backs on the Knowers, then flipping around and turning them on you—we're *fifteen*, you know, we shouldn't be playing a game like this. All the betrayal, the lies, every time we've had to run out of a building because we were afraid it would either blow up or someone would come in and shoot us—come on, we're still kids, aren't we? And now the poison is already in our systems and unless the Knowers can come up with a cure—"

"But why?" Miss Parkins wonders. "Why save us when you simultaneously want to destroy us?"

"We're Knowers, too, and I speak for everyone, I think, when I say that for us, at least, we don't stand for killing people for power. The world doesn't work like that." He pauses. "Okay, maybe it works exactly like that—just look at Europe in the nineteenth century—but maybe it shouldn't."

"Well." Ms. Parkins is quiet for a long time, so the only sound I can hear is my heartbeat inside my head. "Then thank you. Sincerely."

The ticking clock in my brain explodes. Fire that burns blue pours out of me and surrounds the room and the room melts like wax off a candle. I think I scream, but I'm not really sure. In fact, I'm not exactly sure of anything that happens after this point.

Chapter Thirty Four

If you get scared of the space
between now and those days,
then I will take you away,
somewhere fear has no place.
We'd make ashes of our clothes
and grow a garden out of those
and watch the water as it rose
to bring the ocean to our toes.

"Islands"
Hey Ocean!

When I was really little—until I was about seven or eight—I would get these headaches sometimes. In hindsight, they weren't that bad, but to a little kid, they were some sort of torture, inhibiting me from playing outside or even school on the worst days. I would pretty much sleep them off, if I managed to fall asleep. I usually couldn't.

Each one would take on some sort of form, like the pain was personified. Sometimes I would imagine there were fairies living in my brain. Other times, it was a knife cutting across my forehead. Even though I can't remember the pain anymore, even though I can't feel it in my head even if I try, I still see every image of fairies or knives as vividly as I did in the midst of a headache. Especially this one that I only had once, when I had the worst headache I'd ever had that kept me bedridden for three days: there was a herd of gazelles trampling a patch of yellow flowers that may have been dandelions.

I flit between two different worlds: the real one and the one I've built in my mind. Is Jacob carrying me, or is it Harry Potter? I can't tell if we're still in Air and Space or in an old, elegant mansion with shining hardwoods and crisp yellow wallpaper. But the lord and lady it belongs to must be aero-enthusiasts because there're a lot of planes in their house. They hang from the ceiling like icicles.

More and more people are around us. They run with us, like we're in a stampede of gazelles. They all talk to each other in static noises and telegraph clicking. I can see the dots and dashes.

"Hey, Bubble, you have to walk for a bit." Jacob/Harry Potter sets me down, and the whole world wobbles on the spot. His eyes aren't green and he's not wearing glasses, so maybe he's Jacob. I don't care, really.

Hallie holds my hand now. Her hair is sparkly. It's blue, like the rest of her. Someone has coated each strand of it in liquid sapphire. She holds me down so I don't float off into space. "Stay awake," she says. Either that or "Stay a snake." Her voice sounds like a frozen cotton ball.

"I'm not a snake," I tell her.

"You're such an idiot," she tells me, so I know she loves me.

Hunter carries a highlighter. The highlighter looks like she's sleeping. Hunter struggles under her weight but doesn't complain. Hunter never complains about anything. The highlighter's eyes pop open, scream, and then close again.

"Is the highlighter okay?" I ask Hallie. "Is she going to die?"

"She's fine," Hallie says.

"Where's Harlow?"

"You'll see her soon."

I don't know if she means because the Day is coming to an end or because I am.

"I'm going to die, too, aren't I?" I ask Jacob/Harry Potter. "I know because I can see the gazelles again."

"You're not going to die," he says.

"Then tell the gazelles to go away."

"Leave us alone, gazelles," he says without question. "Don't pop this Bubble."

To anyone else, it would sound like he's seeing gazelles, too.

After a few years of walking through the aero-enthusiast's mansion with the hardwood floors and the yellow wallpaper, I see Margaret White standing over me. She has three eyes: one blue, one brown, one red. "Back to the Castle," she says. "Immediately."

She sounds like a queen commanding her army.

People buzz around my bed like they're bees. Miss Felding never leaves the room we rest in. She's constantly muttering to herself, tears gently rolling down her pale white cheeks, touching her wrist to our foreheads and brushing her fingers over our hands. She really is beautiful, even when she's crying. Her tears look like beads of glass.

"Are you crying?" I ask her when she comes over.

"Yes, Skylar, I'm crying," she replied. "How could I let her do this to you?"

"The poison is a girl?"

She pushes a strand of hair out of my face, and for a single enthralling second, she looks exactly like Jessamine. Then she moves over to Jacob, who's in a fitful sleep. Then Hallie, whose bed is closest to the window and is intently staring out of it, then Lexie, who hasn't moved in a few minutes.

Margaret comes into the room, followed by a man and an iPad. "How are they?" she asks Miss Felding.

"I don't know, Margaret, you tell me," Miss Felding snaps. I've never seen her so angry, not even when Danny Canter doesn't do his homework or Gemma Fisher talks in class. "How many poisons were in that stuff?" I've also never heard her use the word *stuff*; she's the type of person to say *things,* or perhaps *substances.*

"Eleven." Margaret almost whispers the number, but Margaret never whispers, so I hear it clearly. "Stellan, check their vitals."

The man named Stellan comes to the side of my bed, whispers, "This may hurt a bit, darling, I'm sorry," and puts a thin needle into one of my veins. I barely feel it. He pulls it out after a few seconds and reads the screen the needle is connected to. Everything he reads is then typed into his iPad with lightning-quick fingers. "Good job, Skylar," he says. "You didn't even flinch." He changes the needle and moves over to Lexie, who finally stirs. I inaudibly sigh because I know that she's alive now.

"Why didn't we check where they were first?" Miss Felding breathes.

"I didn't know we had reason to check," Margaret says. Her voice sounds stiff, like it's been sitting in one place for too long. "I thought they would have stayed where they were."

"We should have kept a better eye on them."

"They should have listened to us."

"I beg your pardon, but they're Knowers. Their whole existence depends on not listening."

Margaret doesn't respond to this.

"We should have just told them."

"That would have only made matters worse."

"Why? Because the four of them are stronger than the rest of us put together and they would have found a way to stop you? You needed to be stopped, Margaret."

"Then why didn't you stop me yourself?"

"You would never have listened to me. Never. You don't listen very well, as I have implied."

Margaret takes the iPad from Stellan, looks at it for only a second, and hands it back.

"You can't hold on to the world forever. You have to pass it on eventually."

"Leah," she says sharply.

The room is silent once again.

Then Hallie says, "We broke the Efficacy, you know."

"Alright, Hallie," Miss Felding says, patting her hand.

Hallie pushes her hand away and props herself up. "I'm not kidding. Skylar messed up the firewall."

"She did?" Margaret sounds astonished, but her face doesn't look it.

"You told me not to get mixed up in this, and I don't listen to people," I tell Margaret. It's funny because my voice doesn't sound like it's coming out of my mouth. "Now I'm kind of stuck here for life. But thank you, Margaret White. You messed up my entire life, and I think that my entire life needed that."

She looks at each of us. I've never seen anyone's eyes change color so quickly.

Some time passes, in which I see things in this room that shouldn't be in here, then Stellan—who would be Superman if Clark Kent were a pathologist—comes up with the cure. Or maybe it's not a cure, but at least something that can keep us alive for another few hours. I don't listen to the conversation between him, Miss Felding, and Margaret about how it will work. Too many big words.

I fall in and out of sleep, my mind static like an old broken TV, my entire body made of lead and impossible to move. Jacob murmurs incoherencies in his sleep. (I'm dying, and he's dying, so why do I find this endearing? This isn't the time.) Lexie now tosses and turns like a boat on the ocean. Hallie sits up in bed, curled up in a little ball. Her body looks so small when she compacts it like that. Weird, because she's usually so tall and commanding. Now, she could be an armadillo.

In my lucid dreams, there are lots of gazelles trampling dandelions. And then there are anchors and highlighters and shards of slate and china dolls and a hurricane in the sky that somehow makes the scene sunnier.

There's a single star in the sky, too. I wonder if she's doing okay up there and when she's coming back down. I miss my star, and I've only gone a few hours without her. I try to ask her if I'm worth it to come back, but she won't answer me. I don't want her to, really. I only want one of the possible two answers. I'm asking for selfish reasons.

"Skylar, would you mind another needle?" Stellan asks me.

"Will it make me die faster?"

"No. Quite the opposite."

"Then yes, I would mind."

Stellan ignores me, and then, as he claims, he cures me.

I fall asleep almost instantly—this sleep is deeper. The gazelles stop in their tracks.

Chapter Thirty Five

Now the night
is coming to an end.
The sun will rise
and we will try again.
Stay alive, stay alive
for me.
You will die,
but now your life is free.
Take pride in what
is sure to die.

"Truce"
twenty one pilots

I'm the last one awake. My eyes pop open, and everyone else is already looking at me. And my head doesn't hurt anymore. At least not like before. This dull throb is nothing compared to what it was earlier.

Miss Felding and Stellan rush over to me. Stellan doesn't ask about the needle this time, he just does it. I actually flinch and squeeze Miss Felding's hand, which has slipped into mine.

"How are you feeling?" she asks.

"All the gazelles left."

"That's good?"

"That's great."

"Then great."

"Where's Hunter?" Jacob asks. "Is he okay?"

"He's with the other Eradicators, and I'm quite sure he's fine," Miss Felding reassures him. "But the Eradicators can't know that he's helped us, so he must be with them now."

"Yeah, but is he okay?" Jacob asks. "Did you give them the cure?"

Miss Felding nods. "Stellan sent some over."

Margaret clicks in the room. "Oh, good, you're all awake," she says. "How are you all? Do you need anything?"

"Just an explanation," Jacob says. His eyes are colorful again, bright and full of thunderclouds.

"Of what?"

"What do you think?"

Margaret sighs. "You're far too—"

"If you say 'far too young'," Hallie groans, "I'm going to disembowel you."

Margaret sighs again, but this sigh is filled with less exasperation and more loathing. "I couldn't possibly put all of this on you."

Lexie looks skeptical of this excuse. "You kind of put a lot on us. What's one more sprinkle on the sundae?"

"You almost killed us," Jacob says, "so you totally owe us a reason as to why."

"Haven't you already presumed why?" Margaret asks us. She pulls a chair right in front of Lexie's bed.

"Of course we have," I say. "It was a quick and easy—in perspective—way to get rid of the Eradicators without laying a finger on them. Late enough in the Day that you wouldn't need to worry about authorities again. Really, Margaret, it was quite genius. It would have been foolproof if not for us. You forgot to work an equal but opposite match into your formula."

I look at a clock on the wall; it's eleven-forty-two.

Lexie taps out a beat on her bed frame: pinky, thumb, middle, ring, index. "You want power," she says simply. "And to get that, you needed to eliminate everyone else who had it. And the Eradicators—well, you'd never admit it, but they're just about as powerful as us. Taking them out would mean we would have no competition. No threats."

"And you didn't care who was in your way," I say. "You believed these people were disposable, Margaret. It doesn't matter if they were parents, or sisters, or brothers, or people with real dreams and aspirations and feelings and who want to go to Columbia or smile, really *smile*, when you ask them a question. To you, they were branded as *enemy*."

Margaret is quiet for a very long time before she says, "When you grow up, you will understand that rewards are only given to those who fight for them. I've been fighting from day one. And I will fight until the world caves on itself. I did what I felt was right: put power in hands capable of holding it."

"But you don't need to kill people," Jacob says. "Isn't there anything else you can do? Death ends up leading to more death, and you would just happen to be stuck right in the center of it."

"Look, Margaret," Hallie says, "we're sorry if we messed up things between you and the Eradicators for next Day. Really, we're sorry. But that doesn't mean we—at least I—would take back anything we did today. Even the poison doesn't make me regret taping up the vents or destroying their computer or, come on, licking a Monet painting or making Lexie jump into the reflecting pool. I don't regret it. I would save those people a million times again, even if they shot Skylar. She forgave them, so why can't we all?"

Margaret paces the room now. "You really are the most powerful people in the entire world."

She says *you,* not *we.*

"There will be a thousand more Days like this one, I'm going to warn you. You've only fallen an inch into the rabbit hole."

She looks at each of us, her eyes changing color each time. For me, her brown eyes are just about red. She grimaces slightly, as if her next words hurt her to say.

"The world needs you desperately."

Her breath catches and she can barely speak.

"*I* need you desperately."

And in this moment, this fraction of a second, this blink of an eye that everyone else in the world pays no attention to, I truly feel—inside and out, mind and eyes, head to toe—like I am a Knower.

Miss Felding comes into the room as the clock ticks to eleven-fifty-seven. "Are you feeling up to going downstairs?"

"For what?"

"The Impact."

"Sounds terrifying," Jacob says. "I'm in."

"Then let's hurry."

We move down the creaking stairs of the Castle, which squeak like mice under our feet. It hurts a bit to move like this, suddenly and all at once, but I tell myself, over and over, that I can make it through another three minutes and another thousand years if I have to. Time is only relevant if you allow it to be.

And then we're on the front lawn of the Castle with every other Knower turning and smiling at us. There are the blond twins and Coira, beaming at us, and there's Eula, laughing her honey laugh, and Stellan and Dakarai, and even Margaret just barely smiles and Miss Felding is just radiating with pride in her algebra students, the ones who could have gotten better grades in her classes but had to save the world instead. Or maybe they didn't have to save it. Maybe they just had to make it suck a little less.

"Eleven-fifty-nine," Margaret calls. She stands at the front of the crowd.

"I'm not exactly sure what to expect from this," I say. "There isn't a ball dropping, and we don't have any sparkling juice."

"Man, I could go for some juice," Lexie says. "When we get home, I'm gonna be so tired."

"Or you're going to feel well-rested, if that's how you felt at the beginning of today," Hallie says.

"Nope. We have a global paper due today. I'm gonna be so tired."

"So, next time we're here, I say we go to the International Spy Museum," Jacob says.

"If we're still alive by then," I add.

"Well, that got dark really quickly."

"I just mean . . . Margaret said we're not done, and I highly doubt that this is an annual occupation."

"I guess you're right."

"I know I'm right."

"Can everyone bring phone chargers next Day?" Lexie asks. "Or we all should buy those things that are, like, portable chargers that you don't have to plug in. It would make our lives so much easier."

If Harlow were here, she'd find the scene hysterical, all these scientists and lawyers and future totalitarians spread across the grass of the National Mall on a random day in April, laughing in excitement of the clock's hands turning the wrong way and making everyone repeat said random day in April. She would hold her arms out and wait with her eyes closed—it would be more of a surprise that way, and Harlow just loves surprises.

Hallie seems to be reading my thoughts because she says, "She's going to be fine."

"You think so?"

"You kidding me? That girl's completely unstoppable. Time's not gonna work for her, trust me. She won't let it."

"Thanks, Hallie."

My best friend proceeds to say, "You're something else, Skylar."

"I love you, too."

Isn't it funny how we let those ticking gears rule our lives? Armless hands and a headless face, the molten magma core of the earth, the numbers made of lines that flip by as we give them either way too much notice or not nearly enough—a superficial dictator that only exists because we want it to. We are the ones who make the clock tick and the world turn. The hands won't move unless we tell them to count down our lives with numbers and periods that mean nothing and everything at the same time, in the same heartbeat.

When we throw all that to the wind, we're timeless.

"Ten!" Margaret yells. We pick up, all sounding like children, on nine, eight—

I smile.

—seven, six—

And they smile.

—five—

But we don't really need to smile.

—four—

Aren't we already incandescent?

—three—

"Are you ready?" Jacob asks. His eyes are a storm, and I love them.

—two—

"Not at all."

—one.

"That's what makes it so fun."

ACKNOWLEDGMENTS

I really don't know where to start. I have so many people to thank for getting this book where it is today. It's kind of nerve-racking, if I'm being honest, but pretty exciting.

First and foremost, my parents have been nothing but supportive in the three years since I've started this journey. My dad read it three times to make it perfect, and my mom is my personal cheerleader and the strongest woman I've ever had the privilege to meet. They are my favorite people; everything I am, I owe to them. Words don't work when trying to explain how much I love and appreciate them.

And Max, who only complains a little when I start to ramble or when he can hear me squealing over characters from his bedroom down the hall. A better brother doesn't exist. You are effervescent, Muskrat.

Each of my friends have given me immeasurable confidence. They've been reading *The Knowers* since its birth in seventh grade. They've made fun of the parts that deserved it and gave me only the most honest feedback. They haven't gotten sick of me wrapping my life around a manuscript (and if they have, they haven't shown it). Long nights with Star Wars movies, laughing so hard we're crying at lunch, crying so hard we're laughing in homeroom—you guys are my inspiration.

Ella, Anna, and Finn—you guys are my siblings that aren't actually my siblings. Thank you for cheering me up whenever I need it. (And Ella, thank you for being my star.)

And my seventh grade Scrabble Club, of course. The idea of a nonexistent day struck me while sitting around the green chairs in the library. When I ran it by you guys, you said "it's not terrible". Those three words sparked the largest part of my life.

All of my English teachers taught me to write. My history teachers added hours of extra research to this book because they instilled my love of accuracy. My science teachers were instrumental in concocting a super-smart society built around physics.

All of my "Knowers Artists", as I call them, have influenced me beyond words. Including their lyrics in my work is an honor.

And to my little green composition notebook—you messed up my life, and my life needed to be messed up. Thank you.

ABOUT THE AUTHOR

Nina Martineck has been writing for pretty much all twenty years of her life. She published her first novel, *The Knowers*, at age seventeen, and has since published two more, *The Eminence* and *The Duplicity*. Her short story "The Bug Whisperer" was featured in the Western New York Young Writers' Anthology when she was just ten, and she's since published short fiction in *Just My Cup of Tea Magazine* and *Havoc*, which has featured her on its podcast. She writes and edits for *The Prattler* literary magazine and served as her high school literary magazine's editor-in-chief for two years. She currently studies architecture at Pratt Institute in Brooklyn, NY. In addition to writing, she loves buildings, manatees, singing too loudly, and very hot tea.

Instagram: @the.knowers
Website: https://ninammartineck.wixsite.com/mysite
Goodreads: Nina Martineck
Spotify: sugarbeet6

Other Works by Nina Martineck:

The Knowers
The Eminence
The Duplicity

Marvin the Manatee

Made in the USA
Middletown, DE
12 September 2021